ELYSIANA

ELYSIANA

CHRIS KNOPF

THE PERMANENT PRESS
Sag Harbor, NY 11963

For information, address:
The Permanent Press
4170 Noyac Road
Sag Harbor, NY 11963
www.thepermanentpress.com

Library of Congress Cataloging-in-Publication Data

Knopf, Chris.
    Elysiana / Chris Knopf.
        p. cm.
    ISBN 978-1-57962-198-8 (hardcover : alk. paper)
        1. Eccentrics and eccentricities—Fiction. 2. Barrier islands—
New Jersey—Fiction. [1. New Jersey—History—20th century—
Fiction.] I. Title.

PS3611.N66E49 2010
813'.6—dc22   2009052006

Printed in the United States of America.

For Marty and Judy Shepard

With deepest gratitude

CHAPTER
1

Sᴛʀᴇᴛᴄʜᴇᴅ ᴏᴜᴛ she just fit, slightly wedged, between the padded armrests of the Catalina's backseat. The top was down and the sky was blue. Her brown hair, bleached at the edges, swirled around her face.

She held a lit cigarette. The tobacco, burning hotly in the wind, glowed red at the base of a long tip of ash. Somewhere in the car music was playing, felt more than heard, a subterranean burble rolling along her spine, under her butt and down to the heels of her bare feet. She hadn't eaten in a long time, but the crystal meth was still itching at her nerves, killing her appetite.

She wore a Day-Glo red, orange and yellow shift, sunglasses and a gold signature ring. If asked, she'd have difficulty pin-pointing the exact time, and the precise manner by which she'd lost her underwear and shoes. Or the exact location of the car she was riding in, since all she'd seen was sky for the last three days.

At random intervals a box of Marlboros, thrown from some-where in the front seat, would land on her belly. She smoked steadily, lighting each cigarette with the chrome lighter built into the armrest above her head.

Her legs, most of which extended from the short hem of the shift, were a uniform brownish red, flecked with pale blond fuzz. Periodically, the wind would lift the hem above her pubic mound, which was covered with darker, red-tinted brown hair. Truckers honked their appreciation.

Of the two in the front seat, all she could see was hair—two clumps of long black, wiry hair flapping and twisting in the wind. Whatever she'd seen of their faces was forgotten long ago. She made no effort to recollect, though some images drifted in and out of her mind. Still shots of smoke-screened rooms, shifting colored lights, breathtaking noise.

She vaguely remembered pushing through the congestion, faces coming up and disappearing, looking at her blankly, or with interest, or hostility. Hairy faces, sweaty cheeks and beer breath. The rank smell of perspiration and incense, dope and patchouli. Cigarette smoke, dank and luxurious, burning at her eyes and nose.

A tsunami of amplified music washed away all other sound, though mouths moved and heads nodded agreeably. Shoulders and elbows pushed at her. Chests and breasts, loose under coarse cotton, or slimy synthetics, touched and bumped against her almost as separate things. Hands squeezed her arms, pulling her in to yell in her ear, but she shoved ahead. Hands patted her rump, cupped her midriff, brushed against her breasts. One came up jarringly between her legs, igniting her reflexes. She twisted and dug her fingernails into the hand till it pulled back. She spit at the probable offender and jabbed him with her middle finger.

"Asshole."

She remembered looking around for people she knew and wondering how she got there, or what she took that got her so fucked up. She thought it might have involved a big, fat, red joint at some point. But maybe that was just another phantom, like the tuxedoed jungle animals on the stage playing guitars, or the gloved hands waving to her from the big cafeteria clock on the wall.

Riding in the big convertible, the liquid walls, twirling bananas, naked football players with hydra-headed penises, purple iguanas and household appliances singing in barbershop quartets had quietly slipped away. The audible colors and colorful sounds were gone. She was left behind, nearly blank, with a box of Marlboros and traces of speed the guys up front had given her to keep her from falling asleep, which she believed at the time would cost her the last of her shredded sanity.

It was very peaceful looking at the limitless blue sky on such an ideal summer day. Tranquil to be without memory or feeling. Anesthetized down to the finest fibrils of her nervous system. Without fear or thought. Neutral. Outside the present and disinterested in the world. Zapped.

She remembered water. At some point she'd been swimming in dense blackness through slippery, contaminated water. Fishy, vaporous, congealed. It choked her. She'd vomited on the shore, hands and knees sinking into the brackish mud. Some people crowded around, yelling at her, talking among themselves. She wanted to say something, but her throat was full of puke and a sweet astringent smell reminiscent of carbonic cleaning fluid. Her consciousness was teetering, splintering, ripped by hallucinations and broached by sickening waves of idiocy and confusion.

Hands pulled her to her feet and dragged her into a warm, lighted space. Behind the blur, a broad-faced woman in a cotton dress and apron, with curly brown hair and thick glasses, was staring at her while muttering a sort of soothing reassurance she couldn't quite make out. Behind her was a man with a pot belly and madras shirt, baseball cap, khaki shorts, dark socks and tie shoes. Red hair, bad skin, boozy nose. Grinning behind the woman's back.

She was led to another room. There was a washer and dryer and coats hung on hooks. The floor was fake brick linoleum. It was reminiscent of her grandmother's kitchen. She dropped down to smell it, wondering if it smelled like her grandmother. The woman was still there and helped her back on her feet. The woman pulled at her sopping clothes, clumsy thick fingers unable to unbutton the buttons. She pointed to some towels and a gaudy shift draped over a spindly drying rack, then she left her alone to strip and dry off.

It took her a while to undress because the floor and the walls had lost some of their tangibility. The palms of her hands felt bumpy and her joints seemed less resilient. The nausea, however, was gone and she felt as if her internal organs were now fully under control. From this point forward, she told them, we'll have no more rebellion, no more puking or racing of the heart.

The towel was coarse against her skin. It hadn't been dried in the dryer, she assumed. Frugal people. Use the dryer for something else. Maybe to warm pets. She noticed the man was there in the room with her. He asked her for the towel and she gave it to him. He threw it in the corner so abruptly she wondered why he wanted it in the first place. He grinned at her, nodding his head. Had she said something that amused him? He clamped a hand around her wrist and pulled her up against him. She was nearly overpowered by the sugary alcohol smell of the man's breath. It reminded her of her father.

His madras shirt felt good against her naked breasts. She let herself rest on the sloping upper stretch of his stomach, burrowing in a little to get some friction against her nipples. The man had a hand on each cheek of her butt, digging in with his jagged fingernails. He told her she was a stinking little hippie whore that needed him to shove his cock up her ass so far it'll come out her mouth, if it don't just split her in half like a piece of cordwood.

Something bothered her about that imagery. She backed away from him as he pulled his penis out of his pants, just clear of the enormous water-balloon belly that hung over his belt. He pumped the thing, which looked tiny inside his blunt-fingered hand.

She pinched a piece of the shift and pulled it off the rack. He told her not to be scared, that he wouldn't hurt her. She wondered if she should be, and why she wasn't. Something told her to put on the shift, but she was transfixed by the man, who now looked something like Oliver Hardy. But even more porcine. Porky Pig. He closed in again, saying something about putting it in her mouth. He grabbed her by the hair and pushed her to her knees. She wriggled under his grasp, shocked nearly sober by the sudden violence. The bulbous little purple head bounced in front of her, poking at her lips, bumping off her nose and face. It stank.

"Now you just leave that girl alone. Honestly," said the woman, who was suddenly there in the room again. The man let go of her head roughly, and pushed his erection back in his pants.

"She's just a stinkin' little hippie whore."

"That don't mean you go doin' that, for pity's sake. See what happens when you run around nekkid?" the woman said to her, scoldingly. "Now put on that dress and come on out of there so's we can figure out what to do with you."

Left alone, she slipped into the shift and wiggled out a small window. She landed on the driveway, which she followed down to the street, where the first car, a couple of girls out for a cruise, picked her up. The memory was unclear. A Camaro? Something fast. They were fat girls out feeding their anger and boredom. They had big tubs filled with fried chicken and huge tankards of Coca-Cola. They took her to another bar. Maybe that's where she met the two guys with the frizzy hair. She remembered how good the chicken tasted.

THE CATALINA lurched to a stop, sending her rolling off the seat, into the padded bucket seats in front of her, and down to the floor, the hump punching her in the belly when she hit.

"Jesus Christ!" screamed one of the guys in front. She braced herself for the impact, her mind snapping into awareness with the brutality of a wet slap across the face.

Nothing happened, but the movement had stopped, and an ugly wakefulness began its slow creep back into her consciousness.

"Sorry," said one of the guys.

She sat up and looked around. Ahead loomed the mighty ass end of a tractor trailer. To either side was the tall grass of coastal wetlands. Behind her was a long straight, two-lane causeway leading back to some cruddy pines and the concrete patterns of a four-lane cloverleaf. The guys in front were giggling and swearing with relief, like they'd just gotten away with something, which they had. The one with the zitty, long-nosed face looked back at her.

"It lives."

The other guy looked a little better, though no more familiar. Both had yellow teeth and eyes with too much white around the iris.

"Lookin' good!" the zitty guy yelled, more as a morale boost than a come-on. She knew, from what little awareness she had, that looking good wasn't a realistic possibility. She smiled lamely.

"You, too."

The driver pulled out into the other lane and put all the Catalina's 356 available horses to work getting around the truck. She noticed with relief the absence of oncoming traffic. The torqued-out thrust of acceleration made her feel like her stomach was about to jump out the back.

"Easy boys, still feelin' a little dicey."

She lit a cigarette and squinted at the marshy terrain.

"Where the hell are we?"

The two of them grinned back at her. She wished the driver would stop doing that.

"Been rammin' three days straight. Been all the fuck over the place. Just stopped for gas and smokes. And burgers. You was just starin' so we ate 'em all ourselves. Been fuckin' flyin'!"

"No shit," said the other guy.

"Fuckin' reds, man. Fuckin' reds."

"No shit," the other guy said again.

"Fuckin' reds?" she asked, "I thought it was fuckin' meth."

"That's what we gave you, sweetheart. We ain't messin' with that shit. Fuckin' crystal, no way."

"No way," the other guy agreed.

"So where are we?"

They looked around again and the car yawed off to the right.

"Christ, watch the road."

"We're in fuckin' New Jersey! Yeah! Fuckin' New Jersey!" They whooped as she contemplated being a thousand miles and several days away from her last recollected moments of sobriety.

The road sparkled with sea stones imbedded in the macadam. Brilliant parallel yellow lines ran down the middle. They approached a steeply arched bridge that crossed a broad channel. On either side of the causeway were gray-boarded shacks built on splintery piers, looking like a flock of down-and-out water fowl. Along the horizon to the east stretched a jagged line of buildings. It was the developed north end of the barrier island of Elysiana. A twenty-five mile strip of sand running north to south featuring an assortment of seashore amenities and profound dissociation.

"Fuckin' New Jersey, man. Fuckin' Neeeeew Jersey!"

She stood unsteadily at the curb and watched the convertible whoosh away. They'd offered to let her crash with them and their friends, but she declined. She was nearly sober now, and a little sick, but awake and alert. She wanted all association with the last three days out of eyeshot, at least for now.

She walked across the street to a hoagie shop. It was a single long corridor, with a counter down one side and a row of tables down the other. It was half full of people eating pancakes and eggs, drinking coffee, smoking, speaking *sotto voce*. A few guys looked up as she came in. She sat at the counter.

"What'll it be for you today?"

She leaned forward so the waitress could hear her whisper.

"Can I have a meal, then work it off in the kitchen or something?"

"You don't have any money?" the woman whispered.

"It's a long story."

The woman looked skeptically down the counter at a large man behind the cash register.

"He don't like to give away food."

"I'll work for it."

The woman looked more closely at her.

"He don't like hippies."

"Please."

"Tell me what you want. I'll take care of your check."

"I don't mind working."

"Just shush your mouth and order, while I'm in the mood," said the woman, smiling nervously.

She ordered a huge breakfast when she saw the ten the woman put under the sugar dispenser in front of her.

"Leave a good tip."

It wasn't until she'd mopped up the last puddle of maple syrup that she looked up from her plate and saw a kid behind the counter holding a plastic pail full of dirty dishes. He was staring at her.

"Hi," she said.

He turned abruptly and dropped the pail. The woman who bought her breakfast bent down to help the kid clean up. The old man behind the cash register raised both hands to acknowledge God for one more act of petty cruelty.

She kept two dollars from the change and left the rest on the counter. It was getting bright and warm outside. Except for the jagged edges of her nervous system, she felt okay.

Two dollars, a pack of cigarettes, an ugly dress, and a pair of shades. The sum of her estate on earth. Or at least in New Jersey.

Main Street was wider than necessary and lined with low-slung storefronts, restaurants, a gas station on either side of the street, and a single motel. None of the commercial enterprises resisted the impulse to lend a nautical air to their signage. This is how you knew you were on the Jersey Shore and not a strip development in Illinois.

She squinted into the morning sun and pondered the direction her life should take. A second later she turned right and headed down toward the beach, into the sun. It warmed her face, chest and the parts of her breasts above the scooped neck of the shift. The slate walk was salted with fine, windblown Jersey sand. The air was spring dry and filled with noisy birds she assumed were seagulls based on birds she'd seen circling the Great Lakes, though she'd never before been near the ocean, or even on the East Coast, or farther east than Valparaiso, Indiana.

The houses on either side of the street were groomed to the point of artificiality, as if on a stage set. The lawns were a thick-cropped green, the driveways pearly white pebble stone. An exception was a squalid little two-story wreck set awkwardly back from the house line. Two overgrown red cedars rose above a ragged lawn littered with residential detritus—mattress springs, a baby carriage, derelict autos and rusty tin cans.

Standing at the center of the carnage was a tall, broad-shouldered blond man doing stretching exercises. A surfboard was next to him on the ground. She waited for him to complete the final cycles and make eye contact.

"Going surfin'?" she asked.

He nodded.

"Live here?"

He nodded again.

"Got roommates?"

Another nod.

"Any girls?"

He shook his head.

"I'll clean the whole place, including toilets and defrosting the 'fridge for a hundred bucks. Two days work. Including laundromat if you supply the change."

"We like it dirty."

"Eighty. Forty a day. Cash, up front, each day."

He shrugged, "Okay."

He picked up his surfboard and brushed by her on his way down to the surf.

"I need the first forty bucks."

"Inside," he called back.

"I have a name," she called.

He stopped and turned around.

"So?"

"It's Gwendalynn."

The surfer shrugged and turned again, trotting toward the ocean.

Inside was dark and filled with smells powerful enough to achieve substance. There were pieces of furniture arranged in loose formation around an immense, square coffee table heaped with magazines, take-out boxes, ashtrays, bongs, motorcycle parts, swimwear, and pieces of fruit in various stages of putrefaction. The woven hemp carpet on the floor was peppered with burn marks, as were the lampshades. There were a half dozen aluminum screen doors leaning against the wall, a large, empty fish tank, two partially stripped and reglazed surfboards, and a half disassembled 350-cc Honda where a dining nook should have been.

The stairway to the second floor ran along the back of the living room. Coiled around the banister was a four-and-a-half foot long boa constrictor.

The kitchen was at the back of the house. She steeled herself before entering.

As suspected, dried food splatters were spread across the walls, ceiling and floor. A small mountain range of cups, plates, silverware and cooking utensils—along with some organic material not yet a decorative element—had formed across the sink and counter top.

The appliances were chipped '40's white. As was the linoleum-topped kitchen table. At the head of the table on a bent-legged chair listing severely to the right, was a fat young man wearing an overtaxed pair of gym shorts around his midriff and a fair amount of dried vomit on his chest.

He slept.

"Fuckin' New Jersey," she said, though not loud enough to wake the dead.

CHAPTER
2

Jack Halcyon stood twenty stories above the sand and watched the sun pop out of the ocean. It was a grand entrance, with a gaudy display of light, searing the sky and splashing white paint across the water. For a few minutes, as he watched from the sky-walk, he could lose himself in that slow scorching rise above the perfection of an unobstructed horizon.

The fresh morning breeze, blowing in from the sea, had stripped the atmosphere of the gray-brown haze that sometimes floated over from Philadelphia. The bickering gulls loved to swoop through the cool, brine-scented air, their wings stretched like bleached eagles, soaking up the pale light.

He moved to the edge of the skywalk and spread his arms like the wings of a gull. His face, chest and thighs collected heat from the sun. His back was chilled by the air. His arms caught crosscurrents and he teetered at the brink. The gusts shoved him around. He looked down, gripping a tall metal stanchion mounted at the edge of the building. Twenty stories may as well be a hundred. Enough to do the job. He leaned further out, halfway between control and the pitiless pull of gravity. He became aware of his grip on the stanchion and how it compared to the mass of his body, pulling away, drawn to the shabby landscape below.

He heard the coffeepot whistle, pulling him back toward the Box. The coffeepot sputtered as he poured hot water over a mound of stale Chock full o'Nuts. The coffee aroma freshened the air inside the Box, which usually smelled like a wet sheep dog. He took the cup back outside and dropped into the all-weather recliner, a swayback, redwood and plastic chaise lounge.

He was the only resident of the hotel, by far the largest building and the highest peak south of Atlantic City. It was built at the edge of the ocean in 1928 by a virtuoso of bad timing named Igor Lapp. Lapp named it the Imperial Hotel. Subsequent management had experimented with less majestic names, but local people never stopped calling it the Imperial. For them, it was no longer a building. It was a mountain. A natural landmark.

As he drank the coffee he looked over his naked body. May of 1969 felt more like July, and the last two weeks on the all-weather recliner had worked his melanin into a pigmenting frenzy. His legs were brown. His leg hairs blond. A virtual negative of winter legs, when skin turns white and leg hairs go brown.

The Box had been the hotel's observatory. The interior walls were covered floor-to-ceiling by an Art Deco mural rendering the dawn of creation. Swirling clouds of cosmic dust and bubbling, vulcanizing planets. Sometimes it kept him awake, knowing that in the silent darkness God was giving birth to a whole new universe.

During the Second World War, when the Coast Guard commandeered the hotel, attention turned from heaven to sea, which they believed was infested with German submarines. Everything but the mural had been stripped away and replaced by cots, radios and olive drab file cabinets.

He rose from the all-weather recliner and went back to the Box to pour another cup of coffee. He took it into the bathroom. The shower stall was another Coast Guard holdover. Galvanized metal walls engraved with graffiti:

"Jimmy M. sucks ensign meat."

"Impossible. Ensigns have no meat. Signed Jimmy M."

He showered, and without drying off, climbed into khaki shorts and T-shirt. He checked the length of the stubble on his face. He hated shaving, but a beard was out of the question. It would only make a bad situation worse.

His face was too big. His nose too long, his chin too heavy. His ears approached the grotesque. And his eyes were too far apart. When he smiled, only one side of his mouth would rise. His forehead was scored by a deep, V-shaped crease that started above the bridge of his nose, and ran up through his scalp.

His mother told him he looked French. It was a nice try, and he appreciated it. On a good day, he could imagine himself as Jean-Paul Belmondo.

The shaving soap was supposed to smell like leather, but it reminded him of a rotting cardboard box, or the wooden floor of an old attic. His mother had bought it for him. Several cases, a virtual lifetime supply. He knew someday he'd have to throw a lot of it away, but only after his mother was gone.

When he was done at the sink, he picked out a book from the stack next to his bed and brought it out to the balcony with another cup of coffee. It was one of Anaïs Nin's pornographies, an even better way to stir the morning blood than Chock full o'Nuts. He'd stolen it and a few hundred other books from the lost-and-found at the mental institution where he lived for a few years.

He felt Anaïs Nin's succulent prose warming his face and hands. Really not the best choice, he thought, given the state I'm in. The dislocated, fractured state of New Jersey. Where you could have coastal mornings like this, with a gray-green ocean below and blue airbrushed sky above. And foolish hotels, like the one old Igor built on the eastern edge of the state's easternmost island.

Jack gulped down the rest of his coffee and shifted his swelling erection around inside his khaki shorts. All dressed up, and no place to go, he thought to himself. It was time to start moving. He jogged back into the Box and grabbed his tank suit and towel off the dish rack where they'd been left to dry. He slipped out of the shorts and into the suit in a single graceful movement. He dropped the T-shirt on the floor.

The phone rang. That was surprising, since he'd never heard it ring before. It was a very old phone, installed and forgotten years ago. He listened to it, wondering what to do next. Did he feel violated or relieved? He picked up the receiver.

"Huh?"

"George home?"

"No George."

"No?"

"No. Just Jack."

"Jack? Not George?"

"No."

"Must be the wrong number."

"Do you remember what it was?"

"What?"

"The number you dialed. The wrong number."

"This isn't 609-354-8276?"

"I don't know. It doesn't matter."

"What doesn't?"

"The number. I don't have to know the number."

"What number?"

"Try George again. He's not here."

"You know when he'll be back?"

"He's never here. You have the wrong number."

"Sorry."

"That's okay."

He hung up the phone and eyed it for a few minutes, waiting for another violation. Silence.

The hotel's central stairwell began in the hall outside the Box. Jack bounded down, escaping the threat of another phone call. The stairs were marble. The walls were a dusty brown trimmed in gilt molding. Igor did it dumb, but he did it right. The shape of the central tower rose in a modified H. The top floor sloped inward forming a steep roof, so the windows had to be set into long dormers. The Box, sitting front and center at the top of the tower, interfered with the otherwise symmetrical lines of the roof. The highest point, in actuality, was the peak of an enormous smokestack shooting up from a tiny power plant only a few feet behind the hotel. A giant coal furnace once heated the rooms in winter and the Olympic-sized pool in summer. The pool had been empty for thirty years. Thin lines of tall dune grass grew from a checkerwork of cracks threading the cement bottom. The pipes and pumps once circulating seawater from ocean to pool had long since fused into solid rust.

The transition from the narrow stairwell to the cavernous lobby always made Jack feel a little dizzy. The ceiling above ate into the first four stories of the hotel. The walls were lathered with frescos, trompe l'oeil and plaster bas-relief. The floor space was in keeping with the profligate style of early twentieth-century banks and train stations. At the lobby's center was a two-story, octagonal kiosk the precise purpose of which no one, even Igor himself, ever truly understood.

The hotel was anchored to the earth by an outsized Greco-Roman portico supported by rows of Sequoia-tall, fluted columns. Terraced layers of stone steps poured out from the front entrance and rolled down to the sea, inviting the venturesome, and completing the building's majestic countenance.

Jack took three steps at a time on the way down. At four feet above sea level he hit a broad concrete path. The path took him to the seawall, down the last flight of steps, and out to the sea itself. He was panting hard as he took a level look at the Atlantic. Down here, the breeze was even cooler. The ocean, always slow to accept a change of season, chilled the air. Jack reckoned the water temperature to be on the cooler side of sixty degrees. He shielded his eyes against the glare off the glassy water. It'll be smooth, he thought, but it'll be cold.

He ran across the sand and into the surf. Immediately, his feet were numb. His heart sped up against the circulatory shock, reminding him how stupid it was to swim in the Atlantic Ocean in late May. So what? he told himself. So it's a little cold. So what?

In a few seconds he was into the breakers. He dove through the foam. Slimy plant life clung to his arms as he tried to clear the breakers for the open water. The strong sea smell filled his nose. His internal organs cowered and his testicles tried to climb back up into his body. Why the hell do I do this to myself? he asked himself, again.

Past the breakers, he felt his chest tighten. Swimming alone in a frigid ocean was an easy way to die, he thought, clinically.

His stroke began to smooth out. His arm arched high over the
water. He reached out and pulled a long pull, all the way back till
his hand brushed past his thigh. It was the long distance stroke
he'd developed for the ocean. The long pull for efficiency, the
high arch to clear the choppy waves. He raised his head every
few strokes to fix his bearings on a distant buoy. On the way
back, he would aim for the Imperial.

Movement was important to Jack. He had a plastic plate in
his head. It was put there to cover a section of his skull that
had been pulverized in a car accident. The brain tissue underneath had also been damaged, putting him in a four-year coma.
After his eyes opened, he spent another year as a drooling cata-
tonic, welded to a green, vinyl-upholstered chair. Clear food and
stimulants were delivered through intravenous tubes and the
atmosphere was held at an even sixty-eight degrees. His hair was
trimmed once a week. Every morning and afternoon, two muscular orderlies held him upright for a few minutes to allow blood
to run down into his legs. It wasn't enough. His buttocks and
thighs were laced with decubitus ulcers.

Volunteers came in and out of the room. They would sit
across from him and talk. Some would play cards, some would
read, others paced around the room, acting out dramatic scenes
from Shakespeare and Eugene O'Neill. Teenagers tortured guitar
strings and whispered perverse confidences. But Jack couldn't
speak, and he couldn't move. All he could do was sit on the green
chair with his head bowed and the tip of his tongue protruding
from between his lips.

Four hundred yards off the coast, a sandbar, an anomaly
on the ocean floor, raised a row of telltale breakers. They were
easy to swim through if he was careful not to swallow the salty
foam. He raised his head as he crested a swell and drew a bead
on the buoy. It was getting closer. He kept his pace: pulling
with long slow stokes and filling his lungs at every breath. At
this distance he usually began to feel a sickening fatigue creep
through his body. Nausea and cramping were familiar things, yet
never welcomed. The buoy was only about forty yards away. Jack
knew the total distance—out and back—was about a mile and a

quarter, depending on the tide. He felt the mild wave of nausea pass through him. It was definitely a good day. He picked up the pace.

Up close, the buoy always looked so tall. Jack hooked around and headed back to shore. He felt strong, and the cool, easterly breeze felt icy on his face as he looked over the tops of the waves for the Imperial Hotel. Once oriented, he settled back into his long, lazy-looking stroke.

The Imperial Hotel was only one of two monuments to lunacy authored by Igor Lapp. The other was Jack's mother.

Igor had a terrible time retaining secretarial help. His standards for technical competence would have daunted Katy Gibbs. He believed the key to longevity was a steady routine of high-protein meals, brisk walks and midday sex. So after his morning steak, he would walk from his apartment in Philadelphia to Camden and back. Too busy building architectural absurdities to commit to marriage, he looked to his secretarial pool to complete the third leg of his daily regimen.

Jack's grandmother was a flapper named Elizabeth Annandale. A crack stenographer, she would capture every syllable of Igor's scrambled dictation while staring wistfully out the window. Blind to her secretarial skills, he was deeply grateful for her sexual compliance. It was like a clear shot at immortality. Every afternoon between one and two o'clock they made love in a huge Murphy bed that fell out of the ersatz bookcase behind Igor's giant mahogany desk. A practice they continued right up to the moment Igor dropped dead prematurely at age forty-five from a massive heart attack, his cholesterol-choked arteries closing down as he walked briskly over the Ben Franklin Bridge.

He left everything to his lover and stenographer, who was the only mourner at his funeral. It was an unsettling experience for Elizabeth, and she might have cried were she not so preoccupied with her menstrual cycle. Normally clockwork perfect, she was already a month overdue. Seven months later she was nursing Jack's mother. When asked how she felt about the whole careening series of events, Elizabeth said, "Things occur."

A wave pushed Jack toward shore. He was over the sandbar, at a point where the top-heavy swells would crest and foam. It was just a prelude to the serious surf another 100 feet ahead. He sprinted over the remaining distance.

He felt the rising surge of a breaker. He relaxed his stroke and let the wave take over. As it cascaded forward, he slid down the face, and felt a pleasant surge of acceleration. The Jersey sand was hard beneath his feet. His arms and shoulders felt heavy and pumped full of blood. He was a little dizzy, but already feeling the narcotic effects of a bloodstream full of endorphins. The day had warmed up a lot. He picked up his towel and trotted back to the Imperial Hotel.

Avery Volpe stood at the rail that secured the third highest point on the island and glowered down at the ocean. Beneath his feet was the galvanized roof of the old opera house, a concrete mass squatting impossibly on a forest of pilings along the ocean side of the boardwalk. His eyes were following a seagull soaring toward the north, when he saw a swimmer sprinting through the surf toward the beach. It was Jack Halcyon, that ugly oddball who lived in the hotel, he thought. Out there every morning. He could see the windmill stroke arching high over the waves. One of the fastest ocean swimmers Avery had ever known. But not right. Something off about him.

Avery understood most kinds of trouble. It usually came from aggressive men and boys goaded by reproductive coding into assorted forms of malice and mayhem. This Avery dealt with in an old-fashioned way—with quick, vicious and demoralizing violence. Other trouble was bureaucratic, often in suit and tie, coming from guys coded with a different slant on challenging Avery for domination of his twelve-mile strip of Atlantic sandbar. This Avery dealt with in approximately the same way.

The long, dense hair on his hands moved with the wind like grassland on the Serengeti. Coarser hair was pressed beneath his T-shirt, growing in thickets over mountainous sweeps of muscle, tendon, ligature and bone. At the crown of his head the climate faltered, and only a thin slick of gleaming skin separated the world from the hardest skull in South Jersey.

His back formed an inverted triangle above baggy, threadbare gym trunks. His legs swelled at the thighs, then tapered to stick-like shins that saved Avery from any inclination toward narcissism.

Chewing gum, his jaw moved as if working on a slab of freshly killed herbivore. People stood back a step or two when Avery felt the need to chew a little gum.

He stared intently at the ocean that morning. But for the gulls, it was calm and quiet. Avery disliked a calm ocean. A tormented ocean gave his life shape, making it easier to understand why he had a life in the first place. When it was calm, he had to look for storms elsewhere.

He trotted down to the beach to take in a five-mile run before the beach patrol showed up.

When he got back to the office, his lieutenants said good morning and watched him carefully. Each had been decked at least once during their long association with their captain. It usually happened when Avery sensed someone had lost that edginess of fear in his presence. Many were larger and stronger than him. But as yet, none meaner.

This was the first muster of the season. T-shirts were fresh, faces still white, except for a half dozen black kids who were now milky brown, unlike the color of asphalt they'd be by the end of the summer. Attitudes were optimistic. The bulk of the force was assembling in the ballroom that filled the top floor of the opera house, while the lieutenants hung out in the office, showing off their ascendancy. Typical of the first day, most of the guards were there earlier than necessary. In a few days that eagerness would degrade under the influence of hangovers, sun and physical exertion. Though no one was ever late. To miss a muster was to resign from the beach patrol.

Subgroups jostled and taunted each other. New kids looked wary, conspicuous in unfaded trunks. A few luckier ones knew a veteran or two—recruits from college swim teams or the neighborhood. The veteran loners sought private spots to squat silently, or to methodically organize their gear.

Jack had a spot like this of his own. It was atop a pile of old sails and lobster buoys that once served as ballroom decoration. Some ancient custodian had thrown it all above a big storage cabinet behind the built-in bar. Jack scrambled up there a few seconds before Avery gave his kickoff address.

"Nobody's drowned in the sixteen years I've been in charge of this beach patrol," was the standard opening, modified only to update his tenure, "and nobody's going to drown this year. If anybody does happen to drown on your beach, you're advised to swim out there and drown with them, since you're gonna die anyway from me personally wringing your fucking neck. Outside of that, we have a few simple rules everybody ought to know. If you fuck up, discipline will be handled in the appropriate fashion. To learn what that is, just fuck up. Once.

"As some of you know, we have the longest protected beach in New Jersey with the fewest number of people to protect it. That's because this is just a skinny shit of a sandbar that only holds a limited number of buildings. This means we can't support a beach patrol big enough to adequately guard a beach this long. We've compensated for this by hiring people who believe they are more physically capable than the average lifeguard. You are supposed to be faster, tougher, more disciplined than any other beach patrol on the East Coast. You probably aren't, but you are required to behave as if you were."

Avery then turned the housekeeping over to Johnny Lukeiwitz, the sad-eyed senior lieutenant who'd been with Avery since childhood. Avery and Johnny were a complementary duet, a dance team of opposites. Johnny read the rolls, assigned beaches, reviewed rules, and encouraged the patronage of burger joints and bars politically affiliated with the mayor of Elysiana, who was the official guardian of the beach patrol. Johnny also introduced the rookies to the senior guards who would break them in.

Rookie training had become one of Jack's primary functions, since he was the only senior guard who preferred the salt mines, a stretch of beach furthest away from downtown with the thinnest population and most tenuous contact with the rest of the patrol. Even on clear days it was hard to see the next guard stand to the north. To the south was the federal preserve—uncharted, uninhabited salt and sand wastes, overgrown pine groves, waterfowl protectorates, and no one knew what else since no one was allowed to go in there.

Rookies would always be assigned to low-density beaches manned by second-, third-, and fourth-year guards rotated out from the busy beaches downtown. Jack had started in the mines, and in his second year, asked Johnny to make it permanent. Avery didn't know how he felt about that; no one had ever wanted to be out in the mines full time, away from the boardwalk, the hoagies, the heavier concentrations of available women and girls. But he never interfered with Johnny's assignments.

So every year Johnny brought a fresh rookie over to meet Jack on top of the old storage cabinet behind the bar, as he did that year.

"Mike Ditzler," said Johnny.

Ditzler looked as if he was poised to share something extraordinarily funny. It wasn't until much later that Jack realized Ditzler's face always looked that way, with or without a forthcoming joke.

"Jack is a sixth-year guard," Johnny told Ditzler. "Your main job this summer is to do everything he tells you to do. Understood? If he tells you to dance in the moonlight with a four-peckered pig, you do it, understand? If he doesn't like you, you're gone. No explanations. No apologies. Understood?"

Ditzler jerked out his hand. Taken by surprise, Jack wasn't immediately sure what the gesture meant. Ditzler made a shaking motion and expanded his smile. Johnny looked embarrassed, then relieved when Jack took Ditzler's hand.

"Okay," said Johnny, "let's have a good summer."

Johnny said that kind of thing as if he believed saying it out loud was the only way to ward off evil spirits.

Whether that summer was actually good is still a matter of interpretation and some debate.

CHAPTER
3

"M<small>Y NAME</small> is Gwendalynn," she told the sleeping slob, "and I'm going to clean your house. But only if you pay me. Money."

His head came up off his chest and he opened his eyes, which were shot through with red lines like tiny streaks of electric current.

"Huh?"

"Surfer boy outside said you guys would pay me to clean up the house. Eighty. Forty a day. Cash, up front, each day."

"Fuck no."

"He said you'd pay for it."

"Fuck no again."

"Okay."

She turned to leave.

"How much?" the slob asked.

"Eighty. Up front."

"You said forty up front."

"That was before you cursed at me."

"I didn't curse at you. I just cursed."

He stood up and looked down at himself. Supported by the linoleum table, he staggered across the kitchen and fell into the bathroom.

"Gross," said Gwendalynn.

"Feels worse than it looks," he called back through the bathroom door.

"You shouldn't drink so much."

"This is part of the deal? I take shit from you?"

"You're right. I'm hardly one to talk."

The guy took off his ruined T-shirt and rolled it in a ball as he came out of the bathroom.

"I'm Baxter," he said. "The free spender you met outside is Randy. He rents the place, so if he says you're hired I guess you are. They're two other guys here, but they're at work. Lifeguards. First day."

He sat in a kitchen chair and closed his eyes.

"Do you have cleaning stuff?" Gwendalynn asked him.

"Does it look like it?"

"Give me an extra twenty with the eighty and I'll go get it."

"How do I know you won't just take off?"

Gwendalynn pretended she didn't hear him say that. If she'd heard him say that she'd have to leave the house and never come back and she didn't want to do that. She really needed some money and didn't know how long it would take to find another way to get it. She closed her eyes pretending so fiercely that Baxter got the hint and went upstairs to get the cash. It was an arduous journey for him, twice sidetracked by the threat of upheaval, but eventually accomplished. He stuffed a hundred dollars worth of small bills in her hand, then sailed over to a swayback couch into which he dropped like a felled tree.

Gwendalynn was glad to be out of the house again. She took deep breaths as she walked back up to the row of shops on Main Street she'd passed before, hoping to fill her blood with fresh oxygen to cleanse the fetid reek still hanging in her nostrils.

She stopped at the hoagie shop where the waitress had given her a meal. The woman was at the counter, pouring out two milkshakes from a tall aluminum container.

"Here," said Gwendalynn, putting a ten dollar bill down on the counter. "Thanks for what you did."

The waitress was surprised, but quick on the uptake, snatching the ten off the counter and stuffing it back in Gwendalynn's hand. She was frowning, but looked happy.

"Can't go back on charity, darling. God don't like it."

"Okay," said Gwendalynn. "If it's for God."

"Use it to buy a hairbrush and something to wear, girl. You live around here?"

"Chicago," she said, going back into the sun, rolling up the ten with the other bills in her hand, since she didn't own any pockets. That was the first thing she bought at the general store—a pair of jeans with pockets in all the normal places, a blue chambray shirt, flip-flops and two pairs of panties. And heeding the woman's advice, a hairbrush, along with toothpaste and a toothbrush, and a big fabric bag to carry everything, along with the spray cleaner, Comet, a bucket of sponges and several rolls of paper towels.

Baxter was sound asleep on the couch when she got back to the house, and stayed that way for the next two hours while she cleaned the bathroom. When she finished, she locked the bathroom door so she could lie down in the bathtub and sleep for a few hours, which she did until awakened by a loud knock.

"Have to pee," said the voice on the other side of the door.

Gwendalynn woke up before she remembered where she was, causing a painful surge of panic and disorientation. She lay frozen in the bathtub until she heard another knock.

"You dead in there?"

"I don't know."

"How 'bout it?"

She regained enough of her mental footing to pull herself out of the bathtub and open the door. It was Randy, hair wet, back from surfing. She gathered her fabric bag and cleaning equipment off the floor, then dropped it again so she could splash some water on her face.

"Sorry," she said into the bathroom sink, "I haven't slept much lately."

He waited silently for her to finish and take herself and her things out of the bathroom so he could close the door. She looked at the kitchen and wondered if these boys had any speed, but decided it was too dangerous to ask. She'd have to make do without.

It took the rest of the day to clean the kitchen and get most of the way through the living room. By then both Randy and Baxter had disappeared, leaving her gratefully alone in the house, until two other boys appeared, also tall and blond like Randy, wearing matching dark blue swim trunks and warm-up jackets with "Elysiana Beach Patrol" embroidered on their chests. They were carrying paper bags filled with hoagies and beer.

"Take it in the kitchen," she said to them. "That part's done. Gimme a few minutes in here and you can come back."

"You Georgina?" one of them asked her.

"No. I'm Gwendalynn."

"I thought Georgina was Randy's girlfriend."

"I'm not his girlfriend. I'm just cleaning the house."

"What's Georgina going to do?"

"That's up to Randy."

She took the boa constrictor and slung it over her shoulder so she could dust the banister, working briskly before the snake could coil around inviting body parts. One of the blond guys set aside his provisions so he could slide it off her shoulder.

"You got to stay in your cage, baby," he said to the boa, dropping it into the aquarium.

"You must know snakes," said the other guy.

"Plenty," she said.

She hurried through what she thought would fulfill her obligation, at least toward the living room, and left the house before the blond guys were done eating. It was getting close to dusk, and she wanted to find a place to sleep while she could still see where she was going. She walked toward the ocean, instinctively, since she'd never seen an ocean before. She heard it before she saw it, making her wonder how people felt about the noisy breakers. They must like it, she thought, since the closer you got to the water, the bigger the houses.

Once there she was a little disappointed. The waves were smaller than she thought they would be, having based her expectations on photos she'd seen of surfers riding down the slopes of twenty-five foot waves off Hawaii. But she liked the color of the water, and the fine texture of the sand, now being raked smooth by a machine that came out at dusk every night to clean up debris and obliterate footprints and sandcastles constructed during the day. She took note of that, and headed south along the beach toward a rise of scrub-covered mountains of sand, which she assumed would be unmolested by giant mechanized sand rakes.

An hour later, having walked several miles down the beach, she discovered a path that led deep into the dunes, which she followed until it almost became a forest of rangy cedars and tangled vines. She caught sight of a small hollow away from the beaten path, toward which she made her way with some difficulty, rewarded by the sight of a sand bed scooped out of a grass-covered mound. She lay in the sand, using her fabric bag as a pillow, closed her eyes and immediately fell asleep, remaining there for eighteen hours until awakened by hunger and thirst and the shock of a large green fly plunging its ravenous mandibles into her forehead.

"Son of a bitch!"

CHAPTER

4

Petey Amato was excited by the potential of the new eight-track car stereo technology. Most of the devices were being retrofitted below the dashboard where it only took seconds to extract. He already had several stored in the attic with a few hundred AM and AM/FM radios, hub caps, fuel pumps, gear boxes—standard and automatic—carburetors, chrome air cleaner covers, starter motors, door trim, hood ornaments, and a thousand other parts he'd culled from the herds of cars and trucks arriving and departing with the tourist trade every day. After Labor Day he'd switch back to fixed assets—stereo components, cameras, TV sets, jewelry and silver tea sets found in abundance in the summer homes clustered downtown, and strung out to the south, thinning quickly in density up to the entrance to the federal preserve.

Petey had rigged one of the units to a home stereo, using a twelve-volt transformer swiped out of an old wooden cruiser docked at the Sea Side Marina at the southern end of Half Moon Bay. He was playing Jethro Tull as a kindness toward his nominal girlfriend, Clarice, who had mistakenly seen the band at the Bright Line, a folk joint outside Philadelphia. A mistake for both Clarice and the boys in Jethro Tull, who needed the full square footage of the tiny stage for their Marshall amplifiers, forcing the band to stand in a small area down on the floor that was supposed to hold the first three rows of seating. Clarice had a center spot in what would have been row four.

She'd heard that the band specialized in traditional English folk music, and featured a flautist from Blackpool. Clarice had tried to play the flute in high school because she thought women playing the flute looked delicate and ethereal, but never mastered the embouchure. The resulting breathy squeak coming from her bedroom prompted her father, a steamfitter at Bethlehem Steel, to smack on her door and tell her to quit torturing the cat.

Clarice needed more emotional support than that from her father, whom she blamed for the abandonment of her musical career.

Her injured self-esteem found a balm in Moroccan hashish, happily provided by Petey Amato, the dark-skinned Italian kid from her history class who'd managed a fair amount of academic success without ever taking a test or turning in any homework. She didn't know that his teachers were terrified of him, and in an unspoken conspiracy, had moved him quickly and fluidly from elementary school to middle school and straight through high school, leaving him unburdened by a formal education beyond a rudimentary grasp of handwriting and an appreciation of Aaron Burr, who'd actually shot some other important fucker and gotten away with it.

For Clarice, one of the few patrons of the Bright Line that night who survived without permanent hearing loss, it was an epiphany. What kind of epiphany was unclear, even to Clarice, who could only sleep with Jethro Tull playing continuously on the record player until her roommates told her she had to leave the house. By then she was sleeping with Petey, who failed to see electric flute and overdriven guitar amplifiers as much of a sleep aid. In deference to him, Clarice gave up Tull at bedtime in exchange for free use of Petey's hashish inventory, which would have annoyed him if he hadn't been so preoccupied with his growing commerce in the emerging eight-track technology.

Petey and Clarice lived in an apartment above a row of storefronts built along the Northern Channel at the top of the island. It was the only structure to survive Hurricane Donna in 1960, having been anchored to a concrete breakwater meant to secure a line of docks that were never built. Igor Lapp had failed to take a sounding of the channel, which was too shallow to accommodate the ocean liners he envisioned would bring thousands of beach lovers down from Manhattan to stay at the Imperial Hotel, four blocks away.

Petey first took an interest in the location looking down on the roof from the hotel, where he lived every summer with his friend Jack Halcyon when the two were growing up together in Philadelphia. Petey hadn't appreciated this seasonal routine until it was suddenly truncated by the accident. So the first summer Jack was in the convalescent home, his mother blasted by grief and the hotel shuttered, Petey came down and slept in houses left empty during the week, then in the dunes on the weekends. He repeated that approach the next summer, then after that, never left.

Drawn to the north end of the island, he finally wrangled a year-round lease on the apartment above the incongruous little row of shops. He liked having a view of the Northern Channel, but appreciated the building more for the extended attic space, accessible through a hatch of a closet in the main bedroom.

Since 1960 several homes had been built along Igor's breakwater—larger and more expensive than the ones blown into the bay, whose value the owners believed was diminished by the commercial complex housing Petey's apartment, undervaluing the close proximity of ice cream cones, tuna hoagies and cheese steaks, surfboard wax—and from the gift store, assorted ceramic representations of sea serpents, petrified starfish, miniature lighthouses, mugs formed out of the heads of fishermen, Cape May diamonds, conch shell ashtrays, and slices of cedar trees branded with statements like "God bless people who run around in circles, for they shall be known as wheels."

Petey had never been in the gift store, but he'd stolen a lot of merchandise from the surf shop, whose proprietor was usually asleep on a cot behind the counter, having breakfasted every morning on whole grain cereal and wheat germ, and a healthy bowl of Petey's hashish.

The only thing Petey loved more than stealing things was surfing, so it was gratifying to combine his two favorite pastimes. His surfboard had been delivered to him on the roof of a Plymouth Barracuda several seasons before, when some kid had the bad judgment to park it overnight at the curb under Petey's bedroom. He'd never surfed before, or ever thought about surfing, but the unsecured surfboard was too much of a temptation.

After letting it cool off for a season, he took it down to the ocean one day. Unlike Clarice, whose lack of musical aptitude had betrayed her, Petey was a natural surfer, getting upright and staying there for almost thirty seconds on his first try. Heretofore escaping any kind of addiction, even to his most potent merchandise, Petey was completely hooked, seizing every opportunity to relive that first glorious rush, to refine his skills and add to his repertoire of rips, slashes, cutbacks and carves.

In a further blessing, some of the best surfing in New Jersey was off the beaches at the northern end of the island. The fluid dynamics of the Northern Channel, enhanced by a long ocean jetty built with huge black boulders, shaped the sea floor into a series of gullies and sandbars. These were strategically arrayed to create at least two coherent breaks, graduated in intensity, one for experienced surfers, the other for novices.

Petey always started with the outside break, and only rode the inside on his way in for the day. Or night, since he found after hours more dangerously appealing and less crowded, having only to share the water with other serious surfers, among whom he was generally regarded as the best on the island, with the possible exception of Randy Calvert. Like Petey, Randy never officially competed, yet showed the same skill and commitment, surfing day and night, always alone and aloof, patient and unerring in his ability to pick out the heavies—the biggest rideable waves. Instinctively, Randy and Petey never rode the same wave, and always kept plenty of water between them, sometimes filled with lesser lights, sometimes only empty seas.

It was the night surfing that had cut into Petey's normal working hours, forcing him to find ways to optimize his stock, to focus on higher ticket items that led to faster, more profitable turnover. Which is why the new eight-tracks seem to hold so much promise.

"How's it sound?" he asked Clarice as she emerged from the bedroom, still mostly asleep.

"Kind of thin. Something wrong with the stereo?"

"It's not the stereo. It's an eight-track. It sounds thin because it's supposed to be playing in a car."

"Then why's it playing on the stereo?" she asked, staring into one of the kitchen cupboards as she tried to remember what she'd hoped to find there.

"It's a test. I wanted to hear what it sounds like. It's the new eight-track cartridge system."

"Sounds like . . ." she searched for something to say besides thin, but then the memory returned. "Coffee."

"You're not gonna hear anything if you're high."

"I'm not high. I'm half asleep."

Petey watched her stumble around the kitchen making coffee. She was wearing a translucent baby doll camisole that rode up above her naked butt when she leaned into the 'fridge. He particularly liked that feature of hers, ample, just shy of overweight. Rounded and pale. Smackable. It compensated for a lot.

"I'll put one in the truck. You can listen to it there," he said.

"I'm all ears. Soon as I wake up."

He disconnected the equipment and brought it all up to the attic to store among the other contraband. Petey was meticulous in keeping the living area free of stolen goods, at least anything stolen within the last year, believing that the Elysiana Police Force lacked the imagination to gaze upward in the course of a house search, should anything so unlikely ever happen.

This was one of the areas where Petey would have benefitted from an actual education. It might have helped him appreciate the capabilities of the local cops. Especially the summer cops, mostly ardent law students for whom the job meant vacation money and a chance to flesh out their resumes, impressing future employers with their courage and respect for the rule of law. The population of the island went from about five hundred to twenty-five thousand for three months out of the year, so there was a big demand for summer cops, exacerbated by competition from beach patrols up and down the Jersey coast. The situation was even worse in the summer of 1969, when the recruiting inventory among law students was at an all-time low, the '68 Democratic convention having cemented a prevailing notion among the young that uniforms of any kind, especially accessorized by a side weapon, were inherently fascistic.

Norm Harlan, the island's council president, to whom the police force reported, followed the same logic. He only recruited law schools who maintained a Patton's Commandos unit on campus, an unchartered national society that even student military organizations like the ROTC, Semper Fi and the Pershing Rifles regarded as dangerously retrogressive. This guaranteed a stable recruitment pool, automatically receptive to Norm Harlan's save the New Jersey Shore from hippies and communists sales pitch, and one with a higher than average number of people for whom the label fascist would not be too big a stretch.

The summer of 1969 saw a hardening at the political poles, and was thus an invigorating time for Harlan, whose political affinities were never threatened by ambivalence or doubt. He marked the end of free America with the first term of Franklin Roosevelt, a man he regarded as the great betrayer, and all subsequent presidents lesser betrayers, until the blessed second coming of Richard Nixon in the fall of 1968.

Norm Harlan was a short man, with a large head that sat neckless and balding on his shoulders, and glasses that bobbed on the ridge of his nose when he squinted. Though he'd lived his whole life on the one by twenty-five mile sun-drenched island, he'd managed to remain pale and fleshy, looking as if he'd spent the same lifetime in the basement of an embalmer.

He was born in the back of a cab on the way to the hospital on the mainland. His father decided they'd save the cost of a hospital stay by heading straight back to the island, figuring the hard part was already over with. Since then, Harlan's off-island experience consisted of two years of community college, a daily forty-five minute drive to and from Atlantic City.

After graduating he hadn't seen much reason to leave Ely siana, given the patronage job his father had arranged for him with the public works department, which required little in the way of effort, since virtually all the public works on the island were developed and paid for by the State of New Jersey or the Army Corps of Engineers, leaving him plenty of time to study the decline of American civilization, delving deeply into primary sources like *Time Magazine* and the *CBS Evening News*. He supplemented this by examining the vacationers who flooded in every summer, bringing with them entrepreneurs like Petey Amato who flowed in with the tide, like camp followers feasting on the economic by-product of a huge expeditionary force.

Harlan saw Nixon's election as a harbinger, signaling the summer of 1969 as a time of change, a resetting of the fulcrum under the universe unbalanced sixteen years ago when Avery Volpe was promoted from lieutenant to captain of the beach patrol. Avery was the football coach at a teacher's college on the mainland and had long been the prior captain's protégé and designated successor, a status he'd conveyed to Mayor Black prior to retiring. Since the beach patrol reported directly to the mayor, it was his responsibility to name the new captain and not the council president's, an administrative anomaly that caused Norm Harlan such agonizing frustration and resentment as to border on abject despair.

All other public safety departments reported to the council president. The police and bay constables, roads and parks, paramedics and ambulances, taxes and administration. But not the beach patrol, by far the most heavily staffed municipal entity. Since the beach patrol reported to Mayor Black, as did the council president, it looked like Avery held the same rank as Norm Harlan. According to the borough attorney, Joanie Sheldon, this wasn't technically true, that Avery was administratively on an equal footing with Marty Romanovski, the chief of police and Harlan's principle supporter. But that mattered little, since whenever lifeguards were on duty, from Memorial Day to Labor Day, between nine and five, Marty's jurisdiction extended only to the edge of the boardwalk that delineated downtown, and to the end of the access roads south of downtown all the way to the salt mines, and up to the federal preserve at the southern end of the island, encompassing the impenetrable dunes along the way, which left the beach and the surf and the ocean beyond in the possession of Avery Volpe, for whom the concept of ownership was pure and absolute.

Hatred for the mayor burned bright in Norm Harlan's meager heart. Issues of authority aside, Harlan thought Black dangerously subject to the evil winds of liberalism, as well as grossly unqualified, having never held public office before becoming mayor. Worse, Black had been a social studies teacher at the high school on the mainland when he won a three-way race against the incumbent and Harlan himself, for whom the loss still caused a painful burning in his stomach every time he thought about it.

During the campaign, Harlan had run a secret but thorough investigation of Clifton Black's teaching philosophy, uncovering damning evidence of blatantly anti-American curricula. What should have been a conscientious study of the Founding Fathers, the Constitution and civil order was instead a dangerous obsession with Roosevelt's New Deal, anti-war protestors and civil rights. In Harlan's mind the usual grab bag of radical left-wing claptrap. Reform of the idiotic borough power structure was not only a matter of good local governance, to Norm Harlan it was a struggle for the very political soul of Elysiana.

Having been isolated from mainland reality most of his life, Harlan's greatest strength was not knowing what he didn't know. It gave him a courage of conviction unattainable to the ordinary citizens who filled Elysiana's beaches, much less the cynical sophisticates he so earnestly despised.

Harlan's office was one of the smallest in the borough administrative complex, cramped and unadorned, with minimum seating or file space, the same office he had during his first job in the public works department. As he advanced through the borough hierarchy he'd been reluctant to give it up for something more spacious, fearing that would draw unwanted attention, even jealousy among those he'd have to supersede someday if he was to successfully wrench control of the island away from the usurper.

That he felt ever closer to achieving that goal proved to him the wisdom of the strategy, though it had zero impact on his relationship with Avery Volpe, who'd never been inside the borough offices, and whose only administrative space was an enclosed area off the balcony above the old opera house where Avery and his lieutenants kept a few desks so they'd have a place to put their bare feet when leaning back in their chairs.

Small as his office was, it was big enough to have a phone, which often rang. Norm had an aversion to face-to-face contact with other human beings, especially those who worked for him, so he relied heavily on other means of communication.

"Harlan here."

"Norman, I can't find her, what are we going to do?" his wife yelled into the phone, forcing him to pull it away from his ear.

"What are you talking about?"

"It's Sweetie. She's gone. I can't find her anywhere. You have to come home."

Harlan had fielded many of these calls from his wife. Her nervous system was in a perpetual state of alarm, whether over a chirping bug in the garage or a misplaced child. Sweetie had been a late blessing to the couple, and even after seven years, the shock of it all still lingered.

"Have you checked the car?" Harlan asked. "That's where she was the last time."

"I checked the car, the yard, every room in the house. You have to call the police. Oh, God, the ocean. You have to call Avery."

"It's the second day of the season," said Harlan. "They'll be busy."

"We're talking about our only daughter!" Paula screamed into the phone. "Call the police!"

"I am the police," he said.

"Then call yourself!" she screamed again, hanging up the phone.

Harlan sighed and gently put the receiver back in the cradle. He counted down slowly from ten to one, then picked it up again to call Marty Romanovski, the chief of police.

"Do me a favor, will you, Marty? Get one of your boys to drive over to my place to help my wife figure out where she put my daughter."

"You know how she can be sometimes," said Marty, blowing the steam off a fresh cup of coffee he'd just bought at the hoagie place under Petey Amato's apartment.

"If she gives you a hard time, shoot her."

"Roger that, boss."

CHAPTER
5

GWENDALYNN SHOT bolt upright and slapped her forehead, killing the greenie and causing a young girl, who'd been sitting several feet away watching the greenie zip around Gwendalynn's sleeping head, to scream, which startled Gwendalynn enough to scream herself.

"Why did you do that?" she asked the girl, catching her breath.

"You scared me when you jumped up."

"Something bit me," she said, looking at the smear of blood and pulverized exoskeleton in the palm of her hand.

"I thought you were dead," said the girl. "You were going to be my latest dead person."

"How old are you?"

"Seven."

"I'm twenty-one and I still haven't seen a dead person."

The girl thought about that.

"I'm going to be twenty-one. Next year, I think."

"Okay," said Gwendalynn. "Then I'm going to be seven. And a half."

"You can't be seven. That's ridiculous," said the girl, though she seemed enchanted by the idea.

"Do you belong to someone or do you live in the dunes?" asked Gwendalynn.

"I live in the dunes. I have a bed and a refrigerator."

"Can you make a cup of coffee?"

"Of course."

"Great. I'll take regular, with cream and sugar."

The girl stood up and picked a small piece of bark off the sand. She brought it over to Gwendalynn.

"Here."

"Thank you, darling."

"Sweetie," she corrected, sitting back down again.

"Okay, Sweetie. You're very particular."

"That's my name. Sweetie Harlan."

"I'm Gwendalynn Rothschild if you talk to my mother. If you talk to my father, I'm Gwendalynn Anders."

"What if I only talk to you?" asked Sweetie.

"Then I'm just plain Gwendalynn."

Sweetie's loose brown curls tumbled down around her bare shoulders. She wore a lime green terry cloth dress over her bathing suit. Her skin was pale, accented by bright red patches on her cheeks and the tip of her nose. By the end of the season she would be the color of oiled walnut. She had her father's round face. It looked a lot better on her.

"I'm always Sweetie Harlan, no matter what."

"That's good. Don't let 'em tell you any different."

Gwendalynn pulled herself up off the sand and rolled her head around her shoulders to stretch out the kinks. Sweetie imitated her.

"Do your parents know where you are?" Gwendalynn asked.

"I don't have any parents. I live in the dunes."

"Okay. Does anyone live in the dunes with you?"

"Only my mommy."

Sweetie leaned forward and shoved her hands into the sand, scooping up handfuls which she watched run through her fingers.

"I'd like to meet your mommy," said Gwendalynn.

"She's very nervous."

"Really. About what?"

"Everything," said Sweetie. "My daddy said it's her disposition."

Gwendalynn gathered up her fabric bag and slung it over her shoulder.

"I'd appreciate it if you'd show me how to get back to the ocean. I gotta clean up some skuzzy bedrooms today."

Sweetie looked to her right, then her left, then raised her hands, palms up.

"I don't know," she said.

"Well, I got to find a way out. If I can't, I guess I'll have to live with you in the dunes."

Gwendalynn started to retrace her steps in the sand, noticing they'd been somewhat obscured by a pair of little feet. She was glad to hear Sweetie fall in behind, and gladder still to see their tracks intermingled all the way to the beach. The sun sat well above the horizon, spreading white light across the surface of the ocean, hurting Gwendalynn's eyes. She'd experienced the same thing looking out over Lake Michigan, and again felt a small disappointment that the sun was no grander over this infinitely larger body of water.

A red Jeep drove out of the glare across the wet sand along the water's edge. It was moving slowly, with a driver and a passenger, each wearing the lifeguard T-shirts Gwendalynn had seen on the two blond boys who lived with Randy and Baxter. The passenger was scanning the water with a pair of binoculars, so it was the driver who first spotted Gwendalynn walking out of the dunes. The Jeep turned off in her direction.

"Hey, Sweetie," said the driver, Johnny Lukeiwitz.

"Hey, Johnny. What're you doing here?" asked Sweetie.

"Nuthin'. Just driving around. Who's your friend?" he asked.

His partner in the Jeep was talking on a handheld radio, telling somebody they'd found the little girl.

"Just plain Gwendalynn," said Sweetie. "She lives in the dunes."

"Really," said Johnny. "Got a house in there?"

"Just a bed and a refrigerator," said Gwendalynn. She scooped up the little girl and dropped her in the lap of the guard in the passenger seat. "Love to tell you more, but I'm late for work. See you, Sweetie. Tell her mother to keep a better eye on her," she added to the guys in the Jeep.

She was twenty feet down the beach when the Jeep pulled up next to her. She kept walking.

"Her father wants to know where you found her," said Johnny.

"She found me. In the dunes. Woke me up."

"You're not allowed to sleep in there," said Johnny's partner.

She looked over at him, then forward again as she continued walking.

"Just taking a nap, boys. Don't get all excited."

"Her father's the council president," said Johnny.

"He's the boss of the world," said Sweetie.

Gwendalynn veered west away from the waterline as a signal to the lifeguards that the conversation was over. That's why she didn't see them turn around and head for a breach in the dunes wide enough to allow the Jeep to pass through to Ocean Avenue, and then travel a block over to Norm and Paula Harlan's house.

It was only a few years old, built on sunken piers twelve feet above the sand. From the wraparound balcony on the second floor you could get a good view of the wetlands to the west and the dunes to the east. The Harlans were among the pioneers who first ventured south into the mines, then completely undeveloped territory between downtown and the federal preserve. Nearly at sea level and once routinely flooded by storm surges, the mines were reclaimed in the 1930's when the Army Corps of Engineers piled up the dunes, a massive undertaking no one in the federal government had authorized, according to a young investigative reporter for the *Sea Breeze*, Elysiana's local paper.

Since the story broke at the beginning of the Second World War, in which the reporter was killed during the invasion of North Africa, not much came of his assertions. This came as a relief to a unit of the corps stationed at Fort Dix, who had decided on their own to build the dunes as a way to break up the tedium of pre-war military service.

Another happy by-product was a new water system for the island that included a water tower, the only structure to challenge the Imperial Hotel for command of the skyline. It was basically a giant green ball mounted on a four-legged stand that would reach about the tenth floor of the twenty-floor Imperial. On a clear day, Jack could see flocks of seagulls through his binoculars resting their wings on the crown of the big ball; and if he'd known or cared, could have picked out Norman and Paula Harlan's house about three blocks east of the tower, where at that moment Johnny Lukeiwitz was pulling in between the piers that held the place twelve feet off the ground.

Johnny scooped Sweetie out of the back of the Jeep and brought her up to the balcony. Paula Harlan exploded out a screen door.

"Oh my God, Sweetie, you scared the living bat shit out of me!" she yelled loud enough to hurt Johnny's ears. He handed over the girl and took a few steps back.

"Only Daddy's allowed to say shit," said Sweetie, pushing herself back from her mother's embrace.

"Where was she?" Paula demanded of Johnny, as if he'd been holding her hostage.

"I guess in the dunes. Some hippie chick found her in there and was walking her home when we picked her up."

"Hippie chick? Oh, God, were you given anything?" she asked Sweetie, clutching her by the shoulders. "Did that girl give you anything to swallow?"

"I gave her a cup of coffee," said Sweetie.

"You don't just give coffee to strangers," said Paula. "It's dangerous. You want some, Johnny? We know him, it's okay dear," she added to Sweetie, whose attention had already been diverted by her miniature kitchen ensemble in the living room, which she could see through the sliding glass doors encircling the balcony.

"I'll make the coffee," she told her mother, pulling out of her grasp.

Paula watched her leave and looked back at Johnny with gratitude.

"You are a hero, Johnny," she told him. "A true hero. And I don't say that to everybody who finds my daughter."

"You gotta put a leash on that kid, Paula. She's a runner."

"She's a doll baby, that's what she is. You gonna come in for that coffee?" she said, taking a step forward in a way that inserted her presence into the outside reaches of his personal space.

Johnny's soft-eyed, melancholic face told nothing of what was on his mind. He just looked at Paula in her flowered muumuu, filled with her abundant but well-defined figure, and her jet black hair, too black for nature, but an acceptable frame for her young-looking face with its high cheekbones and dark gray eyes.

"I'm working."

Paula rolled her shoulders and stuck out her hip.

"So come on back when you're not."

"Yeah, then what?"

Paula took a step back, but left her hip in its forward position.

"Don't get suggestive, Johnny, it's just Paula asking you to have a lousy cup of coffee."

"Next time I need a lousy cup of coffee, I'll look you up," he told her as he bounded down the stairs. She leaned over the railing to watch him go, propped by her elbows, her butt swaying to and fro.

"Johnny, Johnny, Johnny, what a piece of ass," she said to him, under her breath.

"Which piece, Mommy?" asked Sweetie, causing her mother to shoot upright and spin around. "I think he's got a right half and a left, just like me," said the little girl, twisting around in an attempt to examine her own posterior.

"I didn't say that," said Paula.

"What?"

"What you think I said about Johnny."

"You just forgot."

"I didn't."

"You don't have to remember."

"I don't?"

"I'll just ask Daddy," said Sweetie, untwisting so she could run back into the house. "You told me he knows ev-a-ree-thing!"

On the way back to the opera house Johnny stopped at Jack's guard stand, one of only three that secured the mines, a stretch of beach over seven miles long, the most southerly and thus the last outpost of the Elysiana Beach Patrol before you reached the federal preserve. On most days the haze off the ocean made it impossible to see the stand to the north much less hear the sound of a run whistle, a series of short, screeching bursts declaring an emergency worthy of reinforcement from neighboring guards. Downtown, a run whistle could draw thirty guards to a single beach in a matter of minutes. In the mines you saved your breath for the action at hand. Even if the wind was blowing the right way, allowing the whistle to pierce the noise of the surf, you'd be lucky to get the dubious help of a single guy staggering on the scene after a flat-out two or three mile run over powdery New Jersey sand.

If you guarded the mines you learned to be on your own. Luckily, almost nothing ever happened out there, making the physical dangers mostly theoretical. The existential, on the other hand, were perilous.

"Found the kid," Jack heard Johnny say as he pulled his Jeep up to the stand.

"In the dunes?" said Jack.

"Basically," said Johnny. "You knew that?"

"She likes the dunes."

"Tell her to stay the hell out of there. I don't want any more three-day searches. She knows them better than anyone."

"Keep her the hell out of there," said Johnny, pulling away in the Jeep.

"Three-day searches?" asked Ditzler, watching the Jeep disappear down the shoreline.

"Whenever somebody goes missing the cops think they're lost in the dunes. We have to tie lines around our waists. There're no maps."

Ditzler turned around to look more closely at the eastern edge of the dunes that rose like battlements above the beach.

"Sweetie said she knows where they all are," said Jack.

"Who?"

"People who went in and never came out. She offered to show me, but I thought it was better to leave well enough alone."

"Reasonable," said Ditzler. "Except for their everlasting souls, which can be a nuisance."

By that time the sun had baked off the morning haze. It hung at an angle that reflected hot light off the wet sand surrounding the guard stand. The concentration of ultraviolet this early in the season would sear the lifeguards' tender, pale skin fresh from winter habitats. Most were foolishly indifferent to sunscreen, remembering only the last weeks of the last season when they were charred a deep brown thought to be impervious to destructive rays.

Ditzler, on the other hand, had swathed himself in handfuls of Coppertone, and coated his nose with a thick layer of glossy zinc oxide. Jack was the better tanned, though the summer would reverse that status, given Ditzler's leathery olive skin, dried out, etched and flaked, though inherently darker.

Jack took note of another of Ditzler's features the moment they sat on the guard stand together.

"Your toenails are black."

"They are, they are," said Ditzler, sticking his legs out straight so they could both get a better look.

And they were black. Not a surface paint job, but a deep, profound black that penetrated into the toe. A black so black it was almost maroon, with the natural gloss of healthy nails, complete with dark gray cuticles.

"They were supposed to turn back to normal after the ceremony, but you can never trust those damn jungle people. Whom I love, by the way, don't get me wrong."

Jack let it stand at that, at least for the time being. His secondary occupation, after securing the safety of the few people who used his beach, was to indoctrinate rookie guards. Most of them were younger than Jack, like Ditzler, and all tried to impress him with something, whether their athletic or sexual prowess, or experience guarding chlorinated pools in the suburbs, or drinking habits, or toughness in the face of danger. None of which Jack cared about, much less believed in the first place, and simply ignored until the kid realized the stories weren't having the desired effect.

"Ever have to save anybody?" Ditzler asked about an hour later.

Jack hated that question. He thought it voyeuristic, prurient.

"Only once. Gave it up after that."

"So you let 'em drown?"

"Don't let 'em swim. At least not far enough out to be in danger of drowning. If they want to swim in water over their heads, they can go to another beach. Or wait till we're off duty. All the way off duty. In the car and down the street. Then they can swim out there and drown all they want."

"That's a good policy," said Ditzler.

"I don't know about that. It's my policy. The only thing you can die of on this beach is boredom."

"Fantastic. I love boredom. God, to be bored. Someday, I swear, I'll attain that state. It's only a matter of time."

"Talk to me in September," said Jack, standing slowly, unraveling his slender loose-jointed swimmer's body, all triceps, forearms and abdominals, and overbuilt trapezius that lifted his shoulders into a perpetual hunch. He curled his toes over the footrest and slowly bent into the position anyone would recognize as the start of a swimming race.

"Be a trick to reach deep water from here. More likely you'll break your neck," said Ditzler.

"By September, you won't care," said Jack before launching himself out across the sodden Jersey sand in front of the guard stand, a shimmering slick reflecting the first angry assault of the sun as it rose above the wooly gray horizon.

LATER THAT morning the regular gaggle of local kids wandered on to the beach, some of whom took to the gulley wash, the tidal pool that formed immediately in front of the guard stand well within Jack's boundary of safety. Their mothers or babysitters stayed well up on the beach, disguised behind hats, sunglasses and scarves in the cooler early season. Over the summer they'd slowly emerge, steadily peeling off layers of self-consciousness, their bodies baked into cherry-flavored chocolate and moods more tied to the languid cadence of the tides and the influence of celestial bodies, the searing sun and intoxicating moon.

JOHNNY GOT back to the downtown beach directly below beach patrol headquarters in the opera house, in time to see a man in an undershirt, floral swim trunks and black shoes become nearly engulfed by a huge flock of seagulls. They rose and fell above his head in a chaotic swarm of white and gray, squabbling over chunks of white bread the man was tossing into the air like chum from the stern of a Bertram shark hunter. Johnny saw the senior guard on the beach, Joey Zable, climbing down off the stand to trot over to the guy to tell him to knock it off. Avery hated it when people fed the gulls, a sentiment Johnny shared, having been the target of more than one slimy wad of gull shit.

Johnny drove the Jeep between the piers under the opera house where the patrol's small fleet of four wheelers were kept out of the direct sunlight. By the time he got back to the beach the gulls had begun to disperse, but the gull feeder and Joey Zable were still in discussions, which even from a distance looked less than cordial. Johnny started to trot across the dry sand. The other guard on Zable's stand stood up and looked over at the two men, distracted. Johnny looked over his shoulder at the walkway on the roof of the opera house. Avery was up there, hands on the railing, staring down at the budding altercation.

The gull feeder had the archetypical look of what the guards called a shoobie, which in addition to the undershirt and black shoes, was characterized by a pale, untannable complexion and a swollen belly that could be used, as it was that day, as a type of battering ram.

Johnny stopped at the stand along the way and gently told the other guard, a second year rookie, to keep his eyes on the water. The kid snapped his head in that direction, suddenly mindful of Avery's watchful presence several stories above the beach. Johnny patted the kid's calf to reassure him and plucked the can, a torpedo-shaped fiberglass life preserver, off its hook on the side of the stand. He brought it with him when he went to see how Joey was doing.

"Show me the fucking rule," the guy was saying, "the rule that says you can't feed the fucking seagulls."

"Hey, Joey," said Johnny, walking up slowly, "what's up?"

"He wants to feed the gulls."

"You can't feed the gulls," Johnny told the guy.

"The fuck you can't. Show me the rule."

"And you can't use profanity when addressing an officer of the law."

The guy jerked his head back and sneered with incredulity.

"Officer of the law? What, this puke?"

"That's right," said Johnny. "Mr. Zable is a fourth-year guard, and thus has police powers here on the beach. That makes him an officer of the law. I'm his lieutenant, so you can figure out what that makes me."

"Head puke?" the guy asked.

Johnny swung the can by its tether into the guy's face hard enough to pitch him backwards into the sand.

"Fucking shit," the guy yelled, holding his face. Johnny dropped down to the sand, planting his knee into the guy's solar plexus, choking off further illegal complaint.

"I told you, sir," said Johnny. "No profanity, no offensive language directed at the authorities on the beach."

By this time, a few other shoobies had appeared and taken positions around the fallen man. Zable turned toward them and straightened to his full height, his arms at his sides. He looked up and saw Avery at the railing, not moving, but his attention fixed on the scene.

"You're under arrest," Johnny told the shoobie. "You have the right to remain silent, which I'd suggest you do before you get into deeper trouble. You have the right to an attorney, and whatever the rest is," he said, standing and dragging the guy up on his feet by the thin fabric of his white undershirt.

"Arrested? For what?" he said through his hands, cupped over his injured right cheek.

Johnny twisted the shoobie's arm behind his back and used a grip on the back of his neck to propel him through the gathering onlookers, and across the beach toward the boardwalk. Zable fell in behind, walking backwards to keep a warning glare focused on the shoobie posse.

"For feeding seagulls, using profanity and disobeying a member of the beach patrol," said Johnny. "What do you think? That you can behave like that and we're not going to care? This young man," he nodded back at Zable, "is a public servant. He is

here to ensure your safety. He deserves your respect and compliance, not your insults."

"Yeah, you dumb, fucking douche bag," said Joey, without
taking his eye off the other shoobies.

Johnny looked up again at Avery, but he wasn't at the
railing. Then his attention was caught by a pair of borough
cops, in starched light blue shirts, dark blue pants with glossy
strips down the outside legs, black leather holsters stuffed with
chrome .38's, silver badges, and heavy black polished shoes that
sank deep into the dry sand, forcing them to walk in a slow,
dignity-draining duck waddle. Johnny stopped and tightened his
grip on the shoobie's neck.

"Christ," said the guy, causing Johnny to give his head a
little shake.

The cops were still a hundred feet away when Johnny saw
Avery coming toward them at an angle, moving quickly, smoothly
across the sand. He called something to the cops, which Johnny
couldn't make out, but it stopped them in their tracks. They
stood and watched Avery as he closed the distance.

Avery stood between Johnny's party and the two cops, his
hands on his narrow hips, his overdeveloped shoulders rolled
forward, relaxed but ready to unleash. Johnny could hear nothing
of their conversation, but he knew the content. Avery was
reminding them that police jurisdiction began and ended at the
sand line, that on the broad beaches of Elysiana he and his lifeguards held absolute sovereignty, with full authority over any
and all actions and behaviors taking place therein in accordance
with lawfully instituted borough and municipal statutes.

Johnny knew the speech pretty well, having delivered it himself from time to time whenever Chief Romanovski got it in his
head to test Avery's implacable resolve, or a pair of summer cops
were stupid enough to wander into this kind of confrontation,
which was apparently the case here. So it didn't take long for the
two of them to turn around and walk back toward the boardwalk,
with Johnny and his shoobie following behind. Avery stayed in
place with his hands on his hips.

The two cops waited for Johnny at the top of the wide steps that led up to the boardwalk. There he handed over the shoobie, as protocol demanded, giving a description of the events leading up to the arrest and the consequent charges. The older-looking of the two cops wrote it all down in his casebook, while the other cop cuffed the shoobie and avoided making eye contact with either of the guards. When he was done with his statement, Johnny turned without further comment and trotted down the wooden steps. Zable, usually a friendly guy, said "Later, man," and went down to the ocean where he jumped in and swam a quarter mile out and back to purge the sickening aftershock of excess adrenaline.

Norm Harlan watched him swim, as he'd watched the whole drama on the beach unfold from an outdoor table where he'd been plowing through a small mountain of fried clams, now threatening to climb back up his esophagus from an adrenal rush of his own. It was nightmarish to witness the jurisdictional anomaly Norm considered an abomination. Marty Romanovski had kept him informed of every clash, every border skirmish from which the police were forced to retreat, but Norm had never seen such a thing himself. He rarely ventured beyond his office, except when Paula had so jangled his nerves that the only palliative was a full plate of deep fried bivalves and a pitcher of Schmidt's beer.

So it was the dual effects of gastroesophageal reflux and over-excited adrenal glands that caused Norm to be struck by a powerful bolt of moral clarity, the conviction that his role on earth was to be an agent of divine vengeance, with the sacred purpose of cleansing Elysiana once and for all of the radical tyranny of Mayor Black and the malevolent Avery Volpe, and everything they had done to corrupt and degrade the hallowed principles of responsible borough management.

He was about to say "Or may God strike me dead," when his better judgment said to hold that commitment in reserve. Instead, looking down at the plate of clams, he asked the Lord for strength, wisdom and fortitude, intestinal and otherwise.

CHAPTER
6

Technically, the beach patrol's work day ended at five o'clock, but Avery made it a practice to personally release every stand one at a time, driving by in his red Jeep, beginning in the south with Jack's beach, the most remote. Since the guardhouse in the abandoned opera house was at the northern end of the island, where every guard had to check in before going home, this allowed for a symmetrical, orderly dismissal. Jack had the longest journey, which he traveled in the '55 Chevy panel truck he'd found in a garage at the Imperial Hotel. It had been used as a gopher vehicle, doing errands for guests, picking up provisions for the kitchen, taking the hotel manager's family out for a picnic on the mainland. All Jack did was replace the battery and re-shoe the brakes, drain and refill the gas tank and oil sump, and push the starter button. He'd found a set of commercial license plates in the weeds along the bay shore, and jimmied up a registration sticker to make them look legal, which in New Jersey in 1969 was close enough.

That afternoon the Jeep drove by at a little after five o'clock which nearly coincided with dead low tide. This presented a situation to Jack and Ditzler, the custodians of the last wooden lifeboat in beach patrol service. A massive, paint-encrusted sodden arc known for its stalwart performance in storm conditions, due to an unfashionably low center of gravity and a construction that favored seaworthiness over performance. As the guard at the bitter end of the patrol's area of responsibility, Jack had the least number of people to protect, and consequently the least need for nautical aids, which is how he drew the stately tub. Something he deeply appreciated, since none of the fiberglass boats now filling out the beach patrol fleet had anywhere near the displacement needed to ride the big storm waves that late summer nor'easters could stir up, in which Jack, alone among the guards, would drag his official lifeboat out to surf.

All of which was scant comfort when facing the hundred yards of sand over which they had to haul the heavy boat with only a pair of antique wooden rollers.

"Outstanding," said Ditzler when Jack broke the news. "Like Hannibal over the Alps."

It took about a half hour to reach the area just inside the dunes where Jack liked to stow the boat and the lifeguard stand, as far from the reach of high tide as possible, and at the foot of the long wooden staircase and walkway that led over the dunes and down to the tiny parking lot. The spot was also the start point for another path, this one plain sand, that led off into the uncharted regions of the dunes, the path from which Gwendalynn and Sweetie had emerged that morning, which Gwendalynn was now telling Jack and Ditzler they were blocking with their cumbersome wooden boat.

"Pretty rude," she said, and then something else Jack didn't hear through the exertion of the final yank on the oarlocks that dropped the boat stern end down on the sand.

"Sorry?"

"All this beach and you put that boat right in front of the path," she said.

"You're not allowed to go in there."

"Doesn't say you can't."

"Yeah, it does." He pointed to a white sign twenty feet up the path before it made a tight right turn and disappeared into the scrub pines.

Gwendalynn folded her arms and leaned back on her left leg, the fabric bag on her right hip. Ditzler gathered up their cans and knapsacks filled with suntan lotion, rain jackets and dry bathing trunks, and started walking up the steps toward the parking lot.

"I don't care what you do," he said to Gwendalynn. "I'm just telling you."

"If you don't care, why'd you say anything?"

"People get lost in there."

Gwendalynn had already walked around the boat and was heading down the path as Jack picked up the red warning flag out of the boat, the only piece of gear Ditzler had left behind, and started to walk up the steps. Then he stopped and called to her.

"Are you actually sleeping in there?"

She stopped and turned around.

"I have slept in there, yes."

"What if it rains?"

"I'll get wet."

"Have you ever tried to sleep in the rain?" he asked.

"No."

"It's worse than you think."

"Maybe. I'll let you know," she said, turning again and walking down the path.

"I've got some extra rooms if you want to get out of the rain."

She turned again, but continued walking backward.

"Rooms?" she asked, emphasizing the plural.

"Rooms."

"How many?"

"About four hundred."

She stopped.

"Big house," she said.

"It's a hotel. It's closed. I live on the roof," he said.

"Cool squat."

"It's not a squat. It's my hotel."

"Why'd you close it?"

"Nobody wants to stay there anymore."

Gwendalynn sat down in the sand and crossed her legs.

"Sorry. Nobody just owns a hotel," she said.

"My mother gave it to me. She still pays the taxes, otherwise I'd probably have to sell it," he said, then shook his head. "Actually, the deal is I'm not allowed to sell it, but she pays for basic upkeep, so I don't have to. It sounds confusing, but you'd have to know my mother."

"My mother gave me life, then gave me grief. Never a hotel."

Jack sat down, too, on the sandy cedar steps.

"It's because of God," he said.

"There we go. Finally an explanation."

"Why she gave me the hotel. She made a deal with God."

"Pretty good deal."

"I have sheets, blankets and towels. The plumbing still works. I just have to find a room along the hot water line that runs up to the roof."

"How many other people you have living there?"

"Nobody. Just me."

"Must piss off your friends."

"I had friends, but I was out cold for a while, and when I woke up, they'd moved on."

"Must have been a while."

"Four years. Give or take."

"Gee."

"I don't mind. I'm fine as it is."

"Then why should I stay there?"

"It's safer than the dunes."

"Are you?" she asked.

"What?"

"Safer than the dunes?"

Jack frowned as he thought about her question. Then he understood.

"Oh, Christ, yeah. You don't even have to talk to me. I'm twenty stories up. I just need to clear you with the security service."

Then he thought about it some more.

"Just you," he said. "And after you leave, no one else. A one-time event."

"That's a little weird."

Jack stood up and brushed the sand off the bottom of his swim trunks.

"Exceptions prove the rule," he said, heading up the steps, at the top of which Ditzler had reappeared, wondering what had happened to his stand partner. When Jack was halfway there, he looked back again at Gwendalynn, who was still sitting on the path.

"Final chance," he called down. "A one time, never to be repeated offer to you or anyone else ever again, for all eternity."

Gwendalynn pulled herself up, cinched her bag over her shoulder and followed him to the top of the stairs, where they fell in behind Ditzler for the long march over the dunes to the parking area where the panel truck was waiting. It was just beginning to shed heat from the day through the open windows, carrying with it the smell of aging upholstery, lubricating oil and renewed purpose.

DITZLER ADMIRED Jack's Chevy panel truck, mostly for the capacious cargo space in the back, which he had plenty of time to study on the way back to the opera house. Ditzler knew something about salvage, having retrieved his 1966 Alfa Romeo Spider Duetto from an overgrown gorge in a city park behind his parents' house in the Roxborough neighborhood of Philadelphia. It was only a few days after returning from Africa, while taking a nostalgic hike through the ignored and largely forgotten little park, that he found a red convertible hanging nose-down from the upper branches of a tall red oak. Since there were no roads within flying distance, or signs of large mechanical equipment, like a crane, it seemed apparent that the Alfa Romeo had literally fallen from the sky.

Ditzler knew it was a 1600 Spider because he'd seen the grill design during a stopover in Paris on the last leg of his trip home.

There wasn't much else to identify the car, with its sensuous body shape unrecognizably torn and crumpled from its plunge through the treetops. He ran back to his parents' house to get his mountain climbing shoes and rappelling gear, which he successfully adapted to scaling the oak tree. Forty feet off the ground, he was able to reach a spot where he could look in through the shattered glass and convertible top, mostly peeled away, to see with relief that the car was empty.

He climbed higher so he could lower himself to the rear of the Alfa, taking great care to keep his lines clear and his anchors above the drop zone. He studied the rear axle, to which he attached a separate line with the other end tied to a spike in the tree, in case his moving around caused the car to slip before he could figure out how to bring it back to earth.

Fortunately for Ditzler, his father Isaac was an engineer. He knew the basic principles of pulleys and levers and could compute the tensile strength of cable and line. With the help of a winch mounted to the front of Isaac's Jeep Wagoneer, the two of them were able to raise, release, then lower the Alfa gently to the ground. An hour after that they used another winch to pull the car on to a flatbed trailer and tow it carefully out of the woods and into the Ditzler garage.

The reconstruction labor was divided evenly between the two Ditzlers. Isaac handled the tricky task of replacing the car's identification numbers, which had been crudely filed down, with a fresh set in the proper font and Alfa-numeric format. The only hurdle was obtaining a phony registration signed by a phony seller. Through his network of international associations, Isaac convinced a fellow engineer in Italy to send over a copy of the registration documents for his own Spider 1600, which made it relatively simple to develop a fresh version for themselves. The Pennsylvania DOT bought the story, and the documentation, and after a few months of body work, parts replacement and general restoration, Ditzler had a new Alfa Romeo to drive to the tryouts for the Elysiana Beach Patrol.

Aware of his rookie status, and thus vulnerable to the jealousy and sadism that might arouse, Ditzler decided to leave the Alfa with an insurance agent a few blocks from the opera house. It seemed a reasonable trade—a little extra wear and tear on the car in exchange for a low profile. And when a guard inevitably saw him in the car he could just say it belonged to the agent. Not a thoroughly fleshed-out plan, but good enough.

Deception was less an issue at the other end. Ditzler was the only guard living at the Sea Star Marina off Half Moon Bay, which bordered the northwest side of the island. His apartment was above the marina's only building, which included a parts counter, chancellery and office space. Ditzler knew the owners from his teen years, before he went to Harvard, when he would hang around in the summer and help the mechanics repair the outboards and diesels and refurbish starter motors and VHF radios. The apartment had belonged to the owner's mother, recently dead and thus fortuitously available when Ditzler dropped by on first hitting the island.

"Mama was a clean freak," said Sebbie Rosconni, the woman's son, "she wouldn't let you through the door unless you'd been, like, hermetically sanitized. I ain't been up there in ten years. She had a cat, don't know what happened to it. I haven't smelled nothin', but let me know," he'd added as he tossed Ditzler the keys.

There was no dead cat, or any other bodies, and true to Sebbie's description the place was impeccably clean and tidy, even with a year's worth of dust. There were two bedrooms, one not much more than an oversized closet, where Ditzler stashed the old lady's clothes and photographs and any other personal object that might preserve her incorporeal presence in the apartment. The big bedroom was on the east side, and had a balcony that overlooked a stand of weedy sumacs that separated the marina from Half Moon Avenue and the salt marsh beyond.

Ditzler dragged the kitchen table out to the balcony, and a single bed from the small bedroom, and a braided prayer mat where he sat in the lotus position for an hour with a bottle of

Boone's Farm Strawberry Hill wine, meditating on the immense and unnerving magnitude of his good fortune.

IT WAS well after dark and Ditzler was on the verge of passing out on the balcony when the first concussion intruded on his flagging consciousness. His eyes snapped open at the second and the third boom, now strung together by the sound of squealing rubber and overtaxed internal combustion. He moved to the railing in time to see an amorphous shape careening down Half Moon Avenue, bouncing like a pinball from curb to curb, leaving behind a wake of sparks that fanned out like beautiful horizontal fireworks. Seconds later he heard a final boom and saw a flash of light. He hopped over the railing, quickly scaled the first floor and thrashed through the row of sumac. Less than twenty yards down the road a blue International Scout was half off the road, pinned to the earth by a toppled telephone pole and a large transformer, spraying sparks.

Ditzler got there just as a woman opened the driver's side door. She was alone in the truck.

"Are you hurt? Can you move alright? Got to get you out of there immediately," said Ditzler.

The woman, dark-haired, dark-skinned, with light blue eyes and an unusually square jaw, seemed interested. The smell of alcohol spilled out of the truck.

"You think it's going to blow up?" she said, with a hopeful uplift to her voice.

"Yeah, come on. Let's get out of here."

"You go ahead. I'm staying put. I'm dead anyway."

"You're not dead. I'm talking to you."

"I'll be dead when I kill myself, or when my husband kills me, whichever comes first."

"It's just a truck."

"It's not his. I stole it."

"Okay," said Ditzler. "All the better. Can I help get you out of there?"

"Hey, thanks, that's really nice, but I'm fine here."

While she spoke Ditzler reached in and pulled her feet out of the truck, which had the effect of half spinning her around in her seat. She held the steering wheel with both hands.

"I always liked these things," said Ditzler, admiring the Scout's elegantly simple, albeit now slightly mashed-in lines. "Why'd you steal it?"

"Had the keys in the ignition. What are you doing?"

"Taking your hands so I can pull you out of there."

Her blue eyes looked up at him through long black eyelashes.

"Could you drive me to the bay? There's a boat ramp less than a block from here. I could just walk in. Don't need the car."

"Sure," said Ditzler. "No problem. Or I can just chuck you off the breakwater."

"Would you? You're a doll."

"Just give me your hands."

She did and he dragged her to her feet. She wavered a little, but stayed upright. Ditzler reached around her, snatched a wad of paper towel off the seat and wiped down the steering wheel, shift knob and door handles.

"Did you play the radio?"

"Of course. Who kills themselves without music?"

He wiped down the dials and the cigarette lighter. Then he took her wrist and pulled her across the street, and with some effort, through the stand of sumacs and on to marina property.

"Boats," said the woman, looking around. "God, I love boats." She pointed her finger at him. "But not enough to live for, so don't even start."

He held up his hand.

"I understand. I'd die for a good boat, too."

"We have a Boston Whaler. *Had* a Boston Whaler. I have to get used to the past tense."

She staggered a little. Ditzler slipped his arm around her waist to keep her from falling. He noticed she was hot and moist, and emanated a sweaty, sour smell. It was hard for a twenty-two year old like Ditzler to gauge an adult woman's age, but he guessed close to her actual thirty-four. It surprised him that her waist was so tight and trim. As they walked across the gravel yard where the marina hauled out boats for maintenance, her unsteady gait caused his hand to occasionally slip up under her unsupported breast, which he also found unexpectedly ample and firm.

"I think you should come upstairs with me while I get my keys," said Ditzler. "You're a little unsteady. I don't want you to fall."

"Oh sure," she said, "the old just let me get my keys then rape me ploy. You think I just fell off a potato truck?"

"Turnip truck."

Despite the stink of booze, Ditzler could smell her perfume, which he found perplexingly familiar.

"I've smelled you before," he said. "Well, not you, but what you're wearing. You haven't been to the Ivory Coast, have you?"

"I never been to the West Coast. It's probably something my sister gave me. She's a stew. Buys shit all over the world. Whoa, steps."

Ditzler did his best to keep the woman upright as they ascended the narrow stairway that ran along the outside wall of the main marina building. He finally got her through the door and into the apartment's open living area. Once inside, she sank like dead weight down to the floor and rolled over on her back.

"Man am I fucked up," she said.

"Anything other than alcohol?" Ditzler asked as he went out to the porch to retrieve his bottle of Boone's Farm.

The woman brought her knees up and pulled the lower part of her tank top off her belly, which Ditzler noticed was taut and well-defined.

"What, dope? No, unfortunately. Do you have any?"

"No. How about a cup of coffee?"

She shook her head.

"No thanks. Keep me up all night."

She picked up her head and looked around the room for him, finally drawing a bead.

"A cup of tea would be nice," she said, then dropped her head back on the floor.

"That we can do," said Ditzler, pleased for the chance to try one of a hundred or so distinctly flavored tea bags he'd shipped back from Asia. He didn't like tea much himself, but made a habit of collecting samples along the way.

"Thai, Sri Lankan, Chinese?"

"Anything from Totowa? That's my hometown. With just a little lemon. Thanks."

When he made it back to the living room with two mugs of tea it looked like she'd fallen asleep; but when he dropped down to the floor she put out her hand.

"Hm, smells good."

She sat up cross-legged and cupped the mug with two hands. Her long straight hair fell into her face as she drank. Ditzler hoped there weren't any injuries hiding under there.

"You alright?" he asked. "Feel sick or dizzy or anything?"

"Sick *and* dizzy."

"I should take you to a doctor."

"I thought you were taking me to the breakwater."

"I think you should kill yourself after we make sure you weren't hurt in the crash."

She put the tea on the floor and tilted back her head, encouraging Ditzler with a clear view of her face, free of blood, abrasions or contusions.

"Even I know that doesn't make any sense," she said.

"Better yet, wait till you sober up before taking the plunge. Booze can adversely affect decision-making."

"Sounds like college talk. I didn't go. No money. No brains. Just tits and legs."

"They're allowed in college, too."

She looked at him.

"Boys don't need looks if they got a brain," she said.

He laughed.

"A contestable hypothesis," he said.

"Where do you go?"

"Went. Harvard."

She looked at him more closely, trying to bring her blurry vision into focus.

"Perfect."

"How's the tea?"

Red and blue lights flashed outside. Ditzler went out on the porch and saw a swarm of cops and emergency vehicles surrounding the Scout. He played several alternative stories through his mind. If/then scenarios. The first things he'd say would be the most important, so he tried to run the logical sequence of question and answer. Meanwhile, he watched the movement across the street as well as he could from the balcony, looking for cops interviewing witnesses, though he was likely the only person living in the predominantly commercial area, which was part of his calculation. He went back to check on his fugitive.

She was still flat on her back.

"Thanks for stopping the floor from moving around. I thought I was gonna ralph."

"The cops are out there. What do you want me to tell them if they knock on the door?"

She propped herself up on her elbows.

"If you hand me over, you'll be killing me just as sure as tossing me in the bay. Only it'll take a lot longer and be a lot messier," she said, then dropped back down again.

"Your husband?"

"If you knew him you wouldn't have to ask. I'm such a little fool."

It didn't come to that. An hour later the truck had been cleared from the road and all the flashing lights were gone again, restoring the stillness of the night. When Ditzler went back out on the porch the woman followed him, a fresh cup of tea in hand. She sat on the bed and he poured himself the last of his wine.

"I'm Mike," he said putting out his hand. "Mike Ditzler."

She shook it.

"I'm Miss Anonymous. After I finish this tea I'll get out of your hair. For your sake, Harvard."

"You don't have to. Nobody's ever here but me. The guy who owns the marina's mother died here. The place freaks him out. You can rest up and figure out what you're going to do. I got a bedroom I don't use. You're welcome to it."

She didn't answer him right away, but he noticed her draw into herself.

"Cold?"

"A little."

He found a sweatshirt to drape over her shoulders.

"Kindness pisses me off," she said, quietly.

"I know. A sense of obligation. An unwanted commitment to reciprocity. Not necessary here. I've got a couple centuries of karma to rebalance. You can just be along for the ride."

"I guess you get that hippie stuff in college."

"In Thailand, mostly. So much kindness you'd go mad with anger."

"I'll be in your way."

"I've got an extra toothbrush. Never been used."

"Sure. Okay. Why not."

"Great. I'll get you set up, then I got to get some sleep. Have to work in the morning."

He stood up from where he'd been kneeling next to her and stretched out his arms.

"What do you do?" she asked.

When he told her he was a lifeguard she started laughing.

"Perfect. Unbelievably perfect. Do you have a gun?"

With surprising speed she rolled on to the balls of her feet, then stood straight up. She raked her hands through her jet black hair, then shook her head, messing it back up again.

"Sorry," said Ditzler, stepping back to give her room. "No guns."

"Pacifist?"

"I guess."

"Good thing. If you had one I'd shoot you with it, then shoot myself. Be better for both of us."

She walked over to him and grabbed a cheek in each hand. Then kissed him hard and fast on the lips.

"You saved my life, you bastard. I should hate you for it, but I think I'm sobering up."

"Want some wine?"

"Sure."

When she let go of his face he went into the kitchen and dug out his best bottle, the only one with a cork and label rendered in script.

"My mother gave this to me to bring down here," he said, "for special company."

He poured them each a full glass.

"My mother told me if I didn't marry the son of a bitch, it would cast everlasting shame on the family," she said. "My uncle owed him a pile of money. Nothing shameful about selling off your niece to pay your debts, right? Cheers."

They clinked glasses.

The woman downed most of hers and wiped her face off with her sleeve. She held out her glass and Ditzler topped it off.

"You know how women say, 'Ooo, I put too much starch in my husband's shirts. He's going to kill me!' "

"I guess."

"Well, I did a little worse than that, and my husband is going to literally, actually, kill me. Do you understand what I'm saying, Mr. Lifeguard?"

"I think."

"And anybody he finds me with. Do you understand *that?*"

Ditzler thought about it a moment.

"I hear what you're saying."

She just stood there after that, staring at him. He shrugged and smiled and sipped at his wine while she stared.

"Can I show you where you're going to sleep?" he asked her. "I'm getting tired."

She followed him to the big bedroom and watched him change the sheets and put out towels.

"The bathroom's across the hall. I'm on the porch. I'm up at six, out by seven. I hope you stay here till I get back so I can help you figure out what to do. If not, it was a pleasure," he said, shaking her hand again, and then left her.

Back on the porch he stood at the railing for a few minutes looking into the deepening night, searching for flashing lights and barking radios. When it was clear that peace and quiet still gripped the night, he stripped off his clothes and dropped into bed, covered by a sheet and knit cotton bedspread. He lay on his back and started to silently repeat the mantra the Thai rice farmer had taught him to induce a deep sleep. Which, as always, took effect within a minute or two, so he was disoriented when awakened an hour later by a rough shake of the shoulder. He opened his eyes and saw a shape standing over him.

"Are you capable of sleeping with a person without trying anything sexual?" the woman asked him.

"Of course."

She pulled back the covers and he slid over to make room for her on the single bed. His nervous system lit up at the feel of her naked body. She took his left arm and held it hard against her breasts as she backed up against him, her soft-skinned butt pressed into his manhood, which despite an emergency invocation of a different sort of mantra, was rapidly on the rise.

"I need a name," he whispered in her ear.

"You pick."

"How about Miss Annie? Short for Miss Anonymous."

But she was asleep, immobilized, where she stayed through the night while Ditzler lay awake, breathing in the smell of her black hair and African perfume. Eventually dawn broke, heralded by the noisy gulls swarming above the fishing boats. At six o'clock Ditzler finally extracted himself, with some difficulty, since his right arm had gone numb hours before. Miss Annie slept on, a slight frown marring what Ditzler saw in the daylight was an otherwise strong, nearly pretty face fortified by a square jaw and early signs of crow's-feet radiating from her eyes.

He secured the sheet and cotton bedspread over her shoulders and went to get ready for another day, hoping the lack of sleep wouldn't prevent him from catching whatever else the gods might be planning to cast from heaven upon the place beneath.

SANFORD GOETTLEWING found it slightly painful to be battered by the wind coming in from all sides, but it was just too cool to drive a GTO at highway speeds with all the windows down. It helped that he was wearing a baseball cap, the white Yankees logo dyed a deep black to blend in with the rest of the hat. It was held at the temples by paper clips gripping the cap to wavy gray hair bound at the back in a ponytail.

The GTO was also black, inside and out, which on a sunny day would turn the car's interior into a Bessemer furnace. Another reason to keep the speed up. The sound of the wind also seemed to go well with *Axis: Bold as Love* playing on the new eight-track hanging under the dashboard. White noise with feedback and vibrato.

Goettlewing was about to hit the last toll on the Garden State Parkway before the exit to the Elysiana causeway. It was a little past noon and he'd been on the road for over six hours, having left his place in the Berkshire Mountains north of Fitchburg at first light.

He liked getting away occasionally, though it always made him a little nervous to leave home. He took some comfort knowing it was left in the able hands of a shell-shocked deserter he'd inadvertently smuggled out of Vietnam inside a container filled with hashish, Sansui amplifiers and teak furniture.

Goettlewing discovered him when he cracked open the container on the dock at Long Island City. The grunt was too paranoid to give up his weapons or his name, so Goettlewing called him Sergeant Saunders and told him he was to be evacuated from inside the container and sent to a secure position at base camp.

A year of Sergeant Saunders' security measures made it unlikely anyone could penetrate the perimeter of Goettlewing's property. As a bonus, he had an extra hand to work in the garden, feed the dogs and assure the honor of Goettlewing's girlfriend.

Goettlewing had done a lot of traveling already in his lifetime. Too many incursions into rat hole countries, too many blood-baths followed by too many scrambles over hostile borders.

But sometimes matters required his personal attention. He understood that, and took the responsibility seriously. He felt the teachings of Lao Tzu learned in Asia made it clear that doing was as true a route to enlightenment as being. That sitting by the river in meditation would not cause the fish to leap into his arms. That sometimes the highest form of letting go was to get your ass off the ground and behind the wheel of a production hot rod made by the General Motors Corporation.

So when one of his couriers failed to call in to confirm a drop, an extremely rare event, he knew an immediate response was the only course of action. His entire enterprise depended on unquestioning discipline by all agents and envoys. There were no exceptions, deviations and no forgiveness. So the lapse could only mean an unavoidable disruption caused by an external force, or one of his people had decided to commit suicide.

As he slowed to chuck a quarter into the bin at the tollgate he checked his watch. Twelve-thirty. Time to stick another che-root in his mouth. The pacing wasn't a matter of health. He'd only brought enough to last a few days and doubted he could reprovision in South Jersey.

In order to light the cheroot, he had to take his hand off the Colt 1911 .45 semi-automatic sitting on the other bucket seat. Goettlewing loved the feel of the polished metal, and never let the gun stray out of reach. It was a custom inaugurated one night in Jakarta when his dreams were interrupted by a razor-sharp knife making an incision across his throat, fortunately catching on a thick silver chain, thus missing his jugular and providing the opportunity to lash out with a lucky punch above the heart, killing the guy instantly.

He lit the cigar right before reaching the Elysiana exit off the Garden State Parkway. Like all first-time visitors, he was surprised at how long it took to get there over the causeway. The island itself, apparently covered in haze, seem to take forever to rise up along the horizon. By the time it did, the sight of the mainland was lost. And then all he could make out was the blurred outline of the towering Imperial Hotel and the water tower, ten miles to the south, the twin towers of Elysiana. To either side of the causeway was a wasteland of marsh grass, tidal pools and water fowl. Most of the traffic on the causeway was moving in his direction, but cars were also leaving the island. A connoisseur of high-performance Pontiacs, the only car he took note of was a '65 convertible Catalina 2+2 carrying two guys with giant balls of kinky hair that passed him at well over the speed limit. They were shouting something, but he couldn't make it out with all the wind noise, though he saw the driver give his GTO a thumbs-up as they roared by.

CHAPTER
7

JOANIE SHELDON'S steadfast goal during the summer season was to avoid perspiration. She'd spent years refining a handcrafted Sassoon coif, determining that the only hairspray capable of maintaining the posterior cranial mount and forward swoop that outlined her jawline and nearly joined at the chin, reacted badly to the saline composition of sweat, and by oozing into her eyes, would cause a fierce, blinding pain.

Consequently, the Elysiana borough attorney was almost as pale as Norm Harlan, whose office was only two doors away, and the only other borough employee who spent as much time confined to the indoors. Harlan had appointed her, a privilege of his position as council president, as a favor to her sister who was married to Marty Romanovski. A decision he now bitterly regretted, as she continued to insist that the borough charter was clear on the reporting relationships between the mayor, council president, chief of police and captain of the beach patrol. It drove him to investigate her credentials, assuming a woman was unlikely to have a legitimate law degree, despite the diplomas from Columbia hanging in her office. It was a disappointment to learn that she'd not only graduated, but had written for the law review and passed the New York, Pennsylvania and New Jersey bar examinations.

That day he took a different tack.

"How hard would it be to change the borough charter?" he asked her, popping his head in her office door.

Joanie put on the glasses she usually wore hanging from a lanyard around her neck.

"Think repealing the U.S. Constitution."

He came the rest of the way in and sat in a chair in front of her desk. She waved at the door, which he reached back to close, helping to contain the cool air from her window air-conditioning unit.

"First you need a petition signed by two-thirds of borough residents. This just to get the proposal for a change before the borough council. Then the council and the mayor all have to agree to submit the petition to the New Jersey State Board of Municipal Affairs who has to pass on the constitutionality of the motion. Whichever way they decide, there's a three-year cooling off period during which interested parties are allowed, encouraged I'd say, to challenge the decision of the board in state court. If it gets through that phase, the original petitioners are required to form the motion into a plebiscite, which to pass, requires yes votes from three-quarters of registered borough voters."

"Pretty stupid."

"You wouldn't say that if they wanted to eliminate the council president."

Harlan glowered at her from across the desk. He'd slowly grown to despise her Shangri-La's hairdo, white lipstick and artificial tanning cream, which by the end of the summer would give her skin an alien orange glow. He could barely listen to her exaggerated South Philly accent, or the sound of her long white nails tapping on the surface of her desk. Or see the barely concealed look of disdain she felt for him occasionally pass across her mascara-painted eyes.

"You're right, Joanie. I wouldn't like that. Just as I don't like the idea that our founding borough fathers thought it necessary to enshrine—no, entomb—their idiotic notions of local governance inside a locked vault."

Since no one outside the immediate borough authorities knew or cared about these hierarchical arrangements, there were no accepted theories on their origins, leaving Harlan with his own explanation—that the pirates who settled Elysiana in the early seventeenth century thought it amusing to place the beachfront outside the jurisdiction of lawful authority, a condition later inherited by another band of thugs called the beach patrol.

"If it makes you feel any better, I agree with you," said Joanie with just a hint of condescension. "There're all sorts of funny things in that charter that don't make any sense to me, especially having to do with the beach. It exposes the borough to all sorts of liabilities that we're just lucky haven't been tested in court. And, I think personally, create an atmosphere of civic irrationality."

Harlan found himself suddenly liking her better.

"Here, here."

"But changing anything? Not likely in our lifetimes."

Harlan frowned, the cloud resettling over his mind.

"Yours, mine or the mayor's," she added.

That sparked a thought. One so obvious and filled with promise it almost gave him vertigo.

"Joanie, what happens if the mayor becomes sick, or incapacitated. Or even dies while still in office?"

"Oh, you mean succession? The council president assumes the mayoralty, while the council vice president takes over his role. The acting mayor appoints a temporary council member to fill the open spot. I thought you knew that."

"I do, of course I do," said Harlan, wondering why the knowledge had stayed so thoroughly dormant in his brain. "And the acting mayor, of course, has full rights and responsibilities. He can hire and fire."

"Natch. Wouldn't be much of a mayor otherwise."

"Including the captain of the beach patrol. He could fire Avery Volpe."

Joanie herself was then struck by what should have been a self-evident fact.

"Yeah, I guess he could. If he wanted to," she said, quietly, as if the thought was too terrible to speak aloud. She clutched herself by the shoulders as if her sleeveless blouse was now inadequate against the chill from the window AC.

"Not that I'd contemplate such a thing," said Harlan. "Avery's been a loyal defender of public safety."

"Yeah, those members of the public whose heads he hasn't cracked like walnuts."

Harlan smiled at her, suddenly aglow with positive sentiment for his borough attorney. Not such a bad girl, he thought to himself. Might be fun to have her over with Marty and her sister. Have burgers on the deck. See if he could get her high on gin and tonic. Loosen her up.

"Thank God there's nothing wrong with the mayor," she said, shaking off the unease that had briefly gathered around her heart. "Healthy as a horse."

"Here, here to that, too," said Harlan. "Lucky for me. I've got enough to worry about," he added, a broader smile than she'd seen before light up his face.

Harlan slapped the armrests of his chair strongly enough to propel him back on his feet.

"So anyway, sorry to keep bothering you with the civics lessons," he said. "Just trying to be a well-informed council president."

"Nothing to it. Anytime," she said, looking relieved that he was about to leave her alone, and maybe not be back for a while.

During the journey down the fluorescent-lit hallway to his office, Norm Harlan thought his feet barely touched the floor so giddy did he feel as he breathed deep the prospects of a solution, the mechanics of which as yet undetermined, though choked with wondrous possibilities.

Gwendalynn agreed to the studio apartment at the rear of a complex of offices behind the front desk of the Imperial Hotel. Jack offered it knowing that the unit was one of the last places in the building to be occupied, as recently as a year ago, by a full-time security guard, subsequently replaced by an outside service after Jack discovered the guard was also running a wholesale business in hash, prescription drugs, Quaaludes and synthetic peyote. This presented Gwendalynn with the intriguing possibility that he'd left some of his inventory behind. She also fancied the prospect of cooking meals in the little kitchenette that Jack threw into operation by closing a pair of circuit breakers in an adjacent utility closet. He gave her a set of sheets and two enormous terry cloth beach towels emblazoned with the regal crest of the Imperial Hotel. They smelled faintly of chlorox, but were otherwise remarkably well-preserved.

"I'm going to pay you rent," she told him as he handed her a key to a service entrance that was the simplest and most convenient way to get in and out of the massive old hotel.

"If you want," he said. "It isn't necessary."

"It is to me."

"Okay. Get some money and we'll figure out how much," he said, and then turned and left, trotting up the forty flights of stairs, two per story, that led to the Box.

As he made dinner for himself, frying up a mound of fresh flounder that he bought at the commercial fishing docks, Jack struggled to understand his reasons for giving the girl a room, breaking a precedent he'd assumed unbreakable. He often found analytical thinking painful and disorienting. Certain thoughts, or combinations of thought, that should follow a logical path, initiate fresh ideas or draw inferences, would arrive in a random, haphazard fashion. He sensed the process operated on some inaccessible plane, somewhere just out of reach, just over the horizon. He described it to himself as a Thereness. While everything he experienced in the world of the senses, all that swirled within his mind, possessed a Hereness.

He knew it hadn't always been like this. Before the accident, things weren't distinctly here or there. He remembered much of his childhood. Though nothing remained of the years he'd been comatose, divorced from time, neither here, there, nor anywhere.

He brought the flounder out to the all-weather recliner with a large jar of unsweetened iced tea. He never drank alcohol, taking the warnings of the neurologists to heart. The prohibition extended to caffeine, but Jack felt no ill effect from a few cups of coffee a day and an occasional jar of iced tea. He thought it neither enhanced nor interfered with his abiding sense of Hereness, but it did help him stay awake on the lifeguard stand.

Whatever damage the accident had done to his deliberative powers, it seemed to fire a lust for reading, made more so by the need to refill a reservoir of knowledge emptied nearly dry. Almost from the moment his consciousness returned he began to read, beginning with a mildewed copy of *Valley of the Dolls* found with a stack of other notable works on the bottom shelf of his bedside table at the long-term care facility. From there he moved on to Plutarch, Spinoza, Will and Ariel Durant, Josephine Tey, James Michener, Erle Stanley Gardner, Damon Runyon, Mark Twain, Henry Miller, John Dos Passos, Pearl Buck, William Shakespeare and the Hardy Boys, all found on the book shelves in the visitors lounge, donated and otherwise ignored by the grief stricken, or merely bored, families of the facility's residents.

It was an advanced education of sorts acquired between long hours in the twenty-yard rehabilitation pool, where he restored his body through the soothing repetition of stroke, pull and breathe, followed by a flip turn, and further stroking, pulling and breathing, until countless laps were logged and his skeletal form filled out into smooth-muscled vigor, and his eyes regained their lucidity, and his tangled hair nearly obscured the glistening pink swath that cut diagonally across his forehead.

When he finished the flounder he fished around for Anaïs Nin, and became comfortably absorbed into the night, barely noticing the music coming from the nightclub on Imperial Avenue, the street directly behind the hotel. It was one of two on the island belonging to Eduardo Buente, a Cuban exile who'd never been in a Havana nightspot much less run one, but made up for it with an entrepreneurial zeal that stood out even among his fellow *Cubanos*.

With a large dance floor lined with bars and invigorated by live bands imported from Atlantic City and Asbury Park, Shing O'Ling's served a full complement of domestic and imported beers out in front and every imaginable illegal drug out the back. With the national decline in sexual inhibitions Eduardo's prostitution business had flagged, though still strong with traditional Italian and Polish union enforcers working the construction trades up and down the coast, whose deep respect for marriage compelled them to favor a more commercial form of dalliance. Drugs had done the most to make up the revenue shortfall.

Having been born in Cuba, but raised by his Italian mother in North Jersey, Eduardo was also devoutly Catholic, yet never drawn to the easy recourse of his working girls, preferring to harvest what he could from the flow of waitresses and female patrons that flooded Shing O'Ling's Lounge every weekend. Since his wife had just left to spend the summer with her sister in upstate New York, that night had an inaugural feel as he surveyed the floor, simultaneously counting the house and identifying prospects. Which was why his mood was slightly dimmed when he spotted Petey Amato sitting at his usual place at the corner of the north bar, Harvey Wallbanger in hand and eyes filled with the same splendor that had been preoccupying Eduardo.

"Hey, *amico*," said Eduardo, approaching Petey to shake hands, "you know for you it's all on the house."

"You think I'm payin' for this shit?" he said, grabbing Eduardo's hand like he'd just caught a fish leaping above the surface of the water.

"Let the games begin, eh?" said Eduardo, allowing his gaze to sweep the noisy tangle on the dance floor.

"Finest kind," said Petey.

Much about Petey was incomprehensible to Eduardo, though he clearly understood his profit motive, and appreciated the skill with which he retailed a large percentage of Eduardo's product.

"So, are we prepared for another summer of sun and fun?" Eduardo asked him.

Petey downed a sizeable gulp of the Wallbanger.

"How much fun depends on what you got for me, which I say only with the genuine respect I feel for you."

Eduardo noted and warmed to Petey's graciousness. It had been an embarrassment for him when the courier across the street at the hotel suddenly disappeared. This forced him to make up the shortfall off-island, driving all the way to New York City, a place he never liked venturing into.

After locating and personally slitting the throat of the missing courier, Eduardo established a new supply chain with a far more reliable resource, and things promptly returned to normal, until a few days ago when a delivery of hashish failed to materialize. This was a little disconcerting, but he felt it would be remedied in short order, given the reputation of this particular supplier.

"Product is not an issue, *amico*," said Eduardo. "I, too, respect your concern for this, but I assure you, our inventory is—" and not finding the word, used his hands to indicate a limitless flow.

"Far out," said Petey.

"Your drink is looking pale," said Eduardo, snapping his fingers at the bartender who nodded without looking at Petey's glass.

"Here's the trip," said Petey. "Speed isn't the thing it was in '67, '68. Too many bad scenes, people realizing the shit won't let you sleep. Too many strung out, with their teeth fallin' in their beer, bugs crawlin' on their eyeballs, that kind of thing. Grass is still big, bigger even, but I don't do that shit. Too much shipping and handling. Hash, as always, is a personal favorite of mine. Lot of shit comin' in from 'Nam inside stereo equipment and body bags, very high quality, running down prices, but it's still good business. I prefer bricks. I don't trust individual baggies, too much cutting potential, no disrespect to you. I'm speaking for both of us."

Eduardo nodded.

"The contemporary thing," Petey went on, "the real shit of tomorrow, is acid."

He waited for that to sink in.

"This is what the people are demanding," said Petey. "Trips down hallucinogenic lane."

Eduardo continued to nod, deliberating.

"This is not a problem," he said. "I can get this."

"Most of the shit is coming in through surfers with California connections. It's quality, man, hippie-certified. I have to do one better, or I'm out of the game, *capisce*? You need good cooks. Quality control. The shit don't addict, so bad product is the end of the world."

"Everything I do is quality, *amico*," said Eduardo casting his eyes across the interior of Shing O'Ling's, the verification self-evident.

"I know, man," said Petey. "That's why I'm talking to you."

And I'll have my *caballeros* feed you with your own entrails after I pull them out of your ass if you don't, thought Eduardo, but knew that was well enough understood to leave unsaid. He smiled instead.

"My honor."

Petey scooped the fresh Wallbanger off the bar and toasted Eduardo, who nodded in return, then spun on his heel and made a nonchalant beeline to his office phone to call Miami for some consultation on the manufacture and packaging of lysergic acid diethylamide, heretofore needed only to round out a full line, but obviously gaining market significance. It excited him to think about it. Eduardo liked a varied work day and the opportunity to diversify and innovate.

Petey worked on his Wallbanger in a near fugue state of self-satisfaction. Commerce in stolen electronics had been steadily on the rise for at least eighteen months. Spring storms had kept the waves above average and the island's most important hood was eating out of his hand.

He wished his father could see him now. Almost fifty when Petey was born, the senior Amato was a hard nut of an immigrant who'd run his family's wholesale produce business with bitter resolve, chain-smoking unfiltered cigarettes until his brutal barking orders came out as a raspy squawk, who barely noticed he had a son except to show annoyance, until Petey found him one day gasping for breath, partially dressed at five in the morning, preparing to drive into Philly to deal with the farmers and agents in at dawn from upstate New Jersey and Central Pennsylvania.

Petey left him where he lay, curled in front of his dresser, white haired and fragile with his shirt collar up and over-the-calf socks half-raised, still breathing shallow painful breaths, and took the old man's new Ford convertible out of the garage and drove off to find some friends to spend the day drinking and playing pool.

Sitting at the bar in Shing O'Ling's, Petey thought about scooping up one of the new waitresses and making a night of it, but to his surprise felt a qualm or two about Clarice, even though he'd never officially anointed her his girlfriend. Instead he left the club and got back into his black pickup truck, planning to head home when he was distracted by the sudden appearance of a borough police car, its strobes and flashers alight, siren wailing, in pursuit of a small red convertible. This caused him to involuntarily veer off and drive in the opposite direction, trying his best to look nonchalant, a regular citizen of Elysiana meandering home.

The cops in pursuit of the convertible barely noticed Petey's pickup, focused as they were on keeping up with their fleet and agile quarry. Earlier that week they'd seen it around town, its foreignness and sensual form a peculiarity among the big American sedans, station wagons and muscle cars common to the island. When the car darted by this time, they were leaving a hoagie joint routinely shaken down by the cops for free food and coffee, and instinct took over.

Ditzler quickly realized there was a cop behind him, making the same turns and keeping a consistent distance. It wasn't a happy situation. He felt sure, despite a legal registration, that a vehicle picked out of a tree could hardly withstand official scrutiny. But the bigger issue was the fugitive hiding in his apartment, to whom he was transporting bags full of clothing, Tampax, makeup and body lotion. He had no way of knowing, but he had to assume she was a person of interest to law enforcement, making him a clear aider and abettor. On the other hand, God have mercy, maybe they were after the Alfa.

At first the patrol car followed at an unthreatening distance. Ditzler was sure they were calling in his license plate number and waiting for the go-ahead. He kept careful watch in his rearview mirror and on the speed limit, maintaining a reasonable two miles under. He put his elbow out the window to project an innocent calm.

Officer Anskeep and his partner were actually too far away to make out the plate number, though he'd put in a call to the dispatcher who hadn't immediately responded. So he turned up the volume on the radio, turned down the squelch, and tried again. He tried to maintain a discreet distance but found himself edging forward, taken with the Alfa's sexy little rear end. It was almost mesmerizing, watching the nimble car turn corners and accelerate out of the sharp turns, so much so that when the distorted blast of the dispatcher's voice finally burst from the turned-up radio, it so startled him that his right foot slipped off the brake pedal and on to the accelerator, causing the patrol car to surge forward, coming within inches of Ditzler's rear bumper. Ditzler's reflexes, in response, caused his right foot to stick his own accelerator into the floor, rocketing the Alfa forward.

After that, it was off to the races.

Ditzler took advantage of his surprise lead to gain as much airspace as possible before the more heavily powered police cruiser could respond. He let about three blocks worth of boulevard tick off, then hung a hard right on to a cross street. He almost made it to the end of the block before the patrol car made the turn. Ditzler made a left, then another left, hoping to disappear into a matrix of alleys and side streets that served a cluster of pre-war bungalows. It was the kind of driving well-suited to a European sports car, and decidedly not for an amped-up Ford sedan designed for chasing speeders across the Nebraska plains.

Ditzler slalomed through the old neighborhood looking for a place to pull off the road and kill the lights, but nothing was forthcoming. He could hear the sound of the cop's tires groaning around the tight curves, and knew that backup was probably close behind. He found an exit that shot him into downtown Elysiana where he'd recently bought the fresh clothing and feminine hygiene equipment for Miss Annie.

Ditzler stretched out third gear until the tach needle was stuck hard against the pin. He looked in the rearview and saw only the empty Ocean Avenue lit by staggered pale yellow pools from the streetlights above. Relief had just begun to loosen the wire strung around his heart when the cop car popped out directly behind him, lights and siren ablaze.

Mostly by reflex Ditzler ripped the Alfa to the right, tipping on two wheels before regaining control, which slowed him down and allowed the cop to make the turn and pull up close enough to almost tap his rear bumper. Ditzler thought there was maybe one more turn left in the chase before a humble acceptance of defeat, arrest and ruin. He hoped Miss Annie would get word somehow, or figure it out herself, and that his father wouldn't be naïve enough to confess to aiding in the Alfa's illicit restoration.

He shoved the transmission into second gear, burning up the fragile Italian synchros, then brought up the RPM's and touched his heel on the brake pedal, causing the cop to slam on his brakes just as Ditzler popped the clutch and yanked the steering wheel to the left. From Anskeep's perspective there was a red convertible in front of him and then suddenly there was not. In its place was the broad rear end of a Buick station wagon parked on the side of the road. Even with his brakes already engaged, there was no room to stop.

Fortunately there was a lot of car, filled with a heavy V8 engine, between Anskeep and the ass end of the big Buick, which accordioned as the kinetic force of the collision raced forward, ejecting Petey Amato from the front seat through the windshield, clutching the just-extracted eight-track stereo to his midriff so that he hit the street shoulder first, absorbing most of the blow, and cushioning the delicate electronic components.

"What the fuck?" Petey asked himself as he slid across the asphalt pavement. When he looked up all he saw were the strobing lights of the police cruiser, prompting a reaction not unlike Ditzler's as he jumped to his feet with the eight-track tucked like a football under his arm, and sprinted from the scene across the parking lot that served the clam bar where Norm Harlan was having a late dinner. Scrambling over a chain link fence that enclosed the lot, Petey plunged into the region of backyards, swimming pools, carports and neatly trimmed lawns that stretched from there to the northern edge of the salt mines.

Phil Anskeep confronted a quandary. Actually, a whole complex of quandaries. Even halfway inside the station wagon he recognized it as Norm Harlan's Buick, having seen it parked every day in front of the borough administrative building adjacent to police headquarters. It was an easy guess that the swarthy fellow flying from the car didn't have the council president's permission to remove his new eight-track stereo. His subsequent flight from the scene bore that out. Given that Anskeep's cruiser was now mated to the council president's car, it was unlikely the situation could be entirely salvaged, but the moment seemed to favor recovering the boss's new stereo over chasing down the red Alfa Romeo, pursued entirely on a hunch and a whim that he never had a chance to fully call in, and now gone like a cool breeze on a hot summer's day.

"Let's move," yelled Anskeep to his dazed partner. They cinched up their ordnance-laden belts, shouldered open the crushed doors of the cruiser and gave chase again, this time on unsteady, ill-prepared feet.

Petey knew little of the physical condition of his pursuers, but wisely assumed the worst—two Villanova track stars filled with racial hatred for people of southern European stock, petty thieves in particular.

What Petey didn't know, and wouldn't believe, is that his athletic prowess far exceeded the capabilities of the Villanova track team, with shoulders, torso, abdominals and thighs fairly bursting with powerful muscles, fired by the reflexes of a predatory cat and fortified by the endurance of an Ethiopian marathoner.

"Hey asshole, quit running," Anskeep yelled, a command Petey heard faintly in the distance, prompting him to quickly redouble the air between him and the huffing cops.

He kept to the interior of the central block, running beside the long avenues that paralleled the shore, crossing backyards, vaulting fences and waking up watch dogs. He correctly assumed this was a course cops on foot would quickly abandon, giving him the lead time to effect a full escape.

Which would have happened if another patrol car hadn't streaked down a cross street, responding to a winded plea for backup. He saw their lights, but they missed him darting down a short driveway, through a carport, over another fence and into a backyard, where he zoomed by a swimming pool in which a pair of nude men were floating on rafts sipping Bloody Marys.

"Hey, fella, what the hell," one of them called out, but Petey ran on.

With this new development, he started to rethink his escape strategy. More patrol cars would be on the way and being spotted was inevitable. He needed a place to hide.

After scaling the pool fence, he dropped into what looked like an empty lot. He wanted to lie in the tall grass for a while, but feared the guys in the pool might try to pursue, so he ran on. Carefully checking for headlights, he crossed two more side streets, and then found himself enclosed in a yard filled with appealingly dense foliage. Better yet, he knew the house and two of the people who lived there—one directly and one by reputation.

He snuck around to the west side and squatted down under a rangy, untrimmed yew. From there he could see into the house without exposing himself to the street.

As he tried to quiet his breathing he noticed a large red welt on his knee. While assessing the damage, he felt a drop of blood fall on the back of his hand. He felt around his face and came away with his palm slick, red and wet. He pulled his T-shirt out of his shorts and used the tail to wipe the blood from his face. He assumed it was superficial, otherwise he'd be passed out or dead by now. No sense worrying about it till he had to.

He noticed he still had possession of the eight-track dug out of Norm Harlan's dashboard. It didn't seem possible, even to himself, that he'd carried the chunky metal box all this way, but there it was.

He saw Randy Calvert and one of the lifeguards who lived with him move across the living room window and into the kitchen. Lights shown from two of the windows on the second floor. Petey tried to remember the layout of the house. He'd only been there once to meet up with Baxter, one of his regular hash customers. They'd made the transaction in Baxter's room, which Petey thought was on that side of the house, directly above an enclosed outdoor shower.

He settled in to wait, senses alert for flashing lights and siren blasts. All he heard was Jefferson Airplane and the rough sounds of lifeguards and surfers banging around their beat-up cottage, the pulse of the ocean to the east and the chirping clamor of assertive amphibians in Half Moon Bay to the west.

Baxter burst from the side door that led to the outdoor shower. He wore a towel tucked up under the sweeping arch of his enormous belly and a pair of leather sandals. He carried a large plastic cup Petey assumed was filled with beer. He took hold of the shower door, leaned back to pull it open, staggered a bit when the door held firm, then tried again, nearly catapulting himself backwards into a cedar tree before managing to conquer the latch. He belched and called the door a motherfucker as he struggled to secure it from the inside.

Petey waited until he heard water running before trotting over to the enclosure, bending low to stay under the windows of the house. He flipped open the latch and jumped inside.

Baxter had spent much of his life confronting all manner of drug and alcohol-induced apparitions, so having a bloodied, muscular Italian-American surf-crazed drug merchant squeezing into him was less a shock than it should have been. It was more discomfiting to Petey, who like most heterosexual males, was ill-at-ease around fat, wet, naked male bodies. He clamped down on Baxter's windpipe and whispered calmly in his ear, "No sound or I snap your neck."

Baxter nodded. Petey loosened his hold, but kept his grip.

"I need a ride back to my place," he said. "There's some trouble, so it's got to be clandestine."

Despite the headful of Petey's hash, Baxter was clear on the situation.

"Okay, Pete, not a problem. Just need to wash myself up, get the keys and we're gone. Could use a little room here to move around and get that done."

Petey stood back as much as the tight space would allow, but kept his hand on Baxter's throat.

"How's that Thai shit working out?" he asked Baxter.

"Far fucking out. Look at me. Living proof."

"I'm not looking at you, man."

"My eyes. I'm talking about my eyes."

He opened wide so Petey could see.

"Yeah, man. Lotsa pupil. You're truly fucked up."

"This is what I'm saying."

"Okay. I'll be outside waiting. I'll make it worth the trip."

"I know, man. You're righteous."

"I am," said Petey. "Always."

He let go of Baxter's throat and let himself out of the shower stall. Instead of going back to his hiding place he hunkered down a few feet from the side door, poised for possible treachery.

Petey was, at heart, an optimistic person. He loved his mother even though she stopped talking to him after his father died, and he loved his country, despite the fact that they'd tried repeatedly to draft him into fighting a deadly war in a foreign place where they spoke a completely different language. Most of all he loved Elysiana, which was now officially trying to run him down like a dog and put him in jail for God knew how long. Yet somehow he sustained an ongoing sense of good fortune, of faith and hope in the future. So it was no surprise to him that he heard Baxter declare to his housemates, loudly enough for Petey to hear, that he was heading out the door to get some ice cream, and that anyone could order up anything they wanted.

"Mint chip."

"Chocolate fudge."

"The shit that tastes like fried walnuts. You know the one."

Baxter's pale blue Plymouth Belvedere pulled out of the driveway and paused at the curb. Petey ran the distance across the yard like a grunt under fire and dove through the back door on to the plastic-covered seat. Baxter hit the gas and they lurched down the side street.

"Take it easy, man," said Petey. "You're supposed to be subterranean."

"It's the nervous tension."

"So calm the fuck down."

"Definitely."

Petey started to feel a little sick, partly from the blood loss, partly from Baxter's driving. But he kept it to himself as he lurched back and forth on the backseat of the Belvedere, gripping the armrest and praying for a short ride to the north end of the island.

"What happened, man?" Baxter yelled from the front seat.

"A bad trip. Let's leave it at that."

"Okay. I'm happenin'."

"Okay. That's cool," said Petey, feeling around his face and shoulders again, somewhat alarmed by what he felt. "Turn right up here and go all the way to the end of the avenue."

"Off the end of the earth, man."

"Yeah, basically," said Petey, sliding down into the car seat, suddenly consumed by exhaustion.

Baxter sat straight in the driver's seat and obeyed all traffic regulations, at least those he remembered, as he ferried Petey up to his apartment above the cluster of shops.

"Wait here," said Petey, when they pulled up to the exterior stairwell. He ran up the stairs and busted into the kitchen just as Clarice was sucking the last unburned remnants of Petey's private reserve of Guatemala Gold out of the pipe he'd given her for Christmas, a token from his last expeditionary trip to the surf shop on the first floor.

"Jesus Christ," she forced out between her teeth, keeping most of the smoke contained in her lungs, "what happened to you?"

He was going to ask if she'd seen any cops lurking around their building, or any other odd activity, but realized that would be futile. A SWAT team would have to break in through the walls, knock her to the floor and put her in handcuffs before she'd realize they were there.

Instead he dug out another brick of hash, an economical but slightly less satisfying variety recently shipped in from Vietnam, and carved off a piece.

"Don't touch," he said to Clarice, emphasizing the request with the blade end of his knife. She nodded as quickly as her hash-addled brain would let her. Petey ran down the stairs and tossed the chunk into Baxter's car.

"Don't smoke it all in one place," Petey told him.

"Whoa, cool beans."

"I keep my commitments. Keep yours. You never seen me. Not tonight, not ever. I don't exist, dig?" Petey said to him, quietly, leaning through the car window.

"I don't even know who I'm talking to," said Baxter. "Must be an hallucination. Doin' too much dope."

"Obviously," said Petey, slapping the side of the car and running back up the stairs to the apartment, where he cleaned himself up and spent the balance of the night trying to decide whether to hang tough and hope the cops hadn't ID'd him, or make a run for it now. He looked around his cluttered apartment and at the pale rounded form of Clarice passed out on the couch and knew the conclusion was preordained. His life might be a shithole, but it was his shithole and he wasn't going to run from it.

Even if he could figure out where to run to.

CHAPTER
8

G WENDALYNN'S HOUSECLEANING gig at Randy's spun off three more engagements via the owner of the house who'd come by to collect rent and assess the damage and thought he'd stumbled onto the wrong property. Baxter ran into her downtown, gave her the guy's number and told her to raise her rates.

"He's got a bunch of other houses around the island. A rich prick. Get it all up front. And stay clear of his old lady. She's evil."

She never saw his old lady, and saw the landlord himself only once before each engagement when he paid her in full. He was so gracious, kindly and respectful she discounted the jobs by ten percent. It still left her with enough cash to feel strangely flush, especially given the free ride at Jack's hotel, as yet unredeemed. She decided to invest some of the wealth in another pair of jeans, a couple tank tops, an embroidered Indian peasant blouse and an ankle-length skirt made of a crinkly printed material she'd never seen before. And a carton of Marlboros, which she was waiting in line to buy when Sweetie Harlan startled her with a warning on the dangers of cigarette smoking.

"My mommy does it anyway when my daddy's not around," she said to Gwendalynn. "I can smell it in the bathroom even though she's got the fan on."

"You should tell her that never works. The smell gets in the towels. My mother busted me every time."

"I busted the vacuum cleaner when I was helping my mommy clean my room."

"Speaking of your mommy," said Gwendalynn, looking around the inside of the store, "where is she anyway?"

"At my house."

"Oh. And you walked all the way here by yourself? Wouldn't surprise me."

"My daddy drove me."

"Good news. And where is he?"

It was Sweetie's turn to look around the store.

"I don't know. He's always disappearing."

Gwendalynn completed her purchase and took Sweetie's hand. "Wanna go find him?"

She perked up her ears.

"Just listen. He's usually the one yelling."

Gwendalynn walked her up and down the narrow aisles of the old general store, then brought her out to the sidewalk where she hoped to find a frantic parent or at least a cop, but no luck. So the two of them started working their way up the commercial district of downtown, in and out of delis and T-shirt shops and places that sold conch shell ashtrays imported from the Caribbean, tiny ceramic figurines of Lady and the Tramp, saltwater taffy, paperback books, and lamps made of bored-out pieces of driftwood. Coming out of the place that sold cigars, cigarettes and newspapers brought in from as far away as Baltimore, Gwendalynn saw the retreating, agitated stride of a short balding guy in a yellow polo shirt and knew she had her man.

"Looking for this?" she called.

The guy stopped dead, spun around and strode back, his face a brilliant red, both complementing and contrasting nicely with his yellow shirt.

"Goddammit, Sweetie, where the hell were you?"

"I was the hell with her," she said, holding up her hand, still clasped to Gwendalynn's.

"I found her in the general store down the street. Or she found me."

"Thank you," said Harlan, pulling Sweetie's hand from Gwendalynn's.

"Could you kindly stop getting lost, young Madame?"

"I knew where I was," said Sweetie, hugging her father's thigh.

Norm looked up at Gwendalynn hoping to commiserate and instead was struck by what he saw. A slightly round-faced, high-cheekboned young woman with long tangled blond and brown hair, crumpled chambray shirt and loose denim jeans concealing an indeterminate female form; slightly sunburned cheeks and round-framed sunglasses, a woven bag over one shoulder, several shopping bags in hand, and a look on her face that perfectly blended hostile suspicion and good will toward all.

"Norm Harlan," he said, sticking out his hand. "Borough council president."

Gwendalynn wasn't used to handshakes, but she did her best.

"Gwendalynn Anders. Finder of Sweetie Harlan."

"So you've been introduced."

"Twice."

"I found her in the dunes," said Sweetie.

"She did."

Norm frowned at the two of them.

"You're the hippie," he said to Gwendalynn.

"That depends on what you mean by that," she said flatly.

"My wife said a hippie found Sweetie in the dunes."

"Sweetie found me. And I don't know what people mean when they say hippie."

"Me neither," said Harlan.

"Then that settles it. I'm a hippie."

"Didn't mean to offend."

"I'm a hippie, too," said Sweetie, using her free hand to grip Gwendalynn's shirttail.

"You're a dingbat is what you are," said Harlan. "Like your mother."

"That's okay, Sweetie," said Gwendalynn, sweeping the little girl's hair back from her forehead. "Dingbats and hippies get along very nicely. You and your wife need to get a better handle on this kid," she added to Harlan before gently detaching herself from the girl's grip and moving back down the sidewalk.

"Miss," Harlan called after her. She stopped. "Are you working anywhere?"

"I'm working sometimes somewhere."

"How about a steady job. For the whole summer?"

"Looking after Sweetie?"

"I've never seen the kid attach herself like this. You must have a gift."

Gwendalynn studied the pale, pudgy little jerk for signs of paternal association with his daughter and regrettably saw quite a bit. She marveled at how nature could reconstitute genes from such an unpleasant source into a blessed goofball like Sweetie, who stood eagerly nodding her head, her face bright with anticipation.

"What about your wife?"

"She's been wanting this for a while. Her friends all have au pairs, so she wants an au pair."

"Is that what I'd be? An au pair?"

"Be whatever you want to be. Just keep a death grip on this kid."

"I have a place to stay. I want to stay there."

Harlan shrugged.

"Go home at night. She hasn't wandered off in her sleep. Not yet, anyway."

Sweetie nodded her head in confirmation.

"I don't have a car," said Gwendalynn.

"We have a spare," said Harlan. "An old Dodge. Runs fine."

Not knowing what else to do, Gwendalynn walked all the way back and put out her hand to shake again. Harlan took it.

"Okay," she said, "deal."

Sweetie used both her hands to shake Gwendalynn's other hand.

Norm Harlan thrilled at the prospect of a summer free of the panicked phone calls, the shrieks of dismay, the hysterical demands that he "DO SOMETHING!" His growing resentment over Paula's inability to keep track of their only child was only mitigated by knowing it had a lot to do with the kid herself. Whom he also resented for reminding him so much of her mother.

This, he knew instinctively, was the solution, temporarily suspending his feelings about hippies, in his mind the untouchables of American Society. This was one less thing to interfere with his concentration, something he needed fully engaged, unimpeded, free of distractions. This was a time of focus. A time for careful planning followed by great deeds. This was Norm Harlan's time.

"Oh pair of what?" asked Sweetie, pulling Gwendalynn toward their car.

During the weeks that Gwendalynn was cleaning houses for Randy's landlord, Mike Ditzler had been trying to look invisible in a bright red Italian sports car. It seemed to be working because he'd been around lots of borough cop cars and hadn't been pulled over. For this he thanked the old man in Thailand with whom he'd lived above a fetid bog in a grass hut built on shaky wooden stilts. In exchange for English lessons, the old man gave him his own mat in the corner of the hut and a perspective on reality that Ditzler suspected was the only one with a shot at authenticity. Ditzler had been raised an indifferent Lutheran, and knew little about other religions, having confined himself to the math and science departments at Harvard. This was expected of the half dozen prodigies who were in Ditzler's freshman class, most like him barely sixteen, though he was the only one who'd graduate three years later. So an education in spirituality seemed a good reason to spend the next three years roaming the earth.

He encountered the old man at the Bangkok airport straining to carry two large boxes that had been flown in by his daughter who was living in Sydney, Australia. Ditzler smiled his broad camel smile and placed his hands on one of the boxes.

"Let me help," he said.

"I do not want this box to be stolen," said the old man. "It is from my daughter."

"I'm not going to steal it. I don't need your box."

"I have no money to pay you."

"I don't want any money. I have everything I need in my backpack."

"Do you have cruelty in there?"

"I have a horsehair shaving brush in the pack. It was cruel to take it from the horse. So I don't need any more of that."

The old man instantly let go of the box and allowed Ditzler to follow him all the way to where he'd parked his handcart, which turned out to be about an hour's walk carrying the forty-pound box. When they finally arrived Ditzler asked him what was in there.

"Beer."

When Ditzler laughed, so did the old man. Having recently come from Japan, Ditzler bowed when they were done laughing and turned to leave, but the old man stopped him.

"Do you know where you are going?" he asked.

"Back to the airport to catch a cab into town."

"I have room in my house. Wife dead, daughter in Australia. I will give you the honor of helping to pull the cart."

"If I can have one of the beers," said Ditzler, half joking.

"You may have all the beers."

"Nah, just kidding. It's your beer. What's in the other box?"

"A goose down quilt."

Ditzler picked up the featherweight box and laughed again.

"That I can use," he said, still joking.

"You can't have that," said the old man. "My daughter would kill me."

"Okay, let's go then," said Ditzler, waving the old man forward, whom he followed for another four hours, and then took over pulling the cart for five hours more, and thereafter maintained the rotation for two days until they reached the old man's village, which was little more than a few huts built on stilts above swampy salt water wetlands.

A few weeks later, Ditzler asked him if he'd wished a foolish young American with a strong back to appear before him at the airport.

"No," the old man said, "I allowed my mind to be cleared of any hope that I would ever be able to bring my boxes to my house."

"Ah. Not wanting is the way to achieve what you want."

"Either that or plain luck. Doesn't matter as long as everything works out in the end."

For the last few weeks, Ditzler had believed with a sureness of the daily sunrise that he was going to be arrested by the first cop who saw him drive by in the Alfa. And then after that the second, third, and so on. At this point, he was allowing his mind to be cleared of any hope that this was anything but a strange and wonderful bit of plain luck. Which it almost was. After plowing into the rear of the council president's Buick, and then failing to bust or even identify the guy who was in the act of stealing the new eight-track stereo with the new Andy Williams tape still in the unit, Officer Anskeep had been reluctant to report the business with the red convertible, pursued as it was without a call-in, or request for backup, or any justification for the chase to begin with. He had enough on his hands getting his partner to tow the party line, and explain the accident and subsequent inability to bag the suspect, who was surely the same guy who'd been ripping off eight-tracks all over the island ever since people had been putting the damn things in their cars.

Ditzler decided to stop lending the Alfa out during the day, assuming whatever cosmic forces had been invoked to rescue him were nontransferable to insurance agents. So instead he parked at the opera house with the other guards for the morning muster, and occasionally drove it up to the mines with Jack, their signal flag fluttering out the window.

All of which was noted by Phil Anskeep. A development that further complicated his plan for the convertible, which was to catch the driver doing anything that could remotely justify a pull-over. There were protocols to follow in the cold war between borough police and the beach patrol. There were feints and counter feints, subtle maneuvers, occasional shows of force, assertions of power and strategic withdrawals, husbanding resources for the eventual breakout of overt hostilities. Petty harassments were avoided. Intercessions only when just cause was clear. And now, despite the stunt car demonstration, the driver of the red convertible could give further lessons on how to safely operate a motor vehicle in the State of New Jersey.

"That's okay, asshole," said Anskeep, quietly, "I'm watching you. When you fuck up, I'll be waiting."

His partner fervently hoped that day would never come. He was still recovering from a broken nose caused by the accident with Norm Harlan's Buick, and just beginning to experience symptoms of post-traumatic stress disorder, including nightmares of convertibles with articulated joints like giant ants belching flames and trying to run him down in the hallways of his own house.

Ditzler's partner, Jack, marveled at Ditzler's calm and conscientious driving style, enough to remark on it one day.

"Preserving a car this beautiful is a grave responsibility," Ditzler told him. "These things don't exactly grow on trees."

Miss Annie agreed the car was beautiful, even though she could only look at it from the second story window of Ditzler's apartment. He'd told her about the police chase, which worried them both until it looked like nothing was going to happen. Since then, they'd settled into a comfortable domestic pattern. Ditzler would bring back provisions every evening, and Miss Annie would cook dinner and make lunch for him to take the next day. He'd tell her about the day's events, which amounted to little beyond a description of the weather and sea conditions, and she would tell him about whatever book she was reading, which is all she could do in the apartment. Ditzler had a small library, mostly scientific texts on engineering, natural history and physics, most of which she didn't understand but enjoyed reading anyway.

"It's fun to read English words that sound like they're saying something but you don't know what it is," she told him.

He also had a collection of Zen poetry in the original Japanese which he'd translate for her while they sat around sipping wine on the balcony after nightfall.

In a repeat of their first night together she'd start off in her own room, then crawl into bed with him, usually after he'd fallen asleep. After almost a week of this, he asked if she would stop doing that since the nightly unrequited erections were getting painful. She went back to her room, but then an hour later reappeared. She pulled back his bedding and took hold of his penis, which she stroked to fullness, then enveloped with her mouth, sucking slowing and deliberately for the twenty seconds it took to achieve the desired result.

"I'm in love with somebody else, so don't take this wrong," she said. "But you shouldn't have to suffer just because I can't sleep without a warm body next to me."

He was happy to see her mood gradually lift over time until there were moments when she could seem almost lighthearted. Even a joke or two would pop out of her—usually wry and self-deprecating. He liked getting this glimpse into a full person, not just a desperate runaway. At the same time, more of her history began to fill in around their casual small talk, until he could sketch an outline in his mind of a fatherless childhood engulfed by a huge extended family with more wealth than erudition, most assuredly connected to some flavor of organized crime.

Ditzler was ambivalent about pressing her on more recent history. The threat of danger lurked about her, firing his self-preservation instincts along with his curiosity. On the other hand, his easy, low pressure ways had encouraged her to relax and reveal various shades of her personality. He hoped that would continue, since he liked it almost as much as the nightly blowjobs.

She settled that issue herself one evening as she sat with him on the balcony drinking wine and smoking Marlboros.

"I need more air," she said. "Even with all the windows open and the fan on I still feel like I'm not getting enough oxygen."

"Not surprising. You're cooped up."

"But I'm afraid to stick my head out the window."

"We could get you a disguise. Glasses and a moustache and a big nose."

"I'd still be afraid. My husband knows a lot of people, and a lot of them know me, but I don't know them."

"And they're all on alert?"

"I don't know. I don't know if he even knows I've gone missing."

This was an interesting twist.

"Really."

"It's a confusing situation."

"Most of life is."

"But I could try to explain."

"Only if you want to."

"You're a very trusting person," she said.

"You decided to trust me," said Ditzler, "for no other reason than you did. You made an instinctive choice. So did I. Decisions like this are all processed at a level below conscious awareness, but everybody does it every day. Unfortunately, some people's instincts aren't as good as others and they make mistakes. Lucky for us, our instincts were pretty good, at least on this one."

"I like the way all that sounds. Makes me feel smart."

"Well, that's the first thing I think you need to realize. That you're smart. You don't think you are, which seriously undermines everything you do, because you don't trust your own intellect."

"There's that trust thing again."

"The knuckleheads who run your family worked hard to convince you that you weren't very smart. I bet because you're female, which most males want to dominate, so they have to make you think you're not a capable person on your own."

"I hear all of that bra-burning Women's Power stuff. I don't know what I think about it."

"I love the bra-burning part."

Miss Annie said she wasn't even wearing one that night the summer before in Wildwood, which might have been part of the problem. She was out with two of her girlfriends. They always went to Wildwood because their husbands never did. Wildwood was holding true to its name, acting as the South Jersey epicenter of drunken festivity, the place you went when you had a night or two to devote to sexual prospecting or simple debauchery. You had a choice of a dozen clubs or bars, none of which aspired to the slightest pretense of sophistication or style. The accepted motif was neon on the outside, wood flooring, battered furniture, oceans of beer and clouds of cigarette smoke on the inside—lighting low, expectations high.

The Lucky Charm was further distinguished as a lifeguard's hangout drawing from every town south of Atlantic City. The individual beach patrols stayed in packs, identified by off-duty T-shirts, or illegally worn uniform jackets or tank tops of obsolete design, simultaneously marking rebelliousness and tenure on the job.

Miss Annie's friends were married as well, one to a podiatrist who commuted to the hospital on the mainland, the other to a real estate agent on the island. Both men had been lifeguards when they met their wives, local girls for whom the pull of Elysiana was too great to overcome, and so had planted careers as best they could in the sandy soil of South Jersey. Thus engaged, neither was aware that their wives had a thirst for the boys on the beach patrols, and their gathering places, not yet fully quenched.

"I always just went along for the ride," she said. "The only time I get out of the house is when I'm helping out my husband, and that's no vacation. I feel like I'm living in a hole in the ground. Sometimes he'd leave for overnights, and I'd tell him I was gonna go stay with a girlfriend, have a pajama party. This is when we'd take off for Wildwood. Wild is right. Crazy girls out on the town.

"So this one night we're there and they're having a special— Triple Sevens—seven seven-ounce glasses of beer for a buck. But only between seven and eight o'clock. A bell goes off at seven and the place goes nuts. The waitresses are dumping these little glasses down on the table as fast as they can, and everybody's downing them the same way, so you start getting the sound of hundreds of these things banging down on the tables, which of course inspires everybody to bang 'em even harder, until it sounds like you're at the battle of Iwo Jima it's so loud.

"This is also the perfect way to make sure that every one of the guards in there is completely wasted in really short order. Which makes 'em start to compete with each other on who can bang their glasses the hardest and fastest, which gets the juices running. I don't know when the dope running the place figured out Triple Sevens was a bad idea. Maybe this huge brawl gave him a clue. I don't know if you ever seen a couple hundred muscley drunken guys trying to kill each other in a very confined space, but it's pretty scary. The three of us were literally pinned up against this wall, and all I could think of was Eddie reading in the paper about how his wife got trampled in a runaway bar fight and wondering if I'd be dead because of that or if I'd have to wait for him to finish the job.

"Then like something out of a dream this guy just comes through the crowd, and it parts to either side of him, like goddamn Moses at the Red Sea. A little older, and not real tall, but really built, you could tell even with his jacket on, and nobody's laying a hand on him. He just walks up to me and takes my hand and starts to move back through the crazy mob. My girlfriends grab on to my shirt, and we just snake our way through those maniacs, who by now are piling out into the street where the cops are pulling up in their cars and big step vans with blue lights on top, and they got their nightsticks out which they're using to bust up fights and shove the guards into their vehicles. This guy who's leading us out of there just kind of nods at the cops and they also move immediately out of his way. I'm thinking, what kind of super powers does this freaking guy have?

"We get to the end of the block and this guy asks if we're all right, and then asks me if I want to go somewhere else to have another drink. It's obvious he's not talking about bringing along my girlfriends, but they're pretty shook up by now, and more than happy to dump me off and run home to their hubbies. I don't know what the hell I was thinking, but as soon as he asks me to go with him it's a foregone conclusion that I'm going to do that, and that we're going to sit around a quiet little dive for a few hours and then go to a motel right off the boardwalk and spend the night together.

"He told me right off the bat he wasn't married, and I told him off the bat I was. That was the good thing I did. I didn't tell him to who, which was the bad thing. Well, one of the bad things. But I couldn't help it. I had this feeling that being with him was the safest place on the planet Earth.

"Of course like an idiot I spend the whole night chewing his ear off about how unhappy I am and how I never wanted to get mixed up with my husband and all that blah-blah-blah. The guy wasn't the most talkative person I'd ever met, but whenever I let him talk I liked the way it came out. So, I just didn't want to break the mood by telling him about being married to Eddie Buente. Eduardo to everybody else. I'm the only one who can call him Eddie without getting stabbed."

"You're kidding," said Ditzler, suddenly hearing his pulse in his ears.

"Sorry, Harvard. I tried to tell you. I should've told this guy right off, but I didn't want to chase him away. Not that he looked easily chased. I've known some serious bods in my time, but this guy . . . like a whole different level. Like a different species of life."

She looked up at him.

"You're not so bad, either," she said to him, halfheartedly.

"Thank you, but not necessary. No anthropomorphic anxieties here."

"Okay, whatever that means."

"So you never found out," said Ditzler. "What he did, who he was."

Annie had perked up while telling the story, but suddenly looked unhappy again. Ditzler regretted coaxing her along, however gently.

"That was maybe the dumbest thing of the night. I got it in my head to ask him what he did for a living. He hesitated, which of course made me push him a little about it. You know, in a teasing kind of way. Dumb girl shit."

"I think it's a perfectly legitimate question to ask a guy you've just had sex with."

"You have experience with this?" she asked.

"No. Just conjecture."

"I didn't think so."

Annie stopped talking and busied herself with her wine glass. After learning the name of her husband, Ditzler had been silently repeating his favorite calming mantra. He was about to apologize for prying into her life and suggest they just cash it in for the night, when she started up again.

"So I started telling him how much I wished I had a regular job to get me out of the house once in a while, other than working at the club, and how Eddie wouldn't hear of it, that he'd think it was a smudge on his honor, like he couldn't provide for me. I'd ask Eddie, so what's your honor got to do with me having a life, and he takes me by the throat and shoves me up against the wall and says, you have a life, baby, and it belongs to me. This kind of bullshit I've been putting up with my whole life. Can I tell you how sick of it I am?"

"I think that's what you're doing."

"Thank you. I think I am. So this was my mistake, because the topic of working for a living led me into just blurting out to him, something like, so big guy, what the hell do you do for money and he says he's a college football coach, and I said, no shit. Of course you are. Explained all the muscles and scars and crooked fingers."

Ditzler couldn't help but conjure the mental image of the hulking male body in the low light of the Wildwood motel, but not happily. He tried to redirect his mind's eye toward the dark sheen of Annie's taut, spring-loaded frame.

"No mistake in that," said Ditzler. "He just told you what he did."

"In the winter. What he did in the winter. Not what he did in the summer."

Annie was staring at him as if trying to send him a telepathic message. He tried to receive it, then gave up and just asked.

"Okay. What does he do in the summer?"

She looked down at the dune grass that tucked around the four by fours that held up the balcony.

"He's a lifeguard," she said, quietly.

"You're kidding."

"Don't act like that. You wanted to know."

"I didn't want to know. You wanted to tell me."

She was quiet again. Ditzler immediately felt bad. He stroked her back.

"Sorry. You're right. I wanted to know. No big deal for me. I'm a rookie. I don't know anybody but my partner and the guy who runs the place. The big guy."

"Right. The big guy. That's what I called him, too."

"Who?"

"The captain of the Elysiana Beach Patrol. As soon as he said his name, I remembered, damn, I've heard that before. How many Averys are there, anyway? So there you go."

"Holy cow."

Annie smiled a weak smile and dug another Marlboro out of Ditzler's withering hardpack.

"I guess you could say all the cats are now officially out of their bags," she said, with the cigarette in her teeth, flicking the lighter.

Ditzler's mind drifted back to the base camp in the Himalayas where he'd spent a few days hanging out with a team of Sherpas waiting out a snowstorm. He'd tagged along with a pair of German homosexuals who were thinking of making a run at Everest, and wanted to get a feel for the challenge. The experience sparked little interest in reaching the peak, but he did note the camp was probably the most remote and godforsaken place on the planet.

He began to wonder how hard it would be to get back there, and if it was remote enough should his current circumstances become generally known.

"Since you know so much about all this Chinese religion," said Miss Annie, "maybe you can tell me what I did in my former life that this one has to involve so much crap."

He cleared his throat, which had started to dry out again.

"I can do that if you tell me your real name. I think I have the other key facts in the case," he said.

"Sylvia. Sylvia Scillante Buente. Two parts guinea, one part spick—by marriage—one hundred percent fucked."

They sat quietly for a while, until Ditzler's curiosity continued to get the best of him.

"You and Avery still, you know, seeing each other?" he asked.

"Every once in a while. And yes, in the biblical sense, so don't bother asking. And no, he still doesn't know about Eddie."

"Does Eduardo know about him?" asked Ditzler.

"Are you kidding me? Avery's a capable guy, but nobody's tougher than a bullet."

Ditzler wondered if that was true in Avery's case.

"It was the day I was set to go up north to see my sister for the summer, like I always do," said Sylvia, "but for some reason, instead of packing my suitcase and catching the bus, I walk a couple blocks to the Crispin Arms Yacht Club to get a drink, which is the only place on the island I'm positive you'd never see Eduardo Buente, and start ordering sloe gin fizzes faster than the bartender can ask me if I'm a member of the club, which is usually full of old guys who were just as happy to have any halfway decent-looking girl hanging around the bar, membership or not.

"I don't know when it happened, but somewhere in the middle of a half dozen fizzes I get this realization: I'm hesitating to leave because once I do, I can never come back again. No way can I ever go back to living in Eddie's cage. And no way can I stand to be here and not see Avery again, which would be the same as giving him a death curse."

"But at least you left the bar," said Ditzler.

"Sure, once I had a plan, which was to catch that bus, go to Totowa, steal my sister's car and drive it off a bridge. I know this is not a crystal clear plan, but I'd been drinking for a while without adult supervision."

"It's clear enough except the killing yourself part."

Sylvia gave him a look that wavered between kindness and disgust.

"Ditzler, you don't run from Eduardo Buente. And if you do, you don't hide. At least this way I'd get to go on my own terms. Eddie once told me about cutting up a guy who was still breathing and using the pieces for chum. That wasn't just to be entertaining."

Ditzler decided a little more wine wasn't a bad idea. He emptied what they had in Sylvia's glass, and got another bottle and a fresh pack of cigarettes. Once restocked, he asked Sylvia how a trip to North Jersey turned into the demolition derby.

"I started thinking about my sister and how much she loves her little MG, and my friends up there and how bad I'd feel being around everybody when all I was going to do was off myself anyway. So, when I finally left that place and saw the little truck with the keys in the ignition, I had a new plan involving that breakwater down the street."

"Which you thoroughly messed up, which I guess I should thank you for, though the jury's still out on that one."

"Interesting," said Ditzler.

"You think? So, anyway, the main point in bringing this all up is I'm getting those feelings again, this sort of low level panic that if I don't get a little more air and sun on my skin I'm going to entirely freak out of my gourd."

Ditzler poured a tall glass of wine and frowned in concentration before gulping it down. Sylvia misinterpreted the gesture.

"You want to get rid of me," she said. "I don't blame you. Now that you know what you know."

He shook his head.

"No. There's always a way."

Ditzler walked to the side of the balcony where he could lean out and look at the bay water. The idea came so quickly and effortlessly that he didn't trust it at first. Then he almost wished he hadn't thought of it, as the implications sunk in. And then he felt the surge of determination that always followed a new, unrealized idea.

"You said you liked boats."

"I love boats."

"Give me a week," he said, going into the apartment and down the stairs to the pay phone outside the marina office to make a call.

CHAPTER
9

"Norm, you gotta come over here and check this out," said Marty Romanovski over the phone.

"Can't tell me over the phone?"

"No. You gotta see it to get the full effect."

Harlan never liked to leave his office, but liked to take good care of Romanovski, even if it meant feigning interest in the chief's meaningless preoccupations.

"Sure, Marty. Why not."

When he got to the police HQ, Romanovski took him out to the caged area of the parking lot where they kept impounded cars. He opened the trunk of a Chevy Malibu convertible and said, "Ta da."

Norm looked in the trunk.

"What the hell is it?" Harlan asked.

"What's it look like?"

"Chunks of peat moss wrapped in cellophane."

"You're close. Both come from the earth."

"Come on, Marty. This isn't the Sixty Four Thousand Dollar Question."

"No, I'm thinkin' more like a few hundred thousand."

Harlan picked up one of the bricks and sniffed it.

"Don't sniff too hard or I'll have to bust you."

Harlan looked at him.

"Get out of here."

"Yup. That there is a trunk full of a dangerous, addictive narcotic known as hashish. A kind of concentrated marijuana. That brick you're holdin'll cost you nigh on four, five hundred dollars American."

"Well, well, well," said Harlan. "Who's the lucky owner?"

Romanovski referred to his casebook.

"Oleg Petronovich, aka Ollie Pinko."

"One of your people," said Harlan.

"Makes you proud, don't it? Thirty-eight years old, from Paterson, New Jersey, got a sheet long on charges, short on convictions. Looks like a Cosa Nostra employee. Strictly worker bee, given the ethnicity issue."

"Only dagos need apply?"

"Which would make this trunk full of dope sort of an official shipment," said Romanovski.

"What's that mean?"

"Means it's a fair haul upstream in the distribution channel. Close to the source. From here it gets scattered to the semi-pros and amateurs. The little people who don't know or won't say where they got it from, realizing that there's no quicker way for the soul to take leave of God's Earth then to fink on the mob."

"How'd you know it was in there?"

"We didn't until Ollie Pinko became a guest of ours and we just sort of took a look."

"What did you arrest him for?"

"Feeding seagulls on the beach. Officially, assaulting a police officer."

Norm Harlan felt that familiar sensation of fury and frustration surge through his body. Several times a year he and Romanovski found themselves calming the civic outrage of a vacationer who'd been thrown off the beach for an offense that was entirely the product of Avery Volpe's whim. That none of these complainers ever had the balls or financial wherewithal to sue the borough was high on Harlan's long list of disappointments.

"Did he actually smack one of the guards?" Harlan asked.

"Not according to Ollie. He said one of them smacked him. I think it was Johnny Lukeiwitz."

"Another Russkie."

"Polack, please."

"So I guess the usual choice between making a stink from jail or leaving the island and never coming back doesn't apply here," said Harlan.

"Not hardly. My next job is to call the FBI in Trenton. Tell 'em to come down and get this desperado."

"You have to do that?" Harlan asked.

"Christ, yeah. A haul this big, they're gonna want to know. Trust me."

"Immediately?"

Romanovski looked puzzled.

"Yeah, I guess. What do you mean?"

"Well, can you just hold him for a little while so we can talk to him?"

Romanovski's puzzlement deepened.

"Why would we want to do that?"

"To find out who he was bringing the drugs to. Obviously somebody on our island. Don't you want to know that?"

Romanovski struggled with the concept.

"Listen Norm, it'd be like this guy Ollie Pinko was an actual pinko, a Russian spy. The thing you do in that case is call the FBI PDQ. You don't start interrogating him on matters of national security, you know what I mean?"

"But this scum was here to infect our children with addictive narcotics, not drop the bomb on Elysiana," said Harlan, warming to his subject. "Don't we have a right to at least secure the identity of his connection?"

Romanovski mulled that over.

"I guess," he said eventually. "'Cept I'm not too sure old Ollie's going to be much help to us. There's nothing we can threaten him with that remotely equals what his own people could do to him."

"Then it can't hurt to try, can it?

Romanovski shook his head as he thought about it.

"I don't know, Norm. Not contacting Trenton right away might take a little explaining. Plus we're not what you'd exactly call experienced in the skills of interrogation."

"Let me do it," said Harlan. "Just let me see what I can get out of him."

Norm had recruited Chief Romanovski through contacts at Patton's Commandos. At the time, Marty was a day sergeant in Altoona, Pennsylvania, and as it turned out, had never heard of Patton's Commandos, since Harlan's contacts had mixed him up with another Romanovski who'd run a precinct in Queens before being sentenced to life for beating a Sikh cabdriver to death. But Marty had turned out to be a fairly competent chief, liked by everyone on the force as well as Harlan himself, despite the lack of right-wing paramilitary bona fides. One reason being he rarely argued with the council president.

"Okay, Norm, if that's what you want to do. You're the boss," said Romanovski to Harlan's retreating back as he headed into the HQ building.

For his part, Oleg Petronovich was ripe for a distraction, having spent several hours in forced contemplation of his various shortcomings, principle of which was an ungovernable temper that had served him poorly throughout his life. Ollie had entered the organized crime industry on the ground floor and shown sufficient loyalty and focus to secure steady assignments as a courier, collections agent and occasional breaker of small and large bones. It wasn't a profession designed to suppress a hair-trigger temper, but at this point, it was all he knew how to do.

"Hey, Ollie," said Harlan through the bars. "I'm Norm Harlan. I run this place. I'd like to talk with you if that's okay."

Ollie's tiny green eyes stared straight ahead, freezing the air between them. Harlan was unperturbed.

"I know you're probably thinking this is the end of the line, the big trip over the cliff. But that's not necessarily so if you're willing to have a little imagination. And the capacity for some blue sky thinking."

Ollie sat motionless in the empty lockup.

"When do I get my phone call?" he asked.

"You haven't gotten your phone call? Gee, that's no good. I'll have to talk to the officer in charge."

"You're not a cop?"

"Borough council president. Don't go away, I'll be right back."

Harlan went to get Marty Romanovski, who got the lockup officer to bring Ollie to a drab little lounge with a table and chairs used by defense attorneys to meet with their clients.

"Make yourself comfortable," said Harlan. "Can I get you anything?"

"My phone call."

"Right. Have a seat and we'll talk for a second, then I'll go see about the phone call."

They both sat, but only Norm Harlan made himself comfortable.

"Let me ask you something," he said to Ollie. "It looks to me like Marty and his boys have a pretty good case against you. A trunk full of illegal drugs, illegally obtained, proving you to be a serious drug dealer. This is not a situation you're likely to emerge from unscathed."

Ollie shrugged.

"You might be thinking your life has taken a turn for the worse," Harlan went on. "And you might be right. But, sometimes when things look to be the worst there's a little glow in the darkness. A little beam of hope guiding you toward salvation."

"I don't need a chaplain."

"I'm sure that's true, Ollie. But I'm just the borough council president. Not that I don't believe in the Lord Our Savior. Though while He might want to save your soul, I'm the only one in creation interested in saving your ass."

"There's no law against feedin' the seagulls."

"I know that, Ollie. I'm aware of that, believe me. But that doesn't matter now. What matters is the dope in the trunk. Your trunk, your car. Your trouble. All yours because nobody's going to share it with you, that's for sure. Especially not the fellas you were planning to sell it to."

"I wasn't selling anything," said Ollie, then instantly regretted it. Harlan read the expression.

"Of course you weren't selling anything," said Harlan. "You were just making a delivery. You're transport."

Harlan sat back in his chair and folded his arms, watching the big Russian try to regain control over his face.

"Now we've really got something to talk about," said Harlan.

"No more talking without my phone call," said Ollie, also sitting back and folding his arms. The clamor of body language filled the air.

"There's nothing I can do to make you trust me," said Harlan.

"I know that. So let's save your time and my breath and cut to the chase. I want you to bring me to your contact. I want to have a talk with him."

Ollie barked out a single laugh.

"I want to have a talk with Raquel Welch. As likely to happen."

"Raquel can't save you from going to jail."

Ollie snorted.

"Can't save me from feasting on my balls while some fuck uses my head for batting practice."

"No, but I can. That's the thing, Ollie, I'm the only one who can."

Ollie snorted.

"Borough council president?"

"Here's how it goes," said Harlan, unfolding his arms and leaning out over the table. "You give me the name of your contact. I go see him. If he doesn't prove out, we never talk again. If he does, you find yourself in your car heading over the causeway to the Garden State Parkway. I keep the dope, of course, but otherwise, you're a whole man."

"Where do I catch the next rocket to Mars? That might be far enough away."

Harlan tapped out a loose rhythm on the table with his fingers. Ollie looked settled in for the long haul.

"You might have noticed that this isn't a very big island," said Harlan. "It's long, but not very wide. Can't fit all that many people. So certain kinds of people stand out. Like the kind of people who might be capable of receiving a trunk-load of dope. We're going to know who they are eventually. Especially when word gets out that we've got the courier and his whole shipment here at the station. That the courier is singing a merry tune, naming names, giving up everybody from his mother on down. Helping us put together a full sweep of the island as soon as we feel like exerting the effort. Could happen any minute."

Ollie looked skeptical, but he was listening.

"Nobody'd believe that bullshit."

Harlan shrugged.

"Maybe not, but you can't blame us for trying. Be fun to see what happens."

"That's wrong," said Ollie.

Harlan smiled.

"Moralizing from a dope dealer. Interesting."

Ollie slid down deeper into his seat.

"I guess when nothing actually happens, you'll have to think of something else," he said.

"We still have you and the dope. You get put away labeled a snitch. That's good for something."

Ollie frowned.

"I deliver the dope," he said to Harlan. "You watch it all, make your move after I'm long gone. That's the only way it can happen."

"Now who's talking nonsense?"

"That's the only way it's going to happen," he repeated. "No offense Mr. Borough Council President, but you don't know shit about how things are done. I'm still taking a lot of risk."

Harlan tried to put on a convincing look of disgust, in part to camouflage his surprise and glee that the transaction had been that easy. To make sure he wasn't missing something, he went back at Ollie a few dozen times over the next two hours, but the basic shape of the deal stayed intact.

He left Ollie in the room and went to find Marty, who wasn't as pleased with the outcome as Harlan thought he'd be.

"Gee, Norm, we can't do anything like that."

"We can do anything we want. We're the police."

"No, we can't do anything we want. We're constrained by process and procedure, to say nothing of legalities, protocols, political considerations and the Constitution of the United States."

"The Constitution's got nothing in there about chasing down a major drug dealer operating in the heart of our community. I think that gives us the latitude to manage this any way we think best. When we snag this bastard there won't be any talk about process and procedure," said Harlan before abruptly heading back to where Ollie sat waiting.

Marty Romanovski looked a little like there was something wrong with his stomach. Like he'd eaten a bad clam. He followed Harlan slowly, walking gingerly, as if a sudden movement would make him lose his cookies. Which it would, though not because of a bad clam.

"Who's this?" Ollie asked when the two of them came into the room.

Romanovski hit him in the nose hard enough to catapult the big Russian out of his chair, smacking both knees on the underside of the table and his head on the floor.

"The chief of police," he said, quietly. "But you can just call me chief. Or sir."

Harlan pulled up a chair as if nothing had just happened. He looked down at Ollie, who was on his back, still in the chair, holding his face.

"Marty's unsure about our concept. But he's willing to play along if he thinks you're sincere. Are you sincere?"

Ollie got off a nod and a salute, a smart thing to do under the circumstances. Marty dropped a handkerchief on the Russian's chest which he used to stem some of the blood. The gesture matched the chief's revived mood. The punch had fulfilled its therapeutic purpose. And earned the respect of Ollie Pinko, who mistook Marty's behavior as evidence of another uncontrollable temper—a brother under the skin.

Nevertheless, the deal was struck. And both Norm Harlan and Marty Romanovski went home that night feeling like a good day's work was done, especially given the promise of the fine work yet to come.

Ollie Pinko didn't sleep quite as well. A man whose fatalism ran as deep and eternal as the Siberian permafrost, he'd always known his chosen business career would be mildly interesting and lucrative, but short-lived. There was something about Norm Harlan, the pasty fleshball of an American bureaucrat, that chilled his heart. Though grateful the fool had so easily succumbed to Ollie's negotiations, the experience felt like a harbinger of ill tidings to come.

He started to feel as if he was using up all the oxygen in the holding cell. He left the bare mattress and discovered he could open the window. Escape was prevented by an open-weaved webbing of steel mesh, but there was plenty of room to let in the thick summer air.

He lay down again on the bed, feeling the damp breeze over his bare chest. But then the sound of the surf, just a half mile away, began to intrude, blending with the worries and premonitions that feasted on his exhausted mind.

CHAPTER
10

Waking up was a bigger event for Jack than other people. While he'd mostly regained control over his waking consciousness, he'd never quite mastered the transition from sleep to full, daylight awareness. The netherworld in-between persistently reasserted itself, making every morning a tug-of-war, a long swim in viscous fluid, a gasping scramble to the surface.

Often the specters of his dream state lingered, sometimes as fully-formed hallucinations, running riot around the Box, or placidly puttering around the place, cluttering up his bathroom, bedroom and kitchen. Jack had to literally shake them off—close his eyes and bang his head around until he could open his eyes and have only the tangibilities of temporal reality in view.

That morning he'd found himself debating with Bento de Spinoza, the half-blind optician-philosopher squinting at him and bickering about his dream's appalling lack of efficient climate control. Jack rolled around his Navy surplus cot, holding his head and yelling at the kvetching philosopher to shut up and go back to Amsterdam.

That seemed to work. Sweaty and disoriented, Jack stood up from the cot and shook his head one last time, then opened his eyes. He rushed over to the stove and filled the tea kettle, then stuffed the Melitta coffee maker with fresh ground beans and tried to watch the pot into a quick boil. Which it did, with a lusty whistle. Jack took it out to the all-weather recliner to check on the day, already vibrant in pale, diffused sunlight, sharpened by its reflection off the gray-green Atlantic below, spreading out into infinity.

The sea was unsettled that morning. The waves rode into shore in undisciplined formations, merging and chasing each other in foamy disarray. The sky was bright, but colorless, except for where the bright rising sun sprayed a smoky gold leaf across the cloud cover.

The general mood of the ocean discouraged Jack from taking his usual morning swim. He'd often swum in much worse, but there was an alien quality to the wave pattern that might be smart to leave unchallenged. He was also tired and listless after several nights of poor sleep, nights when he'd wake up halfway down the grand stairs of the Imperial Hotel, or naked on the beach, or sitting in the panel truck futilely pushing the start button, his subconscious having had the sense to leave the ignition key in the Box. These moments were not so much unsettling as disappointing—a commentary on his progress to full recovery. It would make the rest of the night pretty much a bust for sleep as he lay in the cot upbraiding his mangled, unruly mind.

Jack wondered how a person could find himself constantly entangled in debates with his own brain. Though he appreciated the inherent ironies and conundrums in even posing that question. If he was arguing with his brain, who was "he"? Just another part of his brain, right? he'd ask. So it was the organ arguing with itself. So which side of the argument should he listen to? Which part was "listening"? Both or neither, separately or simultaneously?

He'd done his time in mental institutions, intimately engaged with people whose brains were in outright rebellion. He sensed the difference in their situations. At least he hoped there was a difference, recognizing that everyone in the place was hoping the same thing.

When thinking this he wished he knew what the piece of his brain that hosed off the macadam at the end of his parents' driveway had been assigned to do. He assumed that the pinky gray chunk had interconnections with some other chunks that made up the central operating unit. Obviously these connections, and the functions they controlled, weren't essential to survival, but had some utility, the importance of which had yet to be entirely borne out.

After a half hour on the all-weather recliner and a big mug of Chock full o'Nuts, Jack's daytime consciousness felt established enough to start the day. He jumped up and trotted back into the Box to make the day's second cup of coffee and almost ran headlong into Gwendalynn Anders, who was already engaged in refitting the Melitta with a fresh filter and pouring the remaining beans inside the grinder.

He staggered back a step or two, then leaned forward and touched her arm. She gently pulled it away, keeping her eyes locked on his, fighting the impulse to gaze south at his naked body.

"Sorry to startle you," she said. "The door was open. I guess I should have knocked."

"I don't need to close the door. Nobody else is here."

"Right. I didn't think of that."

"You're real."

She smiled.

"I like to think so."

She saw him shake his head violently, as if a large insect had just dive-bombed into his mass of wiry hair.

"You looked so peaceful out there," she said, "I was going to bring you another cup of coffee."

"I'm not used to people in my house."

"Hell of a house."

"Not trying to be impolite, but what do you want?" he asked.

She held up a small plastic container.

"Cream?"

"I don't have any. Just some skim milk for cereal."

She smiled a strained, embarrassed smile.

"That'll do. I'm really sorry. I would have called, but I didn't know your number."

"I don't have a number. I have a phone. It rings sometimes, but I don't have a number. Not that I know of."

"I don't have a number either," said Gwendalynn. "Though I guess you know that, since you own the apartment."

"I should put on some shorts."

"I'm sorry. I'm really bothering you. You shouldn't have to do that just because of me."

He brushed past her and went to the back of the Box where he kept his clothes in a gray metal cabinet next to the army cot he slept in when he wasn't sleeping on the all-weather recliner. He dug out a T-shirt and pair of cutoffs. He didn't know how to feel about having another person in the Box. It was a rare occurrence. A few service people to fix plumbing and electrical problems, his sister and her empty-eyed husband one awkward weekend, a pair of ambitious Jehovah's Witnesses, and one rookie guard whom he'd recruited to help carry a stacked washer/dryer unit up the twenty flights to the Box, an act of misguided obsequiousness for which there was no adequate compensation.

Except for his sister, there had never been a girl. Jack didn't know any girls. The opportunity to meet one had yet to arise, given the restricted patterns of his day-to-day life. Not that the void went unnoticed. But the mental circuitry required to engage well enough to sustain the engagement didn't seem operational. In the early stages, Jack was mystified that conversations with women would start with such promise, then quickly wither on the vine. He didn't know why, or why the effect on him was so indeterminate. It was all so confusing, even disorienting, that avoidance seemed the more fruitful tack.

With these incongruities in tow, Jack trotted back to the kitchen where Gwendalynn had brewed a fresh pot of coffee, and dressed the cups and saucers with festive slices of white bread globbed with butter and sprinkles of wheat germ, the best she could do with Jack's available food stocks.

"Breakfast hors d'oeuvres," she said.

He grabbed a kitchen chair and led her out to the roof, giving her the all-weather recliner and taking the chair for himself. He was relieved when she didn't fight him over the gesture. She was wearing a pair of cutoff jeans and a T-shirt nicked out of Paula

Harlan's clothes hamper. She looked like three-quarters legs and one-quarter thick, dried-out semi-blond hair. She blew a stream of air over the top of her coffee cup, creating a swirling, ephemeral vapor trail.

"Are you okay in your apartment?" he asked. "Everything working?"

She nodded.

"It's fine. The finest kind."

"If not, there're other places we could try."

"No shit. Big house you got here."

"I've only seen a little bit of the place since I moved in. I should go look someday."

"You're kidding."

Jack tensed as he imagined himself embarking on an exploration of the Imperial Hotel, something he hadn't done since the summers spent with Petey Amato. Gwendalynn must have seen the reaction.

"None of this was my idea. My mother thought God wanted me to be here. I don't know why. But it's okay. I'm here," he said, instantly regretting how he'd trivialized the central desperate issue of his life.

"At least your parents know where you are," said Gwendalynn.

"Yours don't, I take it."

"They can only know that from me, and I'm not talking."

"You've run away from home."

"Indirectly. So what's your old man, hotel mogul?"

"Forklifts. Before he died. The hotel belongs to my mother. Got it from her father. It's a long story," said Jack, his voice trailing off into oblivion.

"Alright, alright," said Gwendalynn, quickly standing up. "I'm an idiot. Just wanted a cup of milk and what do I do, bring down the whole world. Do you have any drugs?"

"No."

"That's cool. I'm cool. Better that way. I've been clean for a few weeks now. Getting used to reality. Not as bad as I thought it would be."

Gwendalynn sat back down again and concentrated on her coffee. The sun suddenly broke free of a band of clouds along the horizon, blasting high-intensity radiation on to the balcony. It was a bracing shock for both Jack and Gwendalynn. Above their heads the seagulls were in full voice, inspired by the anticipated feast of marooned clams.

"I used to have some pills left over from the hospital, but I never took them so I threw them out," said Jack.

"Painkillers?"

"Anti-psychotics."

"Oh."

"Cuckoo's nest," he said.

"Huh?"

"Psychiatric hospital."

"Oh."

He traced a fingertip across the scars on his forehead.

"Car accident," he said.

Jack went back to studying the new day, waiting out the few minutes it would take for the girl to make an awkward excuse and then a prompt withdrawal. But instead she squirmed deeper into the all-weather recliner and said,

"I didn't know crazy from hitting your head was the same as crazy from natural causes."

"It's not, but they treat you the same," said Jack.

"What kind of accident?" she asked.

Jack felt a faint twinge of panic. This wasn't his favorite subject.

"A car thing. I told you."

"I know, but what kind of car thing? A head-on, side swipe, black ice, hit-and-run, rear ender, solo into a tree or telephone pole, asleep at the wheel, DWI, blowjob, black out, hallucination—those are the only ones I'm familiar with, though I bet there're more."

"Familiar as in first person?"

"Some of 'em," said Gwendalynn.

"The backing out-of-the-driveway game. Other than that, I don't remember."

"What was the backing out-of-the-driveway game?" she asked.

"My father liked to race to the end of the driveway in reverse. When he got there, he'd stop and ask my mother, who was sitting next to him, or my sister and me who were in the back, if anyone was coming. It was hard to see from the driver's seat because of a retaining wall and some bushes. We were supposed to yell 'all clear' if it was safe to keep going."

"Interesting game."

"Not really a game. That's just what I called it in my mind. But that's all I remember. Not the accident itself."

She blew over the top of the coffee mug even though it had cooled down long ago.

"Memories always come back," she said.

"You're an expert?"

"No, but I'm nearly college educated, so I have all the world's learning at my fingertips."

"That's a big responsibility," said Jack.

"When did you graduate?"

"I never went."

"Oh."

"I was asleep."

"Asleep?"

"In a coma. Missed that part."

"Shit, I am way too inside your space," she said.

"That's okay. I know it's a little weird."

"I haven't graduated either. Not yet. So there," she said.

"Makes us even."

"Guess not. Never been in a coma. Unless you include tripping my way through Sociology 101."

"You do a lot of drugs?"

"I did. For some reason, not at the moment. Not even a lousy joint. That last trip was pretty bad. Bad enough to zing me all the way to New Jersey."

"Why'd you do it in the first place?" he asked.

She stared at him blankly.

"To get high," she said.

"How come?"

"Man, you are like Rip Van Winkle. You get high to get high. You don't need a reason."

"Hm."

"You don't believe me," she said.

"No. Sorry."

She reached out and took the front of his shirt in her hand, giving it an occasional tug to emphasize key words.

"Okay, emotional pain, disgust, disappointment, and intense feelings of abandonment. And that's not the worst of it. Is that good enough for you?"

"I don't know what's good enough. Or bad enough," said Jack. "Maybe if I had a normal brain I could experiment, then maybe I'd know."

Jack's mental clock, a device made remarkably more precise by the accident, told him it was time for him to jog down the long flight of stairs to the sea if he was going to take his morning swim, rough water or not. Jack had come to rely heavily on routine as he struggled to retrain his mind for more complex behaviors. He'd rarely confronted a conflict between the rational and the rote. But there he was, dying to go swimming but nailed to the balcony by the presence of the girl from Chicago.

"Are you hot?" he asked her.

She pulled her tank top away from her chest and looked down the scooped neck.

"A little. No sweat yet."

"You want to go swimming?"

"Now?"

"The water's a little cold, but it's a good wakeup."

She looked down at the brilliant green surface.

"Sure. We could dive in from here," she said.

"Not yet. Give it a couple months."

She sat back.

"You're kidding."

"In about six weeks the tides will be at their apex. That's when you dive from here."

She sat forward again and studied the shoreline. She shook her head.

"Sorry, man, I've never seen the ocean till very recently, and I can tell you just by looking that it's not coming anywhere near enough for you to dive into it. There's a front yard, a street, a boardwalk and a bunch of sand between here and there. Unless you can jump like Superman, it's not happening."

Jack immediately wished he'd kept his mouth shut, but it was too late.

"I'm doing it anyway. You have to have faith."

"Or suicidal tendencies."

"Either way, I'm going to dive into the ocean from the ledge four feet in front of where you're sitting. Or maybe jump. Depends on the air currents on the way down."

"Okay, fine. I'm going to sing like Maria Callas by next Thursday, right after I grow boobs like Marilyn Monroe."

Jack looked over at her.

"Your boobs are fine the way they are. Marilyn's were too big."

She lifted the tank top again for a different examination.

"I think that was a compliment."

"So you don't want to swim," he said.

"You go ahead. I'm soaking up the sun while it's still fresh. It's already cooled off by the time it gets to Chicago."

"I thought the summers were hotter in Chicago."

"Yes, but the sun is staler. Scientific fact, you can look it up."

Though traveling at close to the speed of light, the transmission of signals within Jack's brain was slightly delayed as it maneuvered around a cavity in the pre-frontal cortex about the size of an avocado core. This infinitesimal delay might explain why he was often late in identifying important social cues. Nonetheless, that morning he read it right.

"Not when I'm in the company of a solar authority of your eminence," he said as he watched a gull soar high above the concrete-like sand at the water's edge lugging a large clam held within his beak, which he dropped at the arch of his trajectory and watched with Jack as it wobbled unsteadily to earth.

Moments before it could smash into the slick sandy surface an even harder material interrupted its descent.

"WHAT THE fuck," murmured Avery Fox, brushing the pulverized clam off the top of his head, flinging the slimy shell fragments from the tips of his fingers high enough for the agile gull to catch it out of the air.

Avery was almost at the end of his daily run from beach patrol headquarters above the opera house to the end of the island and back again. It was a combination exercise routine and baseline assessment of weather, water and political conditions, a first-pass at potential threats and hazards latent in the coming day.

It was also a good time for general reflection, something Avery indulged in to a far greater degree than most people would suspect. It was easier to assume that whatever worldly success Avery enjoyed was the result of physical power and a willingness to apply it with ruthless abandon. But there was an active mind inside that rock hard shell and that morning it was filled with the warning signs of impending strife, the gathering clouds of municipal warfare.

The latest reading was the shoulder set of the two cops who took possession of the hostile Shoobie that Johnny had swept off the downtown beach. A little too confident, almost defiant. Something like anticipation in their eyes. Not knowing, but instinctive.

It was enough to cause Avery to ring the mayor's doorbell the night before, resulting in more unease than reassurance.

"Everything is lovely, dear boy," said Mayor Black, bending at the waist to bring his towering frame closer to human scale. "It is the best of times."

"Yeah, that's right, mayor," said Avery. "I'm just checking in. We had a little dust-up with a guy on the beach the other day. Some of Marty's people wanted to get more involved than we wanted them to. That kind of thing."

"Oh, such is the world. And ever thus. Care to come in?" asked the mayor, ushering the way with his enormous hand.

"Nah, that's okay. I got things to do. Sorry to bother you."
Mayor Black smiled sweetly.

"These trepidations are normal, Avery," he said, the words
emanating from somewhere deep within his expansive chest, hitting the air with the resonance of a trained basso profundo. "If I
had concerns you'd be the first to know."

Avery made a quick exit, embarrassed. A visit to the mayor's
house—the only three-story stucco and red oak Tudor on the
island—was a rare occurrence and not to be squandered by
vague suspicions or anxieties.

Though burdensome, he tried to keep these thoughts in the
foreground as a defense against another preoccupation, one that
had a habit of disrupting every calm moment. This preoccupation had form. A shapely form, and a face, the hard but hopeful
Italian face of Sylvia Buente.

He'd known who she was long before he saw her and her
friends pinned against the wall by the riot at the Lucky Charm.
Avery's jurisdiction was the narrow, undulating strip of sand and
surf between Elysiana proper and the open ocean, but his awareness of malfeasance encompassed the entire island. Despite political tensions, cops working for Marty Romanovski, local guys,
would call Avery whenever summoned to yank a drunken guard
out of a local joint, usually Shing O'Ling's Lounge. Avery would
dispatch a lieutenant to handle extraction before the cops got to
the scene. One night Avery had to do the job himself. The sight
of Avery coming across the dance floor and a quick flick of the
thumb was enough to propel the guard out the door. Avery then
parked himself at the bar where he could take in the essence of
the place, tease out the underlying dynamics. That's when he saw
the wife of the owner of the place, though she didn't see him.

At that moment Avery's brain patterns—which unlike Jack's
were undisturbed by traumatic injury—were permanently altered.

Avery had never needed anyone outside himself to maintain
his or anyone else's discipline. As a child he used his first steps
to charge the family cat and whap it over the head with a spoon.
One of twelve children, he was never inconvenienced by parental

nurturing or supervision of any kind. He made his bed every day, did all his homework, broke other kids' tibias on the football field and generally kept his own well-controlled counsel.

So no matter how profound his erotic attraction to Sylvia Buente might have been, he never showed the slightest change in demeanor or mood. At least to the outside world. Yet falling off to sleep, shaving in the morning, driving to Wildwood to have a beer, running alone on the beach, she was never out of his mind.

Like Eduardo, Avery assumed Sylvia was out of town visiting relatives. She'd told him as much the last time he'd slept with her at the motel in Wildwood. One of the reasons Avery's wife had left him was his sincere disinterest in her comings and goings. In Sylvia's case he was deeply interested, but thought that unseemly. An invasion of her privacy. Which is why he never let on that he knew who she was. If she didn't want to tell him, he didn't need to know.

So he took the news of her leaving with equanimity. Sylvia had disappeared off the face of the earth, as far as Avery was concerned.

It was hard enough to know how he should feel without wondering about the concept of having feelings. Or worse yet, to be thinking about feelings when the very idea of having feelings was so offensive.

In the past, when burdened by unwanted thoughts he'd exercise his way out of the situation. Run a few extra miles on the beach, add forty pounds to the daily bench press, row out to the ten-mile buoy and back. None of that was working this time. He wondered if that was the first sign of impending decrepitude. He'd turned forty-two at the beginning of that summer. He didn't feel any different, but knew he would soon enough. In fact, he'd been preparing himself since the day he'd sensed the strength of his grip surpassing his father's. They both sensed it, turning a simple handshake into a vast, complex and confusing communication.

Thus, the summer of '69 was a watershed for Avery. The year his physical prowess began its inevitable decline, and the year, coincidentally, his political rivals chose to challenge his pre-eminence, at the very moment he was being ensnared by the enervating influence of love. All of which Avery sensed as a sub-audible murmur beneath relentless ruminations. Though none capable of fully breaking his concentration or weakening his resolve to do what needed to be done, whatever the hell that was, no matter what the consequences. He felt himself the agent of a greater power. Whether divine or profane, a power who called the shots, who set the agenda. It wasn't for Avery to judge.

Running along the beach that morning, he decided those forces were telling him to go to Shing O'Ling's that night to see if he could learn something about Sylvia's whereabouts. How he might do that would have to be improvised on the scene. At the very least he'd have a few drinks, maybe watch a ball game, be no worse for the night out.

The decision made, his mind cleared, his pace increased, and the tawny Jersey sand stretched out before him like a road home.

Mike Ditzler was off that day, being a Wednesday, the day all rookies had off. Saturdays and Sundays were reserved for veterans like Jack. Ditzler had so far spent his free time watching the sun slowly fill his apartment above the marina office, and enjoying the consequences of Sylvia Buente's fitful sleep as she squirmed beside him on the single bed.

After about an hour of this he was driven to rise by a yearning for coffee and a look outside from the balcony. There he spent another hour checking his watch and keeping an eye on the front gate for the arrival of his father, who promised to be there no later than nine in the morning.

Chronically early, he showed up at about eight forty-five in his Wagoneer towing a thirty-foot wooden boat with an exaggerated curved bow, swooping topsides and an ungainly pilothouse which had the look of a Disney cartoon character. As did Isaac Ditzler himself, with hair like electrified balls of steel wool stuck to his head and horn-rimmed half glasses clinging precariously to the end of a nose even broader and flatter than his son's.

Sebbie Rosconni came out to welcome him with a sturdy embrace. Ditzler was too far away to hear what they said to each other, but the body language was what you'd expect from two old friends.

Mike Ditzler went back into the apartment to put on a pair of shorts and a T-shirt and wake up Sylvia to tell her he'd be gone for a little while.

She looked disappointed.

"It's your day off."

"Just be a bit. Make enough eggs for both of us."

Ditzler also got a hug from his father when he went downstairs to meet him. The elder Ditzler wore a broad smile filled with the thrill of the moment.

"It took all night to get the goddamn thing on the trailer but I did it. Your mother screeched at me the whole time."

"Thanks for coming, Dad," said Mike. "What do you think vis-à-vis sea-worthiness?"

"First rate. Hull integrity 100 percent. Systems so-so, but credible. Well within your technical parameters. Creature comforts, not so comfortable. But where's the comfort in sinking?"

"Always the relativist. Remember not to tell Sebbie what I have in mind. In fact, forget all about it yourself. To you, this is just another of your son's acts of lunacy. *Capisce?*"

"Don't throw your Italian around with me. I'm fluent, *mio figlio matto.*"

Mike Ditzler stood back to admire the vessel. He and Isaac had pulled it out of the Delaware River and dragged it to the same garage they'd used to restore the Alfa from the skies. It was actually the fifth derelict boat they'd salvaged, thus named *Entropy V*, since the prior four had quickly fallen apart. But the fifth survived, and rebuilt with about a hundred pounds of epoxy, would probably stay afloat at least through the summer.

While his father watched over the launch of the *Entropy V*, Ditzler went back upstairs to have breakfast with Sylvia and present to her his plan. Unsure how she'd react, he rolled it out carefully, laying out the rationale and overall concept before introducing the core implementation.

"I'm now living on a boat?" she asked.

"You could fit all of Elysiana over twenty times inside the area between here and the mainland. And well over half of that is channels and ponds and open bays. You can move every night if you want and never put a dent in the possible anchorages. We'll have to wait for my day off to make the run, but then you'll be able to live out in the sun as much as you want. You said you'd evaporate into nothing if you stayed indoors. You said you liked boats."

He watched her drop a plate of egg in front of him and sit down with one of her own. Her face looked puzzled. Or maybe angry. He couldn't tell. Especially when she started to weep.

"I don't think I can take too much more kindness. It's going to crack me up into little pieces," she said.

"So you like the idea?"

"It's all I been thinking about all day forever, just looking out there at all those boats with nobody on 'em all week and knowing there's all that water out there like you said. It's like this is a magic trick. I dream it up and you just go out and find it for me."

The last few words were barely intelligible as the tears evolved into out-and-out blubbering.

Ditzler, always hungry, eyed the eggs hoping she'd get over her thankfulness as quickly as possible. When she sampled hers mid-sob he felt released and dove in.

"Great," he said. "I'm glad you like it. My dad did most of the restoration on her. She doesn't look like much but the engine always starts and she's real accommodating underway."

"I don't care if I have to row it. It's a damn boat."

She made up two more plates of eggs and grilled a pound of bacon that they ate on toasted baguettes, all lubricated with overflowing glasses of orange juice and cups of coffee. The sea air had that effect on everyone on Elysiana. It was a geography zoned for eating mountains of food with no negative effects beyond the ongoing lust for more. For Sylvia, the meal also had a celebratory component.

"You are boss, you know that?" she said to Ditzler.

"I am boss. That is correct."

"You and your old man. He's boss, too."

"No, he's definitely not boss. But he is a virtuoso of mad escapades. And the purest heart in the world. Thank God I've got enough of my mother's genes to balance some of that out."

She looked at him intently across the table.

"All the time you're talking to me I don't know what you're saying, but you don't make me feel stupid. In fact, I think my IQ and self-esteem have both gone up about eighty points in the last couple weeks."

Ditzler felt a warm rush of pleasure over her pleasure with him.

Sylvia's expression loosened into a slack-jawed stare, as if her face had just been sprayed with a gentle mist. The smell of her suddenly filled up the kitchen and he noticed for the first time that her denim shirt was unbuttoned to the waist, an uninterrupted line of flesh from throat to belly button peaking through.

"Is that what I think it is?" asked Sylvia, pointing at the front of his cotton shorts.

He put his hand through the waistband and nodded.

"I guess it is."

"Here," she said, standing up and unsnapping her own shorts and dropping them to the floor. "Come over here."

She put her foot up on a kitchen chair and leaned back against the stove as she gathered him up and pulled him toward her.

"Just don't come in me," she said. "I've got enough to deal with as it is."

As he pressed closer she guided him into her. After a minute or two discomfort overcame urgency and they slid down to the floor. Ditzler kicked the kitchen chairs out of the way and cursed himself for not sweeping the linoleum the night before.

And for the next hour Sylvia expressed and Ditzler graciously accepted her heartfelt gratitude and appreciation for all he'd done for her. He knew this meant no change in her attachment to Avery Volpe. He knew exactly what this was and what it meant.

He was also grateful, for a mind that could understand the complexity of human entanglements, and a body that knew what to do with the opportunities those entanglements involved.

He loved seeing Sylvia every morning and every night. And would love even more to see her out of his apartment and on that boat.

CHAPTER

11

NORM HARLAN concentrated on forcing open his pupils. He didn't know if this was possible through sheer will power, but he thought it better than taking off his sunglasses which were making it difficult to see at quarter to one in the morning. Marty Romanovski, sitting next to him behind the wheel of the borough's only plainclothes cruiser, had opted for regular clear lenses. For him the Phillies cap was a good enough disguise, bought for the purpose that day.

They were waiting outside Shing O'Ling's Lounge for Ollie Pinko to show up. Both were fairly certain he would, based on the elaborate precautions they'd taken. Marty checked his watch.

"Five more minutes."

It was close to midnight, the time Ollie had arranged with Eduardo to make the drop-off. This made for a convenient stakeout, slipping the borough's Fairlane into a strategic parking spot in the Shing O'Ling's crowded lot. Officer Anskeep and partner, in Anskeep's own car, were assigned to closely follow Ollie from the impound to the lounge, and report even the slightest variation in the plan. Meanwhile, two patrol cars were stopping every Chevy Malibu that crossed the single two-lane bridge that led to the only causeway off the island.

"Surveillance subject turning into target location, Chief," said Anskeep over the radio.

"Thanks, Phil," Marty radioed back, "we got him. Proceed to secondary position and stay alert."

"Roger that, Chief."

Ollie backed his Malibu up to the kitchen entrance. The door was blocked from view by a shed and a row of trash receptacles. They'd have to trust that the transfer was being made. There was no reason to think it wasn't. Getting rid of the dope and clear of Elysiana was Ollie's only hope of survival.

As Ollie promised, it only took about thirty seconds for him to unload the trunk and beat it out of there. He'd told them Eduardo always did the work himself, heaving the bundles of hash into a rolling bin and covering it with a canvas tarp. From their parking spot, Norm and Marty could identify Eduardo by his slick, jet-black receding hairline as he hustled the dope into the bin before slamming Ollie's trunk, handing him a knapsack and slapping him on the shoulder as a combination thanks and see-you-later.

Norm thrilled to the scene as witnessed through the view-finder of his 200 mm SLR lens. The low light might mean the shot would be a little fuzzy, but he felt in his heart that it would suit the purpose.

"Bingo, baby," he said to Marty.

"An amazing thing to see, you know?" said the chief. "The actual commission of a serious crime. Right here on our little island. Makes you think the rest of the world must be some sorry place."

"The rest of the world is a miserable cesspool, Romanovski. Miserable enough that you and me just might see the end of it. They're plenty of prophesies to that effect."

"Good thing I've stocked emergency supplies."

"Include some proper literature," said Norm, pulling away from his camera. "Ayn Rand, Zane Grey, Edgar Rice Burroughs. When the time comes, books'll burn. You need to pass the learning down to future generations."

"The wife's got all her dad's *National Geographic*s and *Life Magazine*s. Been adding to them all along. That's some cultural record she's got there."

"Just watch out for the black boobies."

"The who?"

"All the naked native photos in the *National Geographic.* You want to cut them out of there before passing that collection along. Don't know what those fools're thinking, putting that sort of thing in a magazine any kid or woman could get their hands on."

"Didn't know they did that," said Marty. "I'll look into it."

Ollie's headlights lit up and the Malibu's tires squeaked over the macadam as it roared out of the parking lot. Norm thought he might have seen the Russian flick a middle finger as he passed, but pretended he didn't.

"Okay, boss," said Marty, putting his camera down on the car seat and reaching for the door handle. "Let's go make history."

Norm reached over and gripped Marty's thigh before he could open the door.

"Say, Marty, let me run an idea past you before we go racing in there."

Marty looked confused but stayed put.

"Okay," he said, tentatively.

Norm took a deep breath.

"Here's the thing. We're facing a delicate situation here. This Buente isn't just a guy who bought a bucketful of dangerous narcotics. He's at the center of a distribution network, the lynchpin to a vast underworld of filth."

Marty's confusion deepened.

"I'm aware of that, Norm. I think that's why we're here."

"Of course we are. What I'm saying is that you, as the number one police officer of this island, cannot be compromised by this situation. In other words," said Norm, carefully enunciating the words, "there can never be any doubt that you've been tempted, or shown the faintest inkling of preferential treatment towards this deviant due to financial gain."

Marty's face cleared a little.

"You're thinking somebody'd say I got a little vig along the way?"

Norm's shoulders dropped with visible relief.

"That's exactly what I'm thinking."

"So how do we handle this? Get Anskeep to go in there?"

Norm shook his head.

"I like that young man, I do. I've already forgiven him for the accident. It'd be unconscionable to have him confront a man like Eduardo Buente. Those Spanish people are ruthless. I think a little on the mental side. It's bred in."

"You're right there. Just think of bullfighting."

"I have to go in there on my own. It's the only way to handle this. I know what you're thinking," said Harlan, holding up his hands, though Marty hadn't mounted much of a protest. "It's a dangerous thing to do. But I'm the borough president. People like Buente have a natural fear of advanced authority. It's in their racial makeup. I'm prepared for him. Mentally, psychologically and in every other way. This is something I need to do for the Borough of Elysiana."

Marty Romanovski shrugged.

"You're the boss, Norm. Do what you gotta do."

He dug around in his jacket pocket.

"Here," he said, handing off his police .38. "You know how to use it?"

Norm scowled.

"Of course I know how to use it. I've been a Patton Commando since weaning."

Norm got out of the car, walked around to the driver's side and stuck his head in the window.

"Just so you understand, my plan isn't to bring him in. All that'd give us is one lousy arrest, and by the next day another scum has taken over the operation. We want the operation. We gotta turn Buente. Make him our eyes and ears. Have him give up the whole sordid mess, then bust him into oblivion. You hear what I'm saying?"

Marty nodded.

"That was going to be my suggestion, Norm. It's what we did back in Altoona when facing similar situations. Rural America. You want to talk about your cesspools."

Harlan slapped the side of the car in sympathy and headed off to Shing O'Ling's. He liked having the heavy little Smith weighing down his nylon jacket, though it made him wish he'd dressed in something sturdier. Something more official looking. More authoritative than white cotton pants, polo shirt and Top-Siders.

When he walked through the front door of the club he hit a smoke-soaked wall of fetid air, electrified by what sounded like the screaming agony of a torture victim coming from the loud-speakers hanging from the exposed rafters overhead. It took a few seconds for his eyes to adjust to the negative image effects of the black lights and flickering strobes. Revulsion joined hands with a vague panic. This was hostile territory. An alien strong-hold. The heart of pre-apocalyptic perversion.

The large open area in the middle of the club was filled with people that looked to be in the throes of ritual psychosis. He'd seen much tamer versions of dance floors on TV, but this was the first time he'd seen the real thing. It was more fasci-nating than he wanted it to be. In particular the way the women were dressed—as if they'd just come off the beach. One of them smiled back at his stare and he quickly set himself to locating Eduardo Buente.

He burrowed his way to the bar where he found a conve-niently open space between two large brass handrails. The bar-tender looked at him blankly.

"Is Eduardo Buente here?" Norm shouted over the music.

The bartender's blank stare hardened into concrete.

"You can't stand there."

"What?"

"That's the waitress station. You can't stand there."

"Oh," said Norm, annoyed with himself for complying so quickly. He took a split second to regroup, then bellied up to the bar between a pair of blond minors sipping gin fizzes out of the same straw.

"Hey, man."

"Learn more responsibility," Norm snarled as he reached across the bar and grabbed a piece of the bartender's shirt.

"Listen, kid," he yelled, "go get your boss. Tell him the law is here, and if he wants to stay open for longer than the next ten minutes to hightail it."

The bartender looked down at where Harlan gripped his shirt as if calculating the force needed to slice the hand free of the arm. Harlan let go and watched the bartender move away, duck under the bar and reappear on the outside, and then disappear into the crowd. On cue another bartender appeared and Harlan ordered a rye and soda on the rocks, which the kid had never heard of, so he brought a Jim Beam and 7UP instead.

It wasn't until Harlan felt a subtle press of weight around his stool that he knew Eduardo Buente had responded to the call, along with two very large men who'd pinned the borough council president to his seat.

"What's this?" Eduardo asked, as softly as he could above the ambient din.

Harlan slipped his finger into the trigger guard of the .38 and shook his shoulders.

"The end of your life if you don't get these gorillas away from me."

Eduardo waved his hand and Harlan felt a sudden release of pressure.

"You've got ten seconds," he said to Harlan.

Harlan took a deep, slow sip of his wretched bourbon and 7UP. Then he motioned for Eduardo to come closer. When the other man bent down he whispered in his ear.

"You've got a half dozen cops surrounding your club waiting to take you into custody for drug trafficking. I'm the Elysiana borough council president. Their boss. You're making the only person on God's green earth who can preserve you from lifetime imprisonment feel . . . uncomfortable."

Eduardo snapped back to full posture and perfect attention and took a closer look at Harlan.

"*Merde*," he said.

"Whatever."

Eduardo put his hand on the bar so he could roll his fingers.

"So, we need to have a conversation, am I right?"

"Oh, yeah."

"Fine. Follow me."

Harlan stayed seated on the barstool long enough to leisurely sip his lousy drink to extinction. Eduardo and his entourage stood like a rigid tableau a few feet away until Harlan was finished, then spun around with choreographed precision and plowed their way across the dance floor toward a door next to a bank of restrooms. Harlan followed at his own pace, several feet and a few seconds behind the herd.

They piled into Eduardo's office at the back of the joint. Eduardo turned and waved his hands as if chasing squirrels away from a birdfeeder. All but one of his gang, the biggest one, filed back out of the room. Stone-faced and silent.

"Him, too," Harlan said to Eduardo.

"You're making a lot of demands for a near-dead man."

"If I'm dead, you're dead. Neither of us wants that."

Eduardo managed a patient little smile as he shooed the big man out of the room.

"So," he said to Harlan, "what is this ridiculousness?"

"Let's skip all the back and forth crap. This place is surrounded by the police. They have a photographic record of you taking delivery of a huge pile of controlled substance. You're a drug dealer, a creature so low that the lowest insect on earth would be insulted to have your lowness compared to his. But I'm not here to trade insults."

Eduardo was clearly puzzled, wondering what exactly they were going to trade.

"I'm here to discuss your future," Harlan went on, "which at the moment is precarious indeed."

"Let's discuss your future as well, shall we? I'm thinking it involves evisceration and a body washed up in the bay."

"Then you'll have to face murder charges as well."

"They'll have to prove it. So you get me for a little recreational hanky-panky. Maybe I have some time away. At least I come back to enjoy the rest of my very long, lovely life. Made lovelier by thinking of the crabs nibbling your rotting corpse."

Harlan's resolve began to flag a little. But on thinking of Marty and the rest of the force out there waiting for his sign, he recovered.

"I don't know how many laws you're breaking with that kind of talk, but keep on doing it," he said, easing back in his chair. "Just makes it easier for me."

Eduardo's smile traveled up into his eyes. He pointed his finger at Harlan.

"I'm beginning to understand what's going on here. Why I'm not already in the tender mercies of your police department. You're here to cut a deal."

Harlan laughed.

"A deal implies an exchange between equals. This is more like a presentation of options from me to you. All you get to do is pick your poison."

That Eduardo betrayed little feeling didn't bother Harlan, though if he'd been aware of the tempest of rage and panic swirling within Eduardo's mind it might have been heartening. Eduardo knew better than Harlan that he was in an unequal negotiation. Made more so by Harlan's fundamental naïveté, for nothing else could have possibly driven him to attempt such a foolishly suicidal mission. An experienced extortionist would know that unless the deal included Eduardo ending his own life at the conclusion of their affairs, the paunchy little municipal bureaucrat and his entire family were already slated to be hunted down and brutally murdered, dismembered, vaporized and ejected as a molecular spray into the atmosphere.

"Very well," said Eduardo, "for discussion's sake, what sort of options do you think I'd be interested in?"

Harlan believed himself skilled at seeing the shape of a man's character. This led him to decide the best approach with the subtle Buente was to come at him head on.

"I want you to beat somebody up for me. Badly enough that they can no longer serve in their professional capacity. If you don't, you go to jail. Option one and option two. Two options."

Eduardo laughed. A rare outburst of genuine feeling. Harlan assumed it expressed Eduardo's relief. (Oh, beat someone up?

Such a trifling in return for my freedom? But of course.) In fact, the joke was on himself. Eduardo knew he'd underestimated the ridiculous Anglo.

"I apologize for laughing, Mr. President. Though it's your own fault for making such a humorous suggestion."

Harlan checked his watch. He didn't want to be gone so long that Marty felt compelled to launch an attack.

"Listen, Mac," he said, "you mean nothing to me. You're just a means to an end. Option one. Or, option two, you're headed for the deepest corner of the New Jersey penal system. Makes no difference to me."

"Hm. Tantalizing selection."

Harlan shrugged.

"And if a person was inclined to accept your first option, which of course I'm not, whose good health is so unworthy as to justify leaving someone so undeserving as myself at large?"

"The mayor."

"I'm sorry, just in case you're recording this, speak up a little."

"The mayor. I want you to tear apart the mayor. Just don't kill him. You probably know how to calibrate that."

"Which mayor?"

"Of Elysiana. Mayor Clifton Black."

This was reassuring to Eduardo. There was a logic to the concept, a familiar shape to it. A government official who wants to destroy a rival official. It was simply business, and not something like a domestic dispute or some sick vendetta. Relief found a hold on his mood.

"Interesting choice, Mr. President."

"When we bust you for the dope we'll want to know who your supplier is. And all your customers. Even if you don't tell us, we'll make sure they hear on the street that you did, since we already know who some of them are."

Harlan checked his watch, thinking it might be a good idea to check on Marty. Eduardo got the message. Decide now or seal his fate.

"If someone was so monstrous as to do this thing you want, how would he know you wouldn't arrest him anyway after the deed was done?"

"You wouldn't. You could try to pin something on me, though it's the word of a drug dealer against a council president. Even if you accept my offer, you'll have to take your drug dealing ways somewhere else, of course. This deal is only for offenses committed up to the present. That shipment we photographed is your last on Elysiana. Get a good price."

Eduardo opened a drawer in his desk. Harlan flinched a little, happy to see it was only to pull out a cigar. Eduardo offered one, which he accepted.

"We agree we're still in the land of hypotheticals?" Eduardo asked.

"I'm not, but if it makes you feel better, sure."

"It does. Thank you."

Eduardo drew in a mouthful of smoke which he shot back out toward the ceiling.

"I have a little story growing in my head," he said to Harlan. "In it, there is a man who has the means and the cruel will to effectively carry out this task. This man is indebted to someone who could never, despite the worst threats, be associated with such a deed. This man, who can have no connection whatsoever to this terrible criminal act, gives the name of the hired gun, if you will, to the parties initiating the project so they may contract with him directly."

Harlan shook his head.

"No thanks. My leverage is with you. Not some unknown from Bayonne."

"Not Bayonne, Mr. President, Elysiana. He lives here among us. And I will give you all the leverage you will need. I think this is the best you will be able to do here. And the importance of discretion cannot be overstated."

While Harlan thought about it he worked on the cigar. A good device to have in a negotiation, he realized. A credit to

Buente and something to remember the next time he put his
budget in front of the borough council.

For his part, Buente used the silence to jot down a few lines
on a pad.

"This is the name and address and a brief resume. I think the
activities listed there will provide adequate inducement."

Harlan got up from his chair and took the sheet of paper.
Another greaseball, he thought, reading the name. Figures.

"If it doesn't, expect to see my beautiful face again toot sweet,"
he said to Buente.

"Of course. Though remember," said Eduardo, his face dark-
ening, "anyone willing to bring down a mayor will have little
compunction about working his way down the chain of command. I suggest you stay as loyal to your arrangements as you
are to your ambitions."

Harlan calmly folded the paper and put it in his back pocket.
Eduardo made no move to shake hands on the deal and Harlan
felt no insult. In fact, he felt no more words were needed, and
was half way toward the door when Eduardo cleared his throat.

"There is one more thing you might be able to help me with,
since you are the council president."

Harlan stopped and turned around.

"Yeah?"

Eduardo's gentility was back in place.

"You know that hideous building across the street, blocking
my view of the ocean and presenting an obvious threat to public
safety."

"The Imperial?"

"Yes. I've tried for years to have your council take up the
issue to no avail. There'd be no better way to end the decade
than by condemning and blowing up that monstrosity like they
do every other week in Atlantic City."

Harlan laughed.

"You got balls, Buente."

Eduardo shrugged.

"What's a negotiation without a few flowers to decorate the deal? The resolution is already before the council. It's only awaiting a vote."

"Some negotiator," said Harlan, "I'd've given you that one for free," and then made it out the door. He squeezed past the big statue in the gray suit and strode through the tangled throng.

He still carried the lit cigar, spewing an aroma the kids in the bar associated only with doddering grandparents and pedophiles. Neither association shared by Avery Volpe, who nonetheless looked up from his scotch in the shot glass in time to see the council president move like a pinball across the dance floor. He traced Harlan's route back toward the other end of the club where he saw Sylvia's husband standing with his hands in his pockets, his white linen sport coat flaring out like a plume, staring at the council president's back with ill-disguised venom.

"She leaves every summer for some place, I don't know where," the bartender was saying as the music died down, the DJ mercifully taking a break. Avery forced himself to refocus. "The boss doesn't exactly share his wife's vacation plans with the staff."

Avery nodded.

"The boss is too busy hauling in all the tuna to be worrying about his fucking wife," he said, tossing down the scotch and setting the glass back down on the bar for a refill.

The bartender held his face in neutral. It was only his second season at Shing O'Ling's, but he knew enough to let that sort of inference settle where it fell.

Avery hadn't asked Sylvia for an accounting of her comings and goings and never would. Yet something told him she would never have left for an extended period without telling him. Avery was the last man to presume an importance greater than the one he felt he deserved. But this was more a matter of logic and reason. It didn't fit.

"So, the lady's a friend of yours?" the guy sitting to the right of Avery asked.

Avery let his gaze drift in that direction. What he saw was a guy with a face that had seen a lot of sun and absorbed a lot of abuse. Notably under the chin, which featured a long jagged scar. Past fifty, Avery thought, but still capable, given the lean muscles in his arms and the alert way he sat on the bar stool, as if ready to launch if the need presented itself. Avery had done two years in Korea, so he recognized the look. Military, but on the fringes. A skinny cigar between his lips. Comfortable in denim and ponytail. And comfortable intruding on Avery's conversation, something few ever thought worth the risk.

"Never met her. Just used to seeing her here," said Avery. "She a friend of yours?"

Goettlewing shook his head.

"Never been here before. Just down for the sun and sand," he said, not even trying to hide his disingenuousness.

"Sun's free. The sand belongs to me," said Avery, taking a sip of his scotch. "You're welcome to its responsible use."

Goettlewing toasted him with his drink, something clear in a tall thin glass.

"Thanks for the briefing. Who's the civie in the nylon jacket?"

Avery set the shot glass on the bar as delicately as he would a crystal egg. He sat back in the bar stool and looked at the glass, then wrapped it in his right hand, and with a subtle jolt, crushed it almost back into the sand from whence it came.

"Enjoy your stay in Elysiana," he said, then left.

He didn't mind going home to his apartment above the hoagie place in the center of downtown. It was his natural state. The apartment's arid austerity had a purifying effect. It was the most expensive two-room apartment on the island, merely for the fact that it came with daily maid service. The maid didn't have much to do, since Avery rarely used the galley kitchen and kept the place so stripped down there was little to collect dust or suffer much in the way of disturbance. But it was one of his few indulgences, maybe the only one, to come home every day to the precision of a clean, well-ordered environment.

The only environment in which he was able to get a good night's sleep, disturbed only by visions of Sylvia Buente working the tables, guiding dinner patrons through the thicket of tables, menus clasped to her chest, hips rolling under silken fabric, eyes pleading into the air for anything that might resemble some sort of reprieve, some faint hope of rescue.

WITH EVERY mile put between Elysiana and Ollie Pinko's Malibu his mood lifted another inch. What began as a desperate hope was firming into certainty.

First and foremost, he was free. He had a car and a knapsack full of Eduardo Buente's money, now belonging to a person or persons unknown to Ollie who lived way beyond his professional pay grade. It was enough to fund a new set of ID's, a plane ticket and a simple dwelling in a quiet faraway place, already picked out. Unlike other people in Ollie's line of work, he was always prepared for this eventuality. Likely his status as an outsider freed him emotionally from any sense of place or permanence. That and a streak of practicality, an efficient administration of his career.

He was still unsure about Harlan's designs on Buente. Little about the experience made a lot of sense. He never bought Harlan's story, or the man himself. Ollie's survival instincts had refined his judgment of character to the level of a trained pro-filer. The only thing he knew for certain was that Harlan made good on his word to let him go. After that, he knew all bets were off. Buente's bust would put a curse on his head that would be immediate, comprehensive and everlasting.

In the face of such absolutes, there was no time for half measures. And no need. Fate had decided on a new life for him, and he felt more and more cheered by the prospect as it slowly settled into his mind.

As if to signal approval, fate allowed a jet to pass close over-head on its way to landing at Newark Airport. Ollie took his eyes off the traffic on the New Jersey Turnpike longer than it was safe to soak in the beauty and power, the promise exuded by the giant lighted bird.

He checked his watch. A guy he knew who forged ID's would undoubtedly be home asleep. Ollie could be at the guy's house on Staten Island in less than a half hour, even with the perennial construction going on around the Goethals Bridge. He turned on the radio for the traffic report, which was encouraging. So he switched over to WABC and slumped happily back in the bucket seat.

A low rumble slowly rose above the radio. It was another plane, this one taking off above the turnpike as it made a slow bank to the west. Ollie rolled down the window so he could keep the plane in view as he negotiated what had always been an approach ramp to the Goethals Bridge. Though not technically that night, since the ramp had been diverted as part of a rerouting project involving a petrochemical plant that sprawled messily around the base of the bridge. The sole late night crewman had arrived only a few minutes before, and realizing he'd neglected to re-block the entrance, was on his way back down for that purpose. He waved at Ollie, thinking he was one of his colleagues, who like most people in America in 1969, drove a full-sized Chevrolet.

Ollie didn't catch the guy's wave, absorbed as he was by the roaring jetliner up in the sky. He did see the end of the ramp, but his visual acuity, confused by low light and the velocity of his approach, failed to note that beyond the edge was nothing but fetid North Jersey air, made more so by the pool of liquid industrial waste below, into which Ollie's Malibu plunged with the authority of an Olympic high diver.

By the time the night crewman arrived back on the construction scene, there was barely a ripple on the surface of the greasy, yellow-green pool. He looked back down the ramp, and mentally scratched his head, then calmly made the assumption that he'd been seeing things, or he'd missed the guy leaving, or the third option which, with any luck, would only reveal itself at some distant time in the future, when his involvement in the matter would be far easier to obscure.

CHAPTER
12

D~AWN WAS~ just starting to throw a faint glow above the Atlantic Ocean when Gwendalynn reached the Harlans'. As she became familiar with the family's routine she noticed that Sweetie would usually be up and about hours before her parents, time she often spent wandering the dunes or peering in the windows of the few neighboring houses. One morning Gwendalynn had picked her up on Ocean Avenue, halfway to the northern end of the island. The little girl told her she could usually get to a deli on the fringes of downtown to buy a pint of orange juice to drink on the way back before her mother woke up, or realized she wasn't in her bedroom.

That day she was patiently waiting in the kitchen for the timer on the range to say the TV dinner was ready. Gwendalynn kissed her on the forehead and got the coffee going.

"Your mom still asleep?"

Sweetie shook her head.

"She's gone."

"Really? Where'd she go?"

Sweetie shrugged.

"I dunno."

"How 'bout your daddy?"

"He didn't come home last night. He's gone, too."

Accustomed as she was to the Harlans' impressionistic parenting, this was a little shocking.

"You're kidding."

Sweetie shook her head.

"It's okay. I know how to use the oven. *Ob*viously," she said.

"Crap."

Gwendalynn went through the house, inspecting all the bedrooms, and saw it was true. No P's on the premises.

When she got back to the kitchen Sweetie had one of Swanson's finest steaming on the kitchen table. She'd poured Gwendalynn's coffee and put out the cream and sugar.

"I tasted your coffee," said Sweetie. "Yuck-o-rama."

"Was your mom here last night?"

"Yup. She left an hour ago."

"Her car's still under the house."

"She walked away."

She let the girl eat her chicken, peas and mashed potatoes while she pondered the situation. Paula had probably run out to visit a neighbor, or something like that, and would be back momentarily. Or maybe she'd finally shot a rod and was already halfway to Marrakech after murdering her husband and burying him in the dunes.

"Let's take a walk," she said to Sweetie, who was dumping the aluminum TV dinner tray in the trash.

"Sure. Let's get some orange juice."

It was much lighter outside. The sky was clear and the air already moisture-laden. Gwendalynn listened for the sound of voices above the wet rumble of the ocean. She took Sweetie's hand and went down the street to the three other houses that stood within this remote area of the mines. It appeared empty, but the walk had taken them closer to the parking area that served the path Jack and Ditzler took every day to the mines. Parked there was a red Jeep—of a type she recognized. Still holding hands, they walked the rest of the way down the street.

The Jeep was parked facing the dunes. At first, it looked to Gwendalynn like the guy in the driver's seat was asleep; his head hung back, his left arm draped loosely over the door. When they got closer, some instinctive impulse caused her to plant

Sweetie at the edge of the lot so she could go the rest of the way on her own.

Gwendalynn approached the Jeep from the left side and saw the rapid rise and fall of a brunette woman's head immediately above Johnny Lukeiwitz's lap. His right hand held the object of her interest which from a closer angle appeared more than capable of achieving adequate prominence on its own.

"Paula Harlan," said Gwendalynn, with equal parts disappointment and good cheer.

Paula left her task with a violent urgency. Her mouth was still in mid-suck, causing an audible pop that was so loud Gwendalynn hoped Sweetie hadn't heard it from the other side of the parking lot.

"Jesus Mother of Mercy, you startled me," said Paula.

Johnny stuffed himself back into his swim trunks before the echo from the pop had fully decayed. He looked fairly uncomfortable, for a variety of reasons.

"You left a seven-year-old girl with a history of pathological wanderlust alone in that house. You should be ashamed."

"She was asleep."

"She was baking a TV dinner."

"She doesn't know how to do that."

"Where's Harlan?" Gwendalynn demanded.

At the mention of the name, Johnny began a careful study of the surrounding mountains of scrub-covered sand.

"He was at the office all night. Listen, young lady," she started to point her finger at Gwendalynn, who just stared at it until Paula put her hand back in her lap. "You're not telling him, are you?" she asked, abruptly changing her tone.

A vast, furious sadness welled up within Gwendalynn, a familiar feeling, but one she'd kept at bay since that night in Chicago when some kid hiding behind long ropes of slimy black hair handed her that immense joint wrapped in red paper and soaked in DMT.

"I'm taking Sweetie back to the house," she told Paula in a low, firm voice. "When you're finished here, you might think of getting your head out of your cunt and start spending some time with her before she completely forgets you're her mother."

And then she walked away.

"Why's your face all red?" Sweetie asked her, taking her hand again for the walk back.

"Instant sunburn. It can happen to anyone at anytime. But only in July."

"You made that up."

"Two can play that game."

They walked quietly back to the house. When they got there, Sweetie squeezed her hand and sighed. Then she leaned her head against Gwendalynn's arm and that broke the bank.

"I'm sorry," said Sweetie, watching as Gwendalynn dropped into a crouch with both hands on her face to catch the tears. "What'd I do?"

Gwendalynn shook her head.

"Nothing, sweetheart. Sometimes this happens to people, even grownups. I'll be all right in a second."

Sweetie sat down on the couch next to Gwendalynn and held her hand, silently waiting out the tears.

Gwendalynn was reluctant to leave Sweetie at the end of the day. But Paula graced the dinner table with egg noodles, over-cooked chicken and nearly liquefied green beans, and there was no danger she'd be asking Gwendalynn to join them. So she left without comment and drove the aged Dodge down Ocean Avenue at slightly less than ten miles an hour to give herself time to wail in full voice until sufficiently spent to disguise her control failure should she bump into Jack.

"Damn all you fuckers. Damn you, damn you, damn you," she sobbed through her straight, blond-edged hair. "Fuck you to hell and die."

Petey Amato thought the blond hair contrasted poorly with his deep olive complexion. It didn't look real. He took it as a sign of his deepening panic that he hadn't thought that out beforehand. Clarice, of course, loved it.

"You look like Brian Wilson."

"Brian doesn't have blond hair."

"Okay, the cute one. I thought the cute one had to be Brian."

"That's Dennis. I don't look anything like him."

"You do to me, and that's all that matters."

"Maybe I could join the band. The first goomba Beach Boy."

"You'd have to learn to sing. Not that easy at your age."

"I'm twenty-six."

"The vocal chords stiffen up after eighteen. It's biological. Not your fault."

Petey had been distracting himself by calculating the relative merits of murdering Clarice versus killing himself. These conversations didn't help resolve the question.

He'd been locked up in the apartment for about two weeks. He thought it was literally killing him. He imagined the flesh on his face disintegrating, his sturdy frame withering, his mental state spiraling down into the depths.

The most aggravating factor, he knew, was Clarice. He'd never spent more than a couple hours with her at one time, much of which was blessedly consumed by protean sexual activity. He wouldn't understand what the words vapid or idiosyncratic meant if he came across them in the newspaper, but in those two weeks he'd acquired a practical knowledge of their meaning.

He pulled a pair of scissors out of the kitchen drawer, briefly reconsidered murder/suicide, then lopped off all the matted tangle of lurid yellow hair, leaving Clarice to sweep it up off the floor.

"I coulda dyed it back for you," she called to him as he left for the bathroom to shave his head.

This provided a much needed lift. He thought he looked a little like Yul Brynner—the Yul Brynner of *The Magnificent Seven*, his favorite movie. He mugged at the mirror for a few minutes, then went and completed the effect with black T-shirt, jeans and motorcycle boots.

When he got back to the kitchen he told Clarice to make him some dinner, since it was almost midnight, with what he thought was a Russian roll of the tongue, though to Clarice sounding more like Topo Gigio.

"You make me dee dinner Clar-eeze or I stick you wid dees see-zors," he told her.

"Pretty trippy."

He thought to himself, who is this woman, and what is she doing in my apartment? How did she get here and how do I get her back to where she came from? Is she really going to thaw out that steak by running it under hot water?

The first thump coming from the other side of the door to the outside staircase was partially obscured by the sound of the mostly still-frozen steak hitting the cast-iron fry pan. Petey spun his head toward the door when he heard someone yell "Police!" followed by the shattering crash of fire axes splintering the door.

He was out of his seat, over the kitchen table and halfway across the living room before the first two cops were in the apartment, guns held straight out and yelling "Freeze! Get down on the floor!" He covered the rest of the way in a graceful broad jump that sent him through the window, over the concrete breakwater and into the Northern Channel.

The explosion of effervescence above his head was immediately lit up with spotlights, and he could hear muffled demands coming from cops running back and forth at the edge of the breakwater. He hit bottom more abruptly than expected, but was able to shove off with a trajectory that kept him close to the slimy silt covered sea floor which he followed out into the channel. The lights were diffused by the water, but he could see the frantic movement across the surface as they searched for him. He made for the darker water before him, forcing his mind to ignore the urgent pleading of his lungs.

He didn't make it as far as he wanted, but hoped he could roll over on his back and quickly catch a breath without being seen. Which would have happened had Marty Romanovski not been looking in that exact location at exactly that time. With his gun already pointed in the direction of his big Maglite, he was able to immediately send a round over Petey's head.

"The next one goes between the eyes, son," Marty yelled.

Petey didn't hear the bullet pass by over the sound of the gunshot, but he heard it hit the water. He threw up his hands as every light on the breakwater swung blindingly into his face. He began to sink, since all he had were his legs and feet, weighed down by motorcycle boots, to keep him afloat.

"Okay, okay," he shouted. "I gotta put down my arms to swim."

"Come in nice and slow. Stay up where I can see you," said Marty.

He moved in a steady breaststroke toward the converging lights. When he reached the breakwater he felt a rope drop down on his head. He grabbed it and was pulled up and over the rough concrete onto the paved patio that covered the narrow strip of ground behind the building. A cop pulled his arms behind his back and shoved his face into the slate patio, which is when Petey noticed the blood coming from a gash in his forehead made when he smashed through both layers of the open double-hung window.

It explained the sting.

Upstairs, the two cops sent to clear the apartment discovered Clarice leaning against the kitchen counter with her housecoat pulled up to her throat, which left her nether regions free to the air. A view the cops took in before gripping her under the armpits and dragging her to the bedroom where they watched her squeeze into a pair of jeans, a pair of cowboy boots and one of Petey's undershirts. Too much in shock to notice or care about the audience, she woke up a little when one of the cops caught a handful of tit when he gripped her upper arm.

"Hey buddy, watch the merchandise."

"My hand slipped," he said, grinning to the other cop.

"Slipped, right."

With a cop on each arm, she was escorted to the street below. When she got there she saw the patrol cars, a paddy wagon and the borough's undercover car, their full array of lights flashing, turning the scene into a stuttering, stop-action tableau.

When she saw Petey she screamed.

"You shot him, you bastards."

Petey said to shut her mouth and keep it that way or he'd shoot her himself. Which prompted Marty, who was wrapping gauze around Petey's head, to give the half-dispensed roll a sharp little tug.

"Hey, none of that."

The cops lifted Clarice into the paddy wagon and Marty shoved Petey into the back of his unmarked cruiser.

"I didn't do anything," said Petey when they got underway.

"Sure. And the Pope's a woman."

"So what did I do?"

"What didn't you do?"

Petey could see that as a trick question. At least he hoped it was. A hope not well bolstered by the picture in his mind of the cops swarming over his apartment, discovering the attic warehouse, harvesting enough evidence from Clarice's vanity alone to put both of them away well into the next century.

"Don't you have to read me some sort of rights thing?" he asked Marty, just to have something to say.

"Oh yeah. You have a right to shut up and start acting like a smart guinea for the first time in your life."

"What's with the racial shit? No reason for that."

Marty reached back and snapped his hand in front of Petey's face.

"No profanity in this car. It's official borough property."

"Oh, and it's alright to call me a guinea."

"That's right. What I can't call you is an asshole."

Petey suddenly felt weak, cold and sick at his stomach. He'd never heard of shock, but he guessed rightly that he'd lost a lot of blood. He laid his head back on the seat, which turned out to be a bad idea.

"I think I'm gonna barf," he said to Marty.

"Now?"

"Soon."

Marty pulled over and jumped out of the car. He ran around and opened the curbside door, yanking Petey out on to the grass where the event was brightly lit by the high beams coming from the convoy to the rear. Petey decided that moment was the lowest point in his life, a life even then he had to admit had been filled with little but uninterrupted happiness and gratification. He took some consolation knowing Clarice was locked up and out of view in the back of the paddy wagon. He didn't know she was fully distracted by the leering attention of the cop who'd groped her in the apartment, who was now flagrantly studying the thin, straining fabric of the undershirt as it followed the contour of her breasts, a situation the cuffs holding her hands behind her back only exacerbated.

He reached over and flicked a nipple with his index finger.

"You better've killed my boyfriend back there 'cause when he finds out what you just did you're a dead man," she told him.

"Whoa, I'm shakin'."

In reality, she thought, Petey could probably care less. Her father, on the other hand, would care a little too much about defending his daughter's honor, a daughter he'd almost joyfully thrown out on the street. The thought of it almost made her laugh.

It also caused her to throw back her shoulders and sneer in the cop's face, stretching further the capacity of the undershirt to conceal what was underneath. Not being privy to her inner thoughts, the cop took this as an invitation to massage those ample globes, which resulted in Clarice reflexively jerking up her knees, one of which intercepted the soft tissue between the cop's legs with enough force to knock him breathless to the ground, within easy reach of her heavy, sharp-heeled boots.

"I'm not you," she said to the grimacing cop, lowering her boot to the floor, and for the first time, feeling free of her father's disappointment and the shame of unnecessary loss.

CHAPTER
13

Mayor Black stood just shy of six-foot eight. Sixty-three years old, he'd grown a little broader in the beam since teen hood, but not much. His handicap was also more or less the same, a fact grudgingly noted by Scott Mathewson—chairman of the appropriations committee, the best known legislative committee in the New Jersey Senate, and the least, the New Jersey legislative subcommittee on municipal governing charters—who played with him every month on an absurdly verdant private golf course south of Princeton.

Black was a year ahead of Mathewson at Rutgers, though the relationship had formed long before in Elysiana when their parents summered at their homes in downtown, the only settled area on the island at the time. Mathewson was barely half Black's size, a discrepancy no one who knew them ever found advantageous to point out.

"So, Scott," said the mayor as he twitched his hips and tried to draw an imaginary line running perpendicular from his mischosen putter through the center of the golf ball, "Joanie Sheldon's been crawling up my ass lately about our borough charter."

"How's she finding the weather up there?"

"Stormy," said the mayor, before sending his ball to a location on the other side of the green slightly inside the distance from its original position and the pin.

"Any reason why?"

Mayor Black shook his head.

"Probably that fat prick Norm Harlan."

"The agitator."

"The fat prick. I don't know what he's trying to do, but it's irritating."

Mathewson made a sympathetic sound as he chipped his ball in a perfect arc from a grassy spot slightly outside the fairway to a pleasant lay fifteen feet from the thirteenth hole.

"Though no more irritating than that," the mayor added.

Mathewson shrugged as they journeyed over to Mayor Black's ball. They'd started early and the sun was still low on the horizon. It was warm. A fading mist hung above the grass, still thinly glazed in crystal dew.

"Well, let me know if you want me to do anything with your charter," he said to the mayor. "Though it'll cost you."

Mayor Black swung his putter in a broad sweep as he walked over the grass. He looked around at the giant leaf-engorged maples and red oak, awed by the saturated depth of color, so different from the gray-green scrub that was scattered throughout Elysiana proper and choked the dunes and federal preserve in angry, twisted gnarls.

"Joanie tells me it takes an act of God to even propose a charter revision."

Mathewson smiled.

"It does. Unless you're the chairman of the New Jersey legislative subcommittee on municipal governing charters. In which case, it takes a snap of the fingers."

"No kidding."

"The subcommittee on municipal charters was formed by the governor during the war as a way to rejigger term limits, specifically his and his cronies. You might remember Governor Cancelmo. I think he's actually still doing time in the federal pen."

"Emile. Knew his wife. And his mistress."

"He never got a chance to do much with the power he got invested in the subcommittee, but the legislation still stands."

"What sort of powers?"

"You ever going to hit that poor ball? The power to ignore all other powers and just do whatever the crap you want. Nobody's invoked it yet, probably because they don't even realize it's there. I know for a fact the state board of municipal affairs hasn't a clue."

Mayor Black laughed. At Joanie Sheldon and Norm Harlan. And himself, for what he was about to do.

"So, Scott."

"Yes, Cliff."

"If I wanted to eliminate the position of council president, and say, consolidate all executive powers invested in borough government in the mayoralty, I could do that by simply ingratiating myself with the chairman of the municipal charter subcommittee?"

Mathewson nodded.

"Yup. Believe me I'm one of the few in New Jersey who's even aware of its existence much less our powers and prerogatives. Including the chowderheads on the subcommittee itself, most of whom don't know they're on it."

"Capital," said the mayor.

"Let me know. It'd be fun to stir the pot a little."

They finished up the thirteenth hole and waited for the caddies in the cart to swoop down from the tee to carry them on to the fourteenth.

"You said it'd cost me," said Mayor Black. "The charter change."

"One stroke on the last hole."

"Hardly seems fair given your lead."

"Your state government doesn't dispense favors lightly."

"And they say civic courage ended with Lincoln."

"Bravo."

Clifton Black went on to win the game, despite giving up a stroke on the eighteenth hole. Mathewson immediately forgot their deal, so the mayor had to call him up later that week to tweak his memory.

"Sure, Cliff. Give it a few weeks. I'll let you know when I put it through. Next time I get you to lower that handicap."

"Always taking advantage of your elders," said the mayor before hanging up, settling more than just the phone on the cradle.

"SHE WANTS to know if you want any lunch," said Sweetie, looking up at Jack and Mike Ditzler from the water's edge below their guard stand.

"Who?"

"Gwendalynn."

She pointed back toward the dunes where Gwendalynn was lying on a beach towel, waving.

"We'd be honored," said Jack.

"Is that the same as hungry?"

"Starving."

"What do you want to eat?" the girl asked.

"Peanut butter and jellyfish sandwiches," said Ditzler.

"What kind of bread?"

"Whatever the house is serving."

"The house isn't serving anything. Just me and Gwendalynn."

"Then you pick."

"Wonder Bread is good with jellyfish," she said.

"What isn't?"

As Gwendalynn moved into the picture she slipped her arm over Sweetie's shoulders. Even Jack's detoured brain immediately registered the bikini, something he'd never seen her wear before.

It was orange with stylized white and yellow flowers. Her penchant for loose, over-sized denim and chambray had made it hard to make out what kind of body she had under there. The bikini settled the issue. She had a slim but well-defined kind of body. Her skin wasn't as pale as he thought either, and he could extrapolate its tanning potential from the reddish-brown "V" the sun had painted between the open folds of her shirt.

Now late in July, Jack and Ditzler had been braised to the limits of their respective skin tones. Jack was the color of a saddle-soaped leather baseball mitt and Ditzler looked like an Australian aborigine, a status he'd been able to sell Sweetie, having caught her in a rare moment of gullibility.

Gwendalynn looked perfectly secure in her new suit, though it was hard to tell what she was thinking behind her sunglasses. Jack hoped the same was true for him, as he found it difficult not to stare.

"I was thinking of going swimming," she said to him. "What's it like?"

"It's warm today. Off sea breeze."

"I've never swum in salt water. What's it like swimming in salt?"

"Easier than swimming in pepper," said Ditzler.

"Is that the kind of water you have in Australia?" Sweetie asked.

"Come on, I'll show you," said Jack, stepping down off the stand.

Gwendalynn told Sweetie to stay put.

"Should I tie her to the stand?" asked Ditzler.

"Just watch her."

Jack dropped back so Gwendalynn could take it at her own pace. She quickly embarrassed herself by hopping over the tiny remnants of a once mighty ocean wave. She smiled at Jack.

"Lake Michigan has waves. I'm not a total novice."

"Tread carefully."

At that, she stepped forward boldly to meet the slightly scaled-up version of that first wave. It smacked her thighs and blew a cold, sour spray in her face.

She whooped.

"Yuck. That's salty. Sort of. More stinky salty."

"That's the brine. The primordial soup," said Jack.

"More like a lousy chowder."

After getting smacked by the next wave, she whooped again and charged out into the surf, quickly reaching the first gulley wash, a hidden, rip-prone trench that paralleled the shoreline, running the full length of Elysiana and presenting a merciless challenge to the Elysiana Beach Patrol. Jack saw her drop out of sight, her dirty blond hair briefly floating on the surface before being sucked down into the vortex.

He waited.

She popped up in a sputtering spray of invective.

"Holy Jesus Christ."

"It's the gulley," said Jack, reaching her in two powerful strokes. "I'd've warned you if you'd given me the chance."

He took her upper arm and led her gently to the first sandbar, where they could both stand at waist depth. He had a few seconds to explain that the waves out on the bar had a little more meat on them before one crashed over their heads. He held her arm with a grip that left four distinct red marks, but neither noticed nor cared.

Breaking the surface, Gwendalynn tried to shake clear the waterlogged streams of hair now glued to her face. Jack brushed them aside.

"Go like this," he said, holding his nose and dipping his head backwards into the water. She neatly performed the maneuver the first time.

The next wave forced her to repeat the process.

"Shit, they keep coming," said Gwendalynn.

"For all eternity."

"And this is fun?"

"DIVE UNDER the next one. Not too deep. Straight into the base and just slightly downward. When I say."

"Oh, sure."

He tried to demonstrate, but she didn't follow, so he had to dig her back out of the gulley and help her regain purchase on the sandbar.

"Okay," she said, "this time."

It wasn't a beautiful dive, but it taught her how you could slip through the front of the wave and be brought back to your feet on the other side. Jack stood near, wiping his face and smiling.

"Cool," she told him.

"The secret of the sea is to let her do with you as she will," he said. "All resistance will be met by defeat."

"I'm okay with that. The Atlantic Ocean is bigger than me."

"But not any smarter," said Jack. "It's just a dumb puddle of water."

"And I'm trusting my life to willful dumbness?"

"Brutal, unmerciful dumbness."

She tucked her chin against her chest and dove through the next wave. Jack joined her on the other side.

"I'm getting better at this," said Gwendalynn.

Jack thought her smile looked more authentic than the smiles she'd shared with him before. More toothy, more ear-to-ear. He didn't know that more than the novel sensations of the Jersey surf was at play in her mind. Probably for the better, since she was finally appreciating the desperate disproportionality of his appearance. It made her think of the caricature artists on the boardwalk downtown, who would love to draw his narrow, lined cheeks, stovepipe curly hair and preposterous nose.

The scar didn't help, plainly visible in the sunlight reflected off the ocean water, a pale, hardened line across his face, made more apparent by his skin's deepening tan. Impulsively she reached out and drew the line with her finger.

"Does it hurt?" she asked.

"What a question," he said, but didn't pull away.

She quickly dropped her hand.

"Sorry."

"The body doesn't know how to grow back regular skin. Scars are the best it can do. They seal up a wound, but that's all they can do."

He saw a pink rash spread across her face and blossom over her chest.

"Oh, Christ, I'm really sorry," said Gwendalynn, covering her eyes. "That's way too personal. I'm truly a silly shit."

He grabbed her arm again to steady her through the next wave, but then didn't let go.

"I don't have all my brain anymore," he said to her, matter-of-factly. "Some of it fell out of that hole in my forehead. There's nothing for you to feel bad about. You're just talking to me."

"I know, but Jesus."

He gave her arm a gentle shake.

"Some people put holes in their head on purpose. They think it opens a permanent door to greater consciousness."

"Do you?"

"No."

"I don't think much could have fallen out of there," she said, drawing herself closer and touching his forehead again, more boldly this time.

"That's hard to say. I think the part of my brain that could tell me which parts are gone might be gone itself. I know for sure I lost the years '60 through '63. And my education, though I remember sitting in classrooms. And I can still learn and remember everything from the moment I found myself sitting in a bedroom at the nursing home."

"Freaky," she said, then blanched. "Not that you're a freak. I didn't mean that."

"The first thing I did was take a piss. They had me in diapers. I stripped them off and peed off the side of the bed. Then I tried to read a book that was left on the bedside table. *After Many a Summer Dies the Swan*. Aldous Huxley. It's about a guy trying to achieve immortality. Somebody with a sense of humor must have left it in the room."

"I don't know about immortality, but it looks like you got a will to live."

They'd moved closer to each other as they talked, not only to support themselves against the monotonous assault of the surf. So Jack's face was close enough for her to see a subtle change in the wave pattern behind his eyes.

"I have a will to read," he said. "A will to eat and shit and swim. I have a will to look at the weather, to clean my body and to masturbate. What I don't have is a will to live."

She frowned into his eyes. His words and the look on his face did not belong together. Could there be such a thing as optimistic emptiness, she asked herself before he yelled,

"Dive!"

They dove together under an unusually big wave that broke in a seething frenzy over the sandbar.

"Man, what was that?" Gwendalynn asked.

"The surfers would call it a heavy. The one-in-a-hundred you wait all day to catch."

"You wait," she said. "I've got enough salt up the nose. I'm heading in."

She took one more look into his face and started swimming to shore. Jack followed her a few feet behind, letting her make her way. Sweetie met them at the tide line.

She pointed at Gwendalynn.

"Your suit," she said, the top of which had given up its primary function.

Ditzler went back to examining the horizon but Jack found he couldn't look away. Gwendalynn sighed and calmly put everything back together again.

"Someday you'll have a pair of these of your own, young lady," she said to the little girl, "and then you'll know."

Sweetie frowned and fiddled with the top of her own suit. Ditzler whistled "Ave Maria" and Jack climbed back up the guard stand.

"So, boys," said Gwendalynn, "how 'bout that lunch?"

"*Scyphozoa* all around," said Ditzler.

CHAPTER
14

The next day was Ditzler's day off. Sylvia organized the *Entropy* below decks, while Ditzler followed the chart his father claimed to draw from a thirty-year-old memory. It was remarkably accurate, showing key landmarks, like the wreckage of ancient oceangoing barges and the splintered pilings of abandoned fishing colonies, the shacks above long gone. The depth finder on the *Entropy* was less accurate, and Ditzler felt more than one bump against the muck-covered bottom. With heart leaping in and out of his throat he kept up a blissful smile for Sylvia's benefit, who eventually felt safe enough to join him in the pilothouse, wearing a baseball hat with her hair pulled in a ponytail through the adjustment strap in the back and a pair of dark wraparound sunglasses.

"You look great," he told her.

"I look like Mickey Mantle."

"Mickey Mantle never looked like you. Not even close."

"He's the only ballplayer I know."

It was still morning, but the fat summer sun had already started to bake the air. The tide was at the highest point of the month—a strategic necessity for getting the *Entropy* safely through the narrower, sediment-choked channels—so the usual brine-rot stench of the marshland was mostly pacified. A million bugs were busy zinging around the clumps of marsh grass playing the law of averages with far fewer but clearly rapacious, trash-talking birds.

Sylvia wrapped her arms around his neck and rested her head on his shoulder.

"Ya saved me again, you old Ditzler, you," she said, her voice barely overtaking the clatter of the inboard diesel.

"Glad you never made it to the boat ramp?"

He felt her nod.

"Me, too," said Ditzler. "Otherwise, we'd've never recommissioned the bonny *Entropy V.*"

Sylvia looked around the inside of the pilothouse. Isaac had thrown a fresh coat of paint on everything paintable and a few hurried layers of lacquer on the wheel and brightwork. It was enough to respect the boat's dignity, but not enough to hide her wear.

"No chance of the bonny old tub sinking, I guess," she said.

Ditzler shook his head, his lower lip thrust forward in a convincing show of confidence.

"Absolutely not. Hull integrity guaranteed by Ditzler marine engineering, backed by the makers of the finest marine epoxy in the world."

"That's comforting, whatever it means."

An hour later Ditzler turned up the last few feet of channel and the *Entropy* steamed into Rudolf's lagoon, thus christened by Isaac Ditzler moments before his son shoved off.

"What's a reindeer got to do with anything?" Sylvia asked at the time.

"Rudolf Clausius. Came up with a mathematical sidebar to fundamental thermodynamics that explained what he called entropy. Just be grateful the old man didn't try to get 'Clausius' in there somewhere."

"I'm only thinking your apple didn't fall too far from that particular tree."

Ditzler's smile opened up a notch.

"I never had a father," said Sylvia. "Just a bastard of an uncle who lived with us and a bunch of cousins. My old man got killed in a factory accident right after I was born. I'd ask my mother, what factory? But she'd start crying, so I stopped asking."

Ditzler wanted to say something gentle and thoughtful, but he had to bring the boat into the center of Rudolf's Lagoon and drop the anchor, a procedure that sounded much easier than it turned out to be. The problem was the anchor chain itself, which after several years of neglect had welded itself into a tangled ball of iron oxide, a natural consequence a lesser mind than Rudolf Clausius' could have easily predicted.

"Son of a bitch," said Ditzler, staring down into the anchor locker. "Get me a hammer."

"Where, where?" Sylvia shouted, alarmed.

Ditzler jumped up and ran to the stern. He showed Sylvia where they kept the tool kit. He pulled out a five pound sledge.

"The sailor's friend."

He went back to the anchor locker and pounded on the rusty rode until his ears rang. While he worked, Sylvia got in some helm time circling the center of the lagoon. The pleasure of the moment was all-consuming.

"Take your time down there," she yelled to him. "I'm liking this."

Ditzler ran back to a lazarette off the cockpit and scooped up a quart of motor oil. He ran back to the bow and poured it over the encrusted rode.

"Just stay clear of the land," he yelled.

"Oh, there's an idea. Why didn't I think of that?" she yelled back.

In much less time than he thought it would take, Ditzler released the rode, dumping the pitted plow anchor a whole ten feet to the bottom.

"Stop the boat!"

Ditzler let out another thirty feet of chain and secured it with a snubber harnessed to the bow cleats starboard and port. He felt the *Entropy* start a gentle drift to the right, then a slight tug. Dug in.

He sat on the deck with the sledge in his lap and tried to catch his breath. Sylvia came out and sat next to him.

"Aren't boats just the best?" she asked.

"Best route to cardiac arrest. If you survive the financial consequences," he gasped out.

She looked over the gunwale.

"Can you swim here?"

"Sure. Just don't touch the bottom. The glob under there will suck you right under."

"No, sir."

As he tried to tell her about the demons living on the slippery sea floor, Sylvia stripped off her sweatshirt, jeans, tank top, panties—and eventually stood naked on the transom, arms spread like a soaring eagle. Then without another word, dove into the water, raising an instant alarm in Ditzler's mind. Not from the remote physical danger, but the taunt of fate it represented. We just got here, he thought, let our luck find its equilibrium.

The seconds piled up as he waited for her to break the surface.

In the silence the buzz of the bugs grew into a pervasive hum. Tiny waves from the splash of her dive lapped up against the hull of the boat.

Ditzler was already airborne over the water when he remembered the engine was still running. Not a problem, he thought as the lagoon rushed up at him, as long as the gearbox is in neutral.

To the casual observer, Petey Amato might seem less brave than oblivious, inured to the obvious hazards involved in jimmying car doors and slipping through unlocked rear windows, surveying available merchandise before making his selection with the care and discrimination of a connoisseur.

Petey himself would be unable to explain his state of mind while in the thrall of burglary. Alert, but never over-stimulated. Keen, but not frenzied. Focused. Curious. Sometimes preoccupied by other thoughts.

But always aware that in an instant everything could change. That all it took was one clumsy in flagrante delicto to burn his criminal ass to the ground.

So maybe it was courage, if it takes courage to acquiesce to one's reason for being, however perilous. By that measure, Petey Amato was brave indeed.

Thus the enormity of the terror he felt as Marty Romanovski and Norm Harlan threw him off the hundred-foot water tower was all that more remarkable. Even to Petey himself. The ropes tied around his upper body were strong enough to hold him, but he had much less confidence in the knot the two officials had formed at the small of his back. Or the security of the bitter end of the line, hoping they'd tied it off—a heartfelt, but unconfirmed hope when they first heaved him over the railing.

The neck-snapping jolt at about twenty feet below the railing tested everything, including Petey's faith in divinity. It took about ten minutes for the pendulum action to subside, by which time Petey had slammed two or three times into the underbody of the giant tank and spun about a dozen revolutions one way, and then three-quarters the other, then cycled down to a gentle, swaying turn just inside 360 degrees.

He couldn't see the two men looking down at him from above, but he could hear them fairly well above the wail in his head and the rumble of the surf just over the dunes.

"You still breathing?" one of them called down.

Petey heard him, but couldn't answer. He assumed he was still breathing, but lacked the lung power to prove it. Anyway, at that moment all his attention was focused on the grip of the rope around his midsection.

"Well, make yourself at home," called the same guy. "It's late and we got to get home and get some rest. We'll be back sometime tomorrow to have a little chat."

Petey suddenly found his voice.

"You're shitting me," he yelled, slightly mortified that it came out more like a squeak.

"You're gonna love it when the sun's up. Can see for miles."

He heard the scrape of their feet as they walked across the metal grid flooring.

"Hey, what the fuck," he yelled, more coherently this time.

"No obscenity. I told you that."

"I beg your pardon, but this isn't a normal situation."

Petey heard the scraping footsteps stop.

"It isn't?"

"Yeah. This can't be officially okay."

"Oh, so you're concerned about your rights?" one of them said. "That's all you scum-buckets think about, isn't it? Your rights."

Petey's night vision had clarified enough to make out the dimly lit ground almost a hundred feet below. He wished it hadn't.

"No, sir. I'm thinking about getting back on that catwalk."

"You don't like it down there?"

"That would be the case," said Petey.

"So you think we should haul you back up?"

"That'd be good. I'd like that fine. I would. Really."

"Well, then that clinches it. We'll see you tomorrow morning."

"Aw, fuck, wait a minute. You can't fucking do that," Petey yelled as best he could through the tightening around his throat.

But all he got back was more sounds of feet shuffling over metal grating and after that a big, black nothing that wrapped around him, the sound of the surf growing louder, along with the hum from an electrical cage below the tower, and the distant wash of traffic from the north part of the island.

For the next hour Petey was afraid. It was a fear of psychotic proportions. All reason departed, replaced by an infantile whine of terror that filled the inside of his brain cavity. He gave himself over to it, swam in it. Felt the voltage pass through his body, triggering involuntary spasms that caused him to swing at the end of his tether. Within the dread was a hard nut of frustration and fury. At the cruelty and implacability of his tormentors, and at himself for allowing events to gain momentum, wresting control over his circumstances.

Yet at the end of that hour the fear began to pass, slowly at first, then rapidly draining away like a breaking fever into sweat-soaked sheets. It seemed likely by then that the rope was going to hold. And being alone meant there was no one to cut the line. At least not at the moment. He was dangling powerless over a yawning abyss in the black of night, but all things considered, it could be worse.

He quickly came to the conclusion that proper police procedure hadn't been followed to the letter. He didn't know much about the technicalities of law enforcement, but was sure none involved tying people up and throwing them over the railings of catwalks a hundred feet above the ground.

As the sun began to lighten the air above the dunes he began to worry about his right arm. Having the rope wrapped several times around his midsection did a good job of distributing the load, but there were still pressure points, the worst immediately below his right shoulder. The building pain had become a distraction, until replaced by the absence of pain, a complete numbness. He'd been able to wiggle his fingers, but now he couldn't tell if the signals from his brain were getting through. He started wiggling the fingers on his left hand just in case.

Thus absorbed he was startled by a sudden tug of the rope. His heart raced in his chest and he heard himself cry out.

"Mornin', son. How'd you sleep?" said one of the voices from the night before.

"My arm's froze," he yelled back.

He felt himself begin to swing again as he moved upward in short bursts of movement. The panic of the night before threatened to well up again, but he forced it back down the hole. Instead he concentrated on imagining himself sitting on the catwalk and attending to his bum arm.

The image took on greater form when he reached the railing and could see two sets of legs braced against the effort of hauling him up. They were breathing hard.

"You're a lot heavier than you look, kid," one of them puffed out.

His free movement in the air finally ended when they pulled him up hard against the railing. It had an oddly dizzying effect, like a sailor feeling terra firma after days on a tossing sea.

He could see one of the guys tie the line off on a support strut, presumably the same one that had held him throughout the night. He'd hoped to see something more substantial. Petey heard what he knew now was the sound of footfalls on the metal catwalk. One set. So only one guy was still with him.

"Come on, man," he said. "How 'bout the rest of the way?"

"I can do that."

"Great. How 'bout it?"

"But I need to hear something first."

"Okay. Whatever you want."

"That's what I want to hear. You're smarter than you look. But you oughta hear what I want first."

"That's okay. I gotta do something with this arm. I can't feel it."

Norm reached over the railing and tested Petey's weight. It'd be an effort, but he'd be able to roll him the rest of the way over the railing.

"I need a favor," he said quietly, moving closer to the back of Petey's head.

"Ask away, man."

"I think I've proven what could happen if you refuse."

"I'm not refusing anything. I'm agreeing. I'm seriously agreeing."

"I need you to beat somebody up. Hurt him bad, so bad he won't be able to work, but don't kill him," said Norm, almost in a whisper.

Petey had been running through a long list of possible reasons for this treatment, but this was a surprise. Though not surprise enough to dull his response.

"Hell, yeah. Let me at 'im. Just give me a name."

Norm let that sit for a moment. Then he said, "It's the mayor. I want him out of the way."

"Mayor of what?" Petey asked, hoping like hell he wasn't talking about Mayor Tate in Philadelphia. The cops in that town were one reason he'd been so happy to find work in Elysiana.

"Our mayor. Cliff Black."

Petey didn't know Elysiana had a mayor, much less that his name was Black, but he took Harlan's word for it.

"Okay. Sure. Local job. No traveling. Can do. So what do you say?"

Harlan got a firm grip around three wraps of the rope with one hand and stuck the other under Petey's belt.

"Do I have to waste my time telling you we didn't have this conversation?"

"Nope. Clear on that."

"Or that this is the last time you hear my voice?"

"Got it."

Petey braced himself for one last show of sadism, but instead felt himself being lugged over the railing and dropped to the metal grating of the catwalk floor.

Relief rose from deep within his chest and exploded out into the blue sky above. Harlan was saying something to him, but it took a few moments for him to hear.

"If you don't mind, I'm going down ahead of you," the guy was saying.

"Before that I'll just tie up your legs a bit to give you something to do while I get a respectable head start. Not that I don't trust you."

Petey didn't care when he left. All he cared about was the clear ocean air specked with soaring gulls and the growing ache in his arm as the tension of the ropes was slowly released. He felt the first tentative wiggle of his fingers.

Harlan stood up over him, his face backlit by the rising sun.

"You got to August fifteenth to get it done. That's about two weeks."

Petey nodded.

"Then I want you gone. Far away and forever. *Comprendo?*"

Petey nodded again.

"Gonna be a scorcher," said Harlan, gazing up at the same sky as Petey had lost himself within.

For Petey, clearer thinking accompanied the flow of blood. The flush of joy replaced by an appreciation of his circumstances. A formerly fearless person, Petey now knew the world could be a place of genuine fear, not a theoretical concept, but a real thing of substance and mass.

"Crap," he said to the new day, beautiful though it was.

CHAPTER
15

GWENDALYNN ANDERS, on the other hand, woke up in a state of moist euphoria. She was dreaming of the dock at her family's summer place on the Upper Peninsula.

She's lying on the weathered planks with one leg dangling, her big toe grazing the surface of the water. Her little brother is fishing, cursing weakly at the inattention of the local fish.

Her mother is yelling, "Gwennie, your skin is turning into shoe leather. You'll look like a minstrel, then who'll marry you?"

A powerboat buzzes by, the bright lads at the helm waving and catcalling to no one in particular.

"Creep kids," says her father, though he's not there on the dock. She's listening to him in her head.

She pulls herself up on one elbow. A submarine is drifting on the surface of the lake. Nazi sailors are frantically running around topsides. Barking orders at each other. Her brother complains about the effect this is having on his fishing.

"Creep Krauts," says her father, still offstage.

Then he's standing over her.

"Hm, yeah," he says. "Groove-a-delic."

"Groove-a-delic? What the fuck does that mean?"

"Don't speak that way."

"Sorry, Daddy."

Her best friend from boarding school is kissing her face.

"Ick, what's happening?" she asks the girl.

The tiny fish swell up from underneath. She spreads her arms and legs and settles in comfort on a bed of writhing sea life. Jack Halcyon reaches down with his hand to lift her up. She takes it, tentatively. His face becomes serious.

"Groove-a-delic, Gwennie," he says to her. "Don't you understand?"

"Do I have to?"

"Ah," says Jack. "That's why we love you."

The last segment of the dream was the only part she couldn't remember. But she thought it must have been good, considering her mood on awakening.

The window to her room was across from the foot of her bed. It was a towering window wrapped in a huge molded frame. Below the window was her kitchen sink and a small counter where her morning cantaloupe awaited.

The music of sea life and ocean waves flooded the room. The ocean breeze made a ballet of the rustling sheers to either side of the window. The same breeze swept over her body, flat on her back on top of the sheets, naked. It cooled her skin and brushed her hair. It was an embrace by the Atlantic Coast and a postcard from the Upper Peninsula. The universality of wind.

She let her eyes focus slowly on the ceiling. Built out with coffers and massive crown moldings, there was a lot to look at.

It had been almost two months since she'd last flooded her brainpan with hallucinogenic drugs. She hadn't intended to take a break from a four-year routine, but circumstances intervened. She wasn't ready to declare the respite an unqualified success, but was so far delighted with the results. The real world was turning out to be far more congenial than she thought it would be. Not perfect, but more than tolerable.

She ran both hands up her thighs, across her belly, over her breasts and through her hair, where she paused to scratch her head. Then she flopped her arms back on the double bed and re-engaged with the coffered ceiling.

I could lie here for a hundred years, she told herself. *Just like this.*

She only made it another fifteen minutes before sitting up and swinging her legs down to the floor. She ran her hands through her hair again, scratched and stood up, walking on sore, tender feet over to the stove to fill and put a fire under the espresso pot, and then on to the bathroom. The girl in the mirror looked back with something less than her own agreeable mood. She moved in for a closer examination, then decided it wasn't worth it. Things are never what you see, she told herself.

She brushed her teeth, then stuck her head in a bowl of cold water. This served to clear the fog of sleep from her mind and smooth out the kinks that had formed during the night in her long, blond-tinted hair.

By the time she was back in the main room, the top of the pot and the atmosphere of the apartment was full of espresso. She poured most of it into a big ceramic mug decorated with daisies that formed the name "Gwen" given her by Sweetie on one of their shopping trips downtown.

Gwendalynn walked through the French doors to a tiny balcony off the main room. There was a broad weedy lawn between her and a row of houses across the street. She hoped the distance and sleep-filled eyes would shield her nakedness from whoever chanced a look. She wanted to get the full effect of the morning sea breeze blending with the big cup of Medaglia D'Oro.

She stood for five minutes sipping the coffee, then went back in the apartment and grabbed a dank bedspread to throw around her shoulders. She went back to the balcony and sat on an aluminum-framed, nylon-slatted lounge chair retrieved from a dumpster behind the hotel.

When she went back in the kitchen for a second coffee she checked the time. Almost seven o'clock. Jack would be heading out for his daily swim in a few minutes. She usually watched him trot down the grand stairway in front of the hotel, cross the broad lawn and Ocean Avenue, and scramble over the boulder breakwater. She liked the way he moved. Effortless and unself-conscious. Like an athlete unimpressed by his own athleticism. She wished she could go with him, but would never be able to keep up. She could hardly swim at all beyond an awkward doggie-paddle. Swimming was a skill she always admired in others, but found impossible to imagine accomplishing herself, like passing calculus or learning to speak Mandarin Chinese. She thought about walking out to the hotel lawn to cheer him as he passed by, but thought about it too long and missed the opportunity. She decided the next time they spoke she'd tell him what she almost did, and that would be almost as good.

She gathered up her clothes for the day and a plastic bag filled with bathing equipment, and went down a long dark hall to the door that led to a row of outdoor showers Jack had turned on for her. A tall, blackened gray wood barrier blocked the view of the showers from the street. Intended for guests still in their bathing suits to rinse off the worst of the sand and salt before going to their rooms, there was no need for additional privacy, and less need now, since she was the only other person in the hotel. It took about ten minutes for the hot water to come up, but then there was enough to bathe a hundred people. Gwendalynn used the profligacy to full effect, spending twice the time actually needed to wash and rinse out her long hair.

She took the same amount of care scrubbing her body, being careful not to linger too long on the more vital nerve centers. She was aware that not everyone subscribed to the therapeutic nature of masturbation. Beginning with her mother, who hadn't responded as predicted when Gwendalynn first called her into the family rec room to view a demonstration.

There were consequences.

Staying at her father's place at the end of her junior year, the first thing she did was make a fire in the little fireplace in the den to take the chill off the early spring air and pour herself a glass of wine. Then she took a long searing shower, the first in days after the demands of midterms and a relentless social calendar. She spread her wet hair out across the back of the love seat and leaned back to sip her wine, her feet propped on the huge ottoman, one alternately massaging the other.

"Hi, Daddy," she said to her father, who surprised her by striding into the room and flopping awkwardly into one of the overstuffed club chairs that ran perpendicular to the love seat. "I thought you were going out."

"Not in the mood after all. How's school?" he asked Gwendalynn.

"It's cool. It's fine. I mean, it's okay. I'm doing okay. You must've read the reports they send home."

"Never bother. I assume excellence."

She snorted.

"Yeah, right. But keep doing that."

"Have you chosen your field of study?"

"I'm an art major, if that's what you mean."

He almost seemed to lurch back, as if from a gentle blow.

"Art? Are you painting?"

She laughed again.

"No, Daddy. You don't have to paint to study art."

"Hm. Interesting career. Studying art?"

"It's not a career. It's a major," she said.

"Preparing you for . . . ?"

Gwendalynn felt her pleasant mood drain into the love seat and out across the floor.

"Nothing, Daddy. Absolutely nothing."

"Nothing at the cost of three thousand a year."

"I'll pay you back."

He looked exasperated.

"Come on, honey. I just want you to be prepared for life. That's what college is for."

Gwendalynn's father never went to college. Another sore point.

He sat back in the club chair, hands gripping the two arms. His head was large for his body, even when you factored in the impressive girth of his midsection. His hair, still reddish-brown, was swept back in the style of his days in the military. Gwendalynn had rarely seen him without a tie, or a vest, or brilliantly polished shoes. Or a cigarette, which always stirred her own cravings, though never enough to light up in front of him.

"Well, that deserves a toast. What have you got there, Gallo's finest?"

"I don't know. I just poured it."

"I'm thinking of a little rye and soda. On a couple'a rocks. Burgundy for you?"

"Okay. Burgundy for me."

He walked over and took her glass, tossing the remaining sip into the fireplace and replacing it with a full helping from a wine bottle on the dry bar. He put together his own drink and flopped back into the club chair.

"But anyway, things are going well. You're still in that school."

"Yes, Daddy. I'm still in school. Unless I flunked all my finals, which I don't think I did."

He sipped his drink.

"So now there's the whole summer to waste away," he said. "A lot of time off. I wish I had it."

"Mom used to say you could take more time if you wanted to."

"Your mother doesn't know anything about anything. Not then, certainly not now."

Gwendalynn forced herself not to think about what he just said.

"Of course, I'm hardly with it," said her father.

"Yes you are. I can tell by the sideburns."

"You think? Pretty groovy, right?"

"Far out."

"That, too. So I'm told."

"So you're not going out? No prospects?" she asked him.

"Not lately. Not for lack of trying."

Gwendalynn sat back in the sofa and knocked back half of the fruity, vintage Burgundy. She really wanted a cigarette, but didn't know how to work that into the conversation. Instead she bit her nails.

They sat quietly together for a while watching the fire. Then her father looked over at her.

"So, you got a boyfriend?" he asked.

Gwendalynn's mind flashed through a list of possible answers to that question.

"Not at the moment."

"I hear free love is the happening thing on campus."

"The happening thing?"

"That's the current terminology," her father said, mildly exasperated.

"Some people say happening. And groovy. When they're making fun of us."

"Who's us?"

"Kids."

He frowned.

"When I was your age we never called ourselves 'kids.' We didn't want to be thought of as children. We wanted to be men and women."

Gwendalynn put her hand up to her forehead and rubbed.

"Your mother told me," he said.

She stopped rubbing her head and looked at him.

"Told you? About what?"

He examined his rye and soda while fussing with the front of his trousers, trying to get comfortable in the club chair.

"Your little childhood indulgence."

Gwendalynn's heart leaped with alarm, but the steadiness of the hand that held the wine glass betrayed nothing.

"And that is? What are you talking about?"

Her father's face had a look of smug assurance. The alarm in her brain turned to dread.

"You know," he said, wiggling his fingers above his mid-section, "tickling the quim. Polishing the peach pit. Friggin' the figment of your imagination. I assume you still do. On a regualr basis."

Her legs involuntarily slammed together. A cold, hard boulder began to form in the pit of her stomach.

"That's an awful thing to say to me, Daddy," she said.

"Hey, hey, you got me wrong," he said. "I'm cool with this. I'm more than cool. I'm completely accepting. I'm not your mother, I'm completely on your side."

A chilly wave of foreboding washed over her. She slumped into the sofa and sipped her wine.

"Don't scare me so much, Daddy," she said.

"I never want to scare you, honey. You're my little girl."

"Not so little anymore."

"No you're not. You're all grown up. I can see that for sure."

He smiled at her but she couldn't smile back. The fire had died down by now, so Gwendalynn tended to it, hauling in several split logs in the canvas carrier and dumping them on to the smoldering coals. Sparks flew up the chimney and out on the hearth, which she deftly swept back into the fire chamber.

While she was so engaged, her father refortified their drinks, somewhat to her dismay.

"Okay, so I chose not to go out tonight," her father said, handing her the glass of wine. "I could have, believe me. To you I'm a fat old man. There're a lot of skirts at the office who'd jump at the chance to roll in the hay with the business editor. Forty-eight is still a young man."

Gwendalynn felt that leaden ball in her midsection gain another hundred pounds. She took a big pull on her wine, then regretted it as the effect of the alcohol washed over her.

"Young and virile, young lady," he said, stretching the fabric of his pants across his abdomen, revealing the prominent outline of the last thing in the universe Gwendalynn wanted to see. "Keep that in mind."

She rose from the love seat and swept up the bottle of Burgundy on her way out of the room and up to her bedroom, where she dug the one-inch by one-inch square of paper with the tab of acid out of her still-packed duffle bag. She peeled it off with her teeth and downed it with a swig of wine.

Then she put on her work boots and jean jacket and climbed out the window and on to the roof of the garage, and slid carefully on her butt down to the gutter where she'd taught herself years ago to slip over, hang and drop into an overgrown rhododendron. There was a window to the garage next to where she landed which she'd unlocked through some act of strange prescience the night before. The key to her father's Riviera was in the ignition where it always was, so it was only a few seconds

before she was out of the garage and cruising toward somewhere
she hadn't yet fully determined.

MIKE DITZLER was surprised a person could actually swim through
mud. Even the thin, silty mud that covered the bottom of the
lagoon. He was helped by his natural lack of buoyancy, the consequence of an unusually dense body mass that kept him warm
in the Himalayas, and under water acted like a bodysuit of lead,
to great advantage.

He had his eyes open at first, which led to blinding pain until
he was forced to close his lids over half a pound of silt. Now
he was entirely dependent on touch, which greatly complicated
moving quickly through the water.

After a while it became apparent he'd have to surface in the
next ten seconds or likely drown. He kicked his feet furiously
while waving his hands through the muck, blind to the watery
mire, but not deaf.

Because he heard, seconds after beginning a desperate dash
to the surface, a bubbling trill of a sound. He broke the surface
just long enough to take a breath and dive back down. Eyes closed
he could still imagine the sight below. Brown and green clouds
obscuring tall grass covering bottomless blackened sludge.

He heard her again, clearly, immediately below. He thrust
his arms forward like a high diver and kicked his legs furiously,
gaining so much momentum that when he reached her it was
more collision than encounter.

He grabbed a thrashing ankle and pulled. Sylvia followed,
still thrashing. He gained a grip around her waist, losing
several vital seconds feeling for a bathing suit he'd forgotten
wasn't there.

He worked his legs around until his feet were scrambling
through the viscous sea floor. Then he felt something hard, providing some resistance. A piece of driftwood, or maybe the rib of
an ancient wooden dory, he didn't know or care. He just knew
it allowed him to push off the bottom, and with Sylvia's insane
wriggling, make a go for the surface.

Sylvia and her breakfast broke the surface at about the same time. Ditzler feared she'd aspirate her vomit, though he heard more gasping than choking as he dragged her to the *Entropy V*.

Holding her tight around the waist, he stretched the limit of his reach to pull the swim ladder down from the transom. Then he just held on, waiting to regain his strength and for Sylvia to regain her breath.

"Holy Mother of Mercy," she gasped out, "I thought I was a goner."

"You have some kind of lungs," said Ditzler.

"And no sense of direction," she said, spitting out more of what was clogging her throat. "I was going down when I should've been going up."

"Next time, let's discuss before you leap."

"I'm sorry. It must've scared you something awful."

"It did."

She turned in his arms and grabbed the swim ladder, then hauled herself up and over the transom and poured herself into a puddle on the cockpit floor. Ditzler joined her.

"That did it," said Sylvia, still trying to catch her breath. "I'm like now forever obligated to do anything you want no matter what."

"I want you to stay on this boat or tie a rope around your waist when I'm not here," he said.

"See, you're being reasonable again. Where I come from people bitch and yell over a bad parking space or betting on the wrong horse. And here you are saving my life for the thousandth time and you're still just being nice. You're killing me."

"That's a contradiction in terms."

He went below to grab an armful of towels, which he wrapped around himself and Sylvia, pulling her close to him to share body heat and reassurance.

"I love you, Ditzler," she said, after the tremors subsided.

"I love you, too. But I'm not in love with you."

"That's a really good thing, because I'm in love with your captain."

"I know that," said Ditzler.

"I can't help it. Every time I saw him, I loved him more. I don't think he wants to own me. It wouldn't even cross his mind. Maybe I'm stupid, but I want to believe a man can be powerful and good at the same time."

She let her head drop down on his shoulder. She coughed up a little more water, but that was incidental to her true purpose, which was to feel the vast and exquisite things she was feeling.

They spent another hour sprawled out on cushions still slightly damp from the morning dew. When the chill finally broke through Sylvia's addled nerves, she slipped back into her clothes and went to make coffee. Ditzler fell asleep, exhausted by the unexpected exertion. He was awakened a half hour later by the warm breath of steaming Colombian.

"I want to live," she told him as he worked to regain consciousness. "I decided that when I was in the process of drowning. That means I can't live in fear of death. And I can't live a life somebody else decides for me. I don't know how to do any of these things, but at least I know what I want to do. If that makes any sense, which I'm sure it doesn't, even for a smart person like you."

It did make sense to Mike Ditzler. So much so that he was asleep again by the time she came back with another cup of coffee. She set it down next to his head, and then lay next to him, serene.

CHAPTER
16

C LARICE RUBBED Petey's back and licked his ear lobe.

"Baby, you got to get your shit reassembled, because you can't go on like this no more."

"I know," said Petey.

"Okay, so some bad shit happened, what the hey? You're breathing and standing upright like a normal human being, when you aren't curled into a little ball. Though not incarcerated, I might add. So, what's the diff?"

"You're right," said Petey. "I gotta shake this crap."

"You do. 'Cause I love you and all, but don't know what all else I have to do here, you know what I mean? Like, what does a person do with a guy who's like prostate with fear and self-doubt?"

"I don't doubt anything. I'm positive my ass is grass no matter what I do. Is there any beer in this place?"

"How can you think of beer with this level of crisis?"

Petey looked at her long and hard.

"Rather than answering that, let's just say you get the beer."

"Okay, Petey. I understand. We have beer. I know we do."

Petey was on his back on the sofa. He let his arm fall on the coffee table hoping it would land on a pack of cigarettes. He'd been proud of quitting smoking after leaving high school, but all that mattered now was to calm down. The reds had helped, though he was conservative with the dose. Barbiturates had scared him ever since an overdose killed one of his cousins.

On the other hand, he thought, there're worse ways to go. Just go to sleep feeling completely groovy and never waking up. Then he thought, never waking up? Are you fucking nuts? After which he jumped off the couch and paced the floor of the living room, causing Clarice to run back in from the kitchen in alarm.

"What? What?"

"I gotta get out outta here. You gotta drive me to Mexico or something."

"Okay. I can do that. I know how to drive."

He dropped to the floor on all fours and hung his head.

"Unless they catch me. Then what? What sort of sick shit would that mean? Christ, I gotta go farther than Mexico. I gotta go to Rhodesia or Bali Ha'i."

"Can you drive there?"

He looked up, studying her face again for any sign of rudimentary self-awareness.

"Yeah, sure, honey. Course you can."

"Okay. So let's go. Anything but you all upset and depressed."

He rolled over on to his back again, this time on the rug.

Petey wasn't given to blaming fate for his circumstances. He thought a man blessed with his good fortune shouldn't be bitter about one little setback. He believed a man had to take his hits, had to buck up and make his way with as much pride and resourcefulness as he could muster.

But this thing. Way beyond acceptable limits.

He didn't think it would be possible to stay another day in the apartment, though the thought of being out there exposed to all the world made him want to lose consciousness.

The fact was, he didn't know what to do. He didn't know how to think, and barely knew how to breathe.

He needed help. That was all he knew, and wasn't even sure he knew that.

"I need help," he said to Clarice.

Her face softened.

"Oh, baby, I'll help you anyway I can."

"Not that kind of help. I need advice. Psychological assistance, like you get from priests or scientists."

"Oh. Like I can't give advice."

He was sorry it came out like that. He was pretty sure Clarice didn't have a very functional brain, but didn't want to hurt her feelings. Partly out of kindness and partly to spare himself one more source of conflict.

"That's not what I mean. I know you can give advice. It's just your experience in these things is no better'n mine. We need a specialist in figuring shit out."

"I'd do that for you if I could."

"I know you would. I appreciate that. I do. Okay?"

"Okay," she said, richly pleased.

They kept each other company in silence until Clarice couldn't stand the dead air and started quietly humming "Look Into the Sun" under her breath. Petey looked up at her from where he lay supine on the floor and she stopped, catching herself unawares.

It was at times like these she wished Petey was more interested in some of the stuff he sold. This, she thought, was an ideal occasion to take a little journey to a pleasant, faraway land.

"So, who you think gives advice?" she asked, hoping she was in safe territory. "The only guys I know like that are on TV, like Mr. Spock or Walter Cronkite, but they aren't real."

"Walter Cronkite's real," said Petey without opening his eyes. "Only I don't think he's taking appointments."

"You don't know that if you won't even ask."

Petey actually knew what he wanted to do when he first brought up the subject. He wanted desperately to talk to Jack Halcyon, he just didn't know how to frame the logic to Clarice. That the best brain he ever knew didn't actually have all his brains still in his head.

The more formidable barrier was shame. That's what Petey really wanted Clarice to talk him out of. Shame that he'd never visited Jack in the hospital, never talked to his mother, never even dropped off a card or a bunch of crummy flowers. He took the reports from other kids who said Jack was a vegetable sitting in a chair staring at the middle of the air. Just the thought of that made Petey feel dizzy. So it was easy to put off going until a few years went by, and then, what the hell, the guy wakes up.

Nobody thought that was going to happen. Which only made Petey feel worse. What, you couldn't just go over there and show your best friend a little respect?

The tangle of regret, self-recrimination and unease over what he might find guaranteed that he never did.

If self-analysis had been a sturdier component of Petey Amato's psyche, he might have realized that he revered his summers with Jack and Jack's mother. That he loved Jack as his temperamental and morphological opposite. That he held unwavering faith in Jack's judgment and perception of the world, a faith forged from near infancy and reinforced through the years of their friendship. To Petey, Jack was the smartest person who ever lived, because he'd always seemed so much smarter than Petey. And a devoted friend. Kind and loyal. Polite to Petey's alcoholic mother and nasty old man. Patient and interested in whatever interested Petey, no matter how ridiculous and childish in retrospect some of those things were.

The loss, though impossible to equate with the Halcyons', was devastating to the adolescent Petey, who never understood the irreplaceable value the relationship had, only that its absence was something he himself was far too wounded to contemplate.

Until that day lying on his back in his apartment, rubbing his bald head and begging God for a way out of this unholy place in which he'd found himself.

"I need to see Jack Halcyon," he finally said to the ceiling.

Clarice was quiet for a moment before saying,

"The gooner?"

Petey knew he had to be in a weakened state to hear something like that and not just smash her head with the first blunt object that came to hand.

"It was an accident. He's recovered. People have seen him. Nothing wrong with him."

"You told me he was like a turnip for five years."

"So he isn't anymore. He's a lifeguard, for Chrissakes. You think Avery hires turnips?"

Clarice shoved herself deeper into the couch.

"Sorry, Petey. I'm only repeating back what you told me."

He rolled over on his side so he could see her.

"You don't know about Jack. He always knew the right answer to every fucking thing you ever asked him. About anything. He figured out how to build the forts. Found all the paths through the woods so you could ride your bikes and end up anywhere you wanted. Drove us around in his old man's car when we were thirteen or something. Plotted out capers. Knew who in the neighborhood left their beer in the garage. Or when the house was clear for more serious B and E. How to sneak kegs out of the distributors. Showed me how to hot-wire cars. How to go for joyrides without getting caught. How to pick a mark. How to scam the suit and ties at 30th Street Station for spending bread. Got us into every drive-in for nothing. You never had to buy a fucking thing when you were with Jack. Groceries, gas, burgers. He knew everybody. Never paid for anything. The kid was a genius."

"Oh, goodie. A criminal genius."

He rolled on to his back again.

"Ah, shit, Clarice, it's not like that. He just did it for all us other douche bags. Because I wanted him to. Not for himself. Dreamy, weird kid, most of the time. Took a lot to protect him sometimes, never saw the danger."

Clarice didn't look like she was buying it, but she was glad he had some sort of distraction. It was unnerving to see him so lost and unsure. Unhinged from his cheerful confidence. It frightened her, as if he'd somehow contracted an exotic disease, lethal and infectious.

"Okay. Let's go see him," she said. "Where's he live?"

"In the Imperial. But we can't just go see him."

She felt another surge of anxiety.

"Nobody lives there, Petey. You know that."

"Oh yeah? You know better?" he asked. "He lives there. It's his hotel."

Her face softened.

"Sure, Petey. Jack lives there. I just didn't know that."

Petey heard a lilt of indulgence in her voice, but let it pass.

"They're watching everything I do. I can't let them see me with him. I'll have to swim there."

She pointed to the east.

"It's over there. You going to swim through the streets?"

He closed his eyes.

"Yeah, Clarice. That's what I'm going to do. You never seen anything like it. It's like 'Ripley's Believe It or Not.'"

"I don't know Ripley."

"That I believe."

It was late afternoon. But now Petey had a plan, and his mood began to lighten. He decided to kill the time till dark by closing himself in the bedroom and falling asleep. He'd feel better for it and it would save him from more conversation with Clarice.

"Swim to the Imperial Hotel," said Clarice, quietly, at the closing bedroom door. "Good idea. Me, I'll just be flying to Constantinople."

"I WANT to take you to a party," said Mike Ditzler to Sylvia Buente.

"Ha, ha."

He was sitting in the cockpit of the *Entropy V* drinking the beer she handed him in exchange for a pair of overstuffed grocery bags and twenty pounds of block ice brought out in one of Sebbie's inflatables.

"Look in those bags. You'll find something," said Ditzler.

She disappeared for a while and came back holding what looked like a small, hairy mammal.

"This?" she asked.

"It's a wig. My mother sent it to me. She bought it at Wanamaker's. That and a pair of sunglasses. Nobody's going to know who you are."

"Blond does not go with Italian."

"You've been to Wildwood. When did skin tone ever stop anyone down there? You told me Eduardo never let you wear work shirts or cutoffs."

"Yeah?"

"So that's what you wear. Also in a bag."

"This is schizo."

"No, this is counter-schizo. Another way to keep you sane."

"I am sane. I'm lovin' it out here. I mean it, Ditzler, I'm truly lovin' it."

It was after seven in the evening. The sun was starting to close in on the backside of the tall grasses that lined the western edge of the lagoon. The sky was turning a coral blue, which the water, most of the day a gray-green, was beginning to reflect. The cooler air and impending transition to darkness was bringing out the bugs again, some of whom in the fecund saltwater swamp could grow to birdlike dimensions. A big attraction for a different swarm of birds, who were swooping above the grass like crop dusters, partaking of the midair feast.

The low angle of the sun showed Sylvia's skin had indeed realized its tanning potential, radiating a color and tone unachievable by a blond's measly melanin. She was wearing a plain white T-shirt and panties, as if to demonstrate the contrast.

"I know you're lovin' it. But you have to interact with other human beings or you'll become hopelessly anti-social and regress into irrevocable misanthropy."

"That's what I would've said."

"It means you gotta go out and have a little fun," said Ditzler. "And so do I."

"You can go out any time you want. I'm not keeping you here."

"I have to be here to look after you. I saved your life. It's a sacred duty."

"You got that reversed," said Sylvia.

"Not to Buddhists. You save someone, you're obligated to them forever."

"That's significantly screwed-up."

"An obligation which includes bringing you to parties. It's next Saturday night, so we've got two more nights to prepare."

He had to say that last part to her departing back as she went below to make dinner.

"Sweet thought, Ditzler," she called. "But not happenin'."

Ditzler understood the dynamic of the northern New Jersey Italian family unit in the way of a graduate student of anthropology. Decent command of the principles, but minimum field experience. He believed whatever success he'd had guiding his charge was more the result of luck and sincerity than conscious action. He wondered if that was the point. That this situation benefited little from analysis. If he understood the old rice farmer in the hut in Thailand, few situations did.

"I guess that's why they call them balls," he called back down.

She poked her head out the companionway.

"Balls?"

"Girls don't have them."

"Pardon me?"

"You need balls to go out and kill things like woolly mammoths and next door neighbors. Girls need to run away from threats without embarrassment. It's the natural order of things. Perfectly understandable."

"They teach you this at Harvard?"

He snorted.

"Hell, no. Ivy League girls have bigger balls than the football team. And hairier armpits."

She pointed at him with an uncooked chicken leg.

"You don't need balls to have balls, buster."

"He's going to be there."

"Who?"

"The captain. Avery Volpe. Two of the guys having the party are on the beach patrol. Which means most of the guards are going to show up at some point during the night. So according to Jack it's one of those unofficial, unsanctioned, undiscussed occasions when Avery will have his lieutenants maintain security. Keep the guards inside and the cops out. Then make sure everybody gets home okay. Avery has to be there so the cops know for sure the party house is within his protectorate. It's a form of diplomatic immunity."

She sat down on a cockpit cushion and started tapping her knee with the drumstick. He took it from her and brought it down to the galley. He brought back a bottle of wine and two glasses. Sylvia drained the first glass in a single pass and held it out for a refill.

"I can't be seen with Avery," she said, more downcast than defiant.

"You won't be, Blondie."

He picked the wig off the cockpit floor where she'd dropped it and tossed it in her lap.

"Try it on, anyway. The least you could do for Ma Ditzler. You told me you weren't going to live your life in fear. Here's your chance."

She glowered at him, but went along. It took a few tries to get the alignment right, but the result was striking, in Ditzler's mind.

"Whoa, who the hell are you? Where'd Sylvia go?"

"Yeah, right."

"Seriously. Put on the sunglasses."

"Man, you are weird sometimes," she said, but complied.

"Wow."

"Come on."

"Don't move," he said, jumping up and diving down the companionway. He came back up with the mirror from the head, hastily unscrewed from the bulkhead.

He held it in front of her face. She moved her head from side to side and looked over the tops of the sunglasses.

"Like I said," she said, "doesn't go with the complexion."

"But you definitely don't look like you. Admit it."

She cocked her head, vamping at the mirror.

"Jesus, you're persistent."

He bent down, put his hand behind her head and pulled her toward him so he could kiss her hard on the lips. She resisted instinctively, then relaxed and kissed him back.

"Never kissed a blond before," he said, grinning. "Better than I thought."

"Don't get used to it."

By the time they put dinner together the sun had given up, leaving a pale wash of rose-colored sky above the western horizon as a reminder of the day. The bird noise fell with the sun. The bugs brought in a late shift to sing with the frogs and dance with the demons of the salty swamp.

They avoided more talk about the party, but it was decided.

CHAPTER
17

SANFORD GOETTLEWING slept best with his hand wrapped around his army-issue .45. It was as natural a part of the night's routine as an alarm clock and pillow. He'd found a room at a sorry little motel on the fringes of downtown. He could have easily afforded better accommodations at any of the beachfront hotels or Victorian B&B's, but they wouldn't provide the same anonymity. The worse the bed smelled, the safer Goettlewing felt.

Goettlewing loved guns and the practice of personal defense from an early age. Interests he put to good use in boot camp, where he was among the few who managed to intimidate the professional sadists in charge of training America's fighting men.

After the war, when ex-officio military units were being formed to fight global communism, Goettlewing was a natural recruit. As things heated up in Southeast Asia, they took full advantage of his skills and inclinations, while Goettlewing took full advantage of a black market in drugs, weapons and Japanese stereo equipment the likes of which was formerly beyond imagination. Thus when mustered back to the States, it was only fitting to be assigned to a unit in New York City. Thoroughly entrenched in the greatest illicit supply chain in the world, he was now at the center of the greatest demand.

Robust commerce ensued.

Establishing a cover, Goettlewing slipped easily into the sixties boho scene in lower Manhattan, taking over a loft apartment in what was then the dangerous but cheap artists' squat of SoHo. It was the second time Goettlewing had lived in New York, the first as a teenager after running away from home. It was an easy home to run away from, the three room house, more of a shack, in West Conshohocken, a forgotten mill town west of Philadelphia.

Although opportunities to practice his special gifts in and around Philadelphia were plentiful, Goettlewing was drawn to the storied concentrations of crime and mayhem in the city two hours to the north.

He settled comfortably into Hell's Kitchen where his life's work reached full flower. In time, other young exiles from around the country formed gangs with whom Goettlewing held a loose affiliation. Never a joiner, he nonetheless saw some benefit to alliances that extended his reach and provided insulation from other gangsters and the corrupt police force, a practice he returned to thirty years later.

The other advantage was access to the steady flow of teen-aged girls attracted to the version of New York entirely contrived by Hollywood movies. Like the boys, they quickly learned the truth, but in most cases had no means to return home, even if their families wanted them back. One in particular was a runaway from a deeply religious and conservative family in the suburbs who'd been sent in to try to earn money for her destitute family. Her name was Antonia, a name Goettlewing would have barely registered if she hadn't been ovulating the night he introduced her to his bed.

Antonia, though wracked with shame, never considered the dangerous alternative to bearing the child, a decision rewarded by a baby girl. To his surprise, Goettlewing's feelings ran along similar lines. He had little interest in raising a kid, but felt the pull of paternal responsibility, however remotely engaged.

So they made a deal. Antonia went back home with the infant and a convincing cover story, crafted by Goettlewing, of a tragic, short-lived marriage between her and a rash young longshoreman, who a month after the child's birth was crushed beneath a pallet full of grapefruit.

In return for a monthly stipend, Antonia would foreswear any claim on Goettlewing, either his affections or bank account. Her only duty was to send regular updates of the child's progress and development, along with a photographic record. For about thirty years, they held up their ends of the bargain. Then a few years ago all communication stopped. More confused than angry, Goettlewing let the situation simmer, though barely. Holed up in the Berkshires, preoccupied with business, he found little reason to pursue the issue, though the nag of it on his mind would never let go.

LEAVING THE hotel after most of the tourists had left for the beach, Goettlewing stepped outside and took in his surroundings. The light of the sun was suffused by the vaporous atmosphere, but not its heat. It was a regular late July day on the South Jersey shore, when the streets began to melt by ten AM and sweating was futile. Accustomed to the dry, bright mornings in the Berkshires, Goettlewing was struck by the contrast. It triggered an association with other hot, wet climates, notably in Southeast Asia. Ideally so, given the mission.

He stood out on the baking sidewalk and drew in a deep breath.

Nothing like another day in country.

THE PARTY at Randy and Baxter's was more a testament to predestination than a social event. There were seismic communal urges at play potent enough to not only bring the party spontaneously into being, but to generate a gravitational pull that engulfed the entire island.

As with any natural catastrophe, the build-up began almost imperceptibly. Like a low-grade fever lurking just below the awareness of the eventual participants.

Baxter heard about it from one of the guys working the only gas station in the borough, who asked Baxter if there'd be plenty of illegal seafood at the clambake.

"Huh?" said Baxter.

"You know what I mean. Tuna. The tender kind. Fresh and tender. The kind you normally throw back. On normal occasions."

"I have no friggin' idea what you are talking about."

"That's cool. Secret's with me."

The guy backed away and moved down the side of the car to attend to the gas nozzle. Baxter sat perplexed, though taunted by intimations of the truth. It wouldn't be the first time for him. It would be more like the tenth or eleventh time, so he'd had practice divining the social mood of his surroundings.

At the same time Avery and his lieutenants were acknowledging they'd be managing another barely manageable situation in a few weeks. Like wildlife racing to higher ground in the calm before the storm, the senior staff of the Elysiana Beach Patrol sensed a climate shift. And while they felt sure of their ability to contain and control the troops when on duty, every officer knew managing behavior after sunset was a whole different matter.

Eventually, the will of the mob prevailed and the party became established fact, the date set, the general shape of the activities formulated, and the guest list filled in without involving the hosts, who nevertheless succumbed to the inevitable and opened their doors and insurance liability to the onslaught.

The last people on the island to catch wind of the event were Norm and Marty's police force, being utterly disenfranchised not only from the beach patrol, but from the general population, who instinctively withheld that sort of information.

Jack Halcyon, perched among the clouds above, also felt something significant was afoot. Enough to slide a note under Gwendalynn's door inviting her to come up to the Box for a drink, if she was, you know, looking for something to do besides loafing around the apartment.

He'd just made it back upstairs when for the second time the phone rang. It was startling to hear that jangling sound inside the silent Box. He let it ring a few times, then picked up the receiver.

"You've got the wrong number," he said.

"I don't think so, Jack," said Gwendalynn on the other end of the line.

"How did you do that?"

"I'm on the phone at the operator's desk. There's a list of internal numbers pinned to the wall. One of them's 'Observatory.' I figured that had to be it."

"The only other time I got a call they were looking for George," said Jack.

"What sort of drink did you have in mind?"

He paused, pondering the obvious.

"I don't know why I wrote that. I don't have any alcohol. I think I just meant come on up and hang around."

"I thought you said you were going to leave me alone."

He paused again, this time to feel his face heat up.

"I did. You're right again. Sorry," he said, and hung up.

He stared down at the phone wondering if he shouldn't pull the cord out of the wall and throw the thing down the laundry chute. He was about to do that when it rang again. He picked it up.

"I don't mind," said Gwendalynn. "The only two people in this place need to stick together."

"I have a security service watching the outside."

"How did you end up with this place again?" she asked.

"My mother gave it to me."

"My mother gave me an identity crisis."

"You don't know who you are?"

"She's Jewish. Which means, technically, so am I. But my father's an Episcopalian, and that's how they raised me. I don't even look remotely like my mother. It's like none of her genes could be bothered."

"This is America. Everyone's a mutt. You get to pick what you are."

"Then I'm just plain Gwendalynn. Do you prefer white or red?"

"Wine?"

"Of course."

"I can't drink anything. The brain situation."

"Okay. I'm having red. If you come back down here, I'll show you how."

"I don't know what you mean," said Jack.

"That's why you have to come back down."

He put on a pair of white denim cutoffs, sandals and a blue button-downed Oxford cloth shirt and trotted back down the broad, baroque central stairway. The light outside had finally failed, so there was little to illuminate the stairwell, just the faintest glow from the streetlamps surrounding the building at ground level. And something unfamiliar casting jittery light across the base of the stairs.

When he made it to the lobby he saw it was Gwendalynn holding a flashlight. She was leaning against the desk where guests of the Imperial Hotel once checked in. Her long semi-blond hair was combed straight down either side of her face and she wore a shapeless flowered mini-dress and wood and leather sandals.

Before he reached her she turned and walked across the lobby. He followed. She led him through a high arched doorway, through what must have been a lounging area, and through another wide doorway, this one filled with high, glass-paned doors that still swung effortlessly.

As they entered Gwendalynn washed the space with her flashlight. It was cavernous, though amply filled by an enormous mahogany bar where you could sit on red-leather stools and order drinks off glass shelves covering the wall above, improbably accessible only by a towering library ladder.

"I already dug out the vino," said Gwendalynn, taking Jack by the elbow and guiding him to a round table in the corner set at stool height. There was also a bottle of wine and a pair of glasses, and a half dozen candles in crystal candleholders.

Gwendalynn lit the candles with a cigarette lighter, then lit a Marlboro, which she held between her teeth while she popped the cork of the wine bottle. She filled the two glasses.

"I know you can't drink it. Just pretend," she said to Jack as they settled in at the table.

"I haven't been here in a long time," he said. "I forgot about it."

"Must've been something in its day."

"It was always something in my grandfather's imagination." The candles threw a pale, tentative light twenty feet around the table, but died out before hitting the ceiling two stories above or the farther reaches of the huge room. Though they were close enough to clearly see the soaring wall of glass shelves behind the bar, still stocked with hundreds of bottles of rum, bourbon, vodka, gin, scotch, rye, brandy, schnapps, port and limitless choices of obscure aperitifs.

Gwendalynn took a sip of her wine.

"Tasty. Probably some rare vintage worth a scillion dollars. Do you mind?"

"My mother would tell you it's a sin to waste," said Jack.

"She religious?"

"Only since the accident. She feels responsible because until then she didn't believe in God. She said to me, 'Nobody likes to be neglected.'"

"My mother gave up God after she saw my father with his finger in one of the neighbors. That day she crawled into bed and has more or less stayed there ever since. She won't talk to me or anyone else in the family, won't take care of herself or accept help unless it's forced on her. So she's basically committed suicide, for all we get out of her, without the messiness of the actual death part. Episcopalians consider that a sin. I don't know where the Jews stand on it."

"It only matters what God thinks," said Jack.

"Aren't you supposed to avoid religion when you're on a date?" she asked.

"Is this a date?"

"You invited me to have a drink with you. That makes it a date."

"My first date."

"You're kidding, of course."

"When girls ask me where I went to college I say the Friends Society Convalescence and Rehabilitation Center. That's about as far as it gets."

"Maybe we should avoid talking about parents as well," said Gwendalynn. "Way too big a bummer."

"Severe memory loss helps with that."

"That's what dope is for."

"Ah," said Jack.

"What do you mean 'ah'?"

"So not just to get high," he said.

"Not just to get high. A purpose also served by wine, so let's quit with the downers and let me drink some of it."

Which he did, for the next two hours, enjoyed hearing her talk, and watching her sip her wine and light, smoke and fiddle with her Marlboros. They were thus engaged when they heard a sound. An indefinable sound, but nothing they'd heard before inside the abandoned hotel.

"Rats?" asked Gwendalynn.

Jack shook his head.

"Never seen one."

"Don't you have a security service watching the place?" He nodded, still listening intently.

They heard another sound. Something shuffling, or scraping, bumping into things, coming from the far end of the bar.

"Shit, man," said Gwendalynn. "Does this happen often?"

"Never. Everyone's afraid of this place."

"We need to call your security guys."

"I don't have the number. I've never met them. My mother did all that."

A brilliant circle of light shot out from the end of the room. It moved unsteadily, but seemed fixed in their direction. Gwendalynn sucked in her breath. Jack stood up from the bar stool.

"Yo, what's happening?" he yelled toward the light.

It bobbed toward them. Obviously a flashlight, blinding them to everything but the ball of light.

"Hey, Jack," called the flashlight wielder. "It's me. Who's the crack?"

"They didn't see you?" said Jack.

"Crack?" asked Gwendalynn.

"This is Gwendalynn," said Jack.

By this time Petey was close enough to the candles to see without the flashlight. He snapped it off, revealing his darkened form, made more so by their damaged night vision. He was wearing a black wetsuit and grease from the engine block of his pickup that Clarice recovered and rubbed on his face. He had a pair of flippers tied together with a piece of twine and thrown over his shoulder.

"I saw them. They didn't see me. You need to get smarter pigs."

The swim through the Northern Channel had been aided considerably by the ebb tide. He'd cleared the long stone jetty delineating the channel from the northernmost ocean beach in less than an hour, then only had to swim counter to the current for a few minutes before catching the first set of waves toward shore.

In a deep crouch, Petey ran across the sand, then climbed the stairs to the boardwalk and did a belly crawl, sliding down the wall on the other side and taking cover behind a thirty gallon trash barrel. From there it wasn't long before he spotted a drab Ford Galaxy parked at the corner of one of the side streets that bracketed the Imperial Hotel. It was one of a small fleet of Fords he'd tagged long ago as the Imperial's security force, partly out of professional habit and partly in preparation for just this occasion.

He made himself as comfortable as possible behind the trash barrel and waited.

An hour later the Ford started and the lights went on. It pulled away from the curb and turned right, crossing in front of the hotel and making the next right. Petey waited until the taillights flicked out of sight before jumping up and running full out across the street, over the broad lawn and into the giant balls of blue hydrangea growing on either side of the hotel's majestic central staircase.

For Petey Amato the subsequent break-in was too effortless to deserve the classification.

"Gwendalynn wants to know who this is," said Gwendalynn, pointing to Petey, as she watched him climb up the library ladder to retrieve a bottle of Bushmills Irish Whiskey.

"Sorry," said Jack. "Meet Petey Amato. A friend of mine."

"His best friend," Petey called down from the wall of booze.

"Okay, best friends as young assholes. Not for a while now, but I wasn't the one who went to la-la land. I can't believe all this shit is still here."

"You scared the snot out of me," said Gwendalynn.

"Sorry about that," said Petey, pulling up to the table with the bottle and a shot glass. "Tell your boyfriend to get rid of the rent-a-fuzz and people could come right in the front door."

"Not my boyfriend."

"You could still come in the front door," said Jack. "They can't arrest you."

"We'll have to talk about that," said Petey.

Gwendalynn watched Petey pour about four fingers of the Irish whiskey into a large cocktail glass and slug it back with a single throw. He shook his shoulders and belched.

"Still drinkable," he said.

"Apparently," said Gwendalynn.

He took one of her cigarettes out of the pack sitting on the table and lit it with her lighter. A black smudge was left on both.

"How 'bout a shower?" she asked.

He shook his head as he drew on the cigarette.

"Hey, thanks, but I got to deal with the trip back."

A little dead air formed in the bar until Petey realized some explanation was called for. He started with the swim over from his apartment along the channel breakwater. He spoke about the sensation of half swimming and half drifting through the salty water, the difficulty of maintaining his bearing in the dark, exacerbated by the perspective distortions of open water. As he warmed to the tale he pulled off the portion of the wetsuit covering his head, which he'd put on before Clarice greased his face, so the now-exposed skin and his shaved skull encircled the giant black blob that was the center of his face.

Jack asked why he chose to risk his life in a choppy, coal-black sea filled with capricious rip currents rather than simply stroll down the street.

Petey would have preferred keeping things on a quasi-fictional basis forever, but that would have defeated his purpose in coming there. Seeing Jack again made him long for the past. He wanted this to be just another night hanging out, stealing liquor and exploring the caverns and conduits, the boiler rooms and electrical chases that made up the cardiovascular and nervous system of the Imperial Hotel.

He took a deep breath.

"I got my ass in a swirling vortex of shit, man, and that's what this is all about. Truth told, I can't be seen coming or going from here. For your sake, man. I am persona non-fucking grata. I have thoroughly, entirely, unbelievably fucked the duck this time. *And* the horse he rode in on."

"What happened, Petey?" asked Jack.

"It's not what happened so much as what's supposed to happen."

"Okay."

Petey dumped back another shot of Bushmills.

"It's too heavy. I can't even talk about it. How's your mother?" he asked Jack.

"Disorganized."

"So, same old same old."

"Not exactly. The accident was a complicator."

He looked around the cavernous barroom.

"How do you decide which room to sleep in?"

"I'm in the Box."

Petey pointed toward the ceiling.

"Up there? You're kidding."

"The highest point south of Atlantic City. On a clear day high enough to see France."

"He thinks you can dive into the ocean from there," said Gwendalynn, then regretted it when she saw Jack dart a look at her. "I'm on the first floor," she added quickly. "Less of a drop."

"She's in Ricky Bendle's little apartment. The one he had before we caught him selling dope," said Jack.

Petey knew Ricky well. He'd been delighted when Marty's bozo summer cops stumbled into a transaction outside Shing O'Ling's. Nice to have the competition off the island and out of the distribution chain. The thought would have cheered him more if Ricky's name hadn't triggered the sickening recollection of his current circumstances. It must have shown on his face through all the black grease.

"You probably should just tell me what's going on," said Jack, reaching over and squeezing Petey's thick shoulder. "You know you will eventually. Let's get it over with."

Petey slid off his stool and started pacing in front of the long bar.

"I can't do it, that's the fuck of it. I can't even imagine doing anything like it. I said I would. You would, too, if you were hanging by your ass a hundred feet off the ground all night."

Jack got up and led him back to his stool. He poured another Bushmills and took his own seat.

"From the top," he said to Petey.

Petey looked over at Gwendalynn.

"Hey, no offense, but her I don't know for my whole life."

"She's cool."

"You're telling me she's cool? If you're telling me, I trust you."

"She's cool," said Jack, softly.

"I'm cool," said Gwendalynn, tossing him another of her cigarettes.

Petey set the foundation for his story by describing his core enterprise, the illegal acquisition and redistribution of automotive accessories. He didn't think the narrative would suffer from leaving out things like burglary and drug dealing, recently improved upon by the sudden disappearance of Ricky Bendle.

He made a game attempt at linking his career to their childhood capers, mostly masterminded by Jack, and thus appropriately credited. Gwendalynn patted him on the back.

"Proud to know you."

Jack frowned.

"So you got caught," he said.

Petey frowned back.

"Not exactly. I don't know. Something happened."

He did his best from there to describe the bust at his apartment, the brief swim, then the night on the water tower. The strangeness and wonder of the experience still gripped his mind, and found its way into the character of the account. Of all the stories he told that evening it was the most outlandish, yet most believable in the telling, benefiting greatly from Petey's own incredulity.

"Cops?" Jack asked. "You sure?"

"They got uniforms and badges and guns on their belts. They drive cop cars and talk on the radio. All but the top cop, the one without a uniform or a gun, but fuck me dead, one evil scumsucking son of a bitch."

"Marty Romanovski?" Jack asked. "Never seen him out of uniform."

"Nah. I know Romanovski. It's the other one. That fat little douche bag Harlan."

"Hello," said Gwendalynn.

"The borough council president," said Jack.

"I shouldn't even be talking about this," said Petey.

"Too late for that."

"I don't believe this," said Gwendalynn.

Petey pointed his finger at her.

"That's why I shouldn't be talking about it."

"What are you going to do?" she asked.

Petey jumped up off his stool with enough force to knock it over.

"What am I going to do?" he yelled. "What do you mean by that? You think I might consider fucking up the mayor? I've never done anything like that in my entire life. I never even thought about it. I can't even think about it now. Do you know what you're talking about here? Just saying the words makes me want to puke."

"She knows that, Petey," said Jack, calmly. "She's just trying to make conversation."

"Fuck!" Petey yelled, enjoying the feeling of strong words in his throat, and the slight release it gave his anguished heart.

"I didn't mean I thought you'd actually do it," said Gwendalynn.

Jack got off his stool and went over to Petey, put his arm around his friend's shoulders and gave him a little shake.

"Yo, Pete," he said, "let's calm down and think this thing through. That's all we need to do. Think a little."

Petey hung his head and nodded, swallowing hard on the lump in his throat and other signs that he was about to break into tears. Still holding him by the shoulders, Jack said quietly, "And just to keep everything out where it needs to be, Gwendalynn's looking after Norm Harlan's kid this summer."

Petey lurched, but Jack's grip kept him in place.

"Fuck me dead," said Petey.

Jack got everybody settled back at the round table where they sat quietly for long minutes filled with portent and dismay. Petey finally broke the silence.

"So what am I going to do?" he asked.

"Go to the party," said Jack.

"Huh?"

"Randy and Baxter's."

"Not a good time to be pulling my chain."

"You have to turn this whole approach around 180 degrees," said Jack. "By hiding you're doing just what they want you to do. You're out of the way and right where they want you. You're completely in their control. Why would they bother you now? They're just waiting around for you to take care of business, not that you would. And if you did, which you won't, they'd immediately bust you for it, and enjoy you trying to convince a judge and jury that you were hired by the borough council president to assault the mayor of Elysiana."

"Shit," said Petey.

"Wouldn't it feel better to clean off your face and get back out in the world? You gotta show these fascists that you're every bit the killer they think you are. You can't do that cowering in your apartment. You gotta look confident and together. That you're capable of anything. More than capable. You're just picking your time and place. Fitting it into your schedule."

Jack ticked the rationale off on his fingers.

"You get some elbow room, you get mobile again, you take away a little of their control, and you buy the time for your luck to cycle around from bad to good."

Petey's lifting mood seemed to illuminate the inside of the old hotel.

"I like this," he said.

"What better way to express your self-assurance than going to Randy and Baxter's party?"

"Fuckin' A," said Petey, mounting a toast. Three glasses clinked. Gwendalynn downed Jack's to make it official.

Jack had other ideas for Petey, and as the conversation wove into the night, new bearings were set for him, showing a course out of the brooding gloom that had descended over his soul.

Since she was drinking for two, Gwendalynn felt justified in opening and half finishing a second bottle of wine, which was in fact a rare vintage kept behind the bar. One of its more salubrious characteristics was a gentleness of after-effects, which spared Gwendalynn the hangover she deserved in the morning. It didn't spare her, however, or in any way disguise the feelings that listening to Jack's calm counsel fired in her breast.

"Dammit," she said to herself, watching Petey stride out the front door of the Imperial Hotel, and Jack wave to her before trotting up the central staircase on his way to the Box. "Why him?"

CHAPTER
18

T HE MORNING of the day of Randy and Baxter's party was filled with the sounds of people loading overnight bags into their cars and driving away. It was an older neighborhood, comprised of owners and summer renters, with very little turnover, so they all knew what was coming. With the exception of an elderly and thoroughly deranged pair of sisters who lived directly across the street, who watched the neighborhood through binoculars from their front porch, people living within a block's range on all sides pretty well cleared out, knowing protests to the police were pointless when the party was under the unofficial sanction of the Elysiana Beach Patrol.

Consequently, Randy was one of the few people to be shaken out of a deep sleep by the sound of Jim Morrison's arrogant baritone exploding from a pair of guitar amplifiers Baxter had dropped out his bedroom window onto the porch roof.

Five blocks away in the center of downtown, the owner of McCloskey's SeaSide Deli, Beer and Spirits thought the first few thumps from Ray Manzarek's bass pedals was an attack of heart arrhythmia. As the panic subsided, he realized it was actually his cue to start loading the step van with six of the twelve kegs of Schmidt's that he'd brought over from the mainland the day before. It took two trips to get all the kegs, their individual buckets and about a ton of block ice over to the desperate hovel that fat slob of a kid lived in with the surfers and lifeguards.

Though Baxter hadn't actually ordered the beer, McCloskey knew he was the only one on the island, outside of Shing O'Ling's, who could meet the volume requirements. He also knew Baxter appreciated home delivery, and McCloskey's indifference to proof of age when a sale of this magnitude was involved. For his part, Baxter was always ready with a stack of cash to cover both the beer and deposits on the returnables, much of which for a variety of reasons, were never to return.

Avery Volpe, standing on the roof of the opera house, had no cardiological fears on hearing Jim Morrison, though it forced his gaze to shift from the white glare of the rising sun to a point inland slightly to the south of downtown. He didn't like the sound of it. Drug music, was how he framed it in his mind. He hated drugs. It wasn't a matter of taste or moral values, but a matter of public safety. To Avery, drugs were just another variety of trouble that could never be controlled, but had to be contained. At least on his island.

Not a view shared by Sanford Goettlewing, who regarded drugs as a fountain of financial and spiritual well-being. On his way for a jog along the beach, he turned in the direction of the music. McCloskey's step van passed him on the way, so Baxter was busy unloading the kegs when Goettlewing got there.

He stood on the sidewalk with his hands on his hips, his breath barely labored from the jog, and stared up at the two Fender Super Reverbs throbbing on the porch roof. Sensing something, Baxter looked up from one of the kegs and took in the significance of Goettlewing's mangled torso, leathered skin, scarred throat and general deportment in a blinding gestalt.

"Turn it down?" Baxter immediately suggested.

Goettlewing nodded, turned and continued his jog toward the ocean.

He'd been jogging a lot since arriving on Elysiana. It was a good way to stay close to the ground and establish a proportionate sense of the environment. The absolute flatness was another attraction. Having spent years following the pitiless contours of the Berkshires, it hardly felt like running at all.

Thus he'd been able to establish an excellent fix on Shing O'Ling's, the comings and goings of customers and employees, including Buente himself, whose house he'd identified while tracking his daily routine. Three of the five times Goettlewing had followed him home after closing hours, he'd been with a different woman. Knowing that Buente's wife spent the summers with a sister somewhere in North Jersey, he guessed that a good-looking, half-Italian, half-Spanish drug dealing nightclub owner might see some romantic advantage in the situation.

Goettlewing was glad to see the joker left alone once in a while. He hated unnecessary collateral damage.

GWENDALYNN WAS too far away to hear the rise and fall of Jim Morrison's voice, but she might not have heard it anyway, concentrating as she was on being pleasant to Norm Harlan, always a difficult task, now nearly impossible. She smiled at him as he got into his car to go to work, and much to her self-ridicule, wished him a nice day. It made her feel like an animated smile button.

Sweetie noticed that, of course, and clutched Gwendalynn's right hand in both of hers and looked up at her curiously.

"Cut it out. I'm just trying to be nice," she said to the little girl.

"Are you going to be nice to Mommy, too?" she asked.

"Yes. Entirely. Especially extra nice to your mommy."

Paula, as it turned out, was still in bed, now a daily occurrence. It reminded Gwendalynn too much of her mother to bear without some intervention.

"Paula, come on," she said, cheerfully, partly as a way to ward off distant associations. "Let's get up and *carpe diem*."

"I never carp. I can't believe you're saying that. Norm always says that."

"*Carpe diem*. It's Latin. It means seize the day."

"Okay, College Girl. I'm just a stupid wop."

"You're not a stupid wop. You're an unhappy wop."

"I can't believe you just said that to me."

"Get out of bed and Sweetie and I will make us all breakfast, and then we'll go to the beach and shake our behinds at Mike and Jack."

"I like that last part."

"Come on," said Gwendalynn, grabbing Paula's wrist, first yanking her into a sitting position, and then up on her feet.

"I had two years of Community College, you know," said Paula. "I had to go live with my aunt outside Philadelphia. I was in Business Administration. *Carpe shmarpe*."

When they made it to the beach it was low tide. Jack and Ditzler looked like they were a hundred miles away, the image of the guard stand wavering above the white hot reflected light of the sun. Paula groaned under her own weight and an overstuffed beach bag, umbrella and cooler crammed with ice and jelly jars filled with white wine. Gwendalynn made no offer to help, concentrating instead on helping Sweetie decide if the cloud overhead looked like Minnie Mouse or Sander Vanocur.

They established a beachhead at the high water mark, planted the umbrella, spread the towels and drenched Sweetie in suntan lotion at Paula's urgent prompting. The girl took it stoically.

"Excuse me, sirs," said Gwendalynn to the two guards when they finally arrived at the water's edge, "is it safe to swim today?"

"Only for the existentially resigned," said Ditzler.

"Screw Sartre."

"That's Simone's job," said Ditzler.

"What the hell are they talking about?" Paula asked Sweetie.

"Hello, Mrs. Harlan," said Jack.

"Mrs. Harlan is my husband's mother. And she's dead."

"I'm sorry to hear that."

"You're weird," said Paula, trying to make it come out like a compliment.

"You're tan," said Ditzler. "How did you get so dark?"

"I'm a wop. I keep telling this girl, but she won't believe me. I'm the former Paula Prizzi. Two 'z's'. Like Pizza. Prizzi. Wops always look like aborigines in the summer."

"He's an aborigine, too," said Sweetie, pointedly at Ditzler.

Ditzler jumped down off the stand and picked Sweetie up and put her on his shoulders. Then he ran partway into the surf, then back to the beach, then back into the surf again. Sweetie squealed like the child she was supposed to be. The other three watched, puzzled and amused.

"Your friend is weird, too," said Paula.

"I think your friend is exceptionally far out," said Gwendalynn.

"He's not my friend. He's my stand partner," said Jack.

"Not an ounce of fat on him," said Paula.

Gwendalynn twisted her hips back and forth, digging her feet into the silty Jersey sand. She liked the sensation. Jack taught it to her, telling her if you dug deep enough you could lock your knees and stay upright even after falling asleep, a trick the life-guards used to avoid being caught sleeping on duty.

Jack waited until she was comfortably settled in before asking if she was going to Randy and Baxter's party.

"Party?" said Paula.

"Are you asking me to go with you?" Gwendalynn asked.

"If you want to. Sure. I've got a car."

"It's an old truck."

"What kind of party?" Paula asked. "Is that the big hippie happening downtown?"

"Why does everything fun have to be a hippie thing?" Gwendalynn asked.

"You tell me, love child," said Paula.

"Christ."

"I want to go," said Paula.

"You can't go. You have to look after Sweetie."

"The Kimballs can take her for the night. I feed their cat whenever they go to Philadelphia."

"Paula."

"It's not the first time. Janet said she'll take her any time. Don't be such a worrywart. You told me to carp at the diem," said Paula, walking down into the ankle-deep ocean water washing over the dark sand.

"Cool," said Jack, squinting out at the ocean, keeping a careful eye on Ditzler and Sweetie, who were now flopping around in the foamy surf contained by the gulley, the result of larger-than-normal waves at the first break a hundred feet offshore. It was likely caused by an early hurricane-season disturbance far out at sea, raising the possibility of sudden changes in the surf, the worst being a riptide that could empty the gulley in seconds.

"We have to do something about Petey," Gwendalynn said to Jack when Paula was out of earshot.

"We are. We're thinking."

"We need to tell somebody," said Gwendalynn. "Like the mayor, for starters. He might want to know that Norm's hired somebody to rough him up."

"Petey isn't gonna rough up the mayor," said Jack.

"Petey's a criminal," said Gwendalynn, with a slight upswing in her intonation.

"More of a merchant."

"How well do you know this guy?"

"As well as you can. I forgot a lot of my life after the accident, but I remember everything before. Except when I first met Petey, because we were infants. Our mothers took turns looking after us, which for them meant leaving us to our own devices."

"He sure looks like he could hurt somebody."

"It's just the way he looks. I never had to worry about kids picking on me when he was around. A valuable thing when you look like me."

"Shouldn't we tell the mayor anyway?"

Jack climbed down off the stand so he could maintain better eye contact with Gwendalynn without taking his attention off the water.

"If we do, we don't know what'll happen to Petey. Nobody'll believe his story. The cops will just go ahead and bust him and he'll wind up in a cage somewhere. Can't have that."

"He's going to end up there someday."

"Maybe, but not because of something I did."

Gwendalynn was annoyed that Jack's loyalty to his old friend, obnoxious as Petey was, caused her to choke up again.

She crossed her arms and turned her back on him, ostensibly to check on Sweetie. She saw the little girl wave at Paula, motioning her mother to come further out into the water. Paula shook her head and pointed to the spot she was standing in. Immovable. A picture of her own mother leapt into her mind. The clog in her throat grew.

"Dammit all," she said.

"Sorry. I'll think of something."

Gwendalynn turned back to him.

"It's not that. I think you will. I'm just a little fucked up."

Then she ran out into the ocean and struggled out to where Ditzler and Sweetie were playing on the sandbar, grabbed the little girl around the waist, picked her up and squeezed. For once, the kid knew enough to keep her mouth shut and just squeeze back.

AT THE northern tip of the island, on the surfing beach next to the jetty that defined the opening of the Northern Channel, Randy Calvert was testing the strength of the same outside break that held Jack's attention. He was more than pleased by the results. The waves were not only oversized, but seemed to have an extra dose of energy, channeling the underlying power of a deep ocean storm. He could feel it in his legs as he accelerated down the face of the breakers, and in the turbulent seawater that followed when the wave hit the first sandbar and disintegrated, only to be reformed seconds later as it hurtled across the gulley toward the shore.

The timing of this once-in-a-season event could not be more perfect for Petey Amato, recently liberated from self-imposed house arrest, smelling the frenzied ocean in his nostrils, and like a man possessed throwing his surfboard into the back of his pickup and racing down to the beach.

Petey stood at the water's edge and assessed the situation. The first break was farther out than usual, which meant the waves were far bigger than the local rabble of surfers were used to, which meant most of them would be frolicking courageously within the potent, but controllable surf of the second break just outside the near-shore gulley.

Only one other surfer on the island would be out with the storm-swept ocean. And Petey could see him clearly—tall, blond and patient. Given the strength of the surf, Petey would have to move much further down the beach to avoid the possibility of crossing Randy's path. But today, it wouldn't change the prospects for some excellent rides. There were plenty of big waves along the entire Elysiana coast.

Petey hadn't slept much the night before. After walking boldly home from the Imperial Hotel, as far as he could tell unnoticed, he woke up Clarice and allowed her to celebrate the recovery of his *joie de vivre* in her customary way. Given the scale of the turnaround, it took roughly the balance of the night for her delight to be fully expressed. It left Petey with an edge of fatigue that barely dampened the exhilaration that filled his heart.

The heavies on the outside would complete the cure, he decided, and then later he'd sleep like a dead guy for the balance of the day in preparation for Randy and Baxter's party.

Neither Petey nor Randy were disappointed by the day's experience. As if to assure a quality performance, the wind shifted unexpectedly to offshore, keeping the surf orderly, flattening off the chop and organizing the waves into predictable sets. The change in wind patterns was also a surprise to the guys manning meteorological stations from Woods Hole to Kitty Hawk. The readouts from wind sensors on buoys and weather boats out on the ocean gave strong evidence that the Atlantic storm had stalled before making the usual northeast turn on its way to the upper latitudes, and seemed to be drifting back toward the Eastern Seaboard. What felt like a sweet westerly to the surfers was actually the consequence of a sudden drop in barometric pressure off the coast.

Avery Volpe, a sensitive barometer himself, climbed back to the roof of the opera house to get another look at local conditions. The sky was clear and the air fresh, but he didn't like the feel of it. Not for that time of year. He scanned the horizon with a pair of binoculars. He could see to the curve of the earth, though the line between sky and sea was a jagged knife's edge, indicating much bigger water further out. Avery scowled.

"Get me the Coast Guard and tell whoever's in the Jeep to pull the swimmers out of the breakers," he said to Johnny Lukeiwitz when he came back down to the guardhouse.

"What about the surfers?"

"Leave the two on the outside where they are for now. I know those guys. Get the others out."

His contact at the Coast Guard was noncommittal. He told Avery about the shifting highs and lows and the interaction of the two, and lots of other things that added up to the simple fact that he didn't exactly know what was going to happen, but he'd know a lot more in about twenty-four hours. The Coastie promised to call him if anything changed before that. Avery grunted, but took it at face value, the Coast Guard being one of the few institutions he had some faith in.

He went back up on the roof to check on the two surfers and watch the Jeep work its way south toward the mines. Then he turned to the west, running his eyes over the rooftops of Elysiana. The sound of rock music had died down, but he knew that was just another calm before the storm.

But at least one over which he had some control. God would have to look after the sea. Avery assumed it was in the Lord's best interest to leave Elysiana up to him.

CHAPTER
19

GWENDALYNN STOPPED off at the hoagie joint where she'd had her first meal on Elysiana. The woman who gave her the money was there behind the counter. So was her irritable boss and the pale pockmarked kid who'd dropped the tray full of dishes. As before, he stared at her when she came in.

"Well, lookee you," said the woman. "It took me a second to place your face, all tan, scrubbed and fed."

"I need another favor," said Gwendalynn. "Nothing to do with money," she added when the woman raised her eyebrows.

"What doesn't have to do with money?"

"I just need a little advice."

That softened the woman's face.

"I don't know nothin' about nothin', hon, but it won't hurt to ask."

"You gotta know something about lipstick. You're wearing some now."

The woman pursed her lips, as if confirming Gwendalynn's observation.

"I am indeed."

"I want to wear some. I don't know what to get and I can't trust the people at the drugstore."

"How can you not know what kind of lipstick to get, a young woman like you?"

"I've never worn lipstick, or ever put anything else on my face in my whole life."

"Didn't your mama teach you?"

"She's not in the best position to tell me anything anymore. If you could just give me an idea of a color and a brand, I'd be grateful."

The woman shook her head and pursed her lips again, this time trying to hold back whatever commentary was brewing in her mind. Unsuccessfully. "You people so hell-bent on changing the world don't know diddly about the world you already got," she said.

Gwendalynn grinned at her, she hoped like she grinned at her grandmother, which always yielded a favorable result.

"I don't want to change the world. I just want to put some red stuff on my lips so I can feel like a girl instead of a ghost."

She left with a pair of options written on the back of a check. She bought both of them, which felt oddly thrilling, either over the expense or the thought of future cosmetic indulgence.

Clothes were another matter. She knew the parties at Randy and Baxter's weren't occasioned by haute couture, but something made her wish her closet held more than three possible choices.

"Don't get all carried away," she warned herself as she walked into a shop she'd passed many times before, congratulating herself on her indifference to what was inside. She walked out with an embroidered Mexican blouse with layers of ruffles that had a hem about four inches short of her hip-hugging denim cut-offs. The girl running the place assured her the stitching would match either lipstick.

"God, what a silly ass you are," she told herself on her way back to the Imperial, though with less conviction then she might have expected.

There was a note from Jack waiting for her. He said he'd pick her up at eight if she still wanted to go, and to call him if she didn't, or if she'd rather drive herself. Whatever she wanted.

The apartment was full of breezes that swept away the remains of the moldy attic smell that she'd almost cleaned into oblivion. Sunlight followed the air, a rich, late afternoon sunlight that added color to everything it illuminated. Gwendalynn sat on the painted rattan love seat in the tiny living room and gazed about in dumb wonder at the threadbare beauty of the place. She'd always seen her parents' house, the house she grew up in, as an aesthetic standard, for no particular reason other than familiarity. Sitting there in the drug-dealing security guard's apartment at the Imperial Hotel, with its wicker and off-white walls, faded upholstery and musty Persian rugs, made her recognize how little she knew of the world outside Chicago. She felt like she didn't know anything about the world at all, that she'd willfully assumed she was potently perceptive and wise, based on the thinnest possible practical experience.

It was as if she'd lived in a tiny sphere at the center of an infinite number of encapsulating spheres, and that she was only now crossing through the barrier to the next outer shell, itself circumscribed, but of far greater dimension than the insignificant pea at the core.

The thought almost gave her vertigo. She lay down on the love seat and tucked her hands between her thighs, drawing her knees up toward her chest. Uninvited images of her parents assaulted her mind. Mental recordings of conversations, arguments and lamentable declarations played out at an almost audible volume. The moment came when the paths to despair and enlightenment seemed to open simultaneously before her, each beckoning.

Before she could choose the first step she heard a phone ring. It was the one behind the reception desk she'd used to call Jack. Five rings later she answered.

"Is George there?" asked the voice on the other end of the line.

"No George here."

"You're obviously not George."

"Never been."

"I must have the wrong number."

"For you, maybe," said Gwendalynn. "Not for me."

"Heavy."

"When you find George, tell him I said hello."

"So you know George?" asked the voice.

"I'm starting to feel like I do."

"Then you know his number?"

"Nobody knows his number. That's his secret to success," said Gwendalynn, before hanging up.

She waited for the phone to ring again. When it didn't, she went to take her shower, massive life choices in abeyance, eager to experiment with herself in front of the mirror. To take a closer look and see what she could find.

THE SUN set at eight-fifteen PM. With the lawn already filling up, Randy picked out a cluster of five girls to go roust Baxter, who was sleeping off the effects of a head start on the phalanx of kegs. The girls were part of the first wave comprised of the vacationing kids down from Philly for a week or two and house shares of women, often secretaries or teachers pretending to want a peaceful time at the shore, and by now wishing they'd rented in Wildwood or Atlantic City.

Johnny Lukeiwitz had assigned two guards to check ID's to filter out the youngest kids, or at least those lacking the sophistication to manufacture a convincing draft card or driver's license. He picked a pair of guys who were studying to become Lutheran ministers, having had guards in the past repurpose the job into recruiting underage girls for a side function down in the dunes.

On Randy's instructions, the girls all jumped on Baxter as he lay in his bed, and then as he lurched into joyful consciousness, ran back outside. He followed ten minutes later, just in time to see the last of the ruby sunset fade to dark gray. He stood on the front steps of the cottage and surveyed the tank top and T-shirted throng with deep satisfaction. Then, he went back upstairs to re-ignite the sound system. He stacked the record changer with a broad sampling of San Francisco psychedelia, then let the Super Reverbs roar. Every face in the crowd turned to look at him standing on the roof, bracketed by the amplifiers, his arms aloft, his belly proudly swelling over a pair of torn gym shorts, his face to the sky. Bliss.

Taking this as a sign, Ditzler told Sylvia it was probably safe to go in. He'd been circling the block in the red Alfa hoping darkness and a critical mass of people would quell Sylvia's apprehension. As they slowed down to watch Baxter's opening ceremony, Johnny Lukeiwitz approached the car. Ditzler stopped.

"Hi, Mike, made up your mind?"

"We're deliberating."

He reached his hand toward Sylvia.

"I'm Johnny."

"Annie."

Wearing her blond wig, a scarf and a pair of wraparound sunglasses, Sylvia looked like a parody of a woman in disguise. Successfully enough, apparently, since Avery Volpe came up behind Johnny and leaned into the convertible.

"Ditzler. We need another guard to work the function. Nothing demanding. Just keep your eyes out for trouble. Stick around the front of the house. I've got other guys covering the kegs and the sidewalk."

That settled the question. Johnny showed him to a safe spot to park the Alfa, then opened the door for Sylvia. She scurried past him and tucked her arm through Ditzler's.

"Jesus, that was him," she whispered. "I'm out of my fucking mind."

"You need to talk to him," said Ditzler.

She jerked at his arm.

"That wasn't decided."

"Okay, then help me look for trouble. You're deputized."

"What kind of trouble?"

"You'll know it when you see it."

Had she still been out on the sidewalk, she would have seen the approach of Petey and Clarice, by some people's definition, the essence of trouble. Marty Romanovski's, for example, who had spotted them climbing out of Petey's pickup a block west of the house. He immediately called Norm, who'd just arrived home and was reading a note from Paula telling him Sweetie was over at the Kimballs' and she'd gone out with the girls. He was trying to figure out who the girls were when the phone rang.

Norm didn't like what the chief had to report. In the first place, he'd been carefully maintaining his backstory on Petey Amato, that he'd been given up by Buente as the island's true narcotics kingpin. From there, it was relatively easy to convince him to keep both Buente and Amato in operation, at least until they ratted out the entire distribution network. Norm never questioned that Marty was a loyal and dutiful associate, but it'd be a stretch to bring him into an assault and battery on the mayor.

So to keep the story intact, he had to agree that Marty put a man on Amato to track everyone he came in contact with at the party.

"I'm thinkin' Phil Anskeep. He's got sideburns."

"Christ, Marty, every guard there knows Anskeep. Avery'll never let him into that party."

"That's not his jurisdiction."

Norm put his hand over his eyes and shook his head. It'd already been a long day and was about to get longer.

"It wouldn't be much of a surveillance if they all knew a narc was hanging around the beer kegs, now would it?"

"We need to get him a wig."

"Just sit tight. I'll be there in fifteen minutes."

He made it there in ten, but had to park two blocks away. The street itself was now blocked off, and each corner had a pack of lifeguards checking people in and out. Drunk guards had to give up their keys and allow one of the Lutherans to drive them home. Avery didn't like cleaning up a situation inside the party's perimeter, so he instituted outposts that could fall back and raise the alarm. Years before a street gang from South Philly had tried to bust into one of these parties intending to kick some beach patrol ass, or more precisely, crack beach patrol heads with heavy chains and lead-filled saps. After what Avery had done to those black-jacketed kids, the odds were long that another group would take on the challenge, but Avery liked to stick with established protocols.

Thus Norm found himself sitting in the borough's only unmarked patrol car with Marty Romanovski and a jug of black coffee, watching the steady in and out flow of partygoers.

Paula had entered from the other end of the block. Not finding Johnny Lukeiwitz on the first pass through the crowd, she headed for the kitchen of the little house looking for wine. What she found was Baxter sitting yogi style on the kitchen table passing around a huge tubular device that even Paula Prizzi knew was a bong. She'd never smoked anything stronger than Tareyton filters, but with a half dozen cute guys staring at her and the bong held directly in her face, she thought, why not.

She was pleased with herself for not coughing, though embarrassed that she'd let the smoke out too quickly. She made up for it with a few more tokes before passing it along. Emboldened, she went right for the refrigerator and found a gallon of the Gallo brothers finest red.

"Hey, lady, you can pass that around, too," Baxter gasped out with a cloud of hash smoke.

She didn't like being called lady, but got the spirit of the remark. She served all the guys, and got back in the bong line. She managed a couple more hits before Baxter leaned a little too far to one side and collapsed the kitchen table. The jug of wine was on the other side, so as Baxter crashed to the floor the bottle catapulted over his head and sailed through an open kitchen window. The bong wasn't as lucky.

"Whoa, bummer," said one of the guys, picking a tiny pebble of hash out of the fractured bowl.

It was just as well for Paula, who left the kitchen in a far better mood than she entered, good enough to withstand a ten minute wait for the bathroom. Once inside she had a chance to reappraise her outfit, which was the closest she could come to hippie wear—a pair of slightly flared white slacks and a T-shirt from the Steel Pier. There wasn't much she could do with the hair, permed as it was. Or the face, though she was proud to be relatively wrinkle-free. There was one sure way to attract some attention, so while sitting on the john she stripped her bra out from under the T-shirt. She left it hanging from the shower rod and sailed back into the maelstrom.

As if answering a charm, the first back her liberated boobs came in contact with was Johnny's. The lower part of his back, since he stood well over a foot taller. He was engaged with a pair of guards who were holding the jug of Gallo wine and trying to explain that it hadn't actually been thrown from the window.

"While you boys are debatin' this, you can pour me what's left in there," she said to him.

"Jesus, Mary and Joseph," said Johnny.

"And Paula. Make a nice foursome."

"What are you doing here?"

"What's it look like? Here kid," she said, reaching for the bottle and draining what was left.

"Is Norm here?" Johnny asked, wondering how she could have gotten by the centurions on the corners.

"Hell, no, silly. But Gwennie is," she said, pointing to where Gwendalynn was standing in the beer line with Jack Halcyon.

"What'd you do with Sweetie?" Johnny asked, a little harshly.

"We sold her to a band of gypsies," said Paula, with a pout, "for two bits."

Gwendalynn spotted the two of them and strolled over.

"Where's the kid?" Johnny asked her.

"With the Kimballs. I hope," said Gwendalynn.

"What's he doing here?" he asked, pointing at Jack, who was out of earshot.

"What's anybody doing here?" said Paula.

"He's getting me a beer," said Gwendalynn.

"I've never seen him out at night. Shit, I've never seen him anywhere but the beach."

"Gwennie's got her mojo working," said Paula. "Though I'd've picked the one with the black toenails. Much better looking."

"Don't get too drunk," said Gwendalynn.

"I'm not drunk. I'm stoned."

"Jesus," said Gwendalynn.

"And Mary, Joseph and Paula," said Paula.

Jack brought over Gwendalynn's beer.

"Hi, Johnny. Avery told me to tell you the entire police force is split between both ends of the street. And they got the van out."

"And?"

"He said nothing to worry about. Just wanted you to know."

Johnny looked around the crowd.

"Keep an eye on your brothers. No provocations."

"Okay."

Gwendalynn looked reluctant to leave Paula, but Jack pulled her gently away.

"Come on. It's your night off. She'll be okay."

He held her hand to keep from getting separated inside the burgeoning horde. By now most of the vacationers had either sneaked away, been escorted off by one of Avery's boys, or were staggering toward unconsciousness or fumbling sex, or both. They were replaced by an older, larger and more seasoned crowd. Gwendalynn remembered the last time she was tangled in so much humanity, battered by the thunder of over-driven amplifiers and half zonked by secondhand marijuana smoke. But the sensation was far different holding Jack's hand, a dry careful hand, with a strong swimmer's grip.

"Hey, Bax, life is beautiful," she heard Petey yell over the din.

Baxter stood with his arms out as Petey approached, a gesture that must have been permanently imprinted. Petey stopped short of the embrace and reached out his hand. Gwendalynn saw his other hand held a plump platinum blond who looked like she hadn't been out in the sun for weeks, which she hadn't. She smiled sweetly at Baxter and endured the bear hug meant for Petey. Gwendalynn saw Petey lean into Baxter to say something into his ear. Baxter nodded vigorously and put both thumbs in the air. Petey slapped his shoulder and continued to move through the crowd, which gave ground more readily for him than it had for Jack and Gwendalynn. She felt a faint twinge of regret when Petey spotted them and pulled the blond girl in their direction. When they got there, Petey stood behind the girl and held her by her meaty upper arms.

"Clarice, behold Jack Halcyon."

Clarice's face broke into a storm of conflicting reactions. Her smile was genuine, but seemed uncoupled from her eyes, which were a mix of wonder and uncertainty.

Jack reached down for her hand to thwart any Baxter-like greeting.

"Oh, I have heard so much about *you*," she said to Jack, forcing his thumb into a clumsy attempt at a soul handshake. "Helping out Petey was the most incredible thing a person could have ever possibly done."

Jack pulled his thumb free so he could introduce Gwendalynn. Clarice told her she was honored to meet anyone who was cool enough to be friends with Jack Halcyon.

"I am cool," said Gwendalynn. "That's undebatable."

"Was there any hassle getting in here?" Jack asked Petey.

"*Nada*, baby. I've got the aura of invincibility."

Gwendalynn cocked her head at him.

"I think I can see it," she said.

Clarice had both hands clutching Petey's right bicep, steadying herself. Now that she was closer, Gwendalynn could see the pin-prick size of her pupils.

"I've always told you that, man," said Jack. "You are what you think you are."

"That's how I know I'm cool," said Gwendalynn.

"I'm thirsty," said Clarice. "Let's get some beer."

Petey let her drag him toward the beer line, leaving a relieved Gwendalynn to drag her own date toward a far corner of party territory, commandeered from the next door neighbors. This is why they still hadn't made contact with Mike Ditzler, who was stationed at the front of the house with Sylvia, who'd gradually lost much of her anxiety, even though she could barely see through her sunglasses.

Ditzler monitored the party from a vantage point that now included about fifty people who'd started to dance. This made it more difficult to spot brewing antagonisms, a problem he could only solve by joining in himself. Unfortunately, he truly hated to dance. This amused Sylvia.

"First off, Fred Astaire, there's nothing any of those people are doing that a person could call actual dancing. I'd call it the throes of agonizing death. And secondly, when did you start caring what other people think?"

"I don't. Unless it hurts."

"Dancing doesn't hurt anything but your pride," said Sylvia. "And you're not prideful."

"You're right. Let's dance," said Ditzler.

"Not me. No way. I'm stayin' right here."

"I'm not dancing with myself."

"Get yourself a chicky," said Sylvia. "There're a million of 'em standing around."

As Ditzler's distaste for the prospect grew, he was saved by the sight of a red-faced, curly-headed guy in an oversized polo shirt cupping his testicles in one hand and giving the finger to someone across the lawn with the other. This, he felt, constituted the sort of trouble Avery had in mind.

He told Sylvia to stay where she was and moved closer to the guy, who was part of a group of about six, now closing ranks. He tried to see who was on the other end of the gesture, but the dance crowd had suddenly washed across that part of the lawn. The curly-haired guy was on his tiptoes, still giving the finger and yelling fuck you.

Ditzler scanned the area for other guards. Like Petey, he'd made it through life without a single fistfight, using wit and guile rather than physical intimidation. So he knew a lot more about dancing, which wasn't much, than punching people.

It was a great relief to see Joey Zable laughing hysterically over a joke another guard was telling. Ditzler tried yelling for his attention, but the music was too loud. He started to run over there when the dancers seemed to explode in his direction, limbs flailing, people falling like dominos, screaming and shouting.

Ditzler lost sight of Zable right before his legs were knocked out from under him by Paula Harlan, who was rolling across the grass like a piece of timber cut loose from a logging truck. Ditzler managed to avoid landing on her by twisting sideways as he fell. This gave him a clear view of a gigantic kid with long blond hair, mangled into dreadlocks, and a black T-shirt with a huge Day-Glo peace symbol appliquéd to the front. The kid was moving like Godzilla though the dancers, swatting people out of the way with the back of his gargantuan forearms, heading straight for the curly-haired idiot, whose buddies were rethinking their loyalties and beginning to fall back.

Ditzler jumped to his feet, helped Paula regain hers and looked around frantically for Joey Zable. Then he remembered the whistle around his neck, on a chain with his father's dog tags. He stuck it in his mouth and let off a run whistle, signaling a life-threatening emergency.

Zable took in the scene and ran for reinforcements, leaving the area for only a few seconds, but that was plenty of time for the curly-headed guy to drop back himself and snatch up Paula's wine bottle. The big kid in the dreadlocks didn't seem to notice and kept coming, having cleared all human obstacles. Worse, the action had taken a different course, now headed directly for where Ditzler had left Sylvia Buente.

Ditzler yelled at her to get into the house, but she was mesmerized by the scene before her. He ran at the two dummies as fast as he could, yelling futilely for them to back off.

The big kid lowered his head and charged.

Then he flipped over backwards, landing with a sickening thud at the feet of a wiry middle-aged man with long gray hair barely contained under a battered Yankees cap. He had his right hand wrapped around a wad of blond dreads, which he'd apparently used to yank the enormous kid off his feet just as he launched his attack. The man put one leg over the enormous mass, dropped down so the knee of his other leg was planted on the kid's chest, drew his arm back with a yell, then with another yell stuck the kid once in the face.

When the first of the guards arrived, the man in the Yankees cap stood calmly over the unconscious bulk with his palms forward. When they stopped in their tracks he looked over and pointed to the curly-haired guy, then jerked his thumb toward the street, then looked away again, not bothering to watch the guy eagerly comply.

Ditzler had put himself between Sylvia and the battle scene before the *coup de grâce*. Now the man was coming toward them, his palms still raised in peace. Ditzler could see the gaunt intensity of his expression clearly fixed on Sylvia.

The man stood and stared at her for a moment, then moved directly into her personal space. Ditzler tried to get between them, but there was no room.

"Hi, Sylvia," said the man, barely loud enough for the two of them to hear.

Ditzler felt her jump and grab his arm.

"Do I know you?" she asked.

"No," said Sanford Goettlewing, "but I know you."

CHAPTER
20

J OHNNY LUKEIWITZ organized a team of the burliest guys he could find to haul the big kid out to the corner so the volunteer ambulance could drive him to the hospital on the mainland. The effort was little noticed by the partiers, some of whom, like Paula, simply dusted themselves off and dove back into the fray. The night had reached the point where it would take an invasion of flying saucers to mount a meaningful distraction.

Adhering to his protocols, Avery stayed out on the street awaiting a report from Johnny, who was too distracted himself to notice Goettlewing gently herding Sylvia and Ditzler into the living room of the house so they could hear each other over the sound of the loudspeakers.

"I'm not who you think I am," Sylvia was trying to say. "I know everybody knows everybody and we're all like one big happy human race. You can save it for the acid freaks."

"You're Sylvia Scillante and your mother's Antonia. You grew up in Totowa, New Jersey, and you have a half-sister who lives a block from your mother. Her kids are named Vinnie and Charlene."

He reached out to remove her sunglasses, but she reared back and gripped his wrist.

"What is this bullshit?"

Goettlewing took a step back.

"No bullshit."

He continued to back away and turned toward the door.

"Who the hell are you?" she demanded.

He pointed at Ditzler and said, "Keep her safe," before disappearing into the night.

"What the crap was that all about?" said Sylvia, looking up at the ceiling as if the heavens were part of the conversation.

"Keep her safe?" said Ditzler, adrenalin finally sparking a surge of exasperation. "How many terrifying people is one failed suicide victim allowed? What's next, Beelzebub leaping out of a sulfur vent to claim your eternal soul?"

"Hey, coming to this party was your idea." He stared at her until she waved off the comment. "It's not your fault. You're right. I'm cursed."

He took a deep calming breath and was formulating a response when Joey Zable came through the door, looking at them anxiously.

"You two okay?" he asked. "Johnny sent me to find you."

"We're fine," said Sylvia. "Peachy."

"How zoony was that?" said Joey.

"As zoony as it gets," said Sylvia.

"Where's Kung Fu?"

"He left."

"Johnny said you did a good job and can take the rest of the night off."

"Terrif," said Sylvia. "Maybe we should go to a party or something."

Ditzler put his arm around her shoulders and led her back outside. They passed Gwendalynn heading toward the house.

"Hey," said Gwendalynn, "where you been?"

"Avery had me working the party."

"But now we're off," said Sylvia.

"Where's Jack?" asked Ditzler.

"In the backyard avoiding human contact. I just have to pee. I'm Gwendalynn," she added for Sylvia's sake.

"I'm Annie, and I've already pissed myself."

Ditzler told Gwendalynn they were going soon, but that he'd try to say hello to Jack before they did. The area in front of the house was filling up with jostling drunks, pushing them apart. Gwendalynn waved goodbye and said nice to meet you, getting nothing back from Sylvia.

The woman didn't seem much of a fit for Ditzler, but then look at her. What kind of a fit was Jack Halcyon?

Having once slept in Randy and Baxter's first floor bathroom, she knew where to find it. The line was pretty daunting, so she decided to go to the one upstairs. She was stopped by a rope strung across the stairwell. As one of the boys' former employees, she thought she could duck under and go up anyway.

There was a body draped over the top of the landing. When she checked his pulse he looked up at her and smiled.

"What was in that shit?" he asked.

"Never what you think," she answered, patting him on the back.

The doors to all three bedrooms were open. Two were darkened, but she could hear wet smacking sounds in one and barely contained cries of euphoria and shushing sounds coming from the other. In the third, with lights blazing, a naked Randy Calvert sat up in bed with two naked girls and a boa constrictor wrapped around him.

The vision dragged Gwendalynn to the doorway, hypnotized by the beauty of the complex gray-green snakeskin against the curves of flesh, both tanned and pale, the outlines of tiny bikinis. Randy languorously caressed the girls and the boa, alternately kissing the girls and stroking the head of the snake as it traveled in sinuous curls among the entangled body parts.

Randy looked up at her with the same placid smile she'd seen on the guy on the stairs, she guessed for the same reason. He motioned to her to come closer. She shook her head.

He cupped the snake under the throat.

"She's too small to hurt you," he said, his voice rising up from a deep well of tranquility. "It's just a gentle squeeze."

"That's what you say," said one of the girls, wrapping her hand around Randy's penis. She pointed the head at Gwendalynn with a look of invitation.

Gwendalynn shook her head again, violently this time, to shake off the spell and regain hold of her mind. She turned away and stumbled over to the bathroom, which was blessedly empty. She locked the door and bathed her face in handfuls of cold water. After peeing, she ran with eyes and ears averted over the passed-out guy and down the stairs, out of the house and back to Jack, who was still deep in the backyard, still homely, still humane.

She took his hand and put her head on his shoulder. It surprised him.

"Don't ask," she said.

"Okay."

"I think I'm ready to go home."

"Okay."

They headed for the street, following several feet behind Ditzler and Sylvia. Gwendalynn saw Johnny and Avery intercept the other couple, and thus preoccupied, allowed them to slip quietly away.

It was less happy for Ditzler, whose sturdy nervous system had begun to fray around the edges. Still, it wasn't bad to have Johnny shake his hand and Avery nod at him, which for them was paramount to effusive praise.

"Nice work, Harvard," said Johnny.

"I'd've done more if I hadn't been tackled by the council president's wife," he said.

"You're not the first one," said Johnny.

"We gotta get her out of there," said Avery.

"I'll take care of it," said Johnny.

"Let me show you were she is," said Ditzler, looking over at Sylvia with what he hoped was a clear sub-rosa message.

"Sure," said Johnny, stalking off on his long legs toward the house.

Ditzler gestured to Sylvia to stay put, and ignoring the frantic little shakes of her head, followed close behind.

The dancers clustered around the front of the house had formed a circle inside which individuals and couples could turn exhibitionist, usually dropping to the ground and frenetically writhing around like bugs stuck on a pin. Any relationship to cadence or rhythm had long since disappeared, though you'd never convince the dancers of that. Conveniently, Paula took center stage soon after Johnny and Ditzler arrived, executing a kind of synthesis of the Twist and divine rapture. Johnny shook his head, and tagged Joey Zable and two other guards to watch over her.

"Hang back," he said, "but don't let anybody drag her into the bushes."

"You know, she don't move too bad for an old lady," said Joey.

"Just watch her."

Ditzler followed Johnny back out to the street where Avery and Sylvia were talking off to the side, standing close, but in a neutral posture. Avery seemed to be listening, but without making eye contact, striking a balance between attention and indifference.

No one observing could have guessed the intimacy of the conversation itself, which Ditzler prayed was going well, especially the part about how Ditzler had provided safe haven and never laid a hand on her.

He hung back watching them talk. Eventually Sylvia noticed him and leaned into Avery to say something, putting her hand on his arm, the first contact Ditzler had seen her make. Avery nodded at what she was saying, then she left him.

"Don't ask," she said when she reached Ditzler.

"No danger of that."

"It's personal, is all."

"Just tell me good or bad so I know if I have to make a run for it."

"Good enough, considering the circumstances."

"I would if I could figure them out."

"You will, Mr. Egghead. That's what you're good at."

Ditzler put the Alfa's top down to maximize the breeze. As he pulled away from the curb Sylvia slapped him on the arm.

"And stop saving my life. I've got so much Karma commitment built up it'll take me a freakin' thousand years to make up for it."

"Don't worry. I'll clear it with the management of Universal Enlightenment and Understanding."

"You probably could, you pain."

Ditzler drove the Alfa out to Half Moon Bay Drive, which was officially part of the coastal highway, though few thought it worth including Elysiana on their coastal highway itinerary, since you had to drive so far out from the mainland to make the connection and so far back. This didn't discourage the New Jersey Department of Tourism from putting up coastal highway signs, a matter of local pride to a handful of Elysianians, all of whom worked for Norm Harlan.

Ditzler over-revved the Alfa in all four gears as if the RPM's could draw the nervous tension out of his body. Sylvia slid down in her seat and smoked a Marlboro, lit after a dozen attempts.

Behind them cruised a Pontiac GTO, with all the windows down for the same purpose, to clear the air inside the driver's brain in preparation for events yet undefined, but inevitable.

T
HE PARTY had boiled down to the hardcore. It was the custom of the house to pull the taps and flip the dead kegs upside down in the pails. Baxter was both pleased and slightly alarmed to see only three still in action. Most of the people still circulating around the yard were lifeguards and their dates or pickups, and a scattering of French Canadians who'd come down the year before to work construction at the northern edge of the salt mines.

Avery released the corners, letting checkpoint defenders either join the remains of the party or go home. This opened up the street to general traffic and the Elysiana Borough Police.

Out on the street, Avery Volpe and Johnny Lukeiwitz leaned against Avery's Buick Wildcat and quietly assessed the current state of civil order, staring balefully at the cops as they cruised past.

Baxter switched the soundtrack from psychedelic to a mix of Motown and surf music, complementing the shifting mood. This immediately caused an energetic debate on the state of popular music. Two or three of the most passionate told Baxter about a music festival happening in upstate New York, where every great group in the world was going to play, including the Beatles, no matter what the promoters were saying. That and free acid, which Ken Kesey was going to hand out to anybody who could prove they'd bought one of his books.

"Oh, man, we gotta go now," said Baxter, looking out toward the road. "If I could find my car."

"My van's over on the next block," said one of the other guys.

"Cool. Let's blow," said Baxter, who was next seen in a nationally distributed film covered in mud, arms aloft, screaming at the sky.

As the crowd thinned Joey Zable and his crew came to the attention of Paula Harlan. Somehow she'd managed to enlist them in a sing-along with the Beach Boys. The rest of the party, including Petey and Clarice, joined in to the betterment of the presentation as Petey surprised Clarice with a crystal clear simulation of Brian Wilson's falsetto on "Surfer Girl."

After that, both Petey and Joey fought off efforts by Paula to get them to slow dance to Mitch Ryder and the Detroit Wheels. Undeterred, she prevailed upon Clarice, who told Petey not to be such a wet blanket, rewarding the onlookers with a form of interpretive dance that even the most generous commentator would have difficulty interpreting.

Petey enjoyed every bit of it. That night, he would have enjoyed invasive surgery. There was almost nothing Clarice could do to annoy him. So filled with good cheer and a benevolent love for all mankind, that he was moved to offer his services when he heard Joey Zable saying they had to get Paula home before she became dead weight.

"That's okay, man. We got it," said Joey.

"I want to. It's the righteous thing to do."

"Do you know who she is?"

"Of course," Petey lied, not really caring who she was. "Seriously, there's nothing to worry about. I'm the only guy here who hasn't had a drop to drink," which was true, since he was concerned about adverse reactions between alcohol and the grab bag of pharmaceuticals he'd popped in his mouth before leaving the apartment.

Clarice agreed.

"Most definitely," she said, then to Paula, "You want me to take you home, don't you Paula."

"Of course I do," said Paula, grabbing Clarice in an embrace that nearly toppled the two of them into the barbecue.

"Then that's that," said Petey.

"I'm going home with them," said Paula to Joey.

"Not exactly, Paula," said Clarice, though nobody heard her.

Petey got between the two of them so they could walk arm and arm through the scattered clumps of party holdouts, down the front path to the sidewalk, past Avery and Johnny Lukeiwitz.

Johnny went to intercept them, but Avery pulled him back.

"She'll make it to the end of the block. After that it's Harlan's problem," he said to Johnny, who had to comply or risk Avery learning the only secret they had between them.

They actually didn't make it to the corner before Phil Anskeep identified Petey Amato. He immediately called Marty and Norm, who'd moved a few feet in from the corner.

"I got a bead on Amato, Chief. He's leaving the premises with his girlfriend and some other broad, who looks thoroughly loaded. And thoroughly stacked," he added to his partner, fortunately after he'd clicked off the send button on the radio.

When the three drew closer Anskeep got a better look at the broad. He grabbed the radio handset off the dashboard and switched the frequency to Romanovski's private channel.

"Correction on the second woman, Chief. I think it's Mrs. Harlan."

Norm snatched the radio out of Marty's hand.

"What the hell are you talking about, Officer?"

"Shit," whispered Anskeep before depressing the send button.

"Sir, I can see it plainly now. It looks like Petey Amato is escorting both Clarice Jorgensen and Paula Harlan, sir. Your wife."

Norm stared through the windshield of the unmarked car, his mouth slack. His mind raced through a catalog of potential catastrophes, sorted in a rough hierarchy. Even a diagnosis of a fatal disease didn't rise to this level. That would only mean death. This was humiliation. Much worse.

"Has any other officer seen Paula?" he asked Anskeep.

"No sir. The other car's at the end of the block."

"Good. Now listen. Paula's gone under cover to help with this case. This has to be on a need-to-know basis. You and your partner are under strict orders to keep this absolutely confidential, do you understand me?"

"Yes, sir."

"Any slip will be your professional ass."

"Yes, sir."

"You're a good man, Anskeep. I'm counting on you."

"With honor, sir."

He dropped the handset in his lap.

"God Almighty, Marty, what am I going to do?" he asked.

"Gee, I don't know, Norm. She really gone undercover?"

Norm looked at the chief through slitted eyes.

"She's gone fucking mad, is what she's gone. Always unstable. She probably got hooked on drugs. That hippie au pair must have slipped something in her drink. That's what those people do. There's no other explanation. It's satanic."

Marty started the car.

"What are you doing?" said Norm.

Marty looked puzzled.

"Going to pick her up."

"No, I can't talk to her now. I got to think."

"But she's getting turned into a dope fiend. Doesn't every minute count?"

"She's already past saving. I gotta think of my daughter."

"Gosh, Norm, you don't know what Amato's planning on doing to her. You're not considering kidnapping. We got this guy on the hot seat. He might be looking for a bargaining chip."

Norm put his head all the way down on the dashboard.

"You're right. Jesus."

Phil Anskeep came back on the radio.

"The three of them are now in the suspect's pickup truck. Do you want us to follow?"

"Negative, officer," Norm yelled into the radio. "We'll take it from here. Continue to surveil the scene."

Norm sat silently as they fell in behind the truck, following as it went around the next block and turned south on Ocean Avenue. He was rigid with anticipation. Marty kept a careful distance behind the other vehicle. They traveled at the speed limit through downtown, then by the new construction, and then into the sandy wastes of the salt mines.

"He's headed for the federal preserve," Norm whispered, not needing to remind Marty of the jurisdictional implications.

Only a few blocks from the gated entrance the truck's turn signal started blinking. Then the brake lights came on and it made a right turn.

"Isn't this your street, Norm?"

It was. Petey drove Paula right up the short drive. As Norm and Marty slid by they could see her wave at the other two through the windshield, and as she fumbled for her keys, they could hear her slurring out her thanks for a wonderful evening.

"You're the grooviest. I love you. Kiss, kiss."

And then, as she disappeared up the staircase that led to the first floor, something about wishing they could all be California girls.

CHAPTER
21

THE MOON was fat and round and hung above the Atlantic Ocean the way it does when it looks close enough to reach with a good hop. Jack stood on the balcony outside the Box and thought about giving it a try. The reflected moonlight on the sea below was a silver blue carpet. The waves were still growing, the rise and fall of the breakers merging into a continuous roar. The breeze had also grown considerably and shifted toward the north. There were stars visible beyond the glow of the moon, but a black band hid the horizon.

Gwendalynn came out of the Box with two cups of tea. Jack tried to make her take the all-weather recliner, but she said she wanted the chair. They sat quietly and drank their tea, Gwendalynn smoking and Jack humming under his breath.

"I want to ask you about you, but I don't want to pry," she said, finally. "But if I don't ask you'll think I'm not interested."

"Betwixt and between. I feel that way all the time."

"It figures I'd want to know more about the most private person in the known universe."

"You're talking about the Dalai Lama."

"The Dalai Lama doesn't live by himself in a humongous hotel. He talks to people and I'll bet he gets out of the temple once in a while to get a beer and play a little pool."

"The Dalai Lama didn't misplace four years of his life," said Jack.

"Comas make you anti-social? There I go prying again. Sorry."

"That's okay. You're curious. I don't blame you. You're being normal. I'm the one who isn't. I wasn't supposed to come out of it. They usually give you a little shot and call it a day. But my mother never believed the doctors. She put me in a place that does more than keep your body alive until it isn't anymore. Though who knows what really happened. One doctor told me the brain sometimes can rewire itself, if it has enough of the right parts available. Mine must have done that. But it took a while. I was awake before I could move, and then a little at a time, it came back. I couldn't speak for months, then I had to learn all the basic stuff you take for granted. One of the first things I could do, however, was swim. So that's what I did every day for hours. I don't know if that helped or hurt, but it was what I wanted to do. At least it made it easy to get a job as a lifeguard."

"What else do you do, like, during the year?"

"I read."

"They pay you to read?"

"Nobody pays me. It's not a job. I just read."

"Oh. That's cool."

"There was a big insurance payout and my mother already had a lot of money. I don't have to get a regular job, which is good because I can't do anything but swim, read and keep people from drowning."

"I'll bet there're jobs where all you have to do is read," said Gwendalynn, more cheerfully than she wanted to.

"Some of me came back. Not all."

"Oh."

"Colorblind people are rarely completely colorblind. They just can't see parts of the color spectrum, likes greens and reds. Imagine trying to explain to somebody who doesn't see red what red looks like. That's the closest I can get to explaining my mind. There are some things I should have that I don't, and I can't even comprehend what it would be like to have them."

"Just tell me like what, and I promise I won't ask you any more questions," she said.

He took a long sip of his tea.

"You don't have to," she said. "I'll just stop asking questions."

"This might fall into the category of 'be careful what you wish for.'"

"I know."

"I have trouble waking up from my dreams. They stay with me sometimes for the whole morning. That makes me a little anxious. Otherwise, I don't think I'm afraid of anything. Least of all death. Frankly, the idea of death is getting more attractive all the time. It's not that I want to die. I just don't know what makes me want to live. I'm indifferent to time. And space. I know that this balcony is smaller than Texas, but I don't feel the difference. I seek an orderly routine, but I don't care if it's unsettled. I care about people's well-being—their pain and suffering is upsetting to me. Though I'm not sure who 'me' is. I never feel lonely or alienated. I just feel here. Or sometimes there. I like all kinds of people, but I've felt no need to have any around me. This has made it seem impractical to form relationships. Though I'd try if I could figure out which part of me is supposed to do the relating."

Despite the northerly breeze, the air around Gwendalynn suddenly felt dense and weighted with import. For her, sense of space was not a problem. She knew exactly where she was, atop a massive old wreck of a misbegotten building, above the rumbling, infuriated sea, sitting beside a man of grace and misfortune.

She got up and sat on the floor next to the all-weather recliner, resting her head on his thigh.

"Life isn't so bad, you know," she said. "Death is probably just a bag of nothing. At least when you're alive something good can come of it."

"I like the thought," he said.

She stood up and took his hand, pulling him up from the all-weather recliner.

"Okay, I can't do much for your head, but let's see what I can do for the rest of you."

THERE WASN'T much left of the night, but what there was rapidly faded to black, blocking out the moon and stirring up the wind even more as it shifted again from the north to the northeast.

Some time before the muddy dawn Avery's phone rang. It was the Coast Guard officer he'd spoken to before, fulfilling his promise. Avery listened and nodded his head.

He settled the phone back in its cradle and got out of bed. He checked his watch, then set up the percolator to make a jug of coffee. It was an hour before his normal routine. He wasn't going back to sleep so he might as well put the time to good use.

He walked out on the landing at the top of the outdoor stairs that led to his apartment. He recognized the wind, its steady velocity punctuated by random gusts. And the jet-black sky. A classic nor'easter. According to the Coast Guard, fifty percent likely to hit Elysiana in less than twelve hours. All of the South Jersey coast could get some nasty weather, but given Elysiana's unique eastward thrust into the ocean, it was in the path of something on a whole different scale.

"Considering the winds we're clocking now, and the overall speed of the storm, and the likely trajectory," the Coastie had said, "it wouldn't be entirely inappropriate for me to use the word hurricane in this context."

Avery checked his watch again, impatient with the slow progress of time. He foresaw in his mind's eye all the things he'd have to accomplish in the next twenty-four hours, the commands to be made, the men to be deployed, the hard news to deliver across the island.

He stood on the landing with his coffee and waited, already staring down the storm, unyielding and eager to engage the opposition.

It was still dark when Ditzler woke to the sound of the wind whistling through the radio mast of the *Entropy V.* Having never heard that before he struggled to make sense of it. He felt the boat move abruptly to starboard, then snap back on the anchor.

That was when he knew.

He ran to the companionway and looked out. The ambient light from Elysiana showed giant wads of gray-black clouds racing toward the southwest. He checked the barometer, wind gauge and compass just to be sure. Then he went into the pilothouse and turned over the engine.

"What's up?" Sylvia called from below.

"Gotta go. Something's happening."

"What do you mean?"

"Something with the weather. Do me a favor and make sure everything's secured below. Including yourself. Keep a grip on something at all times."

"Sure, Skipper."

While the motor warmed up, he ran below and put on a pair of sneakers and grabbed a rain slicker. When he got back to the pilothouse he turned on the radio and tried to hail the marina, then the Coast Guard, with no luck.

He had Sylvia come up to man the helm and creep the boat forward while he reeled in the anchor. There was rarely much wave action out in the marshes, even with high winds, the maze of channels and islands of marsh grass having a natural dampening effect. What worried him was the three nautical mile's worth of Half Moon Bay they'd have to pass through to get to the marina, in a well-protected cove, but at the southern end of the bay. The Northern Channel was broad enough to let in the big ocean waves, and the wind from the northeast had the entire fetch of the bay to pile them into the entrance to the marina, the worst possible set of circumstances.

Sebbie's inflatable, Ditzler's transport from the night before, was tied to a cleat off the stern. Towing it back in these conditions wasn't an option, so Ditzler cut it loose and watched the wind carry it to the grassy shore.

He took back the helm and Sylvia went below to tie down the loose ends. He moved up the throttle on the motor and argued with himself over the options. It might be better just to stay put in the marsh. Though the anchor would likely drag out of the messy bottom when the wind rose above thirty knots, at which time they'd run aground. After that, the boat would bob up and down and smash its hull against the solid earth beneath the marsh grass.

The marina had docks. And moorings secured with concrete blocks and old V-8 engines. More importantly, he could get Sylvia off the boat.

"Did you tell Avery where you were staying?" he yelled down to her.

"I just said you got me a place that was safe and out of the way."

I have, thought Ditzler. At least one out of two.

The wind was testing its strength, going in random bursts from around fifteen knots to a little above twenty, then back again. Each time the gusts hit the *Entropy* she heeled over and the motor strained. This lit up another alarm in Ditzler's mind. The *Entropy* was a motor boat. No motor, no go.

He yelled to Sylvia to come back up again and retake the helm. He backed off the throttle just enough to reduce the sea motion without losing steerage, then as she took over, he ran for the spare jugs of gas and filled the tank, remembering how a partly filled fuel tank on a boat can be suddenly empty if you're half over on your side. Then he went to the engine compartment and looked at the ancient monster he and his father had rebuilt as carefully as they knew how, often making their own parts and guessing at tolerances specified in operating manuals long lost to time.

The belts were tight, no obvious leaks, and the sound was the same deafening, gasping clatter it always was. He kissed his fingers and laid the tips on the air cleaner cover, then shut the hatch.

"It's not so easy steering this thing with all that wind," Sylvia said when he retook the wheel. "So what's this, a thunderstorm?"

"More than that, I think. It could get a little rough. I think we should put on our lifejackets."

"Really."

"It's just a precaution. You're supposed to wear them all the time. We're a little lax on the *Entropy*."

"They're sort of scratchy."

"You get a ten percent discount on that Karma commitment if you do what I say and pretend it makes you happy."

She patted him on the cheek and went to get the lifejackets.

The sun, wherever it was behind the clouds, had risen, casting the palest of sinister gray lights across the earth. Overhead was an evil quilt of dark gray and smoky brown with bits of morning sunlight trying to shoot through. Ditzler checked his watch, then tried the marina again on the radio and was elated to hear Sebbie come back to him.

"So, the weather," said Ditzler. "What do we got?"

"Nor'easter. Come outta nowhere. Whole coast is scrambling. I think you should come on in."

"I'm coming. Do I dock her?"

"Yeah. I'll clear a slip in front of the office."

"What's the bay look like?" Ditzler asked.

"Chewed up. But I've seen worse."

"You've seen my boat."

"She can do it. Just don't get too close to the shoreline. Make an arc. Head out at about a twenty percent angle on the waves, then turn about and head in when the waves are about dead astern."

"Okay."

"Don't dillydally. This ain't the storm, it's just the previews."

Ditzler moved the throttle around to get the highest revs with the least vibration, tightened the big nut that held the wheel, threw loose stuff around the pilothouse into compartments, battened down the windscreen, shook out his neck and shoulders and yelled for more coffee.

Then he firmed up his grip on the wheel, spread his feet and set his shoulders to the wind.

A half hour later he turned the last corner of the channel and there was the bay, a dark angry washboard tipped in froth.

"Hey, Sylvia," he yelled to her.

"What?"

"I need you to come up here. Bring some pillows."

"We having a pajama party?"

"Yeah. Exactly."

He pulled back the throttle until she reached the pilothouse. He told her to wedge herself in the corner, using the pillows to make herself as comfortable as possible, and to find some handholds.

"We're back in the shit, aren't we Ditzler," she said.

"You like amusement parks?" he asked.

"Who doesn't like amusement parks?"

"Been on the Wild Mouse?"

"Oh, yeah."

"You like it?"

"Naturally."

"Well, here's the thing. The Wild Mouse only lasts about three minutes. You're about to get that same fantastic experience for about a half an hour. How about that, huh?"

"I'm a lucky girl."

He pushed the throttle forward and shoved the *Entropy* out of the channel. They immediately went nearly straight up in the air, then came down again with a crash, water spraying from either side of the hull. Then they were pushed to starboard and the stern lifted to port. Ditzler spun the wheel to port to get the bow back in position just in time to climb the next steep wave and crash back down the other side. Every joint in the little boat began to squeak and groan, and other sounds from below, unidentifiable, rose in raucous complaint.

Ditzler resisted the urge to push the throttle further forward. It wouldn't do any good, only increase the load on the motor and add cavitation as the boat crested a wave and the prop lifted up through the froth.

Ditzler spun and held the wheel, then turned it back again as he struggled to keep the bow at a steady angle to the onrush of the surf, larger and more powerful than anything he'd ever seen on the ocean, and far more difficult to navigate given the tight frequency of the wave pattern. The bow of the boat would barely reach the trough when another wave was upon it, breaking over the bowsprit and smashing into the pilothouse, washing the foredeck in sudsy green water.

He tightened his grip on the wheel and loosened his shoulders. His legs pistoned with the rocking of the cockpit floor. Every few minutes he'd misread the movement and be tossed into the walls of the pilothouse. His right knee and forehead were bleeding, but he didn't lose hold of the wheel and the *Entropy* kept responding like the gallant little derelict he knew her to be.

"Ditzler, this is like much worse than the Wild Mouse," said Sylvia, unsteadily, from her spot on the floor of the pilothouse.

"Sorry. The weather can fool you sometimes."

"Are we done for?"

"No. just a little inconvenienced."

He smiled down at her, daring to take his eyes off the waves long enough to see her face, rigid with dread, her eyes wide and mouth open in a silent scream.

Following Sebbie's advice, he struck out on a northerly course, which he held for almost twenty minutes before looking back toward the bay shore. He'd caught sight of the red and green buoys outside the channel to the marina bobbing crazily in the water. The boat wasn't quite where Sebbie hoped it would be, but he thought, close enough.

"It's gonna get worse, and then it's gonna get better," he said to Sylvia.

"Worse? You're shittin' me."

He waited for a little extra space between waves, but after a few minutes realized he wasn't going to get it.

"Hold on," he said to Sylvia and spun the wheel hard to starboard.

The *Entropy* rose up into the air and heeled hard over, slamming Ditzler into the bulkhead and lifting the propeller out of the water, causing the motor to over-rev and stall out.

The rage of the wind and water seemed incomplete without the sound of the motor. Still glued to the wheel, Ditzler spun the stern into the oncoming torrent and held firm as the *Entropy* came around and surfed down the face of a wave.

The next wave bore the boat off on a different course. Ditzler corrected the wheel and they flew down into the trough. Jack had often taken him and the old wooden surf boat out in big water to ride the waves. Ditzler was always the stern man, the one who popped the oar out of the oarlocks and slid it down the gunwale, converting the oar into a rudder as the boat was caught by the breaking wave and hurtled forward.

This was the same concept, he thought, only the rudder was built right in, and while you were riding the waves you could drink coffee and chat with a terrified woman lying on the floor next to you.

"We're surfing, baby," he said to her. "Hangin' keel."

"I might vomit, okay?"

"Out the door if you can. Don't want to slip."

Ditzler turned the key for the motor and it restarted. He gently moved the throttle forward, bringing the prop into service to help maintain steerage, though most of the forward velocity was provided by the waves.

The channel buoys were hard to keep track of as they rose and fell behind the waves. A challenge made harder by the need to stay locked on the unpredictable wave action that was growing as they approached the shore.

He finally got a clear view of the red nun and eased the boat to port just enough, he hoped, to avoid broaching and still hit the mark. He goosed up the throttle to increase control and began chanting a hymn taught to him by the old man in the hut in Thailand.

"Are we gonna make it?" Sylvia asked from the floor, weakly. "If we're not, I have to start asking forgiveness for everything. I got a lot to ask for, so it'll take a while. Just want to know in advance, if I can."

"We're going to make it. It just doesn't feel that way."

"I'm going to start asking anyway. Can't hurt."

Ditzler found himself repeating that question—are we gonna make it?—within his mind, over and over. To which he answered, of course, naturally, why wouldn't we?

That was when he noticed the *Entropy* having trouble holding her bow forward in the steepening waves. With a relatively shallow keel, most of the responsibility for holding course was born by the rudder, which would lose all contact with the water when the wave crests slipped under the stern.

After a few minutes of this, Ditzler realized that he'd just gone beyond the limit of his and the boat's capabilities, and that the last hundred yards, the worst as Sebbie predicted, were outside their powers to traverse.

It was impossible to send the boat down the channel between the buoys and still keep the waves parallel to his stern. It was one or the other. Which meant either broach and capsize, or run aground on the rocks where the waves would pound the *Entropy* into soggy toothpicks.

He took a deep breath and dropped his shoulders and jaw. He thought of a broad green lawn and a mother stroking the brow of her newborn baby. He thought about his Alfa, and how it accelerated in second and third gears. And his mother's lasagna, the toast of his dormitory when twenty pounds of it would arrive in a cardboard box. He thought these things to make his mind happy and confident.

Composed.

CHAPTER
22

THE NATIONAL Weather Service told Mayor Black it was probably a good idea to evacuate the island. The storm was doing something storms sometimes do—acting entirely counter to expectations. They weren't sure why, but it was likely something related to a shift in the jet stream, which lessened the prevailing high pressure zone that usually kept these storms off the northeast coast. Or something in the Gulf Stream, which had also moved a little to the north, and was feeding tropical depressions into the North Atlantic, and somehow this nor'easter devoured a chunk of that energy. Or some combination of the two, along with the fact that weather sometimes just did what it wanted to do.

The net result, however, was a nor'easter that looked, acted and felt just like a regular hurricane, that was probably going to spare all but a thin slice of the Jersey Shore. The Elysiana slice.

"Lot of probabilities," said the mayor.

"Probabilities are what we do here, sir."

The mayor told his wife to stand down on the bacon and eggs, that he had to go to Borough Hall right away for an emergency meeting. But he'd take a thermos of her best fresh ground coffee.

"Meanwhile, I want you to pack up enough for a couple days and drive to Jed and Julie's. Gladwyne is probably far enough away from this thing."

"What thing?"

"A storm. A humdinger, headed straight for Elysiana."

"Mercy."

While he dressed he called Avery, who wasn't home, and Norm Harlan, who wasn't either. Avery had left for the opera house an hour before, and Norm was sleeping in his office, or trying to sleep through a torment of rage, confusion and self-pity.

He got to both of them on the second try.

"I've already spoken to Avery," said the mayor to Norm. "He wants to meet at the opera house so he can stay close to his men."

Oh, really, thought Harlan. And does he want the mayor to bring him some hot tea and a bowl of porridge?

"Roger that, Mayor Black," he said. "I'll get the word to Romanovski. Anyone else?"

"Get Charlie Abramson. We'll need his road crews and parks people in on this."

"Roger that, too."

"You got half an hour."

"Roger and out," said Norm, and hung up.

"Asshole," said the mayor as the phone went dead.

"Buffoon," said Norm.

JOHNNY LUKEIWITZ met Avery in the parking lot below the opera house and followed him upstairs to the office. They'd been here before, in 1960, when Hurricane Donna came to call. There was a lot of damage to downtown and a boatful of fishermen were lost in Half Moon Bay, but nobody drowned in the ocean. Still, the storm was a lesson on how hard it is to control events on the ground in the face of uncontrollable weather.

Johnny had called the other lieutenants, but they agreed it was fruitless to try bringing in the rest of the beach patrol early. They'd be there on time—it was part of the covenant to hit roll call the day after an unofficially sanctioned party. Most didn't have phones in their squalid apartments and house shares, and given Randy and Baxter's party, half would be sleeping somewhere else anyway.

It also gave Johnny and Avery time to deploy the Jeeps and meet with the borough people. They'd have simple instructions for the Jeep squads. Nobody goes in the water. And if Avery has his way with Elysiana officialdom, nobody goes near it. That was the biggest problem with Donna. Tourists wanting the see the ocean in all its manic majesty, thinking it would be like a theme park, or watching a documentary on TV. Trying to hold people back from the water's edge was a dangerous distraction to the guards, who told them a surge could inundate the whole beach without warning in seconds. The water wouldn't look any different, it just wouldn't stop where it was supposed to.

"This time we put extra Jeeps up in the mines," said Avery. "Pull the guards out of there, except for the last two, and concentrate foot patrols downtown and next to the Northern Channel, keep them close enough to see each other signal and hear run whistles."

"Agreed. I also think we should press other four-wheel drives into service. There're about four among the guards. And parks has a four-wheel-drive pickup."

"We'll talk to the mayor," said Avery.

They went through a hatch up to the roof to take in the situation. The ocean was a disorganized mess. While there were two nominal breaks, the churning surface was almost a continuum from water's edge all the way out to sea. They knew this was partly the perspective from the opera house, that at beach level you'd make out a rough pattern reflecting the contours of the seabed, the rise and fall of gulley and bar. For now. A serious storm surge would make all that irrelevant.

They were leaning on the galvanized railing when the mayor came up out of the hatch. He wore a yellow windbreaker and hadn't shaved, an unusual informality that spoke to his concern.

"What do you think, gentlemen?" he asked, his hands in the pockets of the windbreaker, his eyes on the sea.

"Nobody knows," said Avery. "But it feels serious."

"That's my feeling," said Mayor Black. "I took a pass by Half Moon Bay on the way over. It's erupting."

"I want to close Ocean Avenue," said Avery, in a firm, flat voice. "Keep the beaches totally clear."

"I want to close Elysiana," said the mayor. "I already have Romanovski's men on the causeway turning back traffic."

"All the better," said Johnny. "This time of year there're too many of them and not enough of us. We have to shrink the population, get 'em out of here, and keep those that stay indoors."

"I said I want to, not that I really can," said the mayor. "To make it official the governor would have to declare this an emergency, which he won't do until it is. But we can run around acting like he already has, and that'll help. What we can't do is stop the general population from doing what it wants to do. For a lot of those folks a big storm is nothing but an opportunity to behave like idiots."

They were distracted by vehicles pulling into the parking lot on the other side of the boardwalk. It was Marty, Norm and Charlie. They went back downstairs to gather around a folding table in the office that functioned as a staging area for coffee and sticky buns in the morning and tuna hoagies and cheese steaks after that.

"We can't do it," was Norm's immediate reaction to Avery's proposal to close Ocean Avenue. "Even if we wanted to, I don't have the men."

"I do," said Avery. "I can deploy three-quarters of the patrol to the streets and still have plenty to cover the beaches, since we'll be checking most of the public at the border."

It looked like three-quarters of Norm's blood supply rose to his face.

"No, no, no, and no. Marty?" he looked over at the chief.

"Affirmative on Norm's no," he said.

Norm supported his objections with a battery of underlying legal, social and political principles that he rattled off as if rehearsed, which it was since they formed the basis of an obsessive internal monologue. He seemed to elevate out of his seat and hover over the table as he warmed to his subject.

"We're not maintaining order in the Borough of Elysiana by destroying the very foundations of responsible municipal governance," he declared, in conclusion.

In the silence that followed the sound of the howling ocean slowly intruded. Avery took a piece of gum out of his pocket and started to chew.

"Well," said the mayor. "Excellent tutorial, Norm. Especially helpful under these circumstances. Why don't you get yourself comfortable again and I'll let you all know what we're going to do."

Norm sat down and glared at Charlie Abramson, something he found easier to do than glaring at Avery. Charlie responded the way he always did, with a wide, raffish grin, the expression he used for every occasion, whether you were telling him a joke or the news of his mother's sudden death.

"Ocean Avenue stays open, but the beaches are closed," said the mayor. "Post signs at every entrance to that effect, with a note that violating the restriction will result in arrest. Avery's men enforce it on the beach side, Marty's on the street. Marty's officers will cruise every street in Elysiana with bullhorns telling people we expect very dangerous conditions with destructive winds and flooding, and they are strongly advised to evacuate. But nobody's forced to go. My guess is most of them will take us up on the advice.

"Keep turning people away at the bridge, but also shut down the off-ramps at the parkway and open up both lanes of the causeway to off-island flow. That'll clear us out in half the time. While we do that, Charlie needs to call in whatever favors he's got with people on the mainland to lend us some big trucks for our fleet, preferably filled with sand in case we need to dam off critical facilities, like the power transformer or the borough offices, which must remain operational. While you're at it, see how many four-wheel drives you can muster. Avery'll need the extra capacity, especially down in the mines.

"Get the power company and Bell out here with whatever they can spare. They won't be able to do much if the feeds from the mainland go down, but from what they're telling me we're going to take the brunt, which might mean a lot of local failures they could stay on top of.

"Downtown's almost at sea level, the lowest spot on the island after the mines, but without the dunes to protect it. Avery'll drag at least a half dozen surf boats up on the boardwalk to use for rescue if the surge floods the area. Marty, the bay constables should also be prepared to join in that effort, giving land-based emergencies priority over saving fools who think this is a good time to go fishing.

"Norm, you're in touch with the local HAM operators."

"Yes, sir."

"Enlist volunteers to transfer communications between Avery's men and Marty's. And with Charlie's. Get the frequencies and pass them out to all three services.

"Norm, the moment the storm hits call every state emergency assistance agency you can think of and order up fresh water, tents, rations, blankets, whatever they have. They'll tell you the governor has to make the declaration to release the goods, but it can't hurt to be at the head of the line. I'll do what I can with my contacts as well, but that'll be more top down."

Norm caught the inference, but continued to jot down his instructions.

Mayor Black spread both hands out flat on the table and looked around the room.

"Any questions?"

Marty raised his hand.

"What do we do about looters, sir?" he asked.

"Shoot 'em," said the mayor, in a way that discouraged additional questions.

Johnny's lieutenants were coming in as the group broke up and set off to execute their various tasks. He handed out specific orders and in minutes the Jeeps were fired up and on their way out to the beaches. This break in the routine was immediately noticed by Jack Halcyon, who was trying to stand on the balcony outside the Box and sip his first cup of Chock full o'Nuts coffee. As wind velocity tends to increase with elevation, Jack was already experiencing what would take several hours to reach the rest of the island. From the greater height he could also see the ocean's chaotic wave pattern, featuring breakers that started twice the normal distance from the beach.

He wrapped an arm around a stanchion at the edge of the balcony and took a sip of coffee. Gwendalynn came up from behind and grabbed him around the waist.

"Is it often this breezy?" she yelled in his ear.

"Never," he yelled back. "It's a storm."

"What kind of storm?"

"I think the bad kind."

"You're really worried about this," she said.

Jack didn't know how to explain to her that an aircraft carrier, the USS Enterprise, was floating above the beach between the ocean and the Imperial Hotel. That in and of itself wasn't the issue. It was all the alarm bells and klaxons going off on deck, the frenzied dash to secure airplanes and batten down hatches. It wasn't a good sign.

"You better get to the Harlans'. Wait for my call. And everything you want me to say about last night I'm thinking. I'm not good at expressing some things, but you're going to teach me how," he said, and soon after left her to finish off the coffee and ruminate over why every male thinks it's his special curse to be unable to properly express his intimate feelings, brain damaged or not.

GWENDALYNN'S TRIP to the mines confirmed what Jack was saying. The first evidence was cops with bullhorns warning people to flee the island before it was too late. She observed that all the bullhorn voices had the same familiar pitch and intensity, as if they'd been trained by the people who directed bullhorn yellers in the movies.

Catching snatches of radio reports coming from various patrol cars and maintenance trucks, she gathered the gist. A big storm was coming that might involve wind and flooding bad enough to destroy homes and buildings, and could cause loss of life, a gentle euphemism, in Gwendalynn's mind. She saw herself in charge of instructing the public: "Get out of Dodge or you're dead, you dopes!"

Nevertheless, she was among that percentage the Elysiana officials had predicted would want to stick around, not for the experience, but for the sake of a seven-year-old girl.

"Oh Jesus God, you're here," said Paula, rushing down the stairs to the parking area under the house as Gwendalynn pulled up in the old Dodge. "Marty Romanovski called and said we're all going to be swept into the sea."

"Probably not his exact words."

"That's what he meant."

"Where's Sweetie?" Gwendalynn asked.

"Locked in her room," said Paula, gathering her robe against the nagging wind.

"You're kidding."

"I can't take chances today. The Kimballs have already left for Philadelphia. They woke me up and dropped her right on my bed, if you can believe that. Then Marty called. It's like a nightmare. No, it *is* a nightmare. An actual one."

"Gwendalynn, do you want some coffee?" Sweetie called down from the balcony above.

"How did you get out of there?" Paula yelled.

"You're probably in the safest part of the island, up on stilts and behind the dunes," said Gwendalynn. "But it wouldn't be a bad idea for you and Sweetie to get out of here. You'll still get the wind and there's a lot of glass in your house. Go inland, or up to Philly. Stay with friends or family, like your aunt."

"She's dead. I don't have any friends or family left anywhere but here. Oh, God, I have nowhere to go."

She spun around and ran back up the stairs, clutching her bathrobe to her chest and huffing out big breaths of air with every step. Gwendalynn realized that after last night she probably didn't feel too special. No wonder the Kimballs had to get all the way to her bedroom to wake her up.

Gwendalynn found Sweetie in the kitchen putting slices of cheese on a half pound of burger frying in the skillet.

"It's all I could find," said Sweetie, guiltily. "You can have some."

"It's all yours, kid. Coffee's all I need."

Right then a big gust hit the house with a low thud that trailed off into a shudder. They could hear Paula screaming in the bedroom. Sweetie looked up from the skillet and out the window.

"Gwendalynn?"

"Chop-chop with that burger, young lady. We need to keep moving."

"Where we going?"

"You'll know when we get there."

She went to find Paula, who was immersed in her closet, swimming through hanging skirts, blouses and flare-bottom slacks.

"What do you wear to your own violent death?" she asked Gwendalynn.

"Something sturdy. You could be in the same clothes for a while. Stuff a suitcase if you can. Bring your makeup. And medication if you have any," she added, remembering what she'd heard from the bullhorns.

The wind picked that moment to strip the TV antenna off the roof and fling it clattering to the ground. To Paula the sound might as well have been the roof coming off. She picked up the pace.

Gwendalynn left her and went to check on Sweetie and grab a garbage bag, which she took to the girl's room to fill with clothes, a few books, and indispensable stuffed animals.

When she got back to the kitchen, Sweetie was eating her hamburger at the dining room table set with formal table service and a brace of candles straddling her mother's best placemat.

"Didn't you tell me you like to eat in the car?" Gwendalynn asked.

"When we buy food on the mainland, mommy gives me Tasty-kakes to eat on the way home."

"So bring that burger and let's go ridin'."

They drove Paula's Chevelle and left the old Dodge behind to what Paula declared was a certain death. Sweetie, on hearing this, hugged the bulbous fender and thanked the car for its noble service.

Gwendalynn drove so Paula could lean her head against the window with her overnight bag held close to her chest, moaning softly. Sweetie sat between them and fiddled with the radio, which had given itself over entirely to ominous weather predictions. The words "Elysiana" and "evacuate" came up so often Gwendalynn made her turn it off.

"Okay, okay, we get the picture," she said.

As they entered downtown, Gwendalynn made a detour to see the woman who gave her a free meal and advice on lipstick.

"Oh, go on, there's nothing to worry about," the woman told Gwendalynn. "I was here for Donna in '60 and the Great Atlantic of '44. Those were storms. They're gone and I'm still here."

"They seem pretty serious about this one."

"Only 'cause they know it's coming. In the old days you didn't know till it was at your throat. Didn't have time to get all nervous about it. Better that way."

"Okay. That's a perspective."

Gwendalynn reached over the counter and took the woman's pen out of her apron. Then she wrote a phone number on a napkin and slid it across.

"If you change your mind and need a safe place to stay, call this number. I'll come get you."

The woman looked at the number.

"Where'zis?"

"The unsinkable Imperial Hotel."

Paula looked vaguely panicked when Gwendalynn got back to the car.

"You were gone a long time. I was getting worried," she said.

"I was gone about five minutes."

"Yes, but the wind. It's getting worse. Look at those road signs. Do you think the car will flip over?"

Gwendalynn drove back to Ocean Avenue, then had another thought. She asked Sweetie to help her mother stay calm while they made a couple more stops.

"A couple? Look at that rain. It's going sideways."

She stopped at the SeaSide Deli and bought the last four gallons of water and two boxes full of canned goods, a half dozen bags of potato chips, assorted nuts, a box of ginger snaps, a case of Schmidt's and as much block ice as she could fit in the trunk of the Chevelle.

"Did you get Tastykakes?" Sweetie asked.

The next stop was another backtrack, inspired by the sight of empty beer kegs in the alley next to the deli.

Since Randy and Baxter's street had already been evacuated, they were a leg up on the rest of the island. With the exception of the nuts across the street, who were still on the front porch watching through their binoculars.

The swirling blossoms of charcoal gray cloud above diffused the sunlight into a smoldering, shadowless gloom. There was barely enough light to see the bodies scattered about the lawn or sitting cross-legged in tight clusters, which Gwendalynn knew from experience had been there rapping since the height of the party.

It almost made her woozy to think about.

She wished she had a set of handcuffs to secure Paula and Sweetie to the car, but had to rely on blind faith.

"This is not a time to explore for ice cream," she said pointedly to Sweetie.

Gwendalynn reluctantly left them and picked her way across the lawn, stepping on islands of grass in a sea of paper cups, empty cigarette packs, plastic bags, flip-flops, half-eaten burgers, clam shells, chicken bones, local Pennysavers, T-shirts, bras, athletic equipment, gym shorts, corncobs, hair brushes, Tampax tubes, paper bags, hotdogs, sneakers, strings of beads, tubes of lipstick and small kitchen appliances.

And the occasional human being, whose pulse she'd check before moving on.

She pushed the front screen door through another mountain of debris and entered the fumy, brackish atmosphere inside the cottage. The dreary light outside did little to penetrate the interior. She carefully felt her way through the living room to the kitchen, which was surprisingly clear of casualties, though the walls and ceiling were almost as thoroughly decorated with organic matter as it was the last time she'd scrubbed it off.

She went back to the living room and looked up the stairs, sighing with reluctance.

Randy spared her, somewhat, by appearing naked at the top of the stairs.

"Did you lose your clothes?" she called up.

"My house, my dress code."

"Checked the weather lately?"

"It's windy."

"It's a hurricane. They're trying to evacuate the island. You gotta wake everybody up and get them out of here."

"Hurricane. Dig it. How big?"

"Big enough," said Gwendalynn.

"Of course. The waves we've had. And it's coming here."

He disappeared for a moment, then came back in his baggies. He trotted down the stairs with the surfboard held like a shield in front of him.

"You're kidding."

"You're in my way."

Gwendalynn stepped back down the stairs.

"What about all the people here? They need to know what's going on."

"So tell them," he said, trotting down the front path and out to the sidewalk, turning right and heading for the ocean.

Gwendalynn looked up at the sky and then around the lawn. She took a rough count of about thirty people, and blanched at the thought of counting the ones in the house. She went back to the car and was grateful to find Sweetie and her mother still aboard. She swung open their doors.

"Okay, time for Paul Revere. Sweetie takes everybody on the lawn who's awake and capable of making eye contact. I'll revive the comatose. Paula takes the house. Tell them the Apocalypse is on the way and to seek higher ground. This shack will go over in half the wind they're talking about. If they can't get off the island and have nowhere else to go, they can follow us to the Imperial."

It wasn't the quality warning she would have liked, but they were stretched for time. She assumed they'd heard the bullhorns and by reflex ignored the message, distrusting any official communication. She hoped the three of them would be a more credible source. So she did her best, and at least when she pulled the Chevelle away from the curb her conscience was only partly cloudy.

As they drew closer to the Imperial she began to wonder if Jack would welcome refugees at his hotel. If her judgment of him was correct, he would. She needed her judgment in this to be flawless. Ergo, she decided the question itself was a non sequitur and stopped thinking about it.

"I'd heard there was some maniac living here alone," said Paula as they approached. "I didn't know it was our lifeguard."

"Maniac is too strong a word."

"I'd believe it of the other one. Black toenails, for Pete's sake."

JACK HAD given up all preconceived notions about Mike Ditzler, except to believe him to be very disciplined and responsible, and therefore highly unlikely to miss roll call at the morning muster. When Johnny Lukeiwitz got to the "D's" he gracefully slipped past Ditzler to avoid public notice of the absence, and when he was finished stalked over to Jack's perch on the sailcloth to find out what was what.

"Christ, Jack, where is he?"

"I don't know," said Jack. "He's staying over at Sea Star Marina. Maybe the road's washed out."

"They got boats."

"I don't know. Can't be good."

"I'm assigning you to check on the marina on your way to the mines. Check fast and haul ass back to the beach. We want solid coverage on the southern flank."

"Thanks."

Johnny went back to his position next to Avery to give instructions—coverage assignments, communications protocols, rules of engagement with civilians, a fairly detailed brief, though all boiling down to: keep everybody on the island alive without getting killed yourself.

Johnny never had trouble holding everyone's attention, especially with Avery standing next to him. It was even easier that morning, as they all strained to hear his soft voice over the wail of wind and water and clattering window sashes and doors, and the frantic flapping of the U.S., New Jersey and Elysiana Borough flags that Johnny had raised on the roof of the opera house as he did every morning.

As the guards heading for remote beaches began to disperse out of the parking lot, the sign for Hank's Arcade took a brief flight down to Ocean Avenue, disintegrating in the air and cascading down on the guards' cars and Jack's panel truck, smashing into his left front fender, bending the metal into the wheel.

He was behind a Ford Falcon with a two-by-four protruding from the rear window, which he helped extract and then used to bend the fender off the tire tread. By then the other guards had cleared the road and pushed undriveable cars out of the way.

No one had much to say as they worked, struck sober by the portentous start to the day, made more so by the sign itself, a famous survivor of Donna in 1960, the oft-named "Hurricane of the Century" on the Jersey Shore.

Johnny had heard the sign tear away and crash into the cars, and had run down to help clear, reassign rides and assess cuts and contusions. He spared Jack from driving another guard to the beach.

"Go. Send me word when you can."

The trip to the Sea Star Marina meant a quick run across the slender island, then a sharp turn left to the south down Half Moon Avenue. As he drove he felt better about his washed-out-road theory. Built only a few feet above normal high tide, the road looked like it was inches from disappearing under the rippling marsh water.

Focused as he was on the pavement, he didn't notice the condition of the bay until reaching a breakwater where the view was unavoidable.

"Jesus."

As the truck drove into open air the wind socked the side panels and seawater sprayed across the windshield. He downshifted to gain control and punched the accelerator. After passing the boat launch he could see the marina, and the unmistakable flash of red and yellow emergency lights.

He blocked an ambulance coming out of the marina entrance. The driver's glower softened when he saw the beach patrol jacket and swim trunks. Jack jumped out of the trunk and ran up to the ambulance.

"What's going on?"

"They refused treatment," said the driver. "Fine with me. They looked okay."

"Who's they?"

"See for yourself. I've got other things to do" he said, looking pointedly at Jack's truck blocking the way.

There was a patrol car and one of Charlie's big trucks parked up against the docks facing the channel to Half Moon Bay. Jack raced toward them, part of his mind registering the sight of sailboats rocking and bobbing wildly in their slips, elegant towering masts flicked by the merciless wind, their hulls battered from underneath, betrayed by the normally placid little harbor.

Before Jack could reach the channel-side docks someone stepped out in front of the truck and held up his hand.

Ditzler.

Jack jumped out of the truck.

"Hey, what've you been doing?" he asked Ditzler, pointing to the bright red and blue contusion on his right cheek.

"Getting shipwrecked. You?"

"Avery wants us on the beach ten minutes ago."

"I'll get my stuff."

Jack noticed Ditzler's left arm hanging loosely at his side as he walked off toward the marina offices.

"Hey, you're hurt," Jack called after him.

"I can walk," Ditzler called back.

Soon they were back on Half Moon Avenue, guessing at where to drive as the marsh water by now had obscured the road surface. The panel truck had a high road clearance, but there was the danger of slipping off the shoulder and into the drink. Ditzler braced himself against the dashboard and hummed "Surfin' USA."

"Is Avery pissed?" he asked Jack.

"He doesn't know. Johnny ran air cover. What the hell happened?"

Ditzler didn't know exactly where to start, but did his best to put a foundation under the story, beginning with Sylvia's flashy arrival at the Sea Star Marina at the beginning of the summer.

"So this guy, who says he knows this woman Annie, but she doesn't know, pulls you out of the water," said Jack.

"Him and Sebbie. Don't forget it was Sebbie's boat, with him at the helm. All the guy did was haul us into the cockpit."

"So you were on Annie's boat?"

"It's actually my boat. Mine and my dad's. We just lent it to Annie, who's name isn't actually Annie, 'cause she's incognito hiding from her husband, who'd kill her if he knew she'd fallen in love with another man, which he may or may not know by now. She'd been in my apartment, but needed a little fresh air, so hence the boat, which was a fine concept until this storm came in and I didn't know if the anchor would hold in that mucky bottom. Plus I had to get back to make roll call, so I thought we better make a run for it."

"You made the right choice," said Jack. "You gotta respect nature, she's a tricky old bitch."

"She is indeed."

DITZLER HAD made the decision to aim for the channel opening on the theory that surviving a broach was more likely than a full out encounter with the shore, where they would have been crushed in minutes against the rocks. As the *Entropy* started to turn up into the wind, her beam parallel to the wave, Ditzler caught sight of a boat, it's hull in full view as it flew over the chop, trying to make way out into the channel.

Holding firmly to the wheel, he used his other hand to pull Sylvia to her feet. He kissed her face.

"Get on the high side," he yelled into her ear. "When I tell you, jump."

"Into the water?"

"Our chances are better there. The boat'll roll. Trust me."

He gripped the neck of her lifejacket and held her against the port rail. As the boat lost its forward heading, it heeled more and more to its starboard side. Jack had the rudder pinned to the limits, but the bow refused to budge. Water started splashing over the gunwales into the cockpit.

Then the *Entropy* seemed to give up the fight. Ditzler felt the balance under his feet shift irrevocably toward the onrushing water, which started to flow into the cockpit.

He let go of the wheel and grabbed Sylvia's lifejacket with both hands, lifted her off her feet and flung her over the side. The tumbling boat knocked him backwards toward the boarding seas, but a lucky grab on the pilothouse doorjamb stopped him short so he was able to scramble back on his feet, claw his way to the port side and dump himself over the railing just as the boat capsized, rolling him down the hull and into the clutching embrace of Half Moon Bay.

It was worse than he thought it would be in the water, even with the lifejacket holding him slightly above the turbulence. It wasn't the big waves as much as the little chop that slapped him around, splashing in his mouth and up his nose, stinging his eyes. But he could see Sylvia, close enough to reach in a few strong strokes, her face a mask of struggle, terror and determination. He grabbed her lifejacket at a loop behind her neck and convinced her to roll over and let him drag her on her back. It was the only chance he had of making headway against the roiling bay water.

And he did, until he saw the power boat again, this time almost on top of them. He yelled in alarm and was greeted by the sight of Sanford Goettlewing leaning over the coaming with a long dock hook in his hand. For several long minutes the boat and the two in the water did a type of ballet, swinging up and away from each other, then rushing back down into the trough; then as the hook was nearly in reach, darting off in the opposite direction. Ditzler caught sight of Sebbie at the wheel, fighting to maintain a steady position, looking anxiously over the coaming and back toward the whirling propellers.

After a half dozen tries, the hook was suddenly over Ditzler's head. He grabbed it and held on, even as the ball at the end of his upper arm pulled out of the socket and snapped back again when Goettlewing yanked them up against the topsides. He got a grip on Ditzler's lifejacket and in one fierce heave pulled him, with Sylvia in tow, up and into the cockpit.

Sebbie immediately spun the boat stern to wind and pushed up the throttle. Ditzler and Sylvia banged around the cockpit floor, awkward in their lifejackets and weakened to the point of paralysis. Goettlewing steadied Sylvia, then Ditzler, and grinned down on them.

"I like the black hair," he said to Sylvia. "Suits you better."

With the wind, waves and current hard on the stern, Sebbie shot through the channel and into the little marina harbor, and ultimately tied up at a slip in front of the offices and Ditzler's apartment.

A paramedic and a couple guys from Charlie's road crew who'd heard a distress call from Sebbie were waiting at the dock.

While Ditzler and Sylvia were engaged with the first responders, Goettlewing took off in his GTO. Sylvia looked at Ditzler's puzzled face. "Don't ask me," said Sylvia. "You're the boy genius on the team."

"Maybe there's another damsel in distress."

Then Jack showed up. Ditzler told Sebbie to pretend he never saw the girl after he let her into the apartment upstairs. It wasn't a hard sell. There was plenty to keep the marina owner occupied.

THE WIND took a reckless swipe at the truck as they started across the island toward the beach. More debris was tumbling over the ground and filling up the air. Branches, sand and spits of rain smacked against the windshield.

"I can barely move my left arm," said Ditzler. "I hope that doesn't interfere with the day's responsibilities."

"Let's get square with Johnny. Then you ought to get that looked at."

Ditzler had already rigged a sling made from a torn T-shirt. He felt nauseated, which might have been a touch of shock. He decided to ignore it till it went away.

They found some relief from the wind when they reached Ocean Avenue, which ran close to the dunes, providing some buffer from the fury of the nor'easter. The penalty was an increase in flying objects, mostly branches and leaves and unidentifiable things thudding against the side of the truck.

A red beach patrol Jeep came toward them down Ocean Avenue. It held Joey Zable and a nervous rookie trying to appear bored by the whole thing.

"You guys are late," Joey yelled over the racket from the wind.

"Better late than dead," said Ditzler.

"Not according to Avery."

"How's the beach?"

"What beach?"

"The one next to the ocean."

"Not there. And we're two hours off high tide."

"Where'd it go?" asked Ditzler.

"Into the sea. If the dunes weren't there we'd be having this conversation under water."

"So what're we guarding?"

"Avery's unbroken record of non-fatalities."

"Okay," said Jack.

"We've intercepted a half-dozen shoobies already this morning. It's a suicide's holiday."

"This is the mines. Nobody comes here even in good weather."

"We'll be back to check on you in a few hours. That's when the storm is supposed to hit."

"Supposed to hit?"

"Shit, man, this is just the previews," said Joey. "Showtime's at thirteen hundred hours. Better get an anchor for that old bucket you're driving."

He pulled away, leaving Jack and Ditzler with something to mull over.

"Let's go see if we still have a guard stand and a boat. Then take it from there," said Jack.

They pushed the truck through the wind to their usual parking spot, only this time Jack backed in, as if that made them safer.

The air outside had turned semi-solid. The first task was to get the doors open, themselves out of the truck, and the doors shut again. Then the long march across the dunes, over the narrow path, heads down, eyes mostly closed against the pelting, sandy rain. A few times one or the other stopped, astonished at being flung off the path by a gust of wind, then regaining balance and pressing on. It was too hard to hear over the noise, so they stopped trying to talk.

Twenty minutes later they were nearly through the dunes, their progress halted by the bow of the big wooden surf boat proudly docked in the sand.

"Wow," said Ditzler.

"Let's pull her further in," Jack yelled, and they grabbed the oarlocks and dragged the old scow nearly to the top of a grassy mound at the foot of the towering dunes.

The effort was all Ditzler had left, so when Jack said it was far enough he lay down in the dune grass and fantasized about never getting up again.

"You okay?" Jack asked.

"Been worse."

"I'll go check on the stand. You wait here."

Jack half slid back down the dune, shoving his way through the wind, now almost directly on his nose.

He was met by the sight of colossal rolling mounds of foamy water, the sound from which explained why they could barely hear each other. There was a lot of confusion out there, but he could see defined breaks, maybe four, starting far out to sea and reaching to the new waterline, now kissing the foot of the dunes.

The stand was gone. Not as good a floater as the wooden surfboat.

Though to his great relief, no kamikaze shoobies, stoned, straight or plain stupid.

The little knoll that formed the east side of the tuck inside the dunes where they usually stored the boat and guard stand was still above the water. He waded through the swirling pool that surrounded it and climbed to the top, gaining a better vantage point to the north and south. He propped himself up on the wind, leaning out a full forty-five degrees, and scanned terrain both familiar and unrecognizable.

That's when he saw them. Two barely visible black forms, moving in and out of sight as they rose and fell, then disappeared inside a monstrous tumble of seawater, reappearing on the other side, arms paddle-wheeling, heads upright, waiting to be absorbed into the next cascade.

With a mixture of panic and relief, he realized they were off the coast of the federal preserve and heading rapidly to the south on the prevailing current. Outside Avery's jurisdiction, and therefore, nonentities. Deserving no greater attention than a piece of driftwood or a school of fish. An indelible stain on someone else's conscience.

F‌ROM THE moment Petey Amato took a look at the sea he knew he had to join her, not to succumb, but to glide atop her shoulders, unseen, inconsequential.

He'd driven to what he thought was a secluded spot just inside the federal preserve, with access to a path over the dunes to the ocean, though today it held another car. Randy's Volkswagen convertible, the top down, filling rapidly with aerial flotsam and jetsam.

Under normal circumstances he'd be annoyed. Today it felt preordained, a righteous inevitability.

When he got to the water Randy was already out past the closest break, sitting astride his surfboard in his black wet suit, his back to the shore, paddling hard enough to hold the bow of the board at a slight angle to the oncoming waves. Even in a storm surf there was a rhythm of size and frequency, better detected close in. Randy was feeling it out, looking for a hole, a lull that would allow him to jump through to the relatively stable DMZ between breaks.

There was less of a current than Petey would have thought, but it was enough to be sliding Randy steadily to the south. Petey ran north along the narrow strip of sand between the dunes and the exhausted ocean through drifts of cottony foam. At the giant wooden sign warning all to stay clear of the federal preserve, he put on his own wet suit and plunged into the water, dashing for the first break, barely covering fifty yards before a nasty little wave cut him off at the knees and he was surprised to find himself helplessly tumbling along the sandy bottom, the tether to his surfboard nearly slicing through his ankle.

When he finally made it to his feet, he proceeded more deliberately, trying to read the character of the hydraulic forces beneath the more familiar chop and swirl of the ocean. Closing in on a set of bigger waves he flopped down on his board and spiked it through the first roller, teetering at the crest, then regaining balance and sliding down the back side, the break slapping him on the feet. The next wave had already broken, so it was more a matter of holding on and not losing headway inside the turbulence.

He made it to the second break after a sprint across the interval, scooting under breakers and over the lips of the unbroken, timing and luck riding with him all the way to the next interval. The third break was much farther out, and from that angle nothing but a towering wall of gray and white.

Petey looked for Randy, spotting him farther to the south and up closer to the third break than expected. The sight of Randy's form against the wash of the wave provided a scale for judging wave height, which was too high to go over the top. They'd have to go under if they had any hope of reaching the fourth and final organized break. The final and by far the largest within reach of the coast.

Despite the extreme exertion needed to get to where he had, Petey was far from exhausted. Athletic gifts aside, manic energy and a belief in divine destiny had bestowed on him the sensation of limitless endurance. So the pause he took at the feet of the penultimate challenge was purely strategic. Wave walls this size weren't easily breached, over, under or through.

The surfboard was a mixed blessing. It saved him from the constant struggle to keep his head above water, but the same buoyancy made it hard to tunnel under the waves.

After thinking about it a while, he decided there really wasn't much more he could do than move as far forward on the board as possible, keeping the nose down, and hoping the curved shape would push him toward the sea bottom rather than launch him skyward, or simply allow the wave to bulldoze him and the board back into the gulley.

Randy had been in waves like this before, so he already knew Petey's concept had a good chance of working, which it did for both surfers, who emerged a few minutes later on the back side of the third break, face-to-face with an ocean landscape of far greater psychic significance.

The size of a wave is less a matter of dimension than perspective. From the trough of a ten or fifteen footer, it might as well be a hundred.

As if in recognition of the challenge ahead, the interval was calmer than the others, with a deeper gulley and longer fetch. Petey found himself floating in a nearly placid lake of dirty brown foam, and for the first time noticed the sound of the growing wind and the sight of seabirds overhead streaking toward terra firma.

Randy was still about the same distance to the south, sitting once again on his board, and like Petey, enthralled.

Petey was the first to shake off the spell and drop back on his belly, his arms butterflying through the water, gaining speed even as the waves grew in size and ferocity.

Inside, outside USA, he chanted silently to himself. *Inside, outside USA.*

Once the real rollers started to come over him, any connection to time and space dissolved. It was all brine and spume, the basso profundo sounds of tons of water crashing down into more water, crosscurrents and undertows grasping at his body as he clung half on, half off the surfboard. The ache in his lungs and the fierce compulsion to breathe an atmosphere one part water and two parts air.

Inside, outside USA. Inside, outside USA.

He eventually found another respite as he knifed up through the ragged surface into a vast field of swells—ocean waves born in the heart of the storm a hundred miles off the coast, preparing to ride over the suddenly shallow sandbar, which caused the face to flatten and the crest to rise until the top-heavy ridge curls forward and falls, a torrent, a tumbling frenzy with the power to obliterate anything in its path.

Or to propel a glorious set of kamikaze lunatics off the cliff, their wakes like contrails disappearing into the curl as it chases them across the collapsing wave. Had there been an observer on the shore, safely within a concrete bunker above the dunes, he would have seen two black figures, absurdly small against the backdrop of the mountainous surf, racing toward one another on symmetrical trajectories. Then, as if choreographed, darting above and below, crisscrossing, then turning in unison to slide down to the base of the wave, now a mound of churning white chaos.

The observer would have seen the wave appear to gain acceleration as the surfers slipped back into the foam, the advantage of a clean, vertical surface lost as the wave's energy dissipates over the deepening gulley. Though not enough to prevent it from consuming the tiny figures, their hands held high above their heads, their joyous screams almost heard above the ferocious din, until fluid dynamics overcomes divine destiny and they simply wink out of existence.

Randy's boa constrictor, having spent a pleasant day wrapped around the fleshy contours of Randy's girlfriends, knew through the delicate sensors in his skin that there were dangerous natural forces afoot long before his bedfellows heard the bullhorns of the Elysiana Police Force.

His cold-blooded brain was ill-equipped for higher cognitive functions like twelve bar blues or Euclidean geometry, but he knew better than the girls what to do in a hurricane.

Go to ground.

He already had the route worked out, having traveled it several times after escaping from his glass enclosure. Test runs for just such an eventuality.

So he glided over the floor of the bedroom, across the hallway to the stairs, up the spindle and down the railing to the living room, down the newel post and into the kitchen. And then the tricky part—across the linoleum to a tiny hole next to the gas line.

From there he retraced prior slithers to a cool, comfortable little hollow in the dirt under the shabby house, which had been built on cinder block piers in 1943, a year before the big blow, and several years before Donna in 1960, a storm the house had weathered with ease. This gave both the owners and current residents the idea that it could weather anything, an opinion not shared by the snake, who may or may not have felt some vindication as he watched the sub-floor above him lift off the blocks and sail into the air, hover unsteadily, and then take off toward the cloudy sky, breaking up as it flew into chunks of walls, floors and roof, with shingles, surfboards, sheetrock, futons, bongs, canned food, flip-flops, windows, doors and naked blonds and brunettes raining down on the neighborhood below.

CHAPTER
23

Mayor Black phoned Norm to tell him he was calling an emergency meeting of the Elysiana Borough Council. Norm took the call from the corner of his office where he was wedged behind a large file cabinet. He knew the wind specs on the borough offices were 200 plus mph, though knowing that his father was involved in the construction, undermined his confidence.

The constant chatter of the window and the moaning of the superstructure overhead didn't help.

"I'm not sure any of the council members are still on the island, mayor," he said. "I think you told them all to evacuate."

"Let's meet anyway. Joanie can take notes."

"Joanie left four hours ago. You told her to go to Belize. Isn't that somewhere near Cambodia?"

"Then more hoagies for us. My office, twelve noon."

The line went dead, not because he'd hung up, but because the telephone pole a block away snapped at the base and fell on an insurance agency after twirling around for a few seconds on the cables still attached at the top. The office was closed and should have been empty, but the agent who once drove Ditzler's Alfa let himself and another agent's wife back in for a private hurricane party, which wasn't supposed to include being crushed under the laminated roof beams and wood tongue-and-groove ceiling.

Norm groaned at yet another assault on his battered equanimity. Already feeling harried, the meeting above the opera house had only topped things off. The jurisdictional boundaries remained intact, but not with the vigorous endorsement from the mayor he'd hoped for. And this horror with Paula and Petey Amato. The sight of her waving goodbye to them, right there beneath his own home, the home of his only daughter, played over and over in his mind until he thought it would appear before him in fully realized, three-dimensional form. The only bright spot was the imminent prospect of Amato completing his assignment with the mayor, the consequences of which conjured other images, these far more agreeable.

As the storm worsened he considered retrieving Paula and Sweetie and sheltering them within the borough offices, or getting a cop to drive them off the island, but thought better of it. For one thing, he believed the house he built behind the unbreachable dunes was among the safest on the island. For another, it was dangerous out there. Who's to say they'd be safer on the road than twelve feet above a controlled flood plain?

So he sat, enduring the misery of frightening gusts and deafening rain, but feeling nominally secure.

Until the mayor called wanting to have a council meeting. Idiotic old coot, he thought.

The mayor's office was at the other end of the complex from Norm, making the walk seem interminable. There was even a short passageway between two separate borough buildings that had been enclosed in glass, which Norm passed through with his eyes closed, believing if he couldn't see windblown cars or tsunamis hurling toward him it couldn't happen.

The mayor's office was three times larger than any other, providing room for a respectable putting green. Norm paused for him to take the shot before entering, which the mayor missed, unavoidably distracted by the lumpy presence on his doorstep.

"Norm, a pleasure. Want to practice your grip?"

"Don't golf, Mr. Mayor. Can't find the time."

"You're a dedicated man, Norm," said the mayor. "Can't fault you for that."

Norm applied a tight smile as he mulled the meaning of that. So, there were other ways in which he *could* be faulted?

The mayor tried a few more times until he managed to sink one in the cup, which he left there, and went to sit at the round conference table at the other end of the green. Norm joined him, glad to be done with the sight of a man golfing against the soundtrack of a howling wind storm.

"Practice every day, that's my motto," said the mayor. "Come hell or high water. Appropriate motto today."

"The hell part for sure."

"Just took out the boardwalk downtown, apparently," said the mayor. "The opera house looks ready to follow. The beach patrol has fallen back to the movie theater across Ocean Avenue. It's masonry construction, with a second story. Trading an opera house for a move theater. More coarsening of the culture, wouldn't you say?"

Norm might have agreed if he'd ever seen or heard an opera. Though the mayor's grin seemed out of sync with the comment. He was wondering what next to say when Marty Romanovski came in the room, much to Norm's surprise.

"I thought this was a council meeting," he said, looking around for the hoagies.

"It is," said the mayor, "but as it pertains to Chief Romanovski's responsibilities, I thought it was important to have him here."

"Today?" asked Norm, honestly confused.

"The opera house is nearly history, folks," said Marty, with a half smile. "Should please the redevelopment boys."

"Are we here about the opera house?" Norm asked.

"Not exactly," said the mayor. "Before we lost the phones I got a call from Senator Mathewson. You know Scott? Chairman of the appropriations committee and the New Jersey legislative subcommittee on municipal governing charters?" he asked Norm, knowing that he didn't.

"Haven't had the pleasure."

The mayor, already a looming figure at the table, sat back and crossed his legs, which actually had the effect of increasing his physical presence. The other two, in turn, shrunk slightly into their chairs.

"Well, he was concerned, given our situation here, that we have the most efficient and expeditious municipal structure in place to handle the crisis and its aftermath, which we'll be dealing with for a very long time."

No disagreement around the table on that one, though Norm was still perplexed by the import of it all.

"So Senator Mathewson took it upon himself to accelerate a process that he'd initiated some time ago to reform certain outdated municipal charters. Ours in particular, which he's told me is like a pair of buckskin boots at a Broadway opening."

A comingling of elation and fear washed over Norm's heart. The racket outside died away and the universe became the four walls of the mayor's ridiculous office.

"I thought our charter was tighter than Fort Knox," he said.

The mayor batted the air.

"Baloney."

"I think you're making a wise decision," said Norm. "The current structure is untenable and a clear threat to public safety. I think this disaster has put that in sharp relief."

The mayor reached his long arm across the table and gave Norm's shoulder an affectionate swat.

"That's the kind of dedication to public service so rare in today's world," he said. "Selfless, really. Entirely focused on the good of the whole over your own personal ambitions."

Norm had another jarring moment of cognitive dissonance. He so liked the sound of the words, but couldn't help but detect the hint of an underlying threat.

"Thank you, mayor, but I'm not sure where we're going with this."

"Well, you're going to have a lot more of your attention available to assure the fit and fiddle of Elysiana's infrastructure, which I assure you will be a full-time job after this honey of a storm is done with us."

Norm was still looking in the direction of the mayor, but now all he could see was a pair of headlights coming at him with the high beams on.

"Oh?"

"The State of New Jersey has voided our charter. While we work on revisions, I'm eliminating the position of council president and consolidating operational control over public safety by moving the police department under the Office of the Mayor. I know you'll set an unachievable standard as the new director of the Office of Public Works. Charlie's going to be pleased as punch to have all your time devoted to his team, I'll tell you that."

Norm felt an impulse to reach down and yank Marty's .38 out of the holster and start firing, but when he looked it wasn't there.

"I knew you'd be pleased by this," said the mayor. "All the weighty duties that old charter loaded on your shoulders, it must have been a terrible burden."

"It wasn't," said Norm softly. "I could do that job and more. I could do your job."

Mayor Black laughed magnanimously.

"Of course you could, Norm. I wish you were doing it now, but the voters insist on what they insist on, and I'm forced to go along."

At that he rose from his chair and walked to the door of his office. The others followed, but the mayor put his hand on Marty's shoulder.

"You go ahead, Norm. The chief and I want to catch up. Need to get a handle on all the commotion."

"But we need to talk first," said Norm, pointedly at Marty.

Marty smiled at Norm, but stood back, leaning noticeably toward the mayor.

"I'll make sure the patrolmen keep Charlie and his boys up-to-date on things," Marty said to Norm. "Just know that public safety is word one."

"Hear, hear," said the mayor, as he used his broad physique to ease Norm far enough out of the office to shut the door.

Norm walked back down the cool white hall, through the glass-walled passageway, down another stark hallway to his office. He slid back down behind the file cabinet, where he remained immobile, in a state of waking unconsciousness, for the next four hours.

THE IMAGE of Marty's .38 in its usual place in Marty's desk became more and more defined as Norm's mind regained some semblance of coherence. He could see Marty slip it off his belt and drop it in the desk drawer, which he locked with a key from the middle drawer, always with a crack about airtight Elysiana Police Department security.

The odds of it being there were no better than fifty-fifty, he thought, but it was worth a look-see.

Conditions outside had continued to rapidly decay, but that seemed far less relevant to Norm than it had just a few hours before. More inconvenience than hazard. So far the borough offices had held firm, despite the deafening noise, and were partially lit by emergency generators.

Norm put on his windbreaker and took the short walk over to the police HQ offices, which comprised an open squad room and Marty's enclosed office. No one was there. The dispatcher was in a separate room near the holding cells, closeted off from the usual day-to-day distractions. Everyone else was either on patrol or AWOL, a path taken by at least half the summer cops on word that Mayor Black was taking over the force.

So it was child's play to take Marty's gun, sitting there exactly as he'd imagined on a stack of unpaid bills in Marty's right-hand desk drawer. Sliding the gun out of the holster, Norm loved the feel of it in his hand, heavy and slightly oily to the touch. He snapped out the cylinder and counted six rounds, snapped it back and flicked the safety off and on with his thumb.

He still had the keys to the department's unmarked car in his pocket. It was where he left it in the parking lot, windswept but otherwise unaffected by the storm.

Once out on the roads it was a different story. Norm had also lived through prior hurricanes, so he knew the real danger wasn't the wind itself, but all the stuff it brought with it—tree limbs and lawn furniture traveling at a hundred miles an hour, stop signs like scythes, slicing through fences and pedestrians, broken glass invisible in the rain, and ordinary sand, hissing against the side panels of the car and coating the windshield, the wipers scratching permanent arcs in the glass.

He didn't have a comprehensive plan, more of a projected sequence of events, subject to reordering depending on circumstances and opportunity. Each event was represented by a little vignette, episodes of a feature film he'd begun to script in the mayor's office.

The first episode he had in mind was set in a long, narrow apartment above a row of shops along the breakwater bordering the Northern Channel. With a full, unobstructed exposure to the northeast, the light, wood frame structure that would shudder in a five knot breeze was fully tensioned, with a cant toward the southeast you could have seen with the naked eye if it hadn't been raining so hard.

Upstairs in the apartment, Clarice was alone. Petey had left hours ago with his surfboard, leaving her with a fresh brick of Goettlewing's Southeast Asian hash, making Clarice the only person within the active zone of the storm who felt thoroughly relaxed. It took Norm almost an hour to get there, dodging random projectiles and negotiating the white-water rapids that in many places had supplanted Elysiana's streets.

But he remembered the place well, and felt an almost nostalgic warmth come over him as he pulled in front of the gift shop, now boarded up in haphazard fashion, abandoned with little or no expectation of survival.

Norm pulled the gun out of the holster again and rechecked the load, cocking and holding back the hammer, then releasing the trigger to settle it safely back against the live round.

He slipped the gun into the pocket of the windbreaker and fought his way up the outdoor stairs. He tried the doorknob and was pleased to find the door unlocked. He walked down the narrow hall that led to the living room, where he found Clarice sitting cross-legged on the floor, in white undershirt and panties in mid-toke off a delicate gilded pipe Petey had recently lifted from the surf shop downstairs.

With her synaptic pathways slowed to the velocity of number ten motor oil, it took several seconds for her to notice there was a pudgy middle-aged guy standing in her living room with a gun pointed at her forehead.

"Wow," she said.

"Where's Loverboy?" said Norm.

Clarice frowned with concentration.

"Who?"

"The ape who lives here with you. Amato."

"Petey?" she asked, smiling. "I love Petey. He *is* my loverboy."

"Grand. Where is he?"

She concentrated harder. She knew the answer. It was sitting there in a staging area between memory production and the mechanics of speech. She held up a finger, asking for patience.

"Surfing," she finally forced out. "He went surfing."

"Of course he did. Me, I'm planning on a round of tennis right after I dump your bodies in the channel."

As she poked around the bowl of the pipe to see if that last toke had fully extinguished the little chip of hash, a distant, noncognitive sector of her brain, a more primitive region and therefore more resistant to anesthesia, woke up to the imminent threat. It took a few more seconds, but word eventually worked its way back up to the higher functions, which caused her to look at him with as much alarm as half-open lids would allow.

"Huh?"

Norm left her and searched through the apartment, opening closet doors and kitchen cabinets, pulling open the shower curtain and looking under beds and piles of clothes.

"Where'd he go?" he asked Clarice, who'd spent the interval finding her way to her feet.

"Surfing, man. I told you."

He shrugged, and then took the gun out of his pocket again, rewriting the way the next scene would have to play out.

"Whatever you say. I guess one out of two isn't a bad start," he said, leveling the barrel at a spot slightly to the left and down from the top curve of her ample white breast.

While both had been absorbed in their own pursuits, the storm outside had continued apace. One consequence being the ply Petey had nailed over the hole in the window suddenly ripped off and flew away. The screeching sound was immediately followed by an explosion of wind, blasting dead out of the northeast, hurling Clarice into Norm's arms and shoving the two of them over a side table and into the living room wall.

With only a thin layer of loose woven cotton between her flesh and Norm's windbreaker, the unexpectedly intimate contact did more to shake her out of her stupor than the hurricane-force winds or the murderous barrel of a .38-caliber service revolver.

And so it was that Norm sat stunned into inaction as he watched Clarice turn, and in defiance of logic and the violent intent of nature, walk across the living room floor, her platinum hair fluttering behind, step up on the sill of the broken window, and leap.

This was not how Norm had conceived this moment, not in any way. Here he was, yet again slumped to the floor, both his quarries still at large, unpunished, unrepentant and in full knowledge of his conspiracy against the mayor. He felt the crushing weight of all the unfairness that had been visited upon him squeezing strength out of his body, collapsing his will.

He couldn't let that happen. It wasn't going to happen, not to Norm Harlan. Not after all he'd done, all he'd sacrificed and fought to achieve.

With a lusty string of obscenities, he rose to his feet and followed a path twice traveled before, and without hesitation, dove head first through the window, not immediately appreciating the advantage flexible young muscles can have, however impeded by drugs and alcohol, in clearing hazards such as the one hidden under the lapping, encroaching waters of the Northern Channel, which was why he was still preparing to knife into the boiling sea when he dove instead into the slate-covered patio.

Clarice wasn't much of a swimmer, but the wind and waves were in her favor, and she was literally tossed ashore a half block to the west, over the breakwater and into the backyard of an eighty-five-year-old man who'd decided it wasn't worth the effort to try to save himself if God had chosen such a cruel way to sweep him off this earth. He was sitting at the sliding glass doors facing the channel waiting for just that to happen.

Instead, the channel delivered an essentially naked young woman to his doorstep, rejuvenating, at minimum, his faith in predestination.

Norm had a wait of his own, though mercifully brief. Unable to move, or feel any part of his body, he understood clearly what had happened. From the contorted position of his head he could see the sky, and the busy waters in the channel, which would occasionally wash up and break over his face.

He was glad he could close his eyes, because he wanted to hold one last image in place, of Paula and Sweetie to either side of him high atop the opera house as he surveyed the world as it should have been.

HAVING LIVED through a typhoon that leveled over a thousand square miles of palm trees, grass huts and rickety infrastructure, killing countless people in an archipelago in the Indian Ocean— that barely warranted a third page, left column mention in the *New York Times*—Sanford Goettlewing regarded the little squall over Elysiana as a quaint amusement.

Now alone in the motel, everyone including the owner having fled to the mainland, he took a few basic precautions, like moving the GTO to higher ground, which meant driving it up the steps of a little cluster of retail shops the developer had thought wisely to build on short piers. Goettlewing parked it snugly under a canopy outside a T-shirt boutique. Nothing he could do about the wind, but if the water came up, the car had half a chance.

The storm brought cooler temperatures, allowing Goettlewing to comfortably wear his black jeans and T-shirt and grunt-issue boots, and wrap himself in the black slicker and hood tied firmly at the waist by a black silk scarf taken off the body of an old woman in Phnom Penh who'd come closest to killing him in an almost fair fight.

It was close to eight at night when he went outside, pausing to let his eyes adjust to the near pitch black. With no power and only a few generators, mostly to maintain minimal services at the police and fire department HQ's, there was little on Elysiana capable of lighting up the tempest.

Goettlewing chose a Ford Econoline with a stencil that said "Edgar's Electric. You'll always volt for us!" on the door, that was parked next to the motel, which provided some shelter from the horizontal rain while he hot-wired the starter. It had a bit more road clearance than an ordinary car, and he liked the idea of all the cargo space. The poor aerodynamics would have to be dealt with.

He stayed away as well as he could from the main avenues as he worked his way north. He passed one big yellow maintenance truck, but the guy inside the cab looked busy on the radio and took little note of the light commercial van. He calibrated his speed to maintain forward momentum through the water turning the streets into swift running, but well-ordered streams.

The flat planes of sheet metal that made up the bulk of the van's shape were a problem. Goettlewing wasn't sure if the weight in the box was enough to hold the van to the road, especially as it lost traction over the racing water underneath. He shoved the automatic transmission down to L and centered the van in the middle of the road, pushing the accelerator forward to fight back against the rapids.

This was a good strategy until he turned right, just a block shy of his destination, and found himself broadside to the wind with nothing but an empty lot in between.

The van went over like a drunken bull. He shoved open the driver's side door just as the van landed on its side. The wind then performed a sort of valet service by ripping off the door, allowing Goettlewing to crawl more or less unimpeded through the hole and down into the surge-driven water.

He let the water deliver him to the hood of a Cadillac parked in the driveway of an abandoned house. He squirmed around until he was propped up against the windshield and from there tried to get his bearings.

He had only a few hundred feet to go, but it wasn't going to be an easy trip. The storm was in full fury, the wind speed turning the air into a fluid mass. Goettlewing could see where he wanted to go, but he might as well have been looking through a granite wall.

He searched around for a solution, finally spotting a boat trailer behind the Cadillac, complete with boat, already drifting back and forth, barely anchored by the trailer.

Goettlewing scrambled over the roof of the Caddy, across the trunk, over the short bow of the boat and into the cockpit. The boat was open to the air, but through some act of perverse divinity, somewhat protected by a rickety carport. Goettlewing pulled a tiny flashlight out of his backpack and lit the motor, searching for key components. He found them: choke, throttle, air vent on the gas tank, kill switch, and the mechanism that allowed him to drop and lock the motor in the drive position. He pulled the cord and the twenty-five horse Johnson coughed into action.

The only remaining challenge was to push the Caddy down the drive far enough to allow the boat to drift clear of the trailer, then develop some slack on the cable securing the bow to the trailer so he could set it free. The last part took a lot of strength, but Goettlewing was in full force, flush with a lust for impossible circumstances.

He pulled himself into the boat and grabbed the throttle, darting out into the dark, skimming wildly across the choppy flood water, clipping a post light and stop sign along the way. There was just enough draft to keep the prop spinning, though it frequently ground up chunks of street, curb and sidewalk as he

raced across the last stretch of inundated neighborhood to the
nightclub, which actually sat slightly above the water line, the
rise invisible under normal circumstances, but on this night of
material significance.

Goettlewing drove the boat nearly to the front door of Shing
O'Ling's before the keel dug in and halted progress. He killed
the engine and leaped over the bow. As he walked up to the
entrance, he patted around his waist to be sure he still had all
the equipment he'd started out with. When he was only a few
feet away one of Eduardo's sidemen burst out the glass doors
and stood there, hands on his hips, looking sarcastic, enormous
and indomitable.

"Hey, douche bag, this here's private . . ."

The last words disappeared into the wet mash of the guy's
throat, which immediately ceased to function, and soon after the
guy himself. Goettlewing shook out his fist and kept moving.

The inside of the club was nicely lit by a combination of
electric lanterns and candles, and large kerosene-fueled lanterns
enclosed in frosted glass globes, an under-appreciated feature of
the Shing O'Ling ambience.

Tonight it was just enough to shed a gentle, amber glow
over the big open area comprising the long bar, band stage and
parquet-covered dance floor, which Goettlewing reached before
the second of Buente's protection unit rushed at him to the tat-
tat sound of a snub-nosed .38. Knowing the accuracy of the gun
and the likely skill of the user, he barely looked over, investing
a few seconds to flick his Chief's Special out of his pocket, plug-
ging the guy between the eyes, then slipping it back into his
pocket again.

Buente stood at the entrance to his office, leaning against
the doorjamb, his hands in his pockets.

"Welcome to Shing O'Ling's," he said, with a gracious gesture. "The rockin'ist joint in town."

Goettlewing stopped in the middle of the dance floor, about
twenty feet away. He looked around.

"I've seen worse," he said.

"I presume you're not here to get out of the rain."

"Is it raining?"

Buente moved away from the doorjamb and stepped behind the bar. He took down a bottle and held up two shot glasses.

"Tequila?" he asked.

"You take both," said Goettlewing. "You'll need it."

Buente poured a shot and downed it. He returned the other glass and came back with a Browning HP 9mm. He rested the handle of the gun on the bar and pointed the barrel at Goettlewing's chest.

"Have we met?" he asked Goettlewing.

Goettlewing shook his head.

"Hm. Then perhaps we share business relationships," said Buente.

"Do you believe in predestination without the interdiction of the Almighty?"

"That things happen for a reason? Sure. I'm a devout servant of our Father in Rome. If he tells me the Lord has plans for us, it isn't up to me to argue."

"I'm keen on the old guinea myself, but I just can't get behind all that pomp and smelly incense. Of course, Protestants aren't much better. Tight-assed, self-satisfied buggers."

"So, I see. You've come to discuss religion."

"No, illegal drugs."

Buente lit up a beautiful Latin smile.

"Outstanding. That puts me on firmer ground."

"More specifically, the cash that's supposed to be delivered in return for the illegal drugs."

Buente's smile dropped from his eyes without losing hold on his face. He gestured toward Goettlewing with a freshly poured shot of tequila.

"If I'm not mistaken, that's the responsibility of the delivery man."

Goettlewing shrugged.

"He's skipped town," he said to Buente, "with my money. Unless you still have it. Either way, I'm here for my reimbursement."

"This is not of my doing. Honorable people do not blame the innocent."

"So you missed that part in our contract. You fuck me, I fuck you."

"I must be more careful with the fine print."

"Indeed."

Buente's shot put a hole in Goettlewing's slicker, but not in Goettlewing himself, who had already started a classic drop-and-roll maneuver, having drawn his .45 from the holster under his jacket. By the time Buente could re-aim the heavy Browning, Goettlewing had put a round in his left shoulder and another through his right wrist.

A surprised yelp rose from Buente's throat as the gun fell to the bar. With both hands essentially out of commission, he could only stare at the blood gushing from his wrist.

"*Madre*."

Goettlewing walked over and grabbed Buente by the shirt-front, dragged him over the bar and across the dance floor. Somehow along the way Buente was able to get enough of a grip on his wrist to stem the fountain, but not the flow.

"I haven't had time to distribute the product, *Senior*," he said through clenched teeth. "You can have it all back."

"I know I can."

Goettlewing dragged Buente all the way to the entrance of the club, out the door and across the short strip of unflooded lawn to the newly formed river that used to be Imperial Avenue. The wind had begun to sound the way everyone who's ever heard a hurricane says it sounds like: a runaway locomotive.

"At least I die a man of honor," said Buente, as he tried to spit through the pounding rain. Goettlewing gathered up a two-handed grip on his silk shirt.

"Not according to my daughter Sylvia," said Goettlewing, waiting for the import to register before shoving Buente down through two feet of salt water to the pavement below.

CHAPTER
24

As NIGHT fell, Johnny figured he should start releasing the guards, a decision reinforced by the twenty minutes it took him to reach Jack and Mike Ditzler.

They were huddled under their old wooden lifeboat, partially propped up by two half-burnt logs dragged out of a recent bonfire, the rounded hull braced against the wind.

"We've been checking every ten minutes," Ditzler yelled at Johnny's face looking down into the boat. "Seems like sort of a slow day."

Jack saw no reason to mention the two surfers he'd seen briefly that morning. He'd chosen to believe they were merely the residue of a nearly sleepless night before. There was no point in believing anything else.

"To get to downtown you'll have to head up the middle of the island, then take Edith's Path to the borough garage," said Johnny. "The opera house is gone and Ocean and Imperial avenues are under water."

Jack blanched.

"How deep?"

"You'll need a boat to get home."

Johnny helped them haul the surf boat further up the side of the dune before stumbling with the wind on their tails down the path to the truck. Johnny made sure they were underway before speeding off toward the next beach.

Jack and Ditzler decided it made sense to head for the bay before turning north, seeing if they could still use Half Moon Avenue, which they couldn't. A new bay shore had developed, marooning a row of stilt houses that now looked like they were floating on the whitecaps.

"She's okay," said Ditzler, answering an unasked question. "Sebbie will keep her safe."

They wound their way along the littered avenues leading north, switching back and forth to avoid downed power lines and deep water. They saw one yellow maintenance truck, but no one else was on the road.

"I thought it was supposed to end in a whimper," said Ditzler, leaning away from the sound of something big thudding into the passenger door.

The borough garage, Charlie Abramson's domain, had been a wise fallback position for the Elysiana Beach Patrol after being driven from the movie theater. It was set on a slight rise and surrounded by a twelve-foot cyclone fence, which meant it was relatively dry and free of airborne missiles.

Joey Zable checked them in. Avery and all the lieutenants were out patrolling in four-by-fours, where they'd be for the next two days.

For Jack, it was an important moment. He'd lived out the day mostly in a state of Thereness, but for some reason driving into the sheltered compound brought on profound feelings of Hereness.

The faces of the guards, now wearing the deepest tans of the season, were strained with exhaustion and glossy with rainwater, their hair bleached and dried to straw by the sun, pasted over their foreheads and channeling rivulets over sodden beach patrol jackets.

He looked at Ditzler's broad, congenial face, his partial grin in its perpetual state, his dark hair slightly reddened above bright blue eyes, clearly relieved to be out of the direct path of the storm, however briefly.

"You should come with me to the hotel," Jack told him. "It's the safest place on the island."

"No argument. High and dry for this boy."

Jack told Zable he could ferry any guard who needed a place to stay to the Imperial if he could borrow one of the two pontoon boats belonging to the Bay Constables. Zable radioed Johnny who told him to take both of the boats, since there wasn't much the constables could do at this point on the open sea but flip over and drown.

It took about an hour to establish a good launch point for the boats, with access to where the new inland waterways were deep enough to provide adequate draft all the way to the hotel, which now stood as an island tower, surrounded by seawater reaching partway up the central stairway to the grand entrance.

Another hour later they brought Joey and the last of the guards over, securing one of the pontoon boats at the launch point in case others needed to follow.

When Jack reached the front doors of the hotel, he was met by Gwendalynn.

"I've been allocating rooms," she said. "I hope that's okay."

"Anything above the second floor. If the water goes above there, it's the end of the world."

Most people were gathered in the main lobby, burning candles found in the restaurant and drinking from the expansive Imperial stocks. All shared tales of the day harrowing enough to defy future exaggeration.

Jack and Gwendalynn slipped behind the reception desk and through a door to the back offices, which in turn linked up to one of the service stairwells that ran the full height of the hotel.

When the door to the stairwell clicked behind them, they were jolted by the absolute silence, the unrelenting complaint of the wind gone.

"Igor sure built this thing," said Jack.

"We hope."

She gripped his hand as they walked up the forty flights that covered the twenty stories to the top floor, and then one more short flight to the Box, which Jack was glad to see hadn't already flown off to Philadelphia. In fact, it barely tremored from the huge wind outside.

Gwendalynn had brought a bottle of wine in her big bag, which she uncorked before settling into the all-weather recliner, which was now, despite its name, out of the weather in Jack's living room.

Jack lit a candle, then walked past her and looked out the window at the riotous sea. Whatever light was still being generated around the island was just enough to reflect off the surface, now stretching uninterrupted from the foot of the hotel to North Africa.

"See," said Jack, "I told you I'd be able to dive from here into the ocean."

She got up and stood next to him.

"You did. Though just because you can, doesn't mean you should."

"I'm not convinced of that."

"Really."

Jack tried the handle of the door out to the balcony. The velocity of the wind off the ocean was so high it created a Bernoulli effect, making it difficult to shut the door again.

"It would kill you," said Gwendalynn, helping him pull the door shut, then walking back into the room.

Before he could respond, she held up her glass of wine.

"And tell me, why would a person who avoids alcohol for health reasons want to commit suicide?" she asked.

He turned around and slid down to the floor, leaning against the door with his hands clasped over his knees. She walked over to him and sat cross-legged on the floor.

"You can only commit suicide if you're alive," he said.

"And you're not?"

"Not really. Not dead either."

"I'm sorry," she said, "but I have a hard time with that."

"Because you've never been killed."

"And you have."

"I said I forgot the accident, but not what came before."

"Like what, your childhood?" she said.

"I'm talking about the day of the accident. It wasn't."

"Wasn't what?"

"An accident."

"What was it?"

"Something else," he said.

The more Jack spoke about being neither here nor there, the more she felt his presence. She prayed he would stay just where he was, so she could sit next to him, paired under the feeble glow of the candle.

"I don't understand."

"It was the backing out-of-the-driveway game. I think I told you, if you were sitting in the passenger seat, you were supposed to say if it was all clear."

"You told me. The game in your head," she said.

"I'd just turned sixteen. My father was teaching me to drive the car. So there we were, backing down the driveway. Only now I'm behind the wheel and my father's in the passenger seat. I have a different job."

"Oh."

"But I asked what he always asked, 'All clear?' And he yelled, 'All clear' and I kept backing out. Only it wasn't. There was a truck. A big truck. On his side. Explain that to me."

"A mistake."

"I said I remembered what happened, but that doesn't mean the memory is correct. There was no reason for him to say 'All clear' if it wasn't. But if he said 'Not yet,' why did I pull out?"

She felt the weight of his presence gather a few more pounds. Though to be certain he was still there, she reached over and rested her hand on his arm.

"There's a third explanation."

"I wish that was possible, but it's not."

"It wasn't an accident at all. You had a brain tumor that the doctors said was inoperable. So your parents took you to Mexico, where they'd heard about a native healer who could perform a ritual extraction, but before you could get there you were way-laid by banditos, who your father heroically fought off, though not before you'd been slashed across the face with a machete. So you had to be airlifted back to America, where they repaired the wound, but you lost a lot of blood and slipped into a coma.

"What nobody knew was that the shock to your system triggered something in your immune system that caused it to dissolve the tumor, helped along by being in a coma which let it focus all its energy on curing you. So then, when your body was good and ready, you woke up. Of course, while you were out your dad died saving a family of ten from a burning building. The fireman who tried to revive him on the sidewalk reported that his last words were, 'Give the kid the hotel.'"

She took a sip from her wine glass and smiled.

"Okay, that's a possibility," said Jack.

"You don't like it? I got another one. Actually I got a million of 'em," she said.

"Which one is real?" he asked.

She slapped his knee.

"They all are, man. That's the point. Crap happens to us and maybe it's our parents' fault and maybe it isn't. What difference does it make? Since you don't know, you can't know. One reality is the same as any other. You can make it be anything you want. Or better yet, don't pick at all. Stop thinking about it and concentrate on what you can know, that living is better than not living. And that's good enough."

The rain outside rode a bigger than normal gust into the window, making them both turn and look at the glass. The storm had been in a brief lull as they talked, but now it was driving on to the island with cruel and malicious abandon. The radio reports were right—all of Elysiana was engulfed in the greatest weather disaster in the history of the Jersey Shore. It was crushing everything, from the Northern Channel and downtown to the stilt homes along the western shore and the new development on the northern edge of the mines. The dunes, having held their ground, could do nothing to stop Half Moon Bay from washing across the western flank, returning the mines to the floodplain God had meant it to be.

The rain fell on the thicket of pilings that once supported the opera house, and on the bodies of Eduardo Buente and Norm Harlan as they traveled indifferently out to sea.

It fell on Sebbie Rosconni who strained at the dock lines of an antique sloop, striving hopelessly to hold it off the lee piers on which its graceful sheer was battering itself to death.

And the grim and naked skull of Avery Volpe as he sat in his open Jeep with Johnny Lukeiwitz, smiling and slipping a stick of gum between his lips.

And it fell from the right eye of Gwendalynn Anders, who was the first person in Elysiana to detect the exact moment when the wind exhausted its wrath, and the sea, having done what it was going to do, began an orderly withdrawal toward the east; and as she looked at Jack Halcyon, felt her soul finally return to her chest where it belonged.